ALBRIGHT 05/22/2013 C:1
50686014449248
Larson, Leslie,
Breaking out of bedlam

m. mcK.

ALBRIGHT MEMORIAL LIBRARY

W9-ARG-958

(570) 348-3000

www.lclshome.org

BREAKING OUT OF BEDLAM

**Center Point
Large Print**

**This Large Print Book carries the
Seal of Approval of N.A.V.H.**

BREAKING OUT OF BEDLAM

LESLIE LARSON

CENTER POINT PUBLISHING
THORNDIKE, MAINE

This Center Point Large Print edition is published in the year 2010 by arrangement with Shaye Areheart Books, an imprint of The Crown Publishing Group, a division of Random House, Inc.

Copyright © 2010 by Leslie Larson. All rights reserved.

This is a work of fiction. Names, characters, places, and incidents either are the product of the author's imagination or are used fictitiously. Any resemblance to actual persons, living or dead, events, or locales is entirely coincidental.

The text of this Large Print edition is unabridged. In other aspects, this book may vary from the original edition. Printed in the United States of America on permanent paper. Set in 16-point Times New Roman type.

ISBN: 978-1-60285-728-5

Library of Congress Cataloging-in-Publication Data

Larson, Leslie, 1956-
  Breaking out of bedlam / Leslie Larson. -- Center point large print ed.
    p. cm.
  ISBN 978-1-60285-728-5 (library binding : alk. paper)
  1. Older women--Fiction. 2. Aging parents--Psychology--Fiction.
  3. Family secrets--Fiction. 4. Domestic fiction. 5. Large type books. I. Title.
PS3612.A7737B43 2010
  813'.6--dc22
2009053593

For the Marshes

First Book

Property of Cora Sledge

Do not read until I'm dead

THE BLANK BOOK

I got this book from my granddaughter Emma. The cover looks like a gunnysack. It has a dried purple flower on the front, and all the pages are blank. It's supposed to be pretty. The purple pen that goes with it is squishy, like chewed-up gum. "So it doesn't hurt your hand, Gamma," Emma said. I laughed, thinking where my hand has been these eighty-two years, and what it's done. I was polite, though, and asked her real nice what in the world I'm supposed to do with it. "It's for your thoughts," she said. "If you have any memories or reflections you want to write down. Or a poem, maybe, or a sentiment you think is meaningful."

That girl has always worked my last nerve.

They all feel guilty for putting me here, so they're trying to keep me from losing my mind. I also got a jigsaw puzzle (one of the biggest wastes of time I can think of) and an embroidery set (which I have always hated) for Christmas. My son Dean even gave me a paint-by-numbers kit with three kinds of dogs: a poodle, a collie, and a German shepherd. Do they think I am retarded? That I've gone back to my childhood?

They don't know the first thing about me.

I put those other gifts down in the Day Room and they got snapped up like nobody's business. I tucked this book in my top drawer thinking I could tear the pages out if I needed some blank paper. It's thick as a damn Bible. I don't know who in their right mind could ever fill it. Then this morning I got up early, when the light was just starting to come through the blinds. Usually my pills knock me out 'til breakfast, when the walkers and wheelchairs make a slow-motion stampede for the dining room. But this morning was quiet. Nobody calling out from their bed, or knocking a mop around. The phones at the nurses' station weren't ringing yet, the gardeners weren't running their leaf blowers, and the delivery trucks weren't idling outside my window.

This morning I sat straight up in bed like somebody called my name. Lots of times I can't get out of bed at all. I stay there all day, dozing and waking up, dozing and waking up. I might swallow a few more of my little darlings to settle my nerves. Sometimes whole chunks of the day disappear. Fine by me. But today I woke clear as a bell. I did my bathroom business, sat down here at my dressing table, and started to write.

I got a plan. I'm going to write down everything I ever wanted to say. I'm not holding nothing back and I don't give a damn what anybody thinks. Most people don't tell the truth about their lives, including me. I've done things I'm not proud of. I lied to keep myself alive because life is hard and there's things you got to do. But now

10

I got nothing to lose. I'm going to tell the truth, once and for all. I hope those that put me in this place read it when I'm dead—which I have a feeling won't be long. Maybe then they'll see.

The trucks are starting to idle outside now, spitting fumes right into my window. And the inmates are creeping down the hall, yelping like animals fighting to get to the watering hole. Damned if I'm not hungry myself. Those rubbery eggs don't sound half bad.

I got another reason for keeping this book. It's called leaving a paper trail. Something fishy's going on in this place and I want a record in case anything happens to me. That's right. There's whispering, and shifty looks, and things gone missing.

It's all going down here.

I'm using the purple pen.

I've always had the prettiest handwriting.

THE KIDNAPPING

They put me here about three months ago, just after Thanksgiving. By *they* I mean my family, my two sons and my daughter, along with their wives and husband. If you're reading this, you know who I mean.

My girl, Glenda, is the ringleader, the one who started it. She came out to the house when I was not having a good day. It was getting to be winter.

The days were drawing in and all of a sudden it seemed to be dark all the time. I don't know what time she came. After lunch, I think, but I was still in bed. So what? She acted real funny, asking questions that were none of her business. I know she was snooping around, pretending to use the bathroom and staying in there a long time. Opening cupboards and drawers in the kitchen. Can you imagine? She went home and called the boys, Dean and Kenneth, and word spread like wildfire. Within days the whole posse, including my daughters-in-law, swooped down, poking and prying into every nook and cranny.

I knew what they were up to, but I just sat in my chair, watched my program, and didn't say a word. Dean took Glenda into the kitchen and showed her that spot by the stove that caught fire when the grease in the skillet got too hot, then Glenda dragged him into the bathroom to point to where the ceiling was leaking. It dripped right into the tub and I call that lucky and not a problem. They got in my pantry and pulled out food I'd been saving for a rainy day. They went through the icebox, holding their noses, gagging, and making the biggest fuss over a few little things that had spoiled. They had something to say about the newspapers I'd been saving in a corner of the living room, the clothes in my drawers (which aren't exactly new, but it's not like I'm going out to the *opera* every night), and the drain in the kitchen sink which was plugged so I couldn't do dishes in there (but the bathtub worked just fine; you'd be surprised). They even had a tizzy about the ring on the ceiling over my chair from me smoking while I watched TV or read. Big deal. It's nothing a coat of paint won't cure.

You never saw such gasping and groaning and oh-my-goshing in your life. Every so often they'd come back to the living room carrying a bag of Fritos or those marshmallow peanuts I like so much or a tub of ice cream and hold it up like they just found a dead body. "You are *borderline diabetic,* Mommy. You have *high blood pressure!*" they squawked. Like I didn't know. Well, I've always loved salty things—olives, pretzels, salami, potato chips, and cheese curls. But I'm not supposed to have any of that, just like I'm not supposed to have any sugar. Or fat. What's left? Nothing *I'd* want to eat.

They went on and on. When did I last change my clothes? What did I have for breakfast? How did I take a bath with those dishes in the tub? I just shrugged. I wasn't having a very good day *that* day, either, to tell the truth. All that commotion mixed me up. So I just stared at the screen and acted like they weren't there. I knew it was no use explaining that when you get older certain things don't matter so much—like if you wear the same clothes all the time, or if you have your meals at a certain hour, or whether every little corner is spic and span.

The shit *really* hit the fan when they started rounding up my pills. Dean's wife found some in the sugar bowl, then Glenda found some behind the pillowcases in the hall closet. Kenny's wife found the ones I kept in the junk drawer with the matches and keys. It was like a goddamn Easter egg hunt, seeing who could get the most. They cleaned out the medicine cabinet and my bedside stand. They brought them all into the living room and piled them on the coffee table.

I didn't let on, but even *I* was surprised to see so many.

I have pills for my blood pressure, plus blood thinners, cholesterol reducers, and heart regulators. I got what my doctor calls mood elevators, a few different kinds of sleeping pills, and muscle relaxers for when my back goes out or I get those charley horses in my legs at night. I been taking Valium since I went through the change thirty years ago. I got pain pills for my arthritis, which aches me all the time, plus leftovers from when I had my teeth out, gallbladder surgery, my hysterectomy, and that time I fell on the back steps and bruised my ribs. For a while I was having dizzy spells whenever I went outside and I got real nervous around more than a few people, so I got a pill for that, too.

I'd lost track of a lot of those pills I saw piled

in front of me, but I do know I worked hard to get them, going around to different doctors and scraping and bowing and acting innocent—and I couldn't bear to see them taken away from me.

"Mommy, you're hooked!" Glenda hollered. She has always been an exaggerator.

"Each and every one of those pills is from a doctor," I told her. "Fair and square. Legal as can be." The thought that they'd take them away scared the life out of me.

I knew something bad was coming, I just didn't know *what*. Dean stood there like Mr. Clean with his feet wide apart and his arms crossed over his chest. He's been playing the Big Man since he was four years old. Glenda's mouth hung open and her eyes were big as saucers. Kenneth, my baby—well, he couldn't even look at me. And my daughters-in-law! Holy Christ on earth! They clucked and scratched like hens.

My mistake was thinking an adult could make her own decisions. Thinking I was still an American citizen with rights that couldn't be taken away.

Good riddance, I said to my dog Lulu when the door closed and we were on our own again. To hell with them. I tried to put the whole thing out of my mind. I had a few pills left in places they didn't think of looking. Little did I know they were plotting, that the whole thing was one big conspiracy. They put their heads together and they made plans. They talked to lawyers and looked at places to put me. They got everything in order.

I was the last one to know.

MY SO-CALLED HOME

This place is called The Palisades and to this day I don't know what that means or who thought it up. I just hope whoever it is ends up in a shit-hole like this. Then maybe he'll come up with a better name, like Snake Pit, or Hell Hole, or Lock 'em Up and Throw Away the Key. The part I'm in is called assisted living, which means you're supposed to do things for yourself. They tried to tell me it was just like an apartment of my own, only with maid service. Even *they* can't believe I'm that dumb.

Besides Assisted Care, there's Full Care, called B Wing, where the droolers, pissers, and moaners live. They sit in wheelchairs all day with their heads lolled back and their eyes crossed. I'm in A Wing, I'm glad to say. Some people cross over. It's a sad thing when someone says, "Did you hear Joe Blow got moved over there to B?"

I'd rather be carried out in a coffin.

If you saw this place from the outside, you'd never know what goes on behind these walls. It don't look like much, just a low U-shaped building painted grayish blue. It's made of cinder

16

blocks, like a cement igloo, more like a garage or a warehouse than a place for people to live. It's not like a wood house, that you can smell and feel around you, swaying and creaking. No. It's stiff and dry, a bunch of sand hardened into place.

There's a parking lot out front and the usual plants, oleander and those ugly acacia trees that make me sneeze. When I first moved to San Diego there was nothing but marsh and scrub around here, with a few farms where the Japanese raised strawberries. Then they built the Navy base, and the strip joints where the sailors went. Now it's all built up with Wal-Mart and Denny's and Smart & Final—those giant buildings you can't tell apart.

People in this place scream all hours of the day and night, calling out for folks who've been dead for fifty years. It's just like a prison or a lunatic asylum. I got no more rights than if I took a gun and blew somebody's head off. And while I sit here in this ugly little cell, some strangers are living in *my* house (a nice family they tell me), shitting in *my* toilet, and waking up looking out *my* window at *my* little yard. While I'm getting slopped like a hog in a room full of people who don't know their own names, someone is cooking on *my* stove, and sitting themselves down at *my* dinner table, then washing up the dishes in the sink *I* scoured with Ajax so it would stay pretty

17

and white. I keep asking myself what I done to deserve this, but no matter how hard I think, I can't come up with an answer.

There's a piss smell in here that drives me crazy.

They say I'm lucky I got a corner room all to myself, but once you're inside it don't make a damn bit of difference. It's oblong, with a bed, a stand next to it, a dressing table, an armchair, and a TV. That's it. My bathroom's the size of a closet. You feel all the people that's been in this room before, people you don't know and wouldn't want to. People who cried and were sick here; people who, God knows, must have died here—all alone more likely than not, abandoned and forgotten.

There's a sliding glass door that opens onto a courtyard. I can watch the girls pushing big carts of dirty laundry and cleaning supplies, or the dishwasher pushing racks of dirty dishes. Old ladies are wheeled along or plod like zombies. Once I saw an old man open his fly and spray a fountain of piss on a geranium. There's a window high up by the ceiling that runs the length of my bed. The only way I can see out of it is to stand beside the bed on my tiptoes with my chin on the windowsill. There's a loading dock outside. I watch the men spit, smoke, and chew the fat while they work. The big Dumpsters are just beyond it. Twice now I've seen a man with hair like a buffalo eat trash out of the Dumpster like it was peach cobbler.

And who knows what all with things disappearing right and left, people creeping around and doing God-knows-what. All this, and they say I wasn't safe at home.

POISON IVY

There's someone here I hate more than the devil himself. I didn't like her the minute I laid eyes on her, but now it's all I can do not to put my hands around that buzzard neck of hers and strangle her to death. She accused me of something I got nothing to do with. Right in front of other people, she looked me in the eye and accused me. I'm so mad I can't see straight. I can hardly write, but I got to get to the bottom of this. I got to show that I'm innocent as a lamb.

Her name's Ivy, Ivy Archer. Poison Ivy, I call her. But first I got to explain.

We eat at a bunch of little round tables in the dining room, four people to a table. You get no choice or say. You are assigned a table the day you come, and as far as I can tell, the only way you get to change your seat is by dying. I really got lucky. I hit the jackpot. Each and every one of the people at my table is the last person on earth you'd ever want to see shove food in their face.

Ivy is the worst. She is the meanest, most stuck-up, most hateful old bag around. Thinks she's better than everybody else. Why? Don't ask me. Maybe because she goes to the beauty shop once a week to get her hair fixed into a little gray helmet, or has a bunch of pantsuits to show off how *trim* (her word) she is, or wears a passel of brooches and bracelets. She has the nerve to comment on everything I do, everything I say, and everything I eat. "Cora, is that on your diet?" and "Cora, with your size you might want to pass on dessert today." She's always talking about my *size,* like it was an extra head sprouting on my shoulders. *She* goes to that damn exercise class every day, all them old ladies jumping and grunting and bending over. Just the thought of it makes me sick.

Next there's Albert Krol. There are hardly any men here, so a lot of people think we're lucky to have one at our table. The ladies flutter and chirp like sparrows around him. Far as I'm concerned, he's barely alive. He never talks; I don't even know if he *can.* If he ever manages to squawk out a sound, everybody jumps, like the chair or the table just said, "S'cuse me." Long shanks and a face like a mule. Ass that hangs like an empty flour sack. Whatever he drinks runs down the gullies on either side of his mouth. Try eating with that around.

Poison Ivy fusses over him like Jesus Christ himself has come down from heaven to eat at our table. She shoos away the other biddies if they hover around too long and acts like she knows all about his life. "He was distinguished," she says, "a very respected man in his community," but all I have to do is look at his hands and I know what kind of living he made. His claws are as twisted and hard as a crab's. Every finger big as my wrist and the little one whacked off at the first knuckle. All the men in my life had hands like that—including my daddy, my brother, and my husband—so he ain't fooling me.

Plus he is a Polack.

The last person is Carolyn Robertson, a colored lady in a wheelchair. They lopped off one of her legs just below the knee on account of sugar diabetes. My ma had the same thing. They nickeled-and-dimed her toes, then her feet, then one leg and finally the other. But I am getting ahead of myself. Aside from the wheelchair and the missing leg, you can't see nothing wrong with her, but she don't say a word. She just watches us. There are some other colored people here and she stares over where they're sitting like it's paradise and she's stranded on the wrong side of the river. Go on, then! I want to tell her. You can't help feeling slighted when she's silent as a stone around us, but smiles and nods and pats her own kind on the arm, all the while chattering like a parrot.

You should see Poison Ivy's face when she

looks at Carolyn. It's like she's watching a Frankenstein movie. You can tell she just can't *believe* she's sitting there at the table, eating with a n———. You know which word I mean. I won't say it because I know you're not supposed to, but that word is thick in the air. You feel it floating right over our table and you can see it all over Ivy's face like someone wrote it again and again with a grease pencil. The feeling's mutual, I got to say. You can see that, too. Once in a while when Ivy's busy yammering, Carolyn sneaks her a look that would curl your toes.

I'm getting to what Ivy said, but first I got to talk about the food, if you can call it that. Everything tastes the same, like sludge or cardboard. The plates come in two colors: shit brown and puke green. They're Melmac, that plastic stuff that won't break. Looks like something they'd make a fake leg out of.

B Wing people are lined up under the windows in their wheelchairs. Some get their food all ground up in a cup, and they slurp it up through a straw. Doesn't matter what it is—meat, potatoes, beets, or pudding—they grind it all up together. Others open their mouths like baby birds and the nurses poke food in. When I asked the Filipino girl how we were supposed to eat with that around, she looked at me like I was an ax murderer and said, "Why, Mrs. Sledge, it keeps them more *oriented.*"

Figure that one out.

Well, yesterday Poison Ivy sailed in in full regalia. She had a hat that looked like a bucket clamped on her head, her talons had a fresh coat of red paint, and a skein of necklaces swung on her caved-in chest. She'd hardly sat down when she started gibbering like a chimp.

I try not to pay her any mind. Just sitting next to her makes my blood pressure go through the roof, and it's bad enough already. She thinks I'm stupid on account of the way I talk. I'm used to it. Lots of people think anyone with a southern accent is a half-wit.

I ate my Salisbury steak and minded my own business while she kept jabbering to the biddies at the table behind her. When she lowered her voice and they started sneaking looks at me, I took notice.

"What're you looking at?" I finally asked.

"Well, Cora. I'm sure you've heard what's happening around here," Ivy said in her busybody way.

"I don't have the slightest idea."

"Things are turning up missing. You *must* have heard."

A rushing started in my ears. Krol just kept shoveling food into his piehole. But Carolyn laid down her fork and watched us like we were her favorite TV show.

"No, I haven't." I picked up my fork and carried on with my meat.

"Is that right?" Ivy narrowed her eyes and leaned toward me. "You don't know a thing about it?" she whispered, loud enough for the whole place to hear.

"No, I don't!" I slammed down my fork. Even old Krol jumped. "What're you saying?"

Ivy shrugged, the simpering she-devil, but her eyes said everything. She picked up her spoon and pretended to suck up her soup.

"You think *I* have something to do with it?" Blood banged in my ears. "Are you accusing me of stealing?"

Now Krol stared at me with his blank blue eyes, while Carolyn suddenly found her plate real interesting.

"I'm just saying it's funny," Ivy said with a twisted smile. "Funny how this all started happening just about the time you came."

I wanted to crush her bones like an eggshell. My neck started swelling, my heart pounded. Words snagged in my throat. All I could do was gurgle. Ivy's friends hunched around their table like vultures over a dead skunk.

"You got no call to say that, Ivy," I finally managed to spit out. "You're talking out your ass."

She curled up her nose. "No need to use words like that, Cora. You're overmedicated. I'm afraid it's affecting your judgment."

"Overmedicated? What in the hell is that supposed to mean?" My heart was pounding so hard I thought I'd drop dead on the spot.

"Doped up. It's plain as day. You come in here bleary-eyed, slurring your words. It's a disgrace. It gives this place a bad name."

"I didn't ask to be here!" I yelled. All the heads in the room spun toward me. "You listen here, Ivy! I don't know why you're tormenting me, but you're going to be sorry! I'm going to show you, and you'll be eating crow 'til the cows come home!"

I don't remember standing up, but the next thing I knew I was holding on to the edge of the table for dear life. My hands shook, I gasped for breath. Just when I was about to keel over, an aide showed up and took hold of my elbow.

"What's going on here?" she asked. "What's wrong, Mrs. Sledge?"

"She's under the influence," Ivy butted in. "High as a kite."

"Get me out of here!" I screamed. "Take me back to my room!"

And that's the long and short of it. When I got back to my room I figured I might as well be hung for a sheep as a lamb, so I *did* take some pills—enough that I didn't give a shit about anything. I went to bed and—for a little while at least—forgot about this miserable place where I don't have a friend in the world and everybody's out to get me.

THE SPRINGS

Today's Wednesday, the day they change my linens, vacuum my room, and swish out the toilet. Big deal. I came down here to what they call the Day Room to get away from the noise and get a little writing in before lunch. There's only one other person, name of Elsa, over on the other side of the room crocheting an afghan. She churns them out like a factory and gives them to the nurses. Maybe she figures they'll be nicer to her that way. The one she's working on now's the color of Pepto-Bismol. She keeps sneaking looks over here, like she never saw a pen or paper before.

I got to say that I'm starting to get a craving for writing in this book. It's funny, but I think of it more and more. Now that mess with Ivy is distracting me from the real story. I'm keeping my eyes and ears open, but that's neither here nor there right now. What I want to say is ready to bust out of me. It's all fighting to get out at the same time, so I don't know *where* to begin. But I guess it doesn't really matter. It's all got to come out one way or another, so I'll just start at the beginning.

I was born on July 18, 1914, near Neosho, Missouri. Neosho is an Indian word that means clear, cold water because there's a lot of springs back there, and caves, too. Me and my sisters and brother, we're named after rocks, every one of us. Well, except me, really—but that was a mistake. My daddy was always reading about jewels and minerals, and he worked in the mines there, like a lot of the men. There's lead around there, and zinc, and a big tripoli mine that's been there since long before I was born. Tripoli's grit they use for buffing and scouring. We called it soda ash.

Ruby was the oldest, the boss and the brain. She ruled the three of us kids, and half the others in those parts for miles around. She called the shots, organized the games, told everybody what to do and where to go. Nothing changed when she grew up. She was like a locomotive saying Do This and Do That, and if you knew what was good for you, you did it. She married a big lug called Calvin Roberts and she wore the pants in that marriage long before anybody ever heard of such things. Later she got to be a big wheel around Neosho, what she called a pillar of society, and if anybody seen Ruby Roberts coming down the street in her big black Lincoln, they bowed and scraped; they practically got down on their knees and groveled on the sidewalk. She had a hand in everything— buying and selling property, construction, even the town council—and she could make or break people. She had a fur coat, a house with a den *and* a living room, a set of silver that filled a mahogany hutch, and, like I said, that Lincoln that Calvin kept shining like glass. Far as I could see, that's the only work he ever did. Ruby bought him a cabin out there on the lake so he could fish whenever the mood struck him. Don't ask me why, but she was crazy about that man.

Ruby died seven or eight years ago in the old folks home there in Neosho. She went nuts in the end, screaming and bawling like a little baby. They had to tie her up and she got mean, too, giving anybody who rubbed her the wrong way a knock upside the head with her cane. Calvin, he was long gone from cancer. It rotted him from the inside out like a bad potato.

Next was Crystal. She was the pretty one. Curls the color of maple syrup, the reddest lips and the greenest eyes. Everybody fawned and fussed over her. My daddy doted on her. Boys trailed her like lovesick dogs and even *I* got to say that Crystal was a lot of fun, always laughing and telling stories. You'd think she had a wonderful life ahead of her, but that just shows looks aren't everything. She got married when she was eighteen, moved up to St. Louis, and the next time she came through town—about two years later—she was a falling-down drunk. That took everybody by surprise because we were Baptists from way back, and we weren't supposed to cuss or drink or play cards. I never saw my ma or daddy touch a drop of liquor.

Crystal could not stop drinking. She went

through six husbands, and each and every one of them loved her to death, but they couldn't do a thing to help her. The last one, Bill, came around sobbing and saying she was killing herself. Half the time he didn't even know where she was. She'd go on a bender and be gone days and sometimes weeks. He'd find her in some fleabag hotel laying in her own mess.

The last time I saw her was 1951, when I was back home visiting. Bill had found her holed up in some dive down near Pea Ridge, Arkansas. They drove through Neosho on their way back to Joplin, where they were living. Bill idled the car outside my ma's house, didn't even shut off the engine. I went out and leaned in the window. I'll never forget how Crystal looked sitting there in the passenger seat, like a little old woman, nothing more than a skeleton clutching the dashboard with fingers that looked like claws on some poor bird. She turned her head toward me and smiled, and I almost fell down right there and died. She looked like a mummy, her skin shrunk up and yellow, and her lips drawn back from her teeth. Even the whites of her eyes were yellow and, skinny as she was, her belly was swollen up like she was nine months pregnant.

"Toad," she said. "How you doing, little sister?" She smiled and I thought of that beautiful girl. She died a couple of months later, thirty-nine years old.

It's hard to talk about my third sister. I swear, sometimes I think it's the reason for Crystal's drinking, and for the feeling in my heart, which is a loneliness I've had since I was the smallest child. It's the very same feeling I have now, here in this place, like I'm all alone in the world, different from everybody else with not a hint of hope in sight. It's been like that all my life. People have called me lazy, but it's the God's honest truth that a lot of the time I just could not get out of bed. Like I said when I started this book, I'm here to tell the truth. I'm sick and tired of pretending I'm happy.

Emerald Grace was the third baby born into my family. She died when she was fourteen months old, one week before I was born. One week! For the life of me, I can't imagine burying a baby, then having another one a few days later, but that's what my ma did. It explains a lot, when I look back now. The grief I was born into and the hole in my ma's heart that—no matter how hard I tried—I couldn't squeeze into. I think she had a hard time even *looking* at me. She expected to see that little girl who died and instead there *I* was, like one of them cowbirds. You know the ones I mean. The mama bird lays her egg in the nest of some cute little bird—a finch or a warbler—then pretty soon there's a big, fat, dust-colored bird different from all the other ones, with its mouth wide open. The mama bird tries to jam a worm down its throat, but she knows something's not right. The cowbird gets so big it starves the other babies out, and the mama bird's stuck with one big ugly-ass baby that isn't even hers. That's how I felt. Ma had to settle for me because the baby she *really* loved, the one that she'd fed and washed and played with for a whole year, was taken away.

I felt like I knew Emerald Grace, like she was there while I was growing up. A lot of people don't believe in ghosts, but I think they're around us all the time. Not the way people say— white things floating in the air, or cold winds, or doors slamming—but a space that nothing can fill. That's the best way I can describe it. Emerald had a place in our family even though no one ever mentioned her name. We stepped around her as if she was a living body. Her voice was the silence she left when she died, the sorrow in my ma's heart, and sometimes I think that was the loudest sound around, drowning out the rest of us.

I was next, the fourth girl, and by that time my folks had it up to the gills with girls. My own mother told me so. She was ashamed. My daddy, he just grit his teeth and shook his head. If that wasn't bad enough, I was born two weeks late, so big and fat I nearly killed my ma. It was the middle of a scorching summer and her legs swelled up so bad before I was born that she went to the spring and plunked herself down in it for hours at a time. Everybody says that's why I've always loved the water. Ma said I was nearly speaking age when I finally decided to be born, and they half expected me to hop down off the bed, walk on out of the room, and fix myself breakfast. They took me to the butcher and weighed me on the meat scale. Eleven pounds! That big, when everyone else in my family was skinny as snakes.

"She looks like a big old toad!" Ruby said the first time she saw me, and from that moment on, that's what all my kin called me. Even my husband Abel called me Toad 'til the day he died.

Coral Lorene Spring. That's my real name, the one my folks gave me. Like I said, we was all named after rocks. Coral is a powerful stone, and pretty, too—usually red or sometimes white. But whoever wrote out my birth certificate forgot the last letter. Everybody was so busy calling me Toad, nobody noticed 'til I went to school, and by that time it was too late. So people who weren't in my family called me Cora, and that's what I've been ever since. My middle name is after my grandmother, my ma's mother, Lorene LeFlore, who scared the living tar out of me. Far as I was concerned, she was the meanest woman ever to walk the face of the earth. Big as a mountain, arms like a lumberjack, and tiny black eyes that glittered in her big flat face. Some said she was

French, others said Cherokee. According to everybody, I am the spitting image of her.

When I was four years old, my brother Jasper was born and you've never seen such thanksgiving and hallelujahs and jumping for joy in your life. It was like the second coming of Christ. Finally, a boy! Jasper was the apple of everybody's eye, including mine. He was as spoilt as he could be, and us girls waited on him hand and foot. He got married, got a job with Allstate Insurance, and ended up living all over the country.

So that's my family. Ruby, the Brains. Crystal, the Beauty. Jasper, the Boy.

Which one was I?

I was the Fat One. The pig, the cow, the hippo. The Toad. My weight, or my *size*—like everybody likes to call it when what they mean is *fat*— has been the curse of my life. When I was little I didn't play or run or climb like the other kids, even though I could swim like a fish. If I had my way I'd of spent all my time in that river where I grew up, floating with the current. I loved to feel light as a feather fluttering in the water. Otherwise I wanted to be inside, or up in the loft of the barn reading, or later, when I had my kids, away from those other women yakking and shopping and comparing everything—their clothes and kids and husbands and houses. When someone got a camera out, I wanted to run and hide. I can't tell you how awful it is to see a picture of yourself big as a house with normal-size people standing around you, like you are some monument they're posing beside. If it was up to me, I'd tear up every picture that's ever been taken of me.

Me and Jasper's the only ones left.

One more thing. It's hard to put into words, but I'm going to try. Once in awhile—if somebody mows the lawn right when it's getting dark, and I get a whiff of that smell of grass and the sun's going down and the dew's about to break—I remember the feeling I had ever since I can remember, from the time I was the tiniest girl. It's not happy, or sad, it's just the feeling of me, of who I was, and still am. Me: Cora Lorene Spring, before I was anyone else, or took Abel's name I've used for sixty-five years now, or had kids and grandkids, or got put away here in this place. Not fat or skinny, or dumb or smart, or rich or poor, but something beyond that. More. Maybe that feeling is God, or my soul. I don't know, but it's the reason I've managed to stay alive, and still *want* to be alive, despite everything—even my better judgment.

THE QUARTERS

My daughter, Glenda, gave me a roll of quarters so I can tip the girls here if they do something nice for me, like go get me a new towel or clean up a mess I made by accident. I keep them in a candy dish on my dresser. I hadn't used but a few of the quarters because those girls are paid to do their jobs and don't need any extra from me.

A woman down the hall fell and broke her collarbone. They're giving her Percocet, but that makes her goofy (ain't that the point?), so she holds them aside and I give her a quarter a pill. I'd only bought four or five when I noticed my stash of quarters was way down. Sometimes I get a little fuddled up, and I thought maybe I was imagining things.

Then damned if I wasn't in the bathroom yesterday, standing in the tub and having a nice cigarette from a pack I found in the lobby (I'm not supposed to smoke. But that's a whole other story), blowing the smoke out the window when that Filipino girl called Angela came in to change my sheets.

"Mrs. Sledge, are you *smoking?*" she called out. Like she'd say, "Was you eating dead *babies?*" or "Was you robbing a *bank?*"

Quick as I could, I flushed the cigarette (it

wasn't but two-thirds gone) down the toilet, washed my hands, and put a gob of toothpaste on my tongue.

"Angela, how can you even *begin* to think that?"

She gave me a look to show she knew better, so I decided to give her a little hush money. I went over to the candy dish and there weren't but four quarters left! That's when I remembered other things, like how my jewelry box had been askew, and how my closet door was standing open, when I swore it'd been closed when I left for lunch. My underclothes had been tangled up in my top drawer one day, but like I said, sometimes those pills make things fuzzy. Now there's no denying it. I didn't let on, though, because for all I knew, the culprit was standing right in front of me.

"Thank you for your trouble," I said as I put the quarter in Angela's hand. I watched her real close. "I know you're a good girl."

"Oh, Mrs. Sledge! You don't need to do that." She didn't turn a hair and looked me right in the eye. If she was the thief, she was one cool customer. But she might have a lot of practice from going into everybody's room all innocent-like and stealing them blind. It was a little suspicious that I didn't notice them quarters was gone until now. Maybe she thought she had me over a barrel since she caught me smoking.

"You keep that," I said. "That's for helping me

out, because I'm at the mercy of people here. I sure don't want to make no enemies."

"Enjoy those clean sheets!" she said as she waltzed out.

People come and go in this room like Grand Central Station. Half the time I don't know who they are or why they're here. People like Angela coming to clean my room, or bring my mail, or give me treatments. There's janitors come to change a lightbulb or check a faucet, inspectors making sure the smoke alarm works, and even them candy stripers, high school girls who want to read you the newspaper or clip your fingernails.

Those last three quarters huddled in the candy dish like scared rabbits. I started to put them in my wallet for safekeeping, but then I had a better idea. I left them there for bait. I'll get to the bottom of this one way or another. You watch.

VITUS AND THE CIGARETTES

Like I said, I'm not supposed to smoke because of my lungs. Besides that, I can't smoke in my room. Plus it's next to impossible to get your hands on a cigarette. Same with pills: They dole them out each day, and if you want any extra you have to go to the nurses' station and get down on your knees and beg. They have to call the doctor to get permission, and if you're lucky you'll get one, and I mean *one,* pill that's not on your chart. I hardly waste my time anymore. There's people here who got more pills than they know what to do with and a screw loose to boot. I trade them for whatever I got, sometimes just a stick of gum.

I'm a grown woman and I've been smoking since I was fifteen. So if I manage to get a cigarette by hook or by crook, I go out in the courtyard and have me a smoke. There's plants out there, and a brick circle in the middle where they put a statue of Cupid—one of those plaster things from Tijuana—and a wooden bench. For a change of scenery I take my book out there and write, and boy have I been writing! I can't believe it, but this thing is filling up fast. I write like a house on fire, 'til my hand feels like it's been pounded by a mallet. To tell you the truth, it's the only thing that's keeping me going right now.

From time to time some busybody with nothing better to do comes strolling past here and wants to know what I'm doing. I tell them I'm writing my last will and testament. That usually gets rid of them. Except for that little Mrs. Cipriano, who reminds me of a spider monkey. She has a mustache thick as Joseph Stalin's. I lit up when she started to pull up a chair, gave her a shit-eating grin, and blew a cloud of smoke into her poor little shriveled-up face. The old girl can still scoot, I'll say that for her. Scampered across that pavement like her tail was on fire.

Much as I write, I'm still not getting to the meat of things. I want to talk about *me,* what's happened to *me,* but I keep getting distracted by the goings-on here. Like today. I'd no sooner got rid of that spider monkey than here comes another one—a man this time, a big one.

He had on a kelly green sweat suit with white stripes running down the sleeves and legs. I'd seen him a few times from across the dining room, but never close up. Like I said, he's tall, with a lot of pure white hair. He had sandals on. Sandals! Damned if he didn't start heading in my direction. I closed this book and stuck it under my thigh. Lord have mercy, I thought. Here we go again.

"May I?" he said, pointing to the empty space on the bench next to me.

I shrugged. "It's a free country."

"Finally, I find someone who indulges."

He unzipped a pocket of his sweatshirt, pulled out a pack of Parliaments, shook one out, and held it toward me. By that time I was down to the end of my cigarette, so I stubbed it out and took one of his. I wasn't about to pass up a free one. He lit mine with one of those Bic lighters. I wasn't used to that.

"I don't like smoking alone," he said. "It's so much nicer to have company. Vitus Kovic," he said, reaching his hand out toward me. "Pleased to meet you."

He has an accent like Dracula's. His hand was soft as a girl's, but a lot bigger, of course.

"Cora Sledge," I said. "Where in the world are you from?"

For the life of me, I can't remember what he said. Czechoslovakia or Romania or Yugoslavia— one of those communist countries. I snuck glances at him. He crossed his legs at the knee and held his cigarette at the very tips of his fingers. He has dark, deep-set eyes. Not bad looking, not at all. And he talks a blue streak. He was a waiter in some high-class restaurant. Five stars! Nothing like we have here, where waiters are way down on the totem pole. He worked in Germany, France, Switzerland—all over, just about every country you ever heard of. He told me about rivers going through the middle of towns over there in Europe, and little tables where people eat outside, and big churches hundreds of years old.

"Ever see any castles?" I asked. I never been outside this country in my life.

He chuckled. "So many castles, Cora, I've lost count."

Now, Abel had his good points, but conversation was not one of them. Most of the time I was lucky to get a grunt out of him. I'm not used to a man who chats. It got *me* talking. Before I knew it, I'd told him how my kids took everything I owned and put me in this place. I told him all about my house, right down to how I kept a red coffee can for bacon grease on the stove.

He was interested in all of it, asked me where I'd lived, how long I'd been married, how many kids I had. Where did *they* live? I have to say I was flattered by all that attention.

"How about you?" I asked. "Ever been married?"

"Yes," he answered with a faraway look in his eyes. "My wife died many years ago."

"Well, I'm sorry to hear that."

I wanted to ask more—what happened to his wife, did he have any kin in this country, how he ended up in this hellhole—but I didn't want to get *too* nosy. I settled for asking him how long he'd been here.

"Only a couple of months."

I could tell by the way he pursed his lips and stared down at the ground that he doesn't want to be here any more than I do. "Bad business. Bad business," he said, shaking his head. He looked up and smiled. "Say, shall we have another cigarette?"

Well, I was starting to feel funny spending so much time with him there on the bench, but I figured one more wouldn't hurt. When we were done he stood up and held out his elbow to me.

"May I escort you to your room?" he asked.

They got better manners over there in Europe.

GLENDA COMES CALLING

Glenda showed up at my door carrying a basket of dried fruit: figs, dates, prunes, and apricots. Once you hit seventy, people aren't happy unless your bowels are running like a sieve. She set it down on my dresser, breezed over to my armchair, and plunked herself down like nothing in the world was wrong. She was wearing one of her outfits—flouncy sleeves and loose pants you could fit three people into.

"Well, Mommy, you're looking nice today," she said, giving a big smile that showed off the teeth her new husband paid to have capped. "How are you doing?"

I turned away. I couldn't stand to see her face.

"Are you *ever* going to get tired of giving me the silent treatment?" she asked while she picked up each and every thing on my dresser. I liked to choke when she ran her hand over this book, but thank God she didn't open it. "We only want what's best for you," she said with a sigh. "We found the very nicest place we could to make sure you're well taken care of."

That burned me up, but I wasn't going to give her the satisfaction of an argument. "How's Lulu?" was all I said.

"Lulu is just as happy as she can be. Alex is

taking real good care of her. She loves playing with the kids."

She was lying through her teeth. Lulu does not like children and she doesn't like noise. Since the minute I laid eyes on her, I've been able to read that dog's mind. "I've been waiting for you. Let's go home," she said when I found her at the dog pound. When we got to the house she sniffed around a little, then looked me in the eye and said, plain as day, "I'm very happy. I might not *always* be good, but I'll try my hardest." And that's just what she did. Aside from getting into the trash whenever I forgot to close the cupboard under the sink, that dog has been as good as gold. When my great-grandkids come over and chase her around, she comes up to me and says, "This is not my idea of fun. If you don't make them stop, I'll have to bite."

"We got you this private room so you wouldn't have to share with anybody," Glenda went on. "Your meds were way out of whack, Mommy. You couldn't even walk straight. You were disoriented. We were so worried about you. We couldn't go to bed at night without wondering whether you were okay. Now you got someone here to clean your room, and make sure you're getting balanced meals, and managing your meds."

All the time she was talking she kept walking around and fingering everything—the sheets, pillow shams, and bedspread she'd bought me in what's called *bed in a bag*. The curtains on the window alongside the bed were in the same floral print, blurry purples and pinks that call to mind toilet paper. Then she started messing with the special things I keep on my windowsill: a glass spaniel with two puppies connected to her with gold chains (to remind me of Lulu), a violet in a pot no bigger than a shot glass (the only growing thing in the room), and a picture of my kids taken at Sears one Christmas. Finally, she picked up my crystal.

I got to take a detour here to tell you about it.

This rock came from my great-aunt Alpha, who dug it herself in the Ouachita Mountains down there in Arkansas, where my daddy's family's from. They're known for their crystals, some of the most beautiful in the world. People around there wear them, or carry them in their pockets. Say they're sacred, with magical powers for healing, and for seeing into the past and the future.

Aunt Alpha, she used them rocks for scrying, or what you'd call fortune-telling. People came from all over to ask her advice or to talk with people who'd passed on. She had a room at the back of her house where she lit candles, burned some kind of smelly brush, and looked into those crystals to make contact with the other world. She smoked a corncob pipe and kept a thousand cats. Us kids were scared to death of her.

My crystal is what you call a hand holder because it fits right in your palm. It's quartz, like a big lump of ice. One end is pointed and as clear as water. The other end, where it broke off from the ground, is frosty. It's called phantom crystal because of the shapes inside it—pictures like the mountains it came from, a waterfall, and a fish. There's a face with a beard and a broke-off branch. The more you stare into it, the more you see. Pretty soon you yourself are inside the rock, walking between icy cliffs, with that fairy frost swirling around you. Up toward the point, my crystal has two bubbles of water locked in it, like they're dancing with each other, floating to the top. That water's been in there forever. Millions of years.

My daddy gave me that crystal when I was seventeen years old, a few months before I married Abel. That was one of the blackest periods of my life. I was desperate, let's just say that. Young as I was, I was backed into a corner I couldn't see my way out of. It's one of those things I never talked about. Too much pain, and too much torment. But that rock. He gave it to me as something hard, something to hold on to.

I like to hold it against my cheek or neck, or sometimes my forehead. If you're hot or have a fever, it feels like a big chunk of ice. If you're cold, it's like a hot-water bottle. I feel the life inside it, and the place it comes from, the place where I grew up, the rivers and lakes, and the springs bubbling up through the rocks. This far from home, way out here by this ocean that I never even saw 'til I was all grown up, I remember the smells of my family and how my ma's hands felt when she pulled the comforter up under my chin at night.

Sometimes when I stare into it I see the faces of men I might have married, children I might have had, or houses I might have lived in. I see storms moving in and the sun coming out. Lightning strikes, hoot owls, and car wrecks. I don't have Aunt Alpha's gift, but I've asked the crystal what's going to become of me. Or I try to ask those that's passed over to the other side what it's like. If they're happy and what's in store for me. I hold the rock against my temple and ask the dead ones, my mother and father, to protect me. To use what they've learned to guide me and keep me safe.

Your rock, Abel called it, and that's what it is. He'd bring it out of the china cabinet to show people when they came to call. He drove me crazy. He kept a bone he'd found while he was digging out the backyard. Just a chicken bone as far as I could see, but that man acted like it fell out of King Tut's tomb. He always had to show people *something,* even if it meant running out in the yard and pulling an orange off the tree.

I couldn't help but tease him about the shapes

inside. "You don't see that elephant standing there by the circus tent?" I asked, and he'd stare into that thing 'til his eyes bugged out. "And them fields with the cows grazing near a wind-mill?"

I swear, that man had the imagination of a newt. "Oh, yeah. There it is! I can make it out now!" he might say. He looked real hurt when I snorted and shook my head. Poor old bastard. He must have gone fishing the day they handed out brains.

"Put that down!" I told Glenda in no uncertain terms. "It's nothing to be fooling with."

That hurt her feelings. She'd always been closer to her daddy than to me, and I wondered if she felt cheated that he died first. People might not know it, but I hate to be a disappointment to her, even though I always am. Who wouldn't be ashamed to have a mother the size of me who spends half the day in bed? Sometimes I think I should never have had kids in the first place.

Even though she's sixty now, I can see the girl standing there chewing the end of her braid like it was yesterday. She'd fasten her eyes on me while I did the housework until I had to yell, "Quit your looking at me! Go out in the yard!" I'm not proud of it now. No. In fact I'm so ashamed I burst out bawling. I just couldn't help myself. Before I knew it I was heaving and snorting and crying up a storm. I felt like I was coming apart at the seams, like my body was going to fall in pieces on the floor.

"Mommy, Mommy! What's *wrong?*" she yelled. "Oh, no! What's the matter?"

I couldn't even get my breath to tell her. This place is bedlam, I wanted to say. I don't know whether I'm coming or going. I wanted Lulu and my home and every other thing I'd lost. Even her, the girl I hadn't done right by. I'd lost my mind. Life was just too much for me.

"My moods are swinging," I said. "I'm going from hot to cold. I need a couple of my pills."

She came over and rubbed my back until I quieted down. "Tell you what," she said. "It's almost lunchtime. How about I join you in the dining room? I can meet some of your friends."

"I don't have no friends," I said. "I need some pills. Can you ask the doctor?"

Glenda sighed and said, "Let's just try to get through lunch, okay? We'll talk about that later. Come on, before the food's all gone."

I let her push me down there in a wheelchair but I made her stop before we turned the corner so I could get out and walk, otherwise tongues would wag. As it was, we caused quite a stir when we walked in. Heads spun like owls and a hiss rose up from all the whispering. Poison Ivy almost fell out of her chair when the helper came over to make room for Glenda. The meal was tuna casserole, carrot and raisin salad, and melba toast. Normal people get pudding cup for dessert. People like me get fruit cocktail.

Before long, Glenda was talking away, not just to our table but to everybody around us. She was like a movie star, old ladies getting up from their places to come over and ask who she was, rude as could be. Glenda kept smiling, glad-handing everyone and chatting up a storm. Carolyn talked just as natural as you please and Ivy kept interrupting, doing her darnedest to hog the limelight. Glenda even got a grunt out of old Krol.

I spotted Vitus across the room, talking to one of the girls who feeds the droolers. He was leaning against the wall like a playboy, his arms crossed over his chest, smiling and chatting. The girl nodded as she spooned goop into an old woman's mouth. She threw her head back and laughed.

"You're not eating, Mommy," Glenda said. "Is something wrong with your food?"

I pushed it away. "Looks like cat sick. I'm not interested."

Ivy watched the whole thing. She raised her painted-on eyebrows, twisted her chicken-ass mouth into a smirk, and said real low, so just *I* could hear, "I'll be! I see Don Juan likes 'em young!"

I grit my teeth so hard they almost cracked. Vitus waved good-bye to the girl and headed off toward one of the dark-haired boys who takes the dirty plates off the tables and puts them in a plastic tub. Vitus walked right up to this one and put his arm around his shoulder. They talked and laughed like old friends. Before Vitus walked away, he patted the boy on the back.

"See there, Ivy," I said. "He's just a friendly man, that's all. He likes talking to people, no matter who they are." I flopped back in my chair. I was wore out and I wanted to go back to my room, take a couple pills, and crawl into bed.

"Well, that was just delicious," Glenda said in that cheerful way of hers. She looked at her watch, then at everyone around the table. "And I've really enjoyed our conversation, but I'd better get moving before rush hour starts. I have a long drive ahead of me."

In the shuffle of chairs getting pushed out, old butts being hoisted from seats, and old legs trying to straighten out, I forgot about Vitus. When I looked up, damned if he wasn't plowing his way through the tables, coming straight for me. My heart beat like a tom-tom. He didn't look to the right or the left and he was moving fast, taking long strides. As he whizzed past us, something sailed over my head and landed on the table in front of me. I snatched it up and sneaked a look in my hand. It was a white paper napkin folded up into a pellet.

"Your friends are real nice," Glenda said while

she pushed me back to my room. "They're a lively bunch."

"They aren't my friends."

The pellet was burning a hole in my hand.

When we got back to my room, she gave me a bag of snacks—healthy things like yogurt, trail mix, and little boxes of raisins. "It's going to be a couple of weeks before I can get down here again, Mommy," she said, wringing her hands. "Is there anything else you need? Anything I can get for you?"

My sweaty hand was making the pellet soft and soggy. "I need some cigarettes," I said, real pitiful. "Can you bring me a pack?"

Glenda's eyes sparked. "What in the world are you talking about?"

"I'm out of cigarettes. I need some more."

"You know you aren't supposed to smoke!" She started packing her things up lickety-split, not even looking at me. "You have emphysema and high blood pressure! You just got over pneumonia not too long ago! It's your choice if you want to kill yourself, but you'll have to find a way to do it on your own."

"All right then, I will. Maybe you better go now. I need a nap."

I hated to part that way, but sometimes we just don't see eye to eye. Soon as she was gone I opened the pellet. I don't know how Vitus had managed to fold it so many times. It was practically the size of a handkerchief when I spread it out. He'd used a black felt pen, the kind with a real fine point. It bled out into the white tissue, making the writing look fuzzy, like it was alive and quivering. And oh my goodness—that beautiful handwriting. It's the way they learn to write over there in Europe, full of curlicues and flourishes, like the Declaration of Independence, or a handwritten Bible.

I spread it out in my lap. It was short, only four words.

Shall we smoke tonight?

AN EVENING SMOKE

About nine o'clock I was in my room watching *Roseanne*. I looked up at the sliding glass door that opens out onto the courtyard, and there was Vitus standing there. I liked to jumped out of my skin. God knows how long he'd been watching me. He gave a little wave, made the smoking sign, then pointed at the latch. He had on a white V-neck sweater with blue and red stripes around the neck and wrists, them same sandals, and *shorts!* I'm telling you, his legs aren't at all bad—shapely, with muscles like a horse, and just the right amount of hair, not too much and not too little.

When I opened the door, he *bowed!* He brought his hand from behind his back and held up a daisy, what I call a black-eyed Susan. Like I said, they got different manners over there in Europe. It's what you call *charm.*

"Would you care to join me for a cigarette?" he said in that accent that calls to mind a fancy cologne. There I stood in my robe with my hair not fixed. I wasn't sure about letting a man into my room, it being night and all. And I know they'd kill us if they caught us smoking in there. He must have guessed what I was thinking because he said, smooth as silk, "Shall we stroll in the garden?"

What with everything you hear on television, I don't think I've stepped outside after dark for ten or fifteen years. But Vitus waved his arm toward the courtyard like a magician. All of a sudden it was like a movie where music starts playing, and birds commence to singing, and butterflies twit from flower to flower. I saw the stars and smelled the night-blooming jasmine. And I thought, Why the hell not? My life is lived. What difference does it make if I collapse right here and die?

"Oopsie!" Vitus said when I started to walk out. "Aren't you forgetting something?" He put two fingers up to his lips again and gave me a sly look. He's a right devil. All he had with him was a jacket. So I went and got the cigarettes and off we went, pretty as you please.

We sat on the bench by the little Cupid. He took the cigarettes out of my hand and offered me one, then lit it like a gentleman. I don't want to say anything bad about Abel, but that man was *rough*. He had the manners of a mule. He'd just as soon piss in the shower, spit in the sink, or eat with his hands like a caveman. He was the hardest-working man alive, but when it came to couth he wasn't far from the monkeys. Vitus and him are like night and day. He crossed his legs and sat so elegant, with his foot bouncing in the air. Abel always splayed his knees five feet apart so his privates dangled right there for the world to see. Vitus held the cigarette at the very tips of his two fingers, while Abel pinched his between his thumb and first finger like it was a hangnail he was about to chaw off.

When I shivered, Vitus took his jacket and laid it over my shoulders. That smell! The man smell. Abel died going on seven years now, and I'd forgotten the way that scent can get in your nose and down the back of your throat real thick and fuzzy, like fur growing in your pipes. My legs went rubbery and my joints started buzzing.

"I feel a little woozy," I told him.

"Woozy? What is woozy?" His laugh is way down in his throat. When I told him he chuckled. "Shall I call you that, then?"

I said I didn't mind a bit.

We had us another cigarette, and chatted some more. I haven't talked to anybody like that for the longest time. Just easy. Everything, don't matter.

You say what's on your mind and he listens real close. Once in a while a janitor or an aide walked by and turned their heads in our direction. I got to wishing Ivy or one of her cronies would see us.

When we finished our cigarettes, Vitus slapped his hands down on his thighs. "Well, Woozy, I'm sorry to say I have to go. This evening has been delightful, but I must bid you a-doo."

That's how he talks.

I held his elbow as we walked to my room. At my door he held my fingers, just the tips, and gave his little bow.

It wasn't 'til I slid the door closed and locked it that I noticed the cigarette pack still in my hand. It was awful light. I flipped open the box. I was down to two.

MARCOS

Every other day between breakfast and lunch a man named Marcos comes and checks my blood pressure. He listens to my heart and lungs and takes my temperature. When he's done with that, he gives me what I call my hookah—a pipe I smoke through a long tube. I have to suck real deep and hold it as long as I can. It's for my lung disease. When I'm finished, he bends me over and bangs me all over my back, loosening things up. I hock up the biggest load of phlegm you ever saw, and I feel a hell of a lot better.

Marcos is a *technician,* not a male nurse. He wears those light blue pants and shirt, *scrubs,* like a lot of people here. He has a big belly and short bowlegs and a face only a mother could love, with big rubbery lips and bloodhound eyes, as sad as can be. Not at all a pretty man. Still, he struts around like a rooster. His hair's done up fancy, Liberace-style, with so much gunk it glistens. And his jewelry! It'd weigh down a cart horse. Big square rings, three or four bracelets, enough gold necklaces to sink a battleship.

He is a Mexican and a fruitcake.

I'm not just saying that. He told me himself. It's the damnedest thing. He looks real tough. Muscles like Popeye, jaw and forehead like one of them Neanderthals. Scarred-up skin, and a way of squinting that could curdle milk. But when he gets to talking, his hands get loose and start floating and fluttering around in the air. His eyes get to rolling and his eyelashes to batting. He fans the air and bites the heel of his hand and pats down his hair in a way that lets you know he's the biggest pansy who ever walked the face of the earth.

The funniest part is I don't even care.

Marcos has been good to me. The first few months I was here, I didn't want to come out of my room or see anybody or even get out of bed. I could *not* get my mind around what happened to me. I took whatever pills I could get my hands on and half the time I didn't know my own name. Then I got pneumonia. Good, I thought. I finally found a way to die. Every day Marcos came in and took my vitals. He straightened my blankets and opened the blinds. I just laid there and stared at the ceiling. He talked to me while he worked, nothing important, just chitchat. Sometimes he said things that made me laugh. Sometimes he told me tidbits about other people here, or about the doctors and nurses. "Miss Hildegard in 231," he said, pinching his nose, "she don't smell so good." He imitated the doctor we called Dr. Kildare, who thought he was God's gift. Marcos pranced in with one hand on his hip and the other flouncing in the air, then pretended he didn't want to touch me while he took my blood pressure. He fluttered his eyes while he listened to my heart, and puckered up his face when he handed me my medicine. Bad as I felt, I had to chuckle.

After a couple of months when I didn't get well he came into my room and sat on the edge of the bed. Right next to me! He crossed his arms over his chest and said, "All right. What is the problem?"

I told him about how they'd taken my house and my dog and stuck me here, locked me away, and forgot about me. I raved about this place that's hardly better than a prison, except you got to break the law to end up in there and here your only crime is you lived too long, or fell and

57

broke a hip, or left the burner on too long under a pan of soup. I blubbered about how I kept dreaming about my own sweet little house where I lived for forty-two years, and how I expect to wake up in my own bedroom, how I think I'll hear the birds chirping and Mrs. Villagrosa next door calling her Chihuahua to come get his breakfast. I told him how the nightmare starts fresh every morning when I open my eyes and see the damn drab wall, the door to the bathroom, and the toilet sitting there cold and quiet as the electric chair. How it all comes back: them dragging me out of my house and locking me away. I didn't hold back. I was bawling by the time I told him how I didn't have a friend in the world or a reason to live, how I wanted to die, only my body was fighting me every step of the way. How the world was a dark place I wanted to leave. I screamed for him to give me something that would help me go.

He got up and pulled a chair over next to the bed. When I'd quieted down, he took out his wallet and showed me a little torn-up picture no bigger than your thumbnail. His mother. I didn't want to say nothing, but she was the saddest thing you've ever seen. A thin, tired face with big black circles under her eyes, her hair pulled straight back, and sunk-in cheeks that made her look like she already had one foot in the grave. She didn't even smile for the picture.

"She was an angel, my darling angel," Marcos said. His eyes filled up. "Cancer, boom, when she was forty-nine." He made a throat-slitting motion across his own neck. "Every morning, I light a candle and pray. I talk to her all the time. She is with me every moment."

He stood up, put the picture in his wallet, and pushed the chair back over by the dresser. "So you see, it isn't your time." He wagged his finger at me. "When God is ready, He'll let you know."

He snapped on my TV and sat down at the foot of my bed. "Here," he said. "We'll watch a little."

That's when he started watching his soap operas in my room. *Mexican* soap operas, all in Spanish. I couldn't understand a damn word they said, but oh my God, you've never seen so much screaming and bellowing and bawling in all your born days. Sometimes Marcos tells me what they're saying, but most of the time his eyes are glued to the set. He gasps and chews his nails, pulls his own hair, yells in Spanish at the actors. Tears stream down his face. You've never seen anything like it. He is *addicted* to those shows. It's more fun to watch him than the TV.

He could get in a lot of trouble for what he does. He could get fired. I'm not saying anything, though, because I don't want him to stop. We talk and laugh about everything, and I mean *every-thing*. He don't care what you say. Some of it would make your hair stand on end.

Once a week he brings a scale and weighs me. Today was that day. He set it down, got out his damn clipboard, and motioned for me to get up there. Like usual, I pissed and moaned and begged and pleaded. I can't tell you how ashamed I am to step up there and see those numbers spin, dance around 300, and come to rest on that nasty spot.

"Just write down last week minus five," I pleaded. "I feel like I'm getting up on the gallows."

Marcos shook his head. "*Señora,* please." He pointed at the scale. "Every week, the same thing. I am so tired of it. Try and behave like a lady."

"*You* get up here!" I hollered. "It wouldn't hurt you none!" Because if you want to know the truth, Marcos could stand to drop a few himself.

He didn't say a word, just stared at me with those big, droopy eyes. I finally yelled, "Oh, what the hell!" and stepped up on the scale.

He took his time leaning over and looking at the number, then checking his clipboard, then looking at the scale again. Finally, he wrote something down. He waved me off the scale like he was directing traffic.

"Coralita, you have lost two pounds."

You could have knocked me over with a feather. At first I didn't believe him, but when he showed me the chart and I got on the scale again to make sure, I started whooping. I would have jumped up and down if I could have. I was under three hundred! Oh, my God! I hadn't even *tried!*

"I thought so," Marcos said. He took a step back and looked me up and down. "When I came in I said to myself, 'The *señora* is looking awfully *sleek* today.'"

He sucked in his cheeks and posed like a model.

Well, I don't know what got into me. I was so happy and excited I asked Marcos straight out, "Listen here, can you buy me some cigarettes?"

Oh, what an act he put on! He must have learned it from his soap operas. He slapped his hands to his face and let out a gasp, then he stomped his foot and said, "*Señora!* That is against the rules!"

I just smiled. I knew he smoked because I smelled it on him. He smelled real good, like the cologne he used and his hair oil and his soap. But underneath it all I smelled tobacco. Every man I ever loved smoked cigarettes, so to me that smell is like nectar. While Marcos stood there puffing and blowing like a little bull, I said, nice and easy, "You ain't fooling me. Watching Mexican TV in residents' rooms is against the rules, too. But that don't seem to stop you." I gave him my best smile.

"Smoking is bad for you, Cora. Very bad."

"I know. But I want them."

"You have chronic obstructive pulmonary disease! Smoking is not good for you!" He stomped his foot again.

"I don't have but one or two a day."

"Do you know what could happen to me if they found out?"

"I won't tell nobody."

"No! It is wrong! You are a very sick woman. I would never forgive myself if something happened to you." He picked up the scale and started gathering up his things. "Besides, I need this job. I can't afford to lose it." He made for the door.

"You listen here. I am a grown-up woman! I'm a paying customer here, not a prisoner. I can do whatever I want. All they got to do is clean my room and make sure I don't fall down dead and rot two weeks before somebody finds me. Other than that, I'm on my own."

It might not of been the whole truth, but he paused with his hand on the door, and I felt the tide turning. I gave him a shit-eating smile and said, humble as could be, "I'm begging for mercy. There ain't much left in this life that makes me happy. I'm *craving* it. You know what that's like, don't you?"

He let out a big sigh and set his things down. He looked at me a long time before he held out his hand and said, "Give me the money."

I almost did a jig right there on the spot. I hoofed it over to my underwear drawer where I have an envelope with five twenty-dollar bills Glenda gave me in case of emergency. It crossed my mind, with all the funny business going on, that I shouldn't let Marcos know where I kept my money, but I didn't want to hurt his feelings by acting like I didn't trust him. Besides, I wanted those cigarettes.

"Could you get me a few other things while you're at it?" I asked as I handed the money over. "Some potato chips and Doritos? The hot kind. Maybe a couple of those cupcake things with the squiggles on them?"

"There I draw the line!"

"It won't hurt nothing. How'd you like to eat this slop they serve here day in, day out?"

"You are taking advantage of me. Besides, what about your new figure?"

He made his eyebrows go up and down, but I wasn't falling for that trick. "What if your poor mother was in a place like this?" I asked. "Wouldn't you want to know someone was watching out for her?"

He came over and stood toe to toe with me. He brought his face right up to mine until the tips of our noses touched and his big brown eyes were staring into mine. He huffs a lot, like me. I guess we both have a hard time breathing.

"Señora Sledge, you have no shame. For this, I love you."

I gave him a pretend slap on the face, then pinched his earlobe.

He grabbed my hand, kissed the ends of my

fingers, then clucked his tongue. "Look at this," he said, holding up my first two fingers, which are iodine color because of my smoking. "And you ask me to buy you cigarettes!"

"Wait 'til you're my age. You're going to be just the same."

"No! Never!" He held up his hands. He had big, fat fingers with hair on each knuckle. No stains, I had to give him that.

"I'd kill for one right now," I said, and looked at him real pitiful. "I'm having a nicotine fit."

"Devil! You are very naughty." He shook one of those sausage fingers in my face. "Lucky for you, I *too* am a devil. I crave one myself. Come."

He waved me over to the bathroom, pulled me inside, shut the door, put the toilet seat down, and patted it for me to sit down. "Here, be comfortable." He stepped over into the bathtub, slid open the window, and took a pack of Salems out of his smock.

My heart sank. "Is that all you have? Menthols?"

"Coralita, *please.* You are very rude. Did you know that? Do you want the cigarette or not? Because I can easily go smoke by myself in the break room."

"It's like sucking a mint through somebody's asshole."

It's the same thing I used to say to Abel, who started smoking menthols just so I wouldn't steal them. Marcos laughed so sudden a wad of spit flew out of his mouth. "Aye!" he said, wiping off his lips real daintylike. He lit a cigarette and blew the smoke out the window before he handed it to me.

"What brand do *you* smoke, my queen?"

I had two cigarettes left, but I was saving them in case Vitus came over again. That night he'd dropped by was the last one I'd had, and let me tell you, menthol or not, I couldn't wait for the first drag. My whole body was so keyed up, my hands were shaking. I sucked in a big lungful and felt it rinse down through my body like a warm shower. Everything melted. I let out a big sigh of relief.

"Marlboros," I answered when I'd had a few puffs. I relaxed against the back of the toilet. "I tried some of those fancy cigarettes when they came out, Virginia Slims and those that are different colors, but they were too skinny and tasted like toilet paper."

"Marlboros? Disgusting." Marcos stuck out his tongue like he tasted something nasty. He had his elbow up on the windowsill where I keep my shampoo and soap. He smoked in little sips that whistled through his teeth. "They are no good. The *worst*. Why do you smoke them?"

"I just always have." That cigarette was really hitting the spot. "Plus red's my favorite color."

"Mine, too. Here. Put the ash here."

He tipped his cigarette in the sink and ran some water. I did like he said.

"I want some of them magazines, too, when you go to the store. *National Enquirer,* or the *Star.*" I still had three-quarters of the cigarette left, but I was already worried about finishing it.

"You are spoiled. A princess. Did your husband treat you well?"

"Waited on me hand and foot. My wish was his command."

Marcos sighed and put his hand over his heart. He looked out the window. Someone was sweeping—long, lazy strokes. "You must have loved him very much."

"I got used to him. All those years, we lived together as man and wife. Had three kids together, raised them up. You couldn't of asked for a better husband or father. The kids loved him to death." I took a long drag. "Hard as I tried, and good as I knew he was, I just couldn't work up a whole lot of enthusiasm. That's the God's honest truth." I was sipping at the cigarette now, just like Marcos, trying to make it last. "There's been times I hated my own self so bad because of it, but that didn't do no good, either." You don't know how good it felt to finally say those things. There's something about Marcos that brought it out in me.

"Why?" he asked. "*Why* you don't love him?"

I shrugged. "Long story." The cigarette made

me feel cocky and coldhearted. Too bad it was almost gone. "What about your other patients? Aren't they waiting for you?"

He tipped his head back and smoked the last drag down to the filter. His nose holes are real big, and when he smokes they get even bigger. You could slip your fist in one, no problem. He blew the smoke straight up in the air, like a fountain.

"With some of them I'm in and out. Like that." He snapped his fingers. "But with my special patients, like you, it takes time." He winked. "I make up the time on the others. Hello, good-bye, I'm gone."

He held his cigarette under the tap, then snapped his fingers and held out his hand for mine. The snap was so loud my eardrums almost busted.

"I'm not done yet."

"That's it. Finito. There's nothing left."

I wanted another one, but thought I'd better not push my luck. I handed the butt over. "Now, I want to ask *you* something," I said while he ran water on it. "About being *that way.* I need to ask you a question."

He wrapped the two wet butts in a wad of toilet paper. "When you stand up, we put these in the toilet." He started washing his hands like a surgeon, every little inch of them, with the bar of Dove I use on my face.

"What is it, Cora? What do you want to know?" he asked while he scrubbed.

"Don't take offense, now," I warned him.

He shook his hands over the sink and looked around for the towel.

"All these pretty ladies here, the nurses and the ones who make up the rooms and work in the kitchen, all these cute little girls, don't you want to get to know some of them?" I was thinking how so many of them were Mexican like Marcos, and how it'd be natural for them to get together. "Don't you like women? Are you afraid of them?" I was curious as hell. "How did you get to be the way you are? You know, with men and all?"

He pulled the towel off the back of the door, where my hot-water bottle hung along with a pair of underpants I'd rinsed out. I have a problem with my bladder. He took his sweet time drying every finger all the way up to his wrists, all the time acting like I hadn't asked him a question, like I wasn't even in the room. He shook the towel out and hung it up neat, straightening it in a prissy way.

"My mother was the queen of my life!" he bellowed when he turned toward me. "There will *never* be another woman like her. Women—" He kissed the back of his hand, then he turned it over and kissed his wrist. "Women are the rulers of the world! I get on my knees in front of them." He clasped his hands like he was praying. "My wife is the most beautiful woman in the world!"

"Your *wife?*" I gasped. "You have a *wife?*"

He nodded, real serious, and puffed his chest out. "A beautiful wife and a beautiful son. I would *die* for them."

My tongue dangled out of my mouth. "Where are they?" I gasped.

"In Paree." That's how he said it. "My wife is a dancer. My son lives with his mother."

"Well, don't you want to be with them? What about your boy?"

Marcos shrugged and sucked his teeth. He looked at his fingernails. "We have our own lives. My son knows I will always be his father."

"Well, I just can't believe it! How old is he? What's his name?"

"Marcos!" He shook his head like I was the most ignorant person on earth. "He's seven years old." He picked up the wad of cigarettes and motioned for me to get up. "And now the interview is over. I must go."

"But what about these others? These men?" I tried to hoist myself off the toilet. I have to rock back and forth two or three times to get some momentum. "How can you have a wife"—I grabbed hold of the sink and pulled so hard it nearly came off the wall—"and still do these things with men?"

"It is not the same. With these men, it is different. They are my heart, my body. They are blood to me. Water. Now please, Coralita. *Move,* so I can throw this away. I don't enjoy holding these stinking wet things."

He raised the lid and tossed in the butts. While the water swirled I looked at him. My Lord, I thought. Now I've seen everything. He wiped his hands again, patted his pocket to make sure he had his cigarettes, and reached for the door.

"Is there someone you love?" I asked when the sound of the flushing stopped. "Somebody special?"

Marcos looked at the floor. The pores on his face were big. You could tell he used to have pimples. "Yes," he answered, almost under his breath. "There is someone I love."

He didn't seem real happy about it.

"Who?"

He was puffing again. The bathroom was little and we were close together. "A boy, a beautiful boy," he said. "Someone younger."

He tried to reach around me to open the door, but I stood my ground. *"Where?"* I demanded. "Where is he?"

He scowled. "Here. He is at The Palisades."

My mouth fell open. "He *lives* here?"

He huffed with disgust. "No! He *works* here."

"Who?" I demanded, and this time *I* stomped *my* foot. "What's his name?"

Marcos reached around me and jerked open the

70

door. He jostled past me like I was just a rock in the road. I didn't appreciate it one bit. When he got out in the bedroom, he spun around and looked at me. A grin spread from ear to ear.

An ugly man with a beautiful smile can break your heart.

"Renato. His name is Renato."

The way he said that name stopped me in my tracks. It took my breath away. The *RRRR* rolled like a big cat purring, and the long *AHHH* was the sound you make when something feels really, really good—use your imagination to know what I mean. That last part, the *TOE*, was like a kiss good-bye, the last kiss. So sad, and so pretty at the same time. You could feel the sex in it.

My eyes narrowed down to peepholes. "*What's* his name?" I repeated, just to hear it again.

"Re-na-to." He broke it up into three pieces, his tongue and big blubbery lips handling that word like it was a naked body. The hair on the back of my neck prickled.

"Is he Mexican, too?"

A cloud passed over Marcos's face. "I waste my time with you," he said, flapping his hand at me. "You are always rude."

"I'm just asking."

"No. He is Filipino."

"How old is he?"

"Twenty."

That set me back, but since Marcos was already huffy, I held my tongue about the boy's age.

"And you love him?"

"Yes," Marcos said in a grim way, like talking hurt him. "Renato is *mi vida*. My life."

"Well, I just don't get it."

"Then you don't understand love."

He started gathering up his things: the scale, the hookah, the stethoscope, and the blood pressure cuff. He was right, I didn't understand it at all. You'd think after all the years I've lived, everything I've done and heard and read, I'd have a pretty good idea, but while I stood there thinking about Abel and my kids, what I really felt and what I was supposed to feel, *wanted* to feel, I saw that at eighty-two years old I have no better idea about love than I had at fourteen.

"All right," Marcos said when he was all packed up. "Enough. *Adiós, señora.* 'Til we meet again."

"Don't go away mad, now. You know you're my sugar and I love you to death."

That got a smile out of him. "Wait a minute." He held up a finger and came over to me. "Close your eyes, open your mouth, and stick out your tongue."

I did like he said. With my eyes squinched tight, I felt just a little touch on my tongue, then tasted the clove flavor.

"Body of Christ," he said.

"What the hell are you talking about?" My eyes flew open and there he was.

He held up an itty-bitty bottle no bigger than my little finger, then he touched it to his own tongue. "Shhh," he said, holding his finger to his lips. "Don't tell anybody. It's our little secret."

"Don't forget my cigarettes!" I hollered as I watched my twenty-dollar bill walk out that sliding glass door and across the courtyard.

GONE!!!

Some kind of trouble out in the hall woke me up last night. Nurses were yelling, then somebody was running, then there was a lot of banging around—doors slamming and equipment rattling. They must have called the paramedics, because pretty soon the sirens came blaring, and a bunch of feet rushing in, and something rolling, like a gurney. And moans and pleading, and—oh my God, it was like someone falling into the depths of hell. After that I lay listening into the dark. My blood was chilly in my veins and I couldn't keep my legs still. I was tired, dead beat, but my nerves were jittery, so I took a couple of my pills. That made me feel worse, like my thoughts were taffy somebody was stretching all out of shape.

I got to thinking about all the houses I ever lived in—that first one where I slept up under the

73

eaves next to Ruby and Crystal, with Jasper across the hall and my ma and daddy downstairs. That first apartment me and Abel had when we moved to California. We thought we'd found paradise even though our bed pulled down out of the wall in the living room and the sink was so close you could lean out of bed and wash your hands. We conceived Kenneth there on those broken-ass springs.

I thought about that tenement in Michigan where we lived during the Depression, and the Quonset hut we moved to out here during the war, and all the ramshackle duplexes and bungalows and cracker boxes we made do in. Then, of course, I got to my own sweet house, the one I always dreamed about, the one we worked for, the only one I ever *owned*. I know every one of the doorknobs just by feel. I know which corners collect the most hair, how to jiggle the handle to make the toilet stop running, where to knee the back door when it gets stuck in winter. That house saw me through a lot of changes; it watched me grow old. It didn't care if I woke up in the morning with a song in my heart or if I was cast down to the lowest valley. I thought about how a bed is sacred when you sleep in it night after night for years and decades. So is a room, or a house. Anywhere you did something over and over—stepped out on the porch and called your dog, watched through a window for somebody to come home, washed your face first thing in the morning—those places got special power, and special meaning.

I was standing right there at the wall phone in the kitchen when Ruby called to say our ma had died. Same place I was when Glenda told me she was expecting my first grandchild. That's where I listened while the doctor explained that Abel's cancer was everywhere, that there was nothing they could do. "Toad, my goose is cooked," Abel said the next morning in that very same kitchen while I poured his coffee. He knew it, and so did I. He was damn lucky to stay there right up to the end. I came home to the empty house after we buried him and said to Lulu, "We're all alone now, girl. It's just you and me."

By the time I started thinking about this damn place, this hell they call The Palisades, I was bawling into my pillow and knotting up the bed-spread to keep from tearing out my hair. I cursed this place that's no more than a warehouse, a storage bin where people are tossed until the next shipment comes in. My room even has a number, 136, like a motor lodge or a doctor's office. After I was done cursing, I started praying. I begged God to take me home. To put me back in my house and let me live my last days there. I asked to die in my own room, in my own bed, in the hollow shaped by my own body, under blankets stitched together by my own hands and fastened

75

with little twists of yarn. *Please,* God, I prayed. It's the one thing I want.

Right before morning I dozed in that fretful way you do when you been awake all night, dreaming scraps of crazy things and sweating in the sheets. I was so worn out, so nervous and agitated when breakfasttime came, I felt like I had to get out of that room, no matter how bad I felt. So I slid my teeth in and put on my scuffs and started down to the dining room. I didn't bother running a brush through my hair or nothing.

Sometimes I feel like I'm walking all the way to China, it's so far and takes so long and all them nasty fluorescent lights in the hall reflect on the floor that's white, too, everything white, but a dirty white—like snow that's piled up beside the road. You see one horror after another walking by the open doors of people's rooms. Nobody pays any mind to decency. I've seen bare-ass old men with their balls dangling down to their knees, and tattered dog-ear tits like socks with rocks in the end. It's enough to turn your stomach.

I liked to collapsed on the floor by the time I got to my table. I never been so glad to see a chair in my life. I sat there huffing and puffing, trying to catch my breath. When I did, I looked up and saw Poison Ivy's eyes fixed on my face.

"Where have you been?" she asked.

"Last I heard, I don't answer to you. If I want to go out there on the patio and hang upside down from a tree, it's nobody's business but mine. What's it to you, anyway?"

She's got a way of staring that's worse than anything she could say. It makes you feel like dirt. Her eyes flitted to my hair, then ran down the front of my housecoat. For a second I saw myself as she did, and it wasn't a pretty sight. My housecoat was wrinkled from lying down in it, my terry cloth mules could use a wash, my toenails were long and dirty, my hair was matted flat against my head. I couldn't help but run a hand through it.

"You're late getting here," she said when she finished eyeing me.

They already had their food, French toast from the looks of it. My stomach growled. "I had a bad night. I'm not at my best."

I didn't want to look at her no more, and I sure didn't want *her* looking at *me.* I tried to signal the boy to bring my food, but he was cleaning up one of the tables. Like usual, old Krol shoveled in food without showing the least inkling he knew anybody else was around. Carolyn stared off across the room.

Ivy drilled me with her eyes. "Haven't you heard?"

One of the boys came out from the kitchen with a plate, and I waved him over. The French toast looked like a dirty dishrag, but it didn't smell so bad, so I dug in.

"Heard what?" I asked when I'd had a few bites.

77

Ivy made me so nervous I dropped a big blob of syrup down the front of me. That made her snicker.

"I'll bet you never thought you'd be sitting here eating breakfast with the likes of me," I said to get even. I waved my fork at the other two. "Them either."

"The police have been here," she hissed. "There were five more robberies here last night. *Five.* Whoever it was came right into the rooms while the women were sleeping and stole them blind. Took their wallets and everything. Went through their drawers."

I made a point of chewing real slow. I looked off across the room like my mind was a million miles away. I sipped my coffee and wiped my lips. By that time she was clawing the table.

"That so?"

"Yes, it is."

"Well, isn't that something?"

"If you weren't so doped up, maybe you'd care," she huffed. "Coming in here like you just got out of bed. Don't you have any pride? Don't you care about anything?"

I leaned across the table, looked straight into her face, and asked, "Exactly what is it about me you don't like?"

She sputtered. A line of red rose up from between her wrinkly old tits and spread up her neck. "They're asking questions," she rasped.

"They're going to get to the bottom of this. And when they do—"

She stopped dead in the middle of the sentence like she'd been struck dumb. Her voice gargled in her throat and her eyes bugged, staring off across the room.

The old bag is having a stroke, I said to myself. Maybe it's a sin, but a thrill went through me.

But no such luck. "I'll be," she muttered under her breath.

I turned around to see what she was looking at. There was Vitus standing up at his table, waving to me! When I waved back, he grinned ear to ear, brought two fingers up to his lips like he was smoking, and gave me the thumbs-up.

When I turned back to the table, Ivy looked like she was ready to heave her guts out on the plate. I laughed. I'd whupped her up one side and down the other. The two of us watched Vitus push in his chair and walk across the room. After he'd disappeared through the door, I couldn't help but turn and grin into her face. I started forking up that French toast like I didn't have a care in the world.

"You'll regret this," Ivy said as she stood and pushed her chair in. "Take my word for it."

I smiled so nice. "This French toast is to die for." I pointed at hers with my fork. "You should try it, Ivy. Put some meat on those poor old bones."

I WAS ONE of the last to leave the dining room. I dragged myself back down the hall, one foot in front of the other. The empty day stretched out in front of me, with maybe a light at the end if Vitus decided to visit. I was beat by the time I got back to my room. I pushed the door open and the smell I was getting used to came to greet me—the newish carpet, the disinfectant they used in the bathroom, and a faint whiff of gasoline fumes from the parking lot outside my window. Underneath it all was the smell of old people pushed into the same container, people fed and cleaned and cared for like they were all parts of one big body, a body with no past and no memories.

I hadn't gone but three steps when I stopped dead in my tracks. My spine started smoldering and an icy cold fluttered in my stomach. Someone was in my room, I could feel it. But that place was small and all I had to do was look around to see that everything was just how I left it. The bed-clothes were tangled from me getting up. My brush, mirror, and medicine were untouched on my dressing table. The TV and armchair were right in place. My tiny bathroom was empty, so the only place anyone could be hiding was the closet.

I held my breath and swung open the door. Nothing. Just my clothes hanging from the rod and my shoes in a pile on the floor. All right then,

Cora, I told myself. You are imagining things. I used the bathroom, came out and straightened the bed, but couldn't for the life of me shake the feeling that something wasn't right. It hovered in the room, a quiver that made me check the closet again and look under the bed.

I sat on the edge of the bed and looked out the long high window at the dingy sky. As my eyes trailed along the windowsill, I started getting the feeling that comes in a horror movie when footsteps get closer and closer. The dog figurines, the violet, the picture of my kids. Then it hit me smack in the face.

My crystal. It was gone.

EDWARD

I got to put aside everything that's happening here and make time for the things I really want to say. I thought needing to tell would get smaller and smaller as time went on, but turns out it's just the opposite. This story, these things that happened to me, they won't go away. The closer I get to dying, the more room they take up in my head. So after all this time—practically my whole life—of not breathing a word of it, I want to let the cat out of the bag. It might explain the way I am. A secret makes you lonely, knowing things nobody else does. It sets you off to the side, puts you in your own world.

Not a soul knows, at least nobody living. Abel knew, of course, though there was a time I hoped he never would. My sister Ruby knew, her husband, Calvin Roberts, and my ma and daddy. And that man. Edward. He knew.

Denton his last name was. Edward Denton. He lived in town, in Neosho, which was unusual at the time. Most people lived out in the sticks somewhere, worked in the mines or on farms, and just came to town when they needed something. Edward's daddy owned the drugstore on Main Street. There was a soda fountain there at the front, with six stools, red leather with chrome trim. A big fan twirled overhead, and no matter how hot it was outside, it always seemed cool in there. Even the flies seemed to stay away. They sold candy behind the counter, along with magazines and newspapers. Ruby and I *lived* to drink a Coke while we sat on those stools. We felt like queens the few times we did it, like we'd gotten as high as we could get.

The first time I saw Edward was in the summer of 1931. I was seventeen years old and had just finished high school. My daddy went into town every other Saturday to get a haircut. Ruby and I talked him into letting us ride with him. We bumped over the potholes and ruts with our teeth clacking, but the two of us were excited as could be.

We'd saved up a little money. When we pulled

up in the middle of town, Daddy told us, "Be back here at the car in an hour, and stay out of trouble." There was a clock on the tower of the bank right across the street. Our feet itched to be on their way.

Like always, Ruby had a plan. "First we're going to walk up Main, then down Jefferson, then back up First Street."

I knew better than to argue. We looked in the shop windows, then we went into Tweeds, the department store, and walked up and down the aisles. We strolled past the hotel and the bank, then stopped a minute outside the saloon, where the smell of liquor and the sound of men's voices drifted out the door. It was hot. I couldn't wait to get to Denton's Drugstore, where I could cool off, rest my feet, and drink that icy Coke. But Ruby was a busybody. She had to stop and chat with everyone she ran into, while I stood there waiting like a bump on a log. Some things never change.

We finally went to Denton's. It was so bright outside, you could hardly see when you stepped through the door. The floor was white tile; the porcelain sink and shiny equipment made it seem even cooler and quieter. I felt my way onto a stool and heaved out a big sigh of relief. We were the only ones there.

Edward was working behind the counter. We knew everyone around there, so somebody new got our attention. "Lookit him," Ruby whispered while he stood with his back to us, pouring the Cokes. She jabbed her elbow in my ribs and jutted her chin at him. "Looks like the iceman in that outfit."

He was dressed in white from head to toe, cotton pants and a long-sleeved shirt starched stiff, with crisp creases ironed up the legs of his pants and down the length of his sleeves. A white hat shaped exactly like a business envelope, slit open on the long side, rode on his straw-colored hair. His legs were long and his butt so small it could fit in the palm of your hand. He turned around real careful, the Cokes filled to the brim. His black bow tie stood out against the rest of his uniform, like a letter printed on the whitest paper. His eyes were gray, like a lake on a cloudy day.

"You from around here?" Ruby asked after she'd had a few sucks on her straw.

I didn't pay much attention. Ruby was always talking to boys. They liked her and she liked them. I bided my time looking at the candy on the wall behind the counter. I intended to buy some horehound before I left. I loved to feel it dissolve into syrup in my mouth.

"I's born here," Edward said. He had a quiet kind of voice, deeper than you'd expect from the looks of him. By the sound of it I guessed he was a few years older than us. "This my daddy's place."

"Your daddy's Terence Denton?" Ruby said, so surprised her lips unlatched from her straw.

"That's right."

"I didn't think he had no kids." Ruby challenged him in a tone that said she knew more about it than he did.

He shrugged in a way that said Ruby didn't know everything.

"I never saw you at school," she said real sassy.

"I went up in Joplin. Lived with my uncle. I just come down here in summer, on account of my ma being sick."

We all knew about Terence Denton's wife. She was from back East somewhere and laid up in her house all day. No one knew what exactly was wrong with her, only that she was sickly, maybe in the head. In our minds it had to do with her being from the East.

From the moment Edward set that Coke in front of me, I'd been dreading getting to the end of it, and I was halfway done by then, sucking it up the straw in little sips so just a tiny spurt came out. I had to fight myself every step of the way because, for the life of me, my lips were dying to slurp it down in one gulp. I worked that soda up and down the straw like a thermometer, nursing it, giving myself just a little at a time.

Edward turned to me so sudden, I let the brown line of Coke fall all the way to the bottom of the straw.

"What's your name?" he asked me.

"That's Toad," Ruby butted in. "She's my sister."

"Your name Toad?" Edward asked.

I was shy in those days, didn't talk much. All I could manage was to shake my head.

He didn't turn toward Ruby or say nothing, but there was a twinkle in his eye that told me he was making fun of her. That tickled me more than I can say, because I'd never seen anyone stand up to Ruby, and I sure had never seen anybody pay more attention to *me* than they did to *her.* It surprised me so much I couldn't say a word. I just sat there with the straw between my lips, smiling at him because he was smiling at me, smiling because we were sharing a secret.

"Cat got your tongue?" he said.

His dimples flashed the minute he smiled. With his blond hair, gold lashes, tawny skin, and the fuzz on his cheeks catching the light from the window at the front of the store, he looked like he'd been dipped in honey. You know *something* must have been happening for me to forget about that Coke. A good minute had gone by since I'd had a taste.

My sister was having a conniption. "*My* name's Ruby," she chimed in. "I got two sisters and one brother. I'm the oldest."

Edward put his elbows on the edge of the counter and lowered his face so it was level with mine. That damn straw was *still* in my mouth, but my lips had lost their sucking power.

"They call me Toad," I stammered. "But my name is Cora."

"That's more like it," he said with a nod. His smell floated over the counter, like hay warmed by the sun.

This here is a man, I said to myself. A full-grown man, talking to me.

Ruby gave a huff. Her and Crystal had boyfriends up the yin-yang. They tossed them off and put them on to suit their moods. Ruby was already engaged to Calvin by then, so I don't know why she was getting her bowels in an uproar, but she sucked that Coke down to the dregs in two seconds, then started fussing with her purse. She couldn't stand someone else being the center of attention.

"You want to go to the pictures next Saturday?" Edward asked me.

Ruby made to hustle me off. She got her money out, paid (even paid for *me*), took me by the arm, and almost dragged me out of that drugstore—but not before I gave Edward my answer. I knew then that nothing was going to stop me from going wherever I wanted with him; it would take a tractor to pull me away.

"You don't know the first thing about that boy," Ruby said when she got me outside. "You never seen him before in your life."

"I don't need to know nothing," I told her as I blinked out at the row of shops across the way, at the cars nosed into the curb and the shadows of the few trees darkening the pavement. Everything looked different. "I know that's him. He's the boy for me."

That's how it started. So many times I've wondered how different my life might have been if me and Ruby hadn't stopped in for that Coke, if I'd never laid eyes on that boy dressed in white.

THE EMPTY ENVELOPE

This purple pen's been flying back and forth over the paper like I was in a trance. Would you believe I'm almost halfway through this book? But I got to interrupt the story I was telling. I got to write about Vitus and the things that's been happening.

Vitus *did* come over that night my crystal went missing. He showed up at the sliding glass door with one of the pink gladiolas that grow by the gate where the gardener parks his truck. He handed it to me and said, "Well, Woozy. How are we tonight?"

He was wearing linen pants. A natural color, wheat I guess you'd call it, loose fitting. Looking at him, you can't believe he's any older than fifty or sixty. He had on a powder blue shirt buttoned only halfway up. His chest is covered with silver hair, so soft looking you want to touch it. He's got a little bit of a belly, but nothing you'd even notice if you weren't looking real close. You'd think he was about to go on vacation someplace like Hawaii the way he was dressed.

Marcos *still* hasn't brought me my cigarettes. I got to thinking about him being in my room all the time and not mentioning the money I gave him and knowing where I keep things and, well, it's natural for me to start suspecting him. But that's another story. The long and short of it is that when I stepped through the sliding glass door with Vitus, there were only two cigarettes in my pack.

We went to our bench and I told him about my crystal. He'd heard that things were turning up missing. They were talking about it up on the second floor where he lives, too. I told him how special that rock was to me, how it was the only thing my daddy had given me, how much comfort it was in hard times. I didn't tell him what was hard about them, of course.

Vitus listened real serious. "I'm going to help you find it," he said when I was done. "You watch."

When we finished our cigarettes, I asked him if he wanted to come back to my room. No monkey business, you understand, but just for some company, so we could get to know each other better.

He's a perfect gentleman. So he came in and I let him sit in my armchair, and I pulled up the wooden chair I keep beside my dresser. I got out the dried fruit Glenda gave me and he ate some of that, then he saw the TV and asked if we could watch a little. The man who shares his room sits out in the courtyard sometimes. Name of Daniel. He's pencil-thin, with a face so sunk in it makes his false teeth look huge, like he's baring his fangs. He moves all herky-jerky, like a puppet. Anyway, Daniel only likes to watch sports. Vitus doesn't care about things like that, so we watched *Star Trek,* then we watched the news, then he went home.

Same thing the next night. Vitus showed up the same time at my door and said, "Shall we step outside, Woozy?" I smelled his cologne, something spicy. I smelled that man musk, too, and I reached up, just for fun, and patted his face. He sure looked surprised.

Like I said, he is a real gentleman.

The smile slid off his face when I told him all the cigarettes were gone. "What happened to them?"

"They're gone. You and me smoked them all last night."

"Is that all you have? Didn't you get more?"

I was taken aback. Much as I like Vitus, his attitude provoked me. I've always had a quick temper, so before I thought about it, I shot back, not at all nice, "What about you, big spender? Don't *you* have any?"

Soon as I said it, I thought, Lord Almighty, what have I done? His eyes narrowed and his mouth shifted and I held my breath thinking he was ready to let go on me when a big smile broke out on his face. "Why Woozy, you're a feisty one, aren't you?" He laughed. We came inside. "It doesn't matter in the least. It's you I've come to see."

Oh, we had the best time.

I had him sit in the armchair again and got out the snacks. He told me all about being a waiter in Europe. It's not like here at all. Not like the women who work at Sizzler or Denny's, where it's low-class. Vitus made a face and flapped his hands in the air like he was brushing away a fly when I mentioned those waitresses. In Europe only *men* are waiters. They take a lot of pride in it. They train real hard and work their whole lives at it, like a career. They wear nice clothes, suits and ties, and people respect them. And if you work in the grand hotels or five-star restaurants, like Vitus did, you make a lot of money, as much as businessmen or lawyers. He also worked on cruise ships and in the casinos over in Las Vegas. What a life! I sat there with my tongue hanging out, thinking of all those places.

"Woozy, we need a plan," he said after awhile. "We need to get some cigarettes."

"It almost does me in just to drag myself down to the dining room," I said. "If I could think of a way to get more cigarettes, I would have got them. But I'm stuck here, stranded as can be. Nobody'll buy them for me and I sure can't buy them for myself."

I didn't mention Marcos. He's my ace in the hole.

Vitus nodded and rested his chin on his knuckles, thinking. "There's got to be a way," he said after a minute. "What about that bus?"

I snorted. Sometimes they load a bunch of people in a van and drive them like pigs to the slaughter out to some shopping center. I never even *thought* of going on any of those outings.

"I'm not able," I said. "I can't walk to save my life."

"Oh, Woozy. Sure you can."

I shook my head. "You're fit as a fiddle. You can't imagine."

"Well, you and I have to work on that. We'll have you up and about in no time. Really. I know you can do it."

I didn't think it was possible, but I didn't say anything. I didn't want him to think I was beyond hope, even if it was the truth.

"Until you're ready to come with me, I could go and bring back three or four packs. That would keep us going for a while."

"Now you're talking."

Vitus winked at me. "All right, then," he said, rubbing his hands together. "We have a plan. Soon as I get my check, we're in business."

"What check? When do you get it?"

"Oh, it won't be long. My nephew manages my money. He should send it in a couple of weeks." He winked and added, "But I shouldn't be telling you my private affairs."

"Two weeks is a long time. I can't wait two weeks to have a cigarette."

Vitus nodded. "Well, I have to agree. It *is* a long time. But patience is a virtue, dear Woozy."

Of course that set me to thinking. All this stealing made me wary. You don't know who you can trust. But I wanted those cigarettes, and I had a hard time picturing Vitus as a thief.

"Tell me something," I said. "I got a question for you."

Vitus got a twinkle in his eye. He leaned in closer.

I just dove in. "Do you like big women?"

He looked surprised. Not for long, though. He tipped his head and looked at me from the corner of his eye. "In Europe, it's different than here," he said with a smile. "Where I am from, we cherish big women. They are powerful. They are *real* women. Thin, weak women are for men who are not sure of themselves. Frightened men. A strong man, a *manly* man—he wants a woman of *substance,* not a bag of bones." He waved his hands in the air, like he was trying to knock the skinny women out of his sight. "I have always been that way myself. I want a woman who fills my arms when I embrace her."

Boy, oh boy. I have to admit, that got me going. I know there's lots of men who like women my size. Abel was one of them; he wouldn't even turn his head for a skinny woman. But I'd never heard anyone explain it as nice as Vitus. I could tell he meant it, too. He got some color in his cheeks while he talked about it.

I went to the drawer where I kept my twenty-dollar bills. "Take some of my money. Get on that bus and buy us some cigarettes. You can pay me back later."

"Absolutely not," Vitus said. He didn't raise his voice, but you could tell he meant business.

"Don't be like that. Don't let your pride get in the way."

He sighed. "All right, then. But it's just a loan."

"That's better. How much do you think you'll need?"

"Well, ten dollars or so for the cigarettes. And if you want a little—" He put his thumb to his lips and tipped his head back, like he was drinking out of a bottle. "Then maybe twenty or so. We can have a little party—just me and you." He winked at me, the devil. "I enjoy being with you, Woozy. I think we can have a wonderful time together."

"I don't hardly drink," I told him.

"And why is that?"

I told him how I was brought up strict Baptist and we just didn't do things like that. The most I'd ever had was a glass of beer or a swallow of Manischewitz at Christmastime.

"Tsk, tsk." He shook his finger at me. "What about Jesus? Christ himself drank plenty of wine."

He had a point, so I kept quiet.

"God has put these things on earth for us to enjoy, Woozy. Good food. Wine and spirits." He made his eyebrows go up and down. "Each other."

I was just about to open the drawer when he took my hand, led me to the middle of the room, and waltzed me around the carpet. Just one little turn, but oh, my Lord! You could tell he's a wonderful dancer. I got to laughing so hard I could hardly breathe.

"Careful, Woozy. Careful. Stand here a minute and catch your breath." He steadied me, then he lifted my hand, brought it to his lips, and kissed it real light, like I was the queen of England.

"Let me get that money."

"You know what, Woozy? Don't even bother. We can wait until I get my check. It's not my pride, it's just that I'd rather treat you."

"Stop it, now. Don't be silly."

I pulled open the drawer and took out the envelope. It took me a minute, once I looked inside, to make sense of what I was seeing. Nothing. The envelope was empty.

"Woozy! What is it?" Vitus came rushing across the room.

"Gone, all gone," I gasped. "The thief has struck again."

THE NEXT DAY I called Glenda, but she wasn't home. I didn't want to leave a message on her damn machine. I tried Dean then, but of course he was at work, so I explained to his wife how first it was those quarters, then my crystal, and now my twenties. It was like talking to a wall. That girl. Out of all the women Dean could have married, I will never understand why he chose *her.* "Now wait a minute," she kept saying. "Let me get this straight." I don't know what was so hard for her to understand. She thinks I'm goofy, that's the long and short of it. If that weren't bad enough, she had the *gall* to ask me who was *managing my meds* and if there was someone here at The Palisades she could talk with *to get all the facts.* I got so disgusted I slammed down the phone. The only one left then was Kenny, but when I tried to call him, the phone was busy. I wouldn't be surprised if it was that blabbermouth wife of Dean's, burning up the line to let everyone in the family know I'm in trouble again.

All this makes me feel like I don't know

whether I'm coming or going. I took a couple extra pills to calm myself down and now every time I bend over the room spins like a carnival ride. I got to thinking maybe I spent that money without remembering, but I'm not senile or fuddled enough to forget something like that. Nobody's touched those quarters I left in the candy dish for bait. I can't figure that. I tried thinking back, tried to remember if I'd seen anything suspicious, but nothing stands out. My sleeping pills knock me so dead out that anybody could come in, tiptoe past my head, take whatever they wanted, and I'd be none the wiser. Picturing somebody looking down on me when I'm sleeping makes me feel like a wind is howling in one ear and out the other.

I could tell the management here, or call the police, but everybody just acts like I'm an old fool, or a whiner looking for attention, or an addict whose mind is addled with drugs. The good thing is I don't have nothing much left to take. Pretty soon I'll be sitting here on the floor of a bare room in my underwear, and maybe then the robber will leave me alone. Maybe then everybody will see I'm not just crying wolf.

TREATS

"My crystal's gone," I told Marcos when he came for my treatment. "Somebody stole it."

He always calls the windowsill where I keep my rock my *altar.* Silly. He fusses over it, brushes off the dust, pushes his fat finger into the soil of the violet to make sure it has enough water. He picks up the rock and polishes it on his shirt, then he puts it back just so, turning the flat part toward the sun. "Your *rock,* Coralita," he always says, tapping his temple with his finger like he's in on some big secret.

I didn't say nothing about the money because I wanted to see if he acted shifty. He moved that damn cold stethoscope around on my back without saying a word. Cigarettes were real strong on his breath. He listened and moved it, listened and moved it, breathing so loud himself I wondered how he could hear *my* lungs.

"Did you hear what I said?" I asked him.

He nodded, still writing.

"Well, it didn't just *walk* out of here."

You'd think he was a deaf mute. He slung the stethoscope around his neck and took some notes on his clipboard. When he was done with that, he motioned me over to the edge of the bed for my back thumping. I leaned forward and put my head against his chest, then he bent over my shoulder and commenced to pounding, smacking me real firm to loosen things up. It's what you call *intimate* because we're so close. I smelled his armpits and felt the heat coming off his body.

"You know my daddy gave me that rock, don't you?" The pounding made me sound like I was driving over a bumpy road.

"Yes, you told me." He went on with his work, snuffling with that noisy breathing of his.

"What is *wrong* with your nose?" I had to ask after a few minutes. My head was practically in his armpit. "How come you breathe like that? Sounds like you need this treatment more than I do."

"Just let me finish here, Cora," he said. I could tell his teeth were gritted. When he finally straightened up, sweat glistened on his floppy upper lip and his king-size forehead. He gave a big sniff and wiped his nose on the back of his hand.

"I have asthma, Cora. Allergies, too."

"There's Kleenex over there on my dresser. Go get you one and blow your nose. If you're in a bad mood, just say so."

He honked good and loud, then he started writing on his clipboard.

"Did you get up on the wrong side of the bed?" I asked him.

"I feel very tired today, Cora. I have a lot on my mind."

"Like what?"

He glanced around the room, nervouslike. I wondered if he was planning the next thing he was going to steal. He stuck his pen behind his ear and sucked his teeth, a habit that's not very attractive. He didn't once look at me or say a word about that money I gave him for cigarettes.

"Is it that boy?" I asked. "You can tell me. We're friends."

He just kept writing, like my voice was nothing but a fly buzzing around him. He mumbled something under his breath and started setting up the hookah for my lung treatment. His ignoring me got my blood to boiling, so I asked if he knew anything about my rock.

"If I knew anything about your crystal, I'd tell you," he said, motioning me over to the chair where I took my treatment. He *still* didn't meet my eye.

I had to inhale deep on that damn thing and hold in each breath, so I couldn't talk. Meantimes, Marcos wrote on the clipboard.

"Sometimes you notice something a lot more when it's missing than when it's there," I said soon as I put down the pipe.

"Do you think I took your rock, Cora?" he asked suddenly.

"I never said that!" I answered, though to be honest I had my doubts. Why bring it up unless he had a guilty conscience? "I just can't figure out who would want something like that," I went on. "It has sentimental value, because my daddy never gave me many presents in my life, but he gave me that." I tried to get a look at his face, but he had his head down, still writing. "Why'd you ask me that?" I said. "Is there something you're trying to say?"

Finally, he looked at me. He put his hands on his hips and bellowed, "Every time I go into a room to do my job, someone asks me if I *know anything*. Let me ask you," he said, pointing one of his stubby fingers at me. "Do you ask the doctor when he comes here to examine you if he knows anything about your rock? Do you ask the boss up in the front office if she took it?"

"Well, I'll be," I gasped. "Why are you getting so hot under the collar?"

He still hadn't answered my question about the crystal.

"Because only certain people are suspected, Cora. Always the same, the blacks and the Mexicans."

"That's a load of bull!" I yelled. "That's an excuse if I ever heard one!"

"Huh," he grunted, and gave me a look like he didn't believe it for a minute. "Well, who do *you* think took it?" he asked. "Take a wild guess."

"That's just it. I don't know. People here come and go at all hours of the day and night."

He started rolling up the hookah like it was a

snake he was handling. "It is better just to leave," he mumbled. He banged himself on the head a couple of times with the heel of his hand. "Why do I waste my time?" He grabbed his things and headed for the door. When he got there he spun around and said, "I open my heart to you. I spend extra time with you." He sucked in a big lungful of air. His eyes bugged out. "I ask nothing in return." He blew the air out, a big gust. "I am a fool! Insane! *Adiós,* Señora Sledge!"

"Don't you dare leave!" I yelled back. "There's no need to be so touchy!"

He opened the door without even turning around.

"What about my things?" I hollered. "I gave you money! What did you do with it?"

He stormed back. "Thank you for reminding me!" he snarled so fierce that spit flew out of his mouth. His eyes shot sparks. He reached into his carryall and pulled out a paper bag. "Here are your cigarettes!" He slammed a pack of Marlboros down on top of my dresser. He pulled out another one and slammed it down, too. Boom! Like a gunshot. "Here are your cupcakes, and your corn nuts, and your chips." Bam! Bam! Bam! The last one, the bag of Doritos, came down so hard I knew they'd be crushed to dust.

"Oh, and your newspaper!" He whipped the *National Enquirer* out of the bag so fast the pages flew apart and fluttered to the ground like a bird shot from the sky. "And your magazine!" He fired *People* at the floor on top of the newspaper.

"Marcos!" I hollered. "Don't! Don't do like that!" I tried to grab his hands. "I'm sorry, now. Come on! Quit acting crazy!"

He grabbed *my* hand instead. "And *here, señora,* is your change!" He pried my fingers open and shoved the money into my palm. "One dollar and fifty-seven cents. You want to count it now, while I'm here?"

I closed my hand around the money and looked into his eyes. Sometimes I hated myself. Just *hated* myself. I tried to show him with my eyes how sorry I was, but he was too mad to see anything.

"Why didn't you tell me you bought all this stuff?" I bawled. "Why didn't you give it to me right away?"

"I forgot," he said, huffing and puffing. "But I will never forget again." He tore loose from my hand, picked up his things, and stormed through the door.

What an uproar. I slumped down in my chair and stared out the sliding glass door. I felt so bad for doing Marcos like that. Accusing him, after all he'd done for me. He'd just forgotten, and I went jumping to conclusions. Who could blame him for getting so mad? But I couldn't help thinking of those soap operas, the way people were always double-dealing, stabbing each other in the back. And all that gold Marcos wore. Where'd he get the money? You guilty old coot, I told myself. Stop trying to feel better by blaming somebody else. But much as I tried, I couldn't get over the feeling that something wasn't right.

ALONE AGAIN

Vitus cheered me up from that mess with Marcos by showing up at my door with a wicked little smile. He came on through the door, set me down in my chair, and told me to close my eyes. When I opened them, there was a pack of Malboros sitting on one thigh and a twenty-dollar bill on the other. Vitus grinned from ear to ear. "My nephew came though with a little money," he said. "I want you to have this 'til you get back on your feet."

What a week. I was so occupied with Vitus, I didn't get a chance to write here at all. He came with a posy in his hand each and every night. I didn't realize how lonesome I'd gotten, how I missed having a man around. For the first time in forever I remembered how I felt right after Abel died. He passed at home at 4:10 in the afternoon with a whole mob around him: all three kids and their wives, the hospice woman, even the busybody from next door. The mortuary came and got him just before dinner and Glenda stayed 'til bedtime. I didn't want anyone to spend the night. It's funny, but I slept like a stone.

Well, he's gone, I told myself when I opened my eyes the next morning. I swung my legs over the side of the bed and got up, walked around the house like I had for the past forty years. The feeling of him being *not there* was thick in the house—in the bathroom where he wasn't having his morning crap, at the breakfast table where he wasn't slurping his coffee and spreading peanut butter on his toast. All his things lying around the house, in the closets and out in the garage—grass shears, jockey shorts, toothpicks, razor—they didn't have no more use. No one to wear them, use them, curse over them, or care for them. No more seeing him walk out to the driveway to pick up the morning paper, or clean his ears with a bobby pin, or dance a bare-ass jig to make me laugh when he got out of the shower.

Now here was Vitus visiting every night, sitting beside me while we watched TV, sharing some snacks while we had a chat. I got used to the smell of him, the space he took up in my room. My mind got to working. My imagination got the better of me. I tried to curb it because I dreaded the same thing happening to me as before—being left alone, rattling around by myself, losing my mind and slipping off into the ether.

Turns out there was good reason.

Night before last I fixed myself up. Put on my

105

nice earrings even though they pinch the hell out of my lobes, some lipstick, and the gold flats that are a little tight but not bad if I don't have to walk any distance. I got a cotton shift I never even wore out of the closet and slipped it over my head. It has some kind of leaves on it, bamboo or fern. Some White Shoulders perfume, even a little rouge.

I sat down in the armchair and waited. Waited and waited.

He never came.

THE BEGINNING OF THE END

Here I sit, alone in this room, with plenty of time on my hands. For all I know, Vitus is gone for good. I took a few of my happy pills. That's what they're for, isn't it? Depression? Sadness? For when you feel like hell. Whenever I hit bottom, my mind strays back there to the past, where it all began. I feel like the only way I can stand it is to get out in the open. All those things that happened so long ago—that's the story I want to tell.

Edward had a car. I couldn't get over how he'd drive out to fetch me and I'd climb up there and ride around for all the world to see. It was a 1915 Model T Ford, black like they all were, open to the elements, but it could have been Cinderella's coach for the way it made me feel. I prayed that kids I knew in school would see me. I made him drive round downtown Neosho just so people would say, "Lookee there. Is that Cora Spring I see riding in that car?"

The wind whooshing past your ears, the engine sputtering, and your teeth rattling over the rutted road, you couldn't hear a thing, so we didn't talk much. That first time we went to the movies, I don't think we exchanged a word. I'd got myself up in good clothes: white stockings and button-up shoes, a navy blue suit with a tailored top and tight skirt. The buttons had a target pattern, white and blue stripes. Even a hat, a white turban Ruby leant me. We matched: Edward wore navy blue slacks and a white shirt pressed just as perfect as the iceman outfit he'd worn the week before.

The picture was *Tarzan,* I remember that. People packed into the movie house on Saturday afternoons, and there I was, sitting right up front, in the third or fourth row. When the newsreels ended, he took my hand. My jaw went slack, but I didn't look at him. His skin was clean and dry, like the rest of him. I kept my eyes on the screen, breathed in his smell, listened to the music, and felt all those people around us in the dark. In a little while he let go of my hand and started feeling my leg through my dress. He worked his fingers so my dress hitched up little by little, up over my knees. I couldn't move. His fingers pawed my thigh, inching the hem higher and higher, until I glanced down at my lap and saw both my legs were showing. He stroked my leg through the stocking, running his fingers in loopty-loops all over my thigh.

I watched the movie like my life depended on it, though I wasn't taking in a thing. Edward was the same. I sneaked a glance to the side, and his profile was like on a dime or a penny, his eyes glued to the screen, his lips pressed together. There were empty seats on either side of us. From a distance we must of looked like two well-behaved kids enjoying the movie, minding our manners.

He managed to get his hand all the way up to the top of my stocking and worm a finger under it. They didn't have anything like panty hose in them days. You wore stockings with a garter belt, and because my legs were big those things cut into my thigh at the top; there was no extra space. He really had to work to weasel that finger in there, but he kept at it, hoisting himself up on one hip and putting some muscle into it, boring with that finger like an oil rig.

I bolted upright when he hit bare skin. Lord Almighty, I almost jumped out of my seat! I sneaked a glance out of the corner of my eye. Even though his eyes were *still* fastened on the screen, the tip of his tongue was stuck out at the side of his mouth like he was concentrating with all his might. He worked his way in to the second knuckle, then he ran his finger around the top of the stocking, trying to move in deeper, but like I said that stocking was so tight it must have been cutting off his circulation.

Just when I thought something was going to give, I felt a pop and a snap and boy oh boy, his hand plunged in to the hilt. Damned if he hadn't unhitched my garter! Next thing I knew, he was all over the inside of my thigh, grabbing and kneading and squeezing, not hiding it much anymore, rocking me in my seat.

I latched on to the armrests to steady myself and clamped my legs together like a vise. He used his hand like a wedge, trying to pry my legs apart so he could get in there and squeeze more of the flesh at the top of my thigh. He grabbed handfuls, squeezing it like dough. All the time he shimmied his hand up higher, getting so close to my crotch that, if I hadn't been so scared of being caught like that, I would have cried out. He was breathing hard now, his elbow moving back and forth on the armrest between us, pumping like a lever to get him where he wanted.

All this going on and not a soul in that theater had any idea—or if they did they didn't show no sign. Their eyes were too latched on to Tarzan swinging on a tree. God knows who else might have been up to the same tricks. I was too busy with my own state of affairs to pay any mind to anything else.

Edward's fingers inched their way up, got hold of some skin, scooted up and grabbed hold a little higher, like he was climbing a wall. Tight as I kept my legs together, his hand managed to make progress. That's how determined he was. Then his finger, that same one that had snaked into the top of my stocking, nudged the elastic leg of my underpants. It nosed and sniffed like a dog searching for a chink in a fence.

Edward still hadn't looked at me, hadn't said a word. I prayed for the movie to get over. His finger wiggled in through the leg of my underpants. I was in a downright panic by then, sweating bullets. My stocking where he'd undone the garter was dangling loose, bagging around my knee. I felt like I was naked in that movie house, splayed out for everybody to see.

I couldn't take it no more when his finger started grizzling around in my pelt. I slammed both hands down on top of his, trapped his hand through my skirt, and dug my fingers in. It had to hurt. Anyway, he got the message. He pulled his hand back and folded it in his lap. I hooked my stocking, smoothed down my skirt, and folded my hands the same way. We sat like we were in church for the rest of the movie, and for the life of me, I don't remember one thing about it.

Well, that was the beginning of the end. Neither one of us said a word about what went on in the movie house once we stepped out into the bright afternoon. We chatted a little about other pictures we liked, and Edward told me about living up in Joplin. He was going to school to be a druggist, to work in his daddy's store. I studied him, out in that summer light, wondering at his dimples and gray eyes, that gold glow that seemed to come off him, while he talked serious and steady, already sure of himself.

It would've been natural to go to the soda fountain after the picture for a Coke. I wouldn't have minded at all sitting on a stool next to Edward, but he said, "Let's have a drive," and so we did, up and down those back roads 'til we came to a stopping place near a clearing. Lord, what a mauling he gave me—the two of us rolling and banging around in that car like bears. It only went so far, though, then he drove me home in one piece, more or less.

That was around the middle of July. For a month or two he wore a track out to my house. He'd come get me and we drove anywhere and everywhere, always with the same thing in mind. That car was the first nail in my coffin. Every time I got in, I swore it would be the last. I was scared to death and guilty as hell, but before you knew it we'd be tearing out to one of our places, where we'd go at it again, lickety-split. I was head over heels for that boy. He was beyond my wildest dreams. Didn't matter that we hardly talked, that if you asked me I wouldn't have the faintest idea what went on in his head.

All of a sudden, my whole future was laid out in front of me. Once I started keeping company with Edward, any questions I had about what I was going to do with my life disappeared. My life was going to be better than I'd ever hoped. Once him and me got married, we'd live in town, own the drugstore, drive a car. I'd have an inside toilet and electric lights. I saw the kids we'd have, my invalid mother-in-law, the people who'd be our customers. I pictured everything, right down to the linens on my bed and the silverware on my table. I'd get to stay there near my ma and daddy, but I'd still be living in town, which was a damn sight better than scratching out a living in the sticks. All in all, I'd struck it rich. I'd staked my claim and was on my way. If anything came of my and Edward's hanky-panky, well—we'd just get married sooner rather than later, which was fine with me.

You'd think I'd catch on, wouldn't you? But the same things keep happening, over and over. Look at me now, still sitting here alone, wishing and hoping.

TO HELL AND BACK

Last night I fixed myself up and waited for Vitus, just like always. Hair, lipstick, earrings. I sat in the chair and even though the TV was on, I didn't watch it. Every time there was a noise, my eyeballs darted to the sliding glass door. Eight o'clock, nine o'clock. It ate at me. How he came and gave me flowers. How we laughed and talked. How I hadn't seen hide nor hair of him at my door for three nights running. Oh, I spotted him in the dining room all right, chatting and smiling with all the women. He worked the room like he was running for president. He fluttered his fingers at me from across the room, that cutesy wave I'm starting to hate. I tried to signal to him, to wave him over, but he acted like he didn't see. The minute I got myself up and headed over in his direction, he vanished into thin air.

At 9:30 I couldn't take it no more. I hefted myself up out of my chair. I never been out in the hall after dinner, not once, but I had to find Vitus. I had to know why he stopped coming. I didn't know where his room was. I couldn't walk very far. Still, I switched off the TV, changed out of those shoes that kill my feet, found my key, went over there, and opened the door.

I poked my head out. The fluorescent lights

were brighter than ever after having just the lamp in my room. It bounced off them white floors like an ice-skating rink. With all the noise, you'd think a party was going on. It was like a whole city celebrating right outside my door, and every night in my room with the TV on I hadn't even known about it. Buzzing around like a human beehive. Two aides leaned against the wall right across from me, talking with their heads together like they didn't have a care in the world.

In the other direction, a rangy colored man was sliding trays full of dirty dishes into a rack about two doors down. Must have been from the people who ate in their rooms; those nasty plastic dishes were covered in chewed-up food and cold gravy. A doctor brushed past my nose, then a short square woman with a man's haircut pushing some old fossil in a wheelchair. Don't ask me where they were going that hour of the night. I stepped out in the hall, closed the door behind me, and turned the knob to make sure it was locked.

I decided to head down to the nurses' station and see if they'd tell me where Vitus's room was, or at least try to, even though it was about twice as far as the dining room. I felt like I was setting off to the North Pole, but I told myself that whenever I got tired I'd just stop and rest and if worst came to worst I'd call out for a wheelchair and have somebody push me back to my room. So I took one last look at my door, and off I went. I don't mind telling you that I was scared. Scared, and maybe a little excited.

No sooner did I get started than down at the end of the hall I see that scarecrow Nuella Whit headed right for me. She's a beady-eyed woman with a turkey neck and hair so thin you can see her scalp. She's—what-you-call-it? *Hyperactive.* Skinny as a stick because all she does all day is walk and walk and walk, up one side of the building and down the other. It makes you tired just to watch her. She has a little man with her, a Chinese man with a navy blue stocking cap pulled down over his forehead, who she drags by the hand like a pull toy. He shuffles behind her taking teeny tiny steps. "This is my husband, this is my husband," she says over and over to everyone she meets. She don't turn her head or move her lips, and the man, he don't say a word. Maybe he don't speak English. When they get to one end of the hall, they turn around and go back. It's a wonder they haven't worn a groove in the floor. They must walk five hundred miles a day, so I thought they'd stop at night and get some rest, but there they were, same as always.

I'd only gone about ten steps when they whooshed past me. "This is my husband," she said, so fast you could hardly make it out.

I concentrated on putting one foot in front of the other, because I had so far to go. I'd watched a program on TV about people climbing up Mount Everest, where there's no oxygen, and that's just what it felt like, every step like lifting a hundred pounds. TVs played behind a couple doors; when I got about halfway down the hall, I heard an old woman singing that old hymn "God Lifted Me" at the top of her lungs. There was a railing at the end of the hall. I made for it like it was the edge of the pool and I was drowning. When I got there I grabbed hold and leaned on it, huffing and puffing.

I could see down the next hallway from there. Not too far away a guy with the biggest muscles you ever saw was waltzing a mop across the floor. His head was shaved and shaped like a fireplug; his arms were thick as barrels. You could have parked a car on his chest. Tattoos covered his whole body, all the way down to his wrists and ankles. He was blue all over, like he had on a sweater and long pants.

My eyes bugged out. "Why would you do that to yourself?" I asked when he got within hearing range.

He wiped his forehead with the back of his arm and pumped the mop up and down in the bucket.

"What're you talking about?" he asked, none too nice.

"That business all over your skin. That mess you're wearing. If you was one of my kids, I'd skin you alive."

116

"Good thing I'm not," he said, not even looking up from his mopping.

The disinfectant smell was strong, but it still didn't cover up that piss stink that must have soaked into the floor and woodwork. His mop smelled sour, too. He swirled it around like he was icing a cake.

"Didn't it hurt?" I asked when he got so close he was practically mopping my shoes.

"Yeah, that was the good part."

His face glistened. His neck was big around as a missile. He made a little half-circle around my feet, still not bothering to look up.

"You're a smart-ass, aren't you?" I said.

He straightened up, leaned on the mop handle, and looked me full in the face. "Yes, I am," he said, and smiled. Even though he was a young guy, a couple of teeth on the sides were missing. "You are, too. I can tell," he added before he started in on the mopping again.

"You do all these floors?"

"Yes, ma'am. I do. Every night, rain or shine. The whole place. Upstairs and down."

His butt looked hard as a rock. He finished mopping around me and started down the hall I'd just walked up.

"You still didn't answer my question," I said. "Why'd you get them things?"

He looked down at his arms. A big fish with rows of scales curved from his shoulder to his elbow. The other arm had jagged designs, like lightning.

"They protect me," he said.

"From what?"

"Anybody who wants to do me harm."

"You have any cigarettes?" I asked him.

He put his hands on his hips and clucked his tongue. "Why would you do *that* to yourself?" A smart-ass, like I said. "Be careful. The floor's wet," he added before he turned his back on me and went on with his work.

That nasty mop smell hung in the air. The hall where I was going stretched for miles and miles. I could hardly see the end of it. About a third of the way down was the door to the dining room. That's as far as I'd walked since I'd been there; any time I'd been past that, someone was pushing me in a wheelchair. Lucky for me, the railing I was hanging on to ran all the way to the end. Once I got there, I turned left.

When I'd rested up enough, I started off again, taking my little sliding steps and pulling myself along with the railing. An exit sign glowed green at the end of the corridor. I stared at that to keep my mind off how far I had to go. Once in a while somebody passed me. It's a different crew at night, I'll tell you that. During the day it's all them Mexican and Filipino girls that probably got kids they have to take care of at night. Say what you will, but they work real hard and are on the quiet side. Polite even. But the bunch at night are loudmouths. Rough. Half of them look like they just got out of jail, or belong to the Hells Angels. They shouted up and down the halls and grab-assed with each other and generally gave me no respect at all. I might as well have been out on Skid Row, walking around at midnight.

I made it to the dining room door and stood there a minute trying to get my breath. It's no fun not having enough air. Gasping don't do no good. Your heart beats a mile a minute and your body is screaming, but your lungs can't do nothing about it. It occurred to me to turn around and go back to my room, but I was already halfway there, so I fastened my eyes on that exit sign and started my feet going again, like I was crossing the Sahara Desert. My mind got to wandering, about how I always liked the nighttime and how, all those years I was married to Abel, that time was my solace, when I could be alone and think my own thoughts without the kids fussing and fighting and Mama this and Mama that, and Abel, too, blabbing on about his day at work and how I needed to do this in the house or that in the yard. I'm telling you, I counted the seconds 'til they all went to bed. I confess I lived for those nights when the quiet came down and I could read or thumb through a magazine, or just sit there in my chair and look out the window into the dark.

Two women wearing scrubs came by, both of them sucking Popsicles. Popsicles, at that time of night! They hardly glanced at me. I was thinking of the nights when I might step out onto our back porch way late in the night, one or two o'clock. Back then it was still wild where we lived in East San Diego. You might hear an owl hooting or a coyote howling. There were possums, skunks, and raccoons—all kinds of varmints roving around—going about their business of getting food and making love. The night felt alive and the air was so cool. I'd give anything to be able to do that now. To step out on my own porch and stand there in the dark.

The last door at the end of the hall was wide open. When I finally got there, I saw that it was a big, long closet with shelves all the way to the ceiling. A boy was inside, unloading cardboard boxes of toilet paper, paper towels, and toilet seat covers—what we call Texas T-shirts—and stacking them on the shelves. He was small, Chinese or Filipino or something like that, with dark hair hanging down on his neck and a round little ass squeezed into tight jeans. His T-shirt was just as tight. It was sleeveless, deep red with a gold sun spreading across the chest, and so short a band of his brown belly showed all the way around.

He jumped when he saw me standing there.

"Scared you, didn't I?" I said with a laugh.

He didn't crack a smile, just gave me a hurt look as he came over for another armful of toilet paper. He had thick black eyelashes and lips like a big pillow. His skin was hairless as a baby's ass. A pretty boy, no more than nineteen or twenty. When he bent over, I saw that the side of his neck, from his earlobe to his shoulder, was covered with hickeys.

"Who gave you those monkey bites?" I asked.

I was still huffing and puffing, hanging on to the doorjamb of that closet for dear life. He blinked his big, wet eyes and said in a whispery little voice, "Excuse me?" He knew what I was talking about, though, because his hand floated up to those marks on his neck.

I gave him a little smirk to show he wasn't fooling nobody. "I just need to rest here a minute before I walk the rest of the way to the nurses' station. Don't pay no attention to me. I'll just watch you a minute."

He looked worried. "Is there something you need? Are you okay?"

I glanced down at his bare belly. His hips were no wider than my hand. "I'm down there in room 136. I didn't mean to disturb you. I just need to get my breath. Go on with your work."

He finished the toilet paper and started on the paper towels. There was something sleepy about him, graceful, more like he was dancing than filling shelves. He worked faster than you'd think, though. Before you knew it, he'd emptied another box.

"What's your name?" I said when he came back over by me.

He tucked his hair behind his ears and smiled. I thought of his mama, how happy she must have been to have such a beautiful boy. He was sweet that way a mama's boy is sweet, like he's been loved and protected all his life, pampered and kept soft. My Kenneth's a little bit that way.

"Renato," he said in that breathy voice. "My name is Renato."

It was all I could do not to let out a scream. I clamped my hands over my mouth. I didn't say nothing, though, because I didn't want to let on what I knew. I wanted to watch this boy, to see if I could figure anything out.

He started ripping the boxes open, then stomping them flat. He had tennis shoes on, white with black stripes. No socks. I remembered the way Marcos had said his name. Just once, I wish someone would say *my name* like that. I tried to see him like Marcos did. The muscles in his arms, his cheekbones and lips. I pictured Renato's ass bare, like two brown cantaloupes, and his whang hanging down, and even the two of them—him and Marcos—having at it. Marcos climbing around on him, or kissing him, or Lord knows what—whatever it is they do. I probably shouldn't be thinking those thoughts, but I'm only human. No harm done.

For the life of me, I couldn't understand it.

"I better be going," I said when the boxes were all smashed and Renato started gathering them into a pile. "Nice to meet you. My name's Mrs. Sledge. Cora. Room 136."

You could see he didn't give a rat's ass who I was or where I lived. He looked up and nodded, then went back to the boxes. Well, isn't that something? I thought as I pushed off from the doorway, turned the corner, and started down the next hallway.

THE NURSES' STATION was a beehive. People gathered round, coming and going, leaning over the counter, talking and laughing. I even heard a radio playing. The lights buzzed louder and the floor was even more scuffed up than usual. I leaned forward, wishing I could go faster, but all I could do was slide my feet a few inches at a time. It seemed like eons since I'd left my room. I was almost homesick for it when I pictured the armchair in front of the TV, the oval hooked rug laid over the wall-to-wall carpet, and the basket of pink silk roses that Glenda had brought to make things nice.

If they saw me coming, they sure didn't let on. A lot of folks were coming and going: men pushing carts and women in scrubs, all of them raising Cain, talking and laughing. It was loud, I don't mind telling you. Like a big party. By that

123

time I felt like Frankenstein dragging myself forward.

The nurses' station was a hole cut in the wall with a counter between you and the people working on the other side. Three nurses, colored ladies, were behind the desk, which was covered with computers, telephones, charts, and stacks of paper. On my side of the desk two men and a woman, all of them wearing scrubs, leaned over the counter and talked to the three nurses on the other side like they were ordering drinks at a bar. When I finally got there, I flopped up on the counter beside them and panted, glad to have something to rest against while I got my breath.

I was the only white one there. Nobody said so much as boo to me.

A bunch of food was strewn across their desk: bags of chips and a half-eaten sandwich, an open thermos and a sack of candy. A couple of Coke cans, an apple, even a chicken drumstick with most of the meat chewed off. There were pictures of little black kids, one with a big stuffed dog, another in a karate suit, a few that were taken at school, in frames here and there. I spotted an open pack of cigarettes. I had half a mind to reach over there and help myself. One of the men was telling a story and all the ladies were hooting and laughing. The radio blared. Who would of known that this went on every night, right outside all the old folks' doors?

"Vitus Kovic!" I yelled when I got my breath. "I need to know where he is."

I might as well of been an ant screaming. Nobody paid me any mind. One of the women sitting at the desk had fingernails a mile long: white, with red stripes like a candy cane. Red lipstick to match and white beads all braided up in her hair. Tanya Greeley, her name tag said. She was real tall. She glanced at me a split second, then the party went on like before.

I never! I listened for a minute to see what was so damn important. They were talking about their kids. Shawnee this and Jared that. How one had gone to school and bragged that his daddy had brass balls because that's what he'd heard at the breakfast table that morning.

"Listen here!" I rapped the counter with my knuckles. "I need some help! I got a question I need to ask!"

They all went quiet. Six sets of eyeballs turned toward me.

"What are you looking for, honey? What do you need?" Tanya, the one with peppermint fingernails, asked.

They glanced at each other. You could tell they thought I was a crazy old loon.

"I need to know where Vitus Kovic is," I said. "I need his room number."

"Catch you later," one man said. He leaned way over the counter and snatched a hard candy out of the bag before he sauntered away like a big tomcat.

"I got to be going, too," one of the women said. She followed him.

"Me too. Bye-bye." There went the last one.

The party was over. It was just me and the three nurses behind the desk.

"Vitus Kovic," Tanya repeated. "Is he a resident here?"

The one sitting next to her picked up the chicken leg.

I couldn't help letting out a big sigh and rolling my eyes. "Now, what do *you* think? Course he is."

She eyeballed me. Trying to make up her mind if I was crazy or not. The other two just watched. "Who're you, honey?" Tanya asked, like I was a little girl. The beads in her hair clacked when she moved her head. "What's your name?"

"My name is Cora Sledge. I'm down there in 136." I nodded over in that direction.

They stared at me like they were waiting for me to break out in a song and dance. The one standing up reached over Tanya's shoulder and helped herself to a handful of corn chips. They could of at least offered me something.

Tanya looked at her watch. "It's late, honey. Shouldn't you be back in your room?"

"Enough of that *honey* business!" I snapped. "If you are unwilling to help me, I'll just have to find somebody who will. I thought that was your job, but I guess I made a mistake."

The jaws of the two others had been working like cows. Now they stopped chewing and smiled, like what I said was funny. Tanya didn't smile one bit, though. "We can't be giving out residents' information," she said, all business now. "That information is private."

I sure wanted some of that candy. Besides the bag of hard candy there was a pack of peanut butter cups and a box of malt balls. I smelled them. My mouth was watering. The cigarettes were Pall Malls.

"He's a friend of mine," I said. "He's got something I need. He's expecting my visit."

I tried to smile real nice, but Tanya just gave me a hard look. Her friend had a little pity, though (or maybe she got tired of me standing there) because she tapped something on the computer. Her name tag said Marjorie Patterson. She was hefty, with copper-colored hair cropped close to her head and square little glasses that sat on the end of her nose.

"Kovic?" she said. "With a *K?*"

"That's right. *Vitus.*" I got a thrill saying his name.

After a few more taps on the computer, Marjorie said, "What was your name again?"

"Mrs. Cora Sledge."

"He's in Room 247, Mrs. Sledge. Upstairs in the men's wing."

Upstairs. That threw me for a loop. She might as well of said *Siberia.*

I let out a big groan. "How am I supposed to get *there?*" I wailed.

"Shall I have someone come and escort you back to your room?" that smart-ass Tanya butted in. She still had her back up.

I gave her my frostiest look and said, "I just walked all this way. I can't turn around now and go back."

"We can get a wheelchair for you."

She wasn't even worth bothering with. I turned way around and looked at Marjorie. She might not be prettier than Tanya, but she was a far sight nicer. "Could I have one of them candies?" I said, pointing to the bag.

They glanced at each other. The third one, whose name tag I couldn't see, stood there watching the whole show. Tanya shook her head like all this business was beneath her. She swiveled her chair around, took a folder off the top of a stack, and busied herself with that.

"Are you on a restricted diet, Mrs. Sledge?" Marjorie asked.

"No, ma'am, I'm not."

I don't know if she believed me, but she held the bag out. I felt like a kid at Halloween. It was all I could do not to grab a handful.

Marjorie must have read my mind. "Just one," she said.

Well, there was fruit candies in bright foil, peppermints, coffee nips, and root beer barrels. My hand liked to have a seizure trying to decide which one to take. Finally, I chose a butterscotch, because it was a little bigger than the others. I unwrapped it right there and popped it in my mouth.

"Mmm, mmm, mmm," I said, sucking like my life depended on it. "Sure is good. Thank you so much."

Tanya huffed real loud to show I was working her nerves. She gave me a disgusted look, then pretended to be busy as hell, scratching away in that folder with a pencil.

I smiled at her. "Can you do me a favor, honey?" I said, sweet as pie. "Could you throw this away for me?" I held out the candy wrapper.

Those red and white claws snatched it out of my hand like a tiger. She didn't even look up, just slung it into the trash behind her.

"Can you tell me how I get there, up to Mr. Kovic's room?" I asked Marjorie, the nice one.

"Elevator's down at the end of the hall," Marjorie said. "Just take it up to the second floor, turn right, then left, and go until you get to Room 247, about halfway down."

That one little butterscotch was doing wonders for my mood. It melted on my tongue and trickled down. I don't think I've ever enjoyed anything more, even a steak and lobster dinner. I started to think I *might* be able to make it to Vitus's room after all.

Tanya was tippy-tapping on the keyboard like there was no tomorrow. You'd never believe that just a few minutes before she'd been shooting the breeze with her friends like she had all the time in the world.

"Mind if I take a cigarette?" I whispered to Marjorie.

I reached across the counter and was about to snatch one when those striped talons shot out, closed over the pack, and dragged it off the desk before you could say Jack Flash.

"I'm going to act like I didn't see that," Tanya said without taking her eyes off the computer screen.

"Well, how about one more candy for the road?" I asked.

She reached in the bag, grabbed the first candy she found, and held it out, *still* without once looking at me.

At least it was a root beer, which would've been my second choice. I snatched it from her. "Well, I'll be going then. Thanks for all your help. Hope I didn't *inconvenience* you any." That last part was for Tanya.

Off I went.

THE BUTTERSCOTCH GOT me to the elevator. I sucked so hard, it's a wonder I didn't pull my dentures down my throat. I was getting farther and farther away from my room. God knew how I was going to make it back, but I decided to worry about that later.

You would of thought those beat-up elevator doors were a long-lost friend, I was so glad to see them. Proud, too, that I'd made it all that way. I pushed the button, stepped inside, and up I went.

When those doors slid open, I couldn't believe my eyes. It was like a whole different world. A pool hall or a bordello (though I never been in one, of course), or some kind of opium den. The lights were dim and the smell of piss stronger than ever. Some other smell was mixed in, too: a musty smell of lots of bodies, or dirty feet, or clothes that's been worn and worn and never washed. Down near the end of the hall a couple of men were roving around in their bathrobes like zombies. I could hardly see them in the murky light. Turn right around, get back in that elevator, and go to your room, I told myself. But the minute I headed back, the elevator doors slid closed. I was standing there punching the button when one of those zombies came up beside me.

"What're you doing up here?" he asked.

His skin was a funny gray color and he didn't have a tooth in his head. He had blue rubber thongs on his feet. His toenails were the nastiest things you've ever seen: yellow, thick as a plank, and with enough dirt under them to plant potatoes. If that weren't enough, his robe was hanging open and his business was dangling to his knees. My eyeballs liked to fell out of their sockets.

"I was looking for somebody but I changed my mind," I said, punching the button like my life depended on it.

"You looking for Keith?" he yelled, loud enough to be heard over a buzz saw.

"No."

" 'Cause he ain't here."

"I ain't looking for Keith," I said, *still* punching that button.

"You looking for Tony? 'Cause he ain't here, either."

He smelled like earwax and was standing way too close. I figured the elevator must be broken. "Now, you listen here," I said, turning toward him. "I ain't looking for Keith *or* Tony. I'm just trying to get this elevator to come so I can go back to my room."

"They ain't here."

"Don't matter, because I'm not looking for them!" I yelled, just as loud as he had. "I never even heard of them."

"Who you looking for, then?"

I was trying not to look down at his whang, but it was pretty hard to miss. Marcos told me the old men's balls got so long they dangled in the water when they sat on the toilet, and for the first time I was inclined to believe him.

"Vitus. Vitus Kovic."

"Down there." He pointed toward the end of the hall. "Around the corner."

It wasn't doing me no good standing there punching a button that didn't work while staring at an old man's stretched-out scrotum, so I headed off. It hurts me to know that Vitus lives in a place like this that smells so bad and looks so dirty. The man I'd been talking to stayed by the elevator, thank God. When I got near that other zombie who was wandering around, he walked straight up to the wall, put his forehead against it, and started snarling and cussing in a low voice. It scared the tar out of me. If my kids could see me now, I thought, locked up in this loony bin with the likes of these two.

I could hardly breathe when I got to the end of the hall. From there I could see down the next corridor, and this one was worse than the first. More than half the bare fluorescent lights were out, and the ones that *were* working sizzled and flickered like a scene from hell. A lot of the doors to the rooms were open, and TVs blared out, all the racket clamoring at once. I leaned against the emergency exit door, trying to get my breath. A bunch of junk was parked in the hallway—a gurney and two wheelchairs, plus a couple of those carts from the dining hall. Metal folding chairs stood outside a lot of the rooms; a man sat in one not far from me, his legs spread and his hands on his knees.

"You state?" he called out in a froggy voice.

"What's that?" I gasped as best I could.

"This is the *state* floor! *State* residents only! That what you are?"

Right about then I was thinking how nice it'd be to talk to just *one* normal person. I pushed myself off the wall and started toward the geezer in the chair. My knees felt like they were going to give way any second. The floor was filthy, streaked with all manner of who-knows-what. It hadn't been mopped in a century. My heart went out to Vitus. What a treat it must be for him to come to my room. To sit there with my nice rug and flow-ered bedspread and all my things are pretty and clean and sweet smelling compared to what I was seeing now.

"I'm just visiting from downstairs," I panted to the man in the chair. "Looking for Room 247."

Men poked their heads out of their rooms. Pretty soon they came out in the hall like lizards crawling from under rocks.

"She ain't state!" the man in the chair called down the hallway. "She lives down below!"

A fat colored man with red suspenders pulled up a chair next to him and watched me like I was television. Another colored man who was just as skinny as the first was fat came out from across the way and stood behind him. He had oxygen tubes in his nose and dragged a tank on a little cart behind him. Damned if another man, who looked too young to be there, didn't follow him out and join the crowd. This one was white. Nothing was wrong with his body, but when you looked at his face you could tell something inside his head wasn't right.

"Get me a chair," I wheezed. "I need a rest."

The fat man pointed to a folding chair a few doors down and the younger guy went and fetched it. I fell into it.

"Steady, girl," the fat man said. "Take it easy."

They stood in a ring and watched me pant.

"She's headed down to 247," the first one croaked. "Kovic's room." He had food dripped all down the front of his white T-shirt. I could make out egg yolk, ketchup, and something brown. Gravy, maybe.

"How much farther?" I asked when I could talk again.

"You're well nigh there," the big black man said. He had a ring of gray hair around his head. Light from that sorry fluorescent bulb reflected in the bald part on top. The skinny one with the tubes nodded.

"How come I never seen any of you before?" I asked.

They looked around at each other and snickered. "We're *state*," the first one said. He had a thing about it. "Unless we got some extra money coming in from somewhere, we got to eat in our rooms."

"Some of them old bats looking for men ought to come up here," I said. "This is happy hunting grounds."

They giggled and puffed out their chests. Men are the same, no matter how old or sick they get.

"Help me up," I said, sticking my arms out for them to grab. The young one and the fat one got on each side and hefted me up. The little folding chair creaked and moaned. Lord, I was tired. My feet felt like they'd been run over with a truck. But, truth was, I was dying to see Vitus. Now that I was so close I was downright excited thinking about the look on his face when I waltzed in. I imagined how he'd grin and call me Woozy and find a place for me to sit. Treat me like I treated him when he came to visit. I couldn't wait. I would have run if I could.

"Well, I gotta be going," I said. " 'Til we meet again," I called out as a joke.

There were little square plaques with the room numbers beside each door, odd on one side, even on the other. They could have been milestones for as long as it took to get from one to the other, but I just kept plodding along, taking it one step at a time. I could feel that group behind me watching. Seemed like I was disappearing down a tunnel that kept getting darker and darker, and the smell got worse, too—the pee so shrill and strong it made my scalp tingle.

When I got within a couple of rooms from Vitus's, I saw the door was open. Blue light and TV noise spilled out into the hall. He was home! It surprised me how glad I was, how much I'd missed him. Already it seemed like I'd known him all my life. Only two more doors to go! I was racing for the finish line, pushing myself to keep going even though I was ready to fall down flat on the floor. I lunged for the door, caught hold of the jamb, and clung on for dear life, gulping like a fish out of water.

From the doorway I saw the side of a dresser and a small TV sitting on top. All the light came from that. Just beyond the door, a curtain—the kind that hangs from a track on the ceiling in hospitals—hid all but the foot of a bed. There were feet in the bed, covered by a sheet. Someone was watching the TV. The sound was way up loud. Vitus! I took a minute to catch my breath, patted my hair into place, tippy-toed up to the curtain, and peeked around the edge.

I jumped back like I was bit by a snake! I almost screamed bloody murder! It wasn't Vitus at all but that Daniel, laid out like a corpse! His body was stretched like a rope down the center of the bed and his head was cricked up on the pillow. Spooky blue light from the TV played over the folds in the white sheet that covered him. Those big choppers of his glistened like a bear trap.

He turned his head toward me. "Yeah?" he growled.

"I'm looking for Vitus."

The room was no bigger than a cell. Another hospital bed was crammed in the space between Daniel's and the window. The aisle between the two was hardly wide enough for a person to squeeze through. There was a wooden chair in the corner and another dresser at the foot of what I took to be Vitus's bed. The poor devil. Never in a hundred years had I pictured him in a place like that.

"He ain't here," Daniel said when he was done eyeballing me. His head looked so big at the end of that sad little body—like a great white shark head on the body of an anchovy. His eyes shifted back to the TV like I wasn't even there.

"Well, where is he?"

He was watching wrestling: those big fat guys in masks throwing each other around, their dinks wiggling like goldfish in their stretchy outfits. Abel used to watch it, too. I cannot for the life of me imagine why a grown man would be interested in something so fake, but Daniel's eyes were glued to the set. Right when I turned to look, one of them flipped the other over his shoulder. He landed with a thud and a big groan on the mat.

Daniel laughed. A lot of loose stuff rattled

around in his chest. He started coughing. "What do you want?" he asked when he finally stopped.

"None of your business."

"I told you. He's not here."

I was at the end of my tether. "Listen here," I hollered over the noise of the TV. "I come all this way to see him and I need to know where he is!" I felt like I was about to start bawling. "I'm tired as hell! I need to sit down!"

He leered up at me and patted the side of his bed. "Come on over here. Come over here and sit down."

That about turned my stomach. "Turn that damn thing down and listen to me! I need to know where Vitus is. I didn't come here to chitchat with you!"

He grinned broader, the old barracuda. The madder I got, the more he seemed to like it. "Hand me that," he said, pointing with his chin to the remote control on the sheet beside him.

"Get it yourself! I didn't come here to be your servant."

His old claw came out from under the sheet and took the remote. He pointed it at the TV and turned the sound down, but not off. "What's so special about Vitus?" he asked. "What's he got that I don't?"

I snorted. "A lot!"

I can hardly bring myself to tell you what he did next. Without taking his eyes off me and leering like a wolf the whole time, he reached through the sheet and started handling himself.

I was so taken aback it took me a minute to get hold of my senses. "I ain't interested!" I finally barked while he went on kneading and stroking. "If I could get my foot up there, I'd kick that nasty thing off at the root!"

Well, he is the filthiest man alive. "Come on over here," he whispered in a voice akin to Satan's. "Have a seat. I been saving a place for you here on my face." His dirty tongue flicked over his lips.

I turned tail and hotfooted it out of there.

"You're better off with me!" he yelled as I rushed out the door.

I CAN'T TELL you how I got back to the elevator. It was like I was sleepwalking, or living in somebody else's body. All I saw were those grinning teeth and that hand moving on the knot in the sheet, all covered with silvery light from the television. I do remember punching the elevator button, and the doors sliding open right away, thank God. I held on to the railing when the elevator started moving, and I remember thinking I'd never be able to get my breath again, that I'd die right there, and the next person would press the button and the doors would slide open and there I'd be, a corpse on the floor. But the elevator bumped to a stop on my floor and I was still alive. I never in my life thought I'd be glad to see that hallway, but when the doors slid open I almost got down on my knees and kissed the grubby linoleum.

I was dog tired. It hit me like a locomotive. The only time I was ever that dead beat was after having my kids. But somebody smiled on me, because sitting right across from the elevator was an empty wheelchair. I dove for it and sat there panting until I could muster enough energy to get the wheels going with my hands. Let me tell you, it ain't as easy as it looks. I struggled and groaned, but after a few feet it felt like my arms were falling off. I kicked the footrests aside and tried to pull myself along with my feet, but that didn't help much and it was hard to keep the damn thing on course instead of veering off toward the wall.

I looked down the hall toward the nurses' station, but nobody was hanging around anymore. All of a sudden everything was too much for me and I commenced to whimpering, then to sniveling, and before long I was bawling outright. I was just so tired and my room was so far away. I had no idea what time it was, but it seemed like way late in the night, two or three o'clock. The more I cried, the more I got to feeling like a motherless child. I was so alone in the world! For all I knew, Vitus was cozied up in some other woman's room, smoking *her* cigarettes and watching *her* TV. Or worse—cuddled up in her bed whispering sweet nothings in her ear. My kids were with their families. My folks were dead. So was Abel. My friends, what few I'd had, were scattered to the wind.

"Help me! Oh, help me! I need help!" I wailed, pitiful as hell, to whoever might hear me.

That mean nurse, Tanya, came out of the nurses' station and hustled down the hall.

"What in the world is going on?" she said, leaning over me. "What's the matter? Are you in pain?"

"Oh, yes!" I yelled between sobs. "Yes I am!"

"Where? Where are you hurting?"

I was so desperate I grabbed one of her hands and squeezed it in mine. "Everywhere!" I moaned, looking up at her for mercy.

She pulled her hand back and rested it on her hip. "What's wrong with you?"

How could I explain? I looked down at the nice clothes I'd put on, all for nothing. "I need to go back to my room," I squeaked, meek as a mouse. "Would you mind pushing me down there? Room 136." I pointed in that direction.

She wasn't so bad, after all. She bent over and fixed the footrests, then lifted my feet up on top of them. While she pushed me, I pulled off my earrings, got my key out of my pocket, smoothed my pants over my legs, and wiped the tears from my face. I was already thinking about how I was going to turn off the light, fall into bed, and try to forget this whole evening ever happened.

"Here we go," she said when we got to my room. She helped me stand up, which was no easy chore because I didn't have an ounce of energy left. She got under one arm and grunted and groaned.

"Got your key?" she asked when I was finally on my feet.

I held it up for her to see.

"You need anything else?"

She pulled the wheelchair away from me, turned it around, and got ready to push it back down the hall.

"Listen here," I said. "I'm sorry about before. You know, down there when you was working. I might of been a little nicer."

She tipped her head. The little white beads in her hair clicked together.

"Do you sleep with those things in your head?" I couldn't help but ask her.

"You think I'm going to take them out every night and put them back in every morning?"

"Well, do you?"

"No. I got better things to do."

She just stood there, looking at me like she was waiting for something, so I said, "Well, anyway, like I said, I'm sorry." It wasn't easy to say. She smiled, though, so I went on. "And thank you for pushing me down here."

"You're very welcome," she said, and finally smiled. Not long though. She gave that chair a shove and off she went.

I felt like I'd been halfway around the world. I fit the key in the lock, turned the knob, and pushed the door open.

There he was, sitting in the armchair. The footrest up. The TV on. His hand in the bag of trail mix. Grinning from ear to ear.

"Woozy, my dear, where have you been?" He winked at me and pointed to the sliding glass door. "You left it open," he whispered.

My heart did a flip-flop.

That word *joy,* I never thought much of it. But it popped into my mind right then and I wondered at it, how curious it was, made of just three letters, each so different from the other.

You have had it, girl, I thought to myself. You are in big trouble.

LOVE

I only have one page left in this book, so I got to be careful and say only the most important things. When I first saw all those blank pages, I laughed at even the *thought* that someday I'd fill all of them. Now, will you look at me? Already, here I am.

Something's happening inside me. I tried not to think about it, but I can't deny it anymore. I'm scared to say it, because saying it makes it so. It changes things, so there's no going back.

But I have to. So here goes.

I love Vitus.

There, I said it. It hit me last night all of a sudden. He's taken to coming by of an evening again. He brings a little pint of brandy, what he calls a warmer-upper, for us to sip while we visit. While he was watching TV, I looked at the side of his face. A voice in my head said, "There he is, the man you've been waiting for." It was crystal clear. Every cell of my body felt so light I thought I might float up out of that chair and bounce around the ceiling like a balloon. I know without a doubt that I love that man, body and soul.

A lot of people think that old people are just a bunch of dried-up zombies with no feelings left. Well, I am here to tell you that the hunger for love doesn't go away. Not ever. If anything, it gets stronger. We've seen a lot and been through a lot and we're pretty much stripped down to the basics. Eating, sleeping, and loving. We got less time for messing around. We need love more, real love, because we got less distractions to take our mind off what might be missing. No kids or jobs or busywork. We just want someone to look at us and know who we are.

I got no idea what Vitus is thinking. I can't tell. He comes here at night and seems real glad to see me. We laugh and joke and have a good time. He might bring me a little something: a packet of crackers or, like last night, a charm shaped like a ballet slipper. I catch him watching me. He smiles when I look up. Calls me Woozy. Tells me I'm really something. He makes himself right at home here in my room and seems real comfortable around me. It's a warm feeling, like we're happy just to be together.

But I don't know if he feels the same as I do. For all I know about foreigners, this is the way they act toward women, all women, and he don't mean nothing by it.

I aim to find out. The way I feel, if I only have one year, or one month, or just one day, it's better than nothing. I aim to enjoy every minute. I'm way down here at the bottom of the last page, squeezing everything in with little tiny writing. I don't know what's going to happen, but I do know I got to work fast.

Like I said at the beginning of this book, I'm tired of holding back. I've got nothing to lose.

Second Book

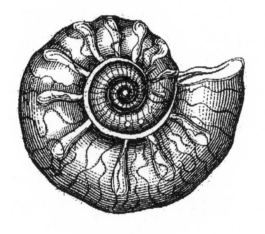

I SPILL THE BEANS

Emma got me this new book. I like it better than the last one—at least on the outside. The cover is light blue with a picture of a cream-colored seashell stamped on the front, that spiral kind called a *nautilus*. It's real pretty.

Inside is a different story. Oh, it looks nice enough: The pages are a buckwheat color, and thick—almost like a cracker. But they're rough, with big flecks of stems, or splinters, or wood chips (I don't rightly know *what* they are) that make my pen snag and the ink spit. I've gotten where I write so fast, I don't have time to slow down for any potholes or bumps in the road. If that's not bad enough, this purple pen is on its last legs. You'd have thought Emma would buy me a new one to go along with this book, but I guess she lost interest, so I'm on the lookout for a new one.

Now that the weather's nicer, I've taken to writing outside. A minute ago one of the girls who work here pushed the laundry cart by and said, "What're you up to, Miz Sledge? You writing a book about all of us?"

I grinned and nodded like the old fool she thinks I am. I wonder if *she's* the one who took my money.

Glenda brought the book on her last visit.

"What's going on, Mommy? You look so nice!"

"You think something's wrong if I don't look like hell?"

Fact is, I lost more weight. Eighteen pounds! Marcos's eyes dangle out of their sockets every time I step up on that scale. I don't know what got into me, but I let the cat out of the bag. Long story short, I told her about Vitus. I just came right out and said, "Maybe I look good because I'm in love."

She didn't know whether to shit or go blind. "What are you talking about?" she asked. She smiled, then she frowned, then her eyes crossed. "Are you serious?"

Even though I have nothing to be ashamed of, my face started burning. I was already wishing I'd kept my mouth shut, but it has a mind of its own. "Serious as a heart attack," I said.

"Why, Mommy!" She leaned forward and laid her hand along the side of my face, like I had a fever. "I just don't know what to say."

"Try not saying anything." My armpits got to itching. I had a hard time looking her in the eye.

"Well, who is he? How did you meet this man?"

"He's just a man," I mumbled. "A man who lives here."

She walked over to the armchair and dropped into it like her knees gave way. She *loved* her father. She was his biggest fan. She ran her hands through her hair and stared at her lap. Lord have mercy, I thought to myself. Here it comes.

When she looked up at me, her face was the color of biscuit dough. "I just don't know what to think about this," she whispered.

I shrugged and waved my hand like it was no big thing, but inside I was panicking. What if Vitus got wind of this? I hadn't let on anything to him—that is, I hadn't said nothing straight out. The way men are, you got to ease into things or it can scare them off.

"What's his name?" she asked like a policeman.

"Don't matter. You don't know him."

Her eyes fired up and the color came back to her face. "Seems to me that if my own mother is *in love* with someone, I at least deserve to know his name."

"Vitus," I muttered.

"Vitus what?"

"Vitus *Kovic!*" I yelled. "I don't need the third degree!"

We stared at each other. She's got them same close-together eyes as her dad.

"Is he a nice man?"

"Depends on what you call *nice,*" I said with a laugh.

She heaved a big sigh and covered her eyes with her hand, like the whole world was just too much for her.

"I thought you'd be happy for me," I said. "I thought you'd be glad I had some company instead of rotting here alone."

Her eyes were red around the rims when she looked up. Her top lip started twitching the way it has since she was six months old. "I'm just thinking of you!" she bawled. "I'm scared for you! I don't know this man! What if he hurt you?"

"If you're so worried about me, what am I doing here in the first place? Last time I checked I was a grown woman with a mind of my own."

"Well, is he good to you? Is he polite?"

"I don't need *polite!* That's not what I'm after!"

"I don't know if you should see him, Mommy," she had the nerve to say. "He might take advantage of you in some way."

"I wish he would!"

You'd think I'd dropped my drawers and did a naked hula on Main Street by the look on her face.

"It's not like I'm going to get pregnant!" I was used to talking to Marcos about these kinds of things. With him I could say whatever I wanted, no beating around the bush. "What are you afraid of?" I asked. "Don't you think I can take care of myself after all this time?"

"Well, how do you know if he's the kind of man you want to associate with?"

Who was she to talk? Three husbands and not one of them worth a plug nickel. "You're not exactly an authority on men," I pointed out. "I'm entitled to make my own mistakes, just like you."

She shriveled up and started bubbling and snotting like a salted snail.

Nobody likes seeing their own daughter hurt. I went over and patted her arm. "Look here, straighten up. Don't cry now. You got to understand that I got feelings like everybody else. You can't just put me away like I'm in a museum and I'm going to sit on the shelf and not say a word or have an emotion for the rest of my life."

"When I was a teenager, you had to see every boy I ever went out with!" she cried, raising her face up so I could see the water streaming down her cheeks. "You and Daddy made me bring him in the house so you could interrogate him. I couldn't go anyplace alone with them and I had to be home at ten o'clock. You never cut me an inch of slack!"

"Well, I never," I said, drawing back from her. "Talk about holding a grudge. You want to get even with me *now,* forty-five years later?"

"You made my life miserable!" she shouted, like she was fourteen years old again.

"Hmpf." I snorted. Two could play that game. "The feeling's mutual."

"You never loved me!"

"That's the craziest thing I ever heard."

"Did you?" she asked in a sneaky voice.

"Of course I did."

"Well, you didn't act like it."

Oh my God. It was like a scene out of one of

153

Marcos's soap operas. I felt like I was being dragged through a knothole.

"Listen here. I love you to death, just like I always have," I told her. "I'm still your mother, no matter what happens. But my life isn't over yet. Long as my heart's still beating, I got to go where it leads me. You got no right to interfere."

You could tell she didn't like it, but she had to give in. I don't regret all the times I wore out her fanny with a switch when she was a youngster. It still pays off.

"I'd like to meet him," she said with a meek little smile.

"Maybe after awhile, when we get to know each other better." I felt silly now that the storm had blown over. "To tell you the truth, I don't know what's going to happen," I said, eating a little crow. "I shouldn't have said anything. Me and my big mouth."

She wiped her face and nodded, poor thing. I pity that girl sometimes, I really do. She's missing something—a backbone or a little fire. But if you're born that way, there's not much you can do about it.

"All right, then. I know you got things to do, so I'm not going to keep you here any longer," I said. Lonesome as I get, I feel antsy when I've been around somebody too long. Besides, I was worn out. "Oh, and Glenda honey, I need some more money."

"Oh, I stopped in the office before I got here," she said.

"Why didn't you tell me?"

"Well, your big news pushed it right out of my head. Anyway, things are missing right and left. They're asking around and keeping their eyes open. They have some ideas about who it might be."

"Who?"

She shrugged. She has the curiosity of a dead fish. "They said just be sure to keep your room locked at all times, even when you're here. And if you have anything valuable, they want you to keep it up there in the office."

"Guess I should put up some barbwire. Like I'm not prisoner enough already."

She sighed. "Is there anything left? Did they take it all?"

I pointed to the three quarters I'd left as bait in the dish on my dresser. "That's it. Everything I got."

"I only have about forty dollars on me right now."

"Better than nothing."

Truth is, my crystal's vexing me more than the money. I've felt unhinged since it went missing. But I didn't want to make a fuss. The long and short of it is, now I got a reason to want to stay here, not forever, but for the time being. I know I pissed and moaned to get out, and I *do* want out, only now there's Vitus. A plan's taking shape in my mind, and until I figure things out, I don't want anybody messing with me.

155

LOSING

I don't dread getting on the scale anymore. When Marcos comes calling, I leap up there like a mountain goat. This week I lost five pounds. Five! When I was done laughing and clapping, I gave him a kiss. He's been pouting since our little tiff. He doesn't give me the time of day.

"Listen here, don't be like that," I told him. "Whatever I done or said that made you mad, I'm sorry."

He just looked at me with his bloodhound eyes.

"What do I need to do to make it up to you?" I asked. "Go out there and lay on the freeway and let the cars run over me?"

He didn't crack a smile, so while he was listening to my heart, I said, "Guess who I seen."

"Please don't talk. I'm behind schedule. I can't hear your heart."

"Your boy. Renato."

His whole face changed, like he'd been sleeping and just woke up. "Where?" he said. "When?"

"Oh, never you mind. You're busy. Got a lot on your mind."

He took the stethoscope out of his ears.

"Got a cute little butt on him," I said. "Jeans so tight I could read the dates on the coins in his pocket."

"Where was he? What was he doing?"

"Don't get your drawers in a twist. He was in the closet down at the end of the hall, filling the shelves up with toilet paper."

Marcos let loose a big blast of air from his mouth and his head seemed to shrink like a leaky balloon. The color drained from his face. He started gathering up his things. "I'm through with Renato," he said in a dead voice. "It's all over."

"How can that be? Just the other day everything was hunky-dory. What changed so fast?"

Big tears rolled down his cheeks and dripped off his poor, ugly nose. I went over and stroked his fat hand and stumpy fingers. "You listen here. I saw that boy. He *is* pretty, but he's not worth all this. Now you just straighten up. What's all the fuss about?"

His bracelets jangled when he wiped his eyes. "Haven't you ever been in love, Cora?" he sniffed.

I went stiff as a board and my lips pressed so tight together I thought my head would pop. "There's somebody I got an interest in, just like you got an interest in Renato." I couldn't believe what came out of my own mouth.

Marcos's eyebrows shot up to the top of his forehead. "What're you up to, Cora?"

"None of your business."

"Cora," he leaned in close and whispered. "Who is it?"

I swatted him. "Now you just forget I said that."

He softened up. I tell you, when that craggy, ugly face of his melts into a smile, he looks like a sweet little boy. I couldn't help myself. I put my arms around that fat belly of his and gave him a big hug. "You're still my sugar, you know that? I wouldn't trade you for the world. If that loverboy of yours gives you any trouble, I'll flay him alive."

I'd seen Renato in the dining room surrounded by girls. The nurses' aides and girls who work in the dining hall simper and frolic around him like May lambs, and he plays along, that cute little thing.

"I'll tan his hide," I added. "I'll give him what for if he does you wrong."

Marcos pursed his blubbery lips. "Loving him is an honor," he said. "No matter what he does."

I shook my finger at him. "You got it bad. Worse than me."

He raised his chin up like he was real proud and made like he was staring off into the distance. His nose holes flared like a stallion's.

"You're a lot older than him," I said. "There's no telling what he might do."

"We are alike, you and me," Marcos said. "We don't hold back. We give everything."

"That's right, we go whole hog," I said, patting his bottom to see if I could get away with it.

He gave me a sad smile. "And so, *señora,* I must go."

I walked to the door with him. He dug around in his bag and took out a can of Pringles. Sodium and calories up the wazoo, but I could have jumped for joy.

"For you, my darling. So you don't waste away to nothing."

"Wait until next time." I winked. "You won't recognize me."

He stepped out the door, but stuck his head in just before I closed it. "You still haven't told me who he is."

"My lips are sealed."

"But maybe I know," he whispered. "Maybe I know more than you think."

THE FOUNTAIN PEN

You might notice I'm using a new pen. I got two: one I found on the counter at the nurses' station, and one I found there in my top drawer where the money was. The purple one with the squishy handle finally gave up the ghost. *Sayonara,* I said when I threw it away. It was like saying good-bye to an old friend.

This new one is a cheap ballpoint, just a thin tube of white plastic with a real fine point. I like it, though. It writes small and pointy, so I can fit more on the page. And it cuts right through those chips and chunks in the paper. I feel like I'm using a needle, or a knife, when I'm writing with it—like I'm ready to get down to business. It didn't have anybody's name on it when I went by the nurses' station the other day (yes, I'm walking a lot more since that night I went upstairs to find Vitus), so I figured it was meant for me. The black ink is good, too. Makes everything I write look important.

The one I found in my drawer is a *fountain* pen! Lord knows where it came from. I can't for the life of me remember where I got it or how it came to be in my drawer, but it's not the first thing I've forgotten about, and it probably won't be the last. There's lots of things I've got as gifts, useless things, things I just tuck away. I figure I uncovered it when I was searching through my underwear for those missing bills. Now that I'm writing in this book, I got use for it, and I'll tell you, it's a doozy.

It's beautiful: a deep wine color with a gold nib. The ink is *brown!* When you write, it looks like a treasure map. But you have to hold the pen just right, and I can't get the hang of it. The ink sputters and splashes and it takes a long time just to write a few lines. Plus it doesn't dry right away. You got to blow on the page. So I decided to use the fountain pen just for show. I lay it on top of my book when I'm done writing and set them both on my dresser.

But I'll use it here so you can see. Look:

Coral Spring
Cora Sledge
Mrs. Cora Kovic

THE LIST

Before I get too far in this book, here's a list of things I want to do. They are part of my plan.

1. Wean myself off these pills.

Ever since they found my pills at the house, everybody has been after me to *get a handle on my meds*. That's how they say it. I hate for anybody to tell me what to do. Always have. But they don't know the half of it. I been taking pills of one kind or another for a good thirty-five or forty years now, sometimes more and sometimes less—sometimes I walked around in a fog for months or even years and sometimes I didn't take hardly any at all, maybe just a pill or two when I had to do something that made me nervous, like go to the kids' open house, or show up at a wedding, or sit through a Christmas dinner with a million people around.

There were days I couldn't see straight by the time the kids came home from school. I cooked dinner in a daze, nodded when they told me about their day. I put the food on the table, cleared the dishes up afterwards, told the kids to brush their teeth and say their prayers and get in bed, all the time high as a kite. Nobody blinked an eye. Later me and Abel went to bed and whatever he wanted was just fine with me. Nothing made much difference. Next day the same thing, and the day after that. A lot of time can pass like that. It just slips on by.

I tried to stop. I made so many resolutions I lost track of them. I flushed pills down the toilet, hid them from myself, even called one of them hotlines, thinking I'd ask for help. I hung up the minute they answered. I prayed, pleaded, and bargained with God. I gave myself talkings-to in the bathroom mirror, called myself every filthy name in the book. But the years went by and I didn't quit. Truth is, it's not easy to kick that stuff. I got used to taking it. I took ten or twelve a day and didn't turn a hair. Long as I could get what I needed, everything was fine.

Except for a few pills I was able to grab and hide here and there, I got cut off all at once when they put me in here. My mind and body went into such a tailspin, it's a wonder I'm still alive. This isn't the time or place to tell you everything about that, but I will say that for a couple of months I was hardly human. I didn't have control of nothing. It was a living nightmare, with every kind of monster and ghoul you can imagine. I finally had to beg for mercy. I went to that damn

Dr. Kildare and said, "Listen here, I'm losing my mind. If you don't give me something I'm not going to make it." It was no exaggeration, and he knew it. So he doled out a few pills. With that and what I've been able to rustle up on my own, I've managed to make it so far.

I'm taking a lot less than I ever did.

A week or ten days ago, I was sitting on a folding chair right outside my door in a band of sun. It felt good soaking into my bones. One of those Mexican gardeners was working on the lawn mower over by the room where they keep their tools. He'd taken it apart and was down on his hands and knees, tinkering. It was that quiet time about two o'clock, when the residents take a nap or watch TV and the workers have finished cleaning up from lunch and are starting to get ready for dinner.

The gardener had a greasy rag hanging out the back pocket of his green uniform. He leaned back on his heels now and then and wiped his hair out of his face. I wasn't thinking much of anything when my eyes lit on the gasoline can beside him. You've seen them—they're metal, about the size and shape of a toaster, bright red. I don't know how long I'd been looking at it when my breath caught in my throat. My chest heaved, my chin wobbled, and before I knew what was going on, I was sobbing. Tears streamed down my face like a river. You know why? Just that goddamn color.

Red. The red of that can was the purest, brightest red I'd ever seen. I'd forgotten that color, and right then it all came rushing back to me: those candy apples they sold at our school fair during Halloween way back when, apples I waited months and months for, saving my pennies so I could sink my teeth into that hard candy, shiny as a fire engine, the crust of red glass that shattered into shards when you cracked into it, that crunched into a heavenly mash of spicy cinnamon and tart apple as you ground it between your molars. That red was Ma's lipstick as she fixed herself up for church, the smell of soap in the air from all of us getting slicked up, and my ma there with her lips parted and her nose inches from the mirror, laying those glossy lines on her mouth while I watched, my heart bursting with love and longing, my own lips tingling like they were the ones being stroked and smoothed with that stick of bright red.

The red of that can brought to mind the frost of blood that covered my little angel the very first time I laid eyes on her and the ember of my cigarette floating in the dark while I smoked alone in my room at night. It was the same red as the kids' scooter laying on its side in the grass when I got up early in the morning and looked out the kitchen window at the backyard. The red pumps and matching handbag I had right after me and Abel got married, the ones I wore when we drove overnight to Las Vegas to see Crystal get married for the second or third time. Lord, I was young then! I remembered the comb of the rooster that ruled the flock of hens back home and the rain boots Glenda loved so much she wore them rain or shine. All that. And me, too. The stone I'm named after. Coral, that high orange-red like the tomatoes Abel grew every year come hell or high water, those beefsteaks as big and heavy as grapefruits, warmed by the sun, smelling like summer, scenting your skin when you reached in to pick them.

It was just a metal gas can sitting on the ground there next to a gardener fooling with the lawn mower, but that color stood out against the grass and sky like a miracle. I hadn't seen a color like that in years. That's when I realized, plain as day, that them drugs was leaving me. I was waking up from a long sleep.

I sat on that metal chair still as a statue, my eyes fixed on that red can, while I thought about all the things I'd missed living in a world with colors as bleached out as a faded snapshot, with now and then just a hint of watery pink or washed-out blue. The sun shifted and a breeze came up. It played in the hair on my arms and the back of my neck. It tickled the creases of my arms and the corners of my eyes like God himself breathing on me. The branches of the trees quivered, the leaves twirled, the clouds slipped across the sky.

Everything around me moved and breathed. I was in the middle of it, sitting in the metal chair.

That started me out. Don't get me wrong: I'm not stopping all at once. That would drive me straight to the loony bin, I know for a fact. But I'm cutting down and keeping better track. I got a system. I keep all the pills in one place instead of stashed all over, and I dole them out little by little. Last week I took one when I got up, one in the afternoon before dinner, and one before I went to bed (along with my sleeping pills). But this week I cut each one in half, and next week I'm going to cut *that* half in half again. See what I mean? If I get to where I'm feeling real nervous, or like I can't take it, then I help myself to a little piece of pill, a half or a quarter, depending on how bad I feel. If that don't help, I take a little more. But those times are getting more seldom, and today, believe it or not, I've made it all the way past lunch on just the one pill.

It's not easy. I wake up in the middle of the night with the sweat pouring off me and the feeling that I been chased up and down dark alleys by an army of zombies. Sometimes the terror in my chest is so strong I have to curl up like a cutworm and pull the blankets over my head. I been *that far* from buzzing the panic button they have that calls the nurses to come and help you. There's times when it feels like ants are crawling up and down my legs, or my insides are fighting to bust out through my skin, or my head is a storm of black water swirling like a whirlpool. The last few days something new has started. Two or three times a day I get a jolt in my brain like a thousand volts just shot through it. My whole body jerks. Don't ask me what *that's* about.

Lord knows what's next.

But I'm noticing things. Little by little. I don't like to admit it, but before—when I was living alone at home—most of the time I didn't know whether I was coming or going. There are blanks, things that don't connect, time I can't account for. Weeks and months I have no recollection of, scraps of memories that don't make sense. I was so mixed-up, so confused in my mind, I was hardly there at all. That's it, the God's honest truth: I was a stranger to myself, somebody I hardly recognized.

I try to figure out when I lost track of myself. Must have been my late twenties, early thirties. Now that my brain is clearing up, I'm getting to know myself a little now. Thoughts passing through my mind, they're new to me. Feeling things, seeing things. Like a newborn baby. It scares the living shit out of me. You might wonder, Why now? and believe me, so do I. Something happened to me is all I can say. Vitus is part of it, and coming to this place. Getting to this age of my life. Thinking I got to the end and finding there's still a ways to go. It's only these flashes I have, flashes of remembering myself like I used to be, that make me feel that some part of me is still out there somewhere, alive.

Which leads me to the second part of my plan:

2. Get to walking.

Ever since that night I walked up to Vitus's room, I found out how far I can go by just putting one foot in front of the other one. Let me tell you that seeing the people around here, people with their legs swollen up, or missing altogether, or dangling like limp noodles from their bodies— not to mention the ones stuck in wheelchairs parked in a puddle of piss—has convinced me that, hard as it is, I got to keep moving. They'll never let me out of here if I can't get around, so every day I go a little farther, even if it's just a few steps. I stop and rest whenever I need to, but I'm finding out that I can do more and more.

I walk out there in the courtyard, down the hall, even out to the lobby. There's always a lot of people hanging around there, those that's parked in their wheelchairs by their keepers, others that's waiting for visitors, and all the people coming and going—deliverymen and salespeople, workers coming on or off their shifts, and kin visiting. Like a circus, or a freak show.

A few tattered magazines about five years old

are always laying around on the tables. I thumb through them while I watch the people and rest up for the trip back to my room. One toothless old man, Mr. Speck, has tried to escape out that front door so many times he has to wear a plastic band around his ankle that sets off an alarm the minute he steps outside. Before they put it on him, they found him wandering in the parking lot over by Arby's Steak House. Which goes to show you it's a human instinct to want your freedom.

3. Get me some new clothes.

I am sick to death of pastels, elastic waists, and baggy knits.

Why is it that, once you turn sixty, you're supposed to wear the same colors as babies? Pale pink and powder blue, dingy yellow and that pukey lavender that turns my stomach. You see it all over here: old ladies walking around like wedding mints or Jordan almonds, milquetoast pastels that drive you to the depths of depression.

I want some patterns. Flowers. Stripes or triangles or polka dots. Bold prints. And some bright colors. Scarlet, peacock blue, royal purple. Fuchsia, poppy, watermelon, chartreuse! But oh no. When you're fat, you're supposed to wear *dark* colors. Flat black, navy blue, and shit brown. That's about it. Otherwise, somebody might *notice* you.

If the colors aren't enough to gag a maggot, the

styles will. Loose saggy pants that you step into like a barrel, long tops shaped like flour sacks that hang almost to your knees, dresses made of yards and yards of fabric that flap around like a tent. No tucks, no curves, no nothing. You might as well be a zeppelin for all the shape you have.

The worst are them sweat suits. Glenda is *determined* I wear them. She bought me three of them. One dogsick green, one the color of pus, and one like chewed-up bubble gum. That last one has elephants embroidered on the front. *Elephants!* And you know what they're doing? *Exercises!* Jumping jacks, sit-ups, and touching their toes.

I feel like a cottonball in them, like a used Q-tip, or a big wad of toilet paper. They're sexy as a cold turd. *No* man in his right mind would want to look at *anybody* wearing a sweat suit, much less wonder what's underneath.

I want dresses that button down the front. Nice collars, maybe a little zipper under the arm, so you can cinch it tight across the bust. I've always had nice big boobs. They might be drooping a little low, but if I get the right kind of brassiere I can hitch 'em up into attention-getters, especially if I get a low-cut dress. That's what I want. Scoop necks, square necks, and V-necks. Show some skin. A little lace. I want some jewelry, too. Bangles and dangles, a big gold necklace. It doesn't have to be expensive, just the kind I used to get at the dime store. Rhinestones and glass beads, sparkly stuff. Live a little.

BUT I BEEN going on long enough. All this talk of bangles and baubles is holding me back. I'm getting good at this writing. I can fill pages and pages without turning a hair. But I keep interrupting myself. I want to get back to the real story, even though it hurts a lot more than talking about what color pants I want. If I don't get it down now, I never will, so as soon as I get back from breakfast I'm going to get at it.

MY PREDICAMENT

You see, I dreamed it first. For about a week that summer of 1931, no matter what I was dreaming, I felt somebody watching, hovering around the edges. I couldn't see anyone. They didn't take part in the dream. They were just there with me, seeing what I saw, feeling what I felt. A presence that stayed just out of sight. It was a wonderful feeling, a true blessing, because that loneliness I always had—feeling different, or fat, or not what I should be—disappeared, at least in my dreams. She (even then I sensed it was a she) was there with me, looking out through my eyes. I didn't understand it, not at first. I thought it was just some new turn my dreams had taken, something I ate, or a passing fancy.

The next clue came in the night, too. First, I dreamed my ma took the rug beater and gave my breasts a good whomping. It hurt so much I went and lay down on my belly in a dry creek bed full of gray rocks the size of cantaloupes. I was tired and wanted to sleep, but no matter how hard I tried, I couldn't push those stones out of my way enough to get comfortable. All night long I fought those rocks, shoving them right and left, trying to shift around, and when I finally woke up I was lying on my belly just like in the dream, only it was my own boobs I was grappling with.

That morning when I woke up my tits were sore as hell, like they had been dragged up hills and down dales, all over creation. I could hardly touch them. Heavy as millstones. You'd think I might've started getting the idea, but I didn't give it a second thought.

Within a few days I started getting hungry. I've always had a healthy appetite, but this was something altogether different. If I just *saw* food, it was all I could do to keep my hands off it. When it was time to sit down and eat supper, I could hardly keep still while we said grace. The minute we said amen, I liked to broke somebody's arm reaching for the food. My pride was gone. I shoveled it down like an animal.

The minute I was done eating, I was just as tired as I had been hungry. I felt like I'd knock down anything that got between me and my bed, and if

I couldn't get to that, I'd just lay down wherever I was and fall into a dead sleep. When I woke up it was time to eat again, then it was time to sleep, just like that. Only other thing I wanted was Edward and, though I'm ashamed to say it, I wanted only one thing from him—and I wanted it just as bad as I wanted to eat or sleep. I pawed the ground in front of the house waiting for him to come pick me up, and a couple of times we barely turned the corner before I made him pull over and get down to business.

I was scared, oh, I was scared. I had no idea what was happening to me, but all them urges was eating me up, and I didn't have the energy to think. On top of that I started being able to sniff like a hound dog. I smelled things far, far away— meat stewing in a neighbor's house, a dead fish floating in the creek way out yonder, onion grass sprouting in the field, my sisters having their monthlies. The walls smelled like chalk, the floor like pine, sweaters like the sheep they came from. It was like things that had been quiet started yelling all at once, only with odor instead of sound.

My clothes didn't fit. It wasn't gradual. It happened overnight. I got up one morning and couldn't get the zipper on my skirt to close. I tugged my blouse over my sore boobs and wrestled every one of the buttons into their holes. When I finally got it fastened up, I bent over to put my shoes on and the seam down the back ripped open from my neck to my waist. You know what? I *still* didn't get it. I was eating so much it made sense I'd be gaining weight, or so I told myself. The last thing I wanted to see was the truth. Who would?

When I missed my period, something I never did since I commenced at twelve years old, I *had* to take note. Everything I'd been shoving to the back of my mind came rushing out and I couldn't have been filled with as much dread if I'd walked to the edge of a chasm, peered over, and saw hell itself roiling and churning, waiting for me to fall in. Oh Lord, what a panic! Every day it didn't start I was more frantic than the last. I couldn't tell a soul, and I had to go on with my day like nothing was happening: take care of the chickens and the cow, help my ma with the washing and cooking, drag my weary ass up and down the stairs like nothing unusual was happening with my body.

How I begged and pleaded with God! I promised if He'd give me my period I'd never open my legs again. I went to the toilet every half hour to check if it had come. Every little cramp or twitch down there made me dance with joy. But no luck.

Then a funny thing happened. To this day I can't explain it, but that was when it was like someone hit me over the head with a hammer and knocked some sense into me because I suddenly knew, for sure, that I was in trouble. Deep, deep trouble, the deepest trouble I'd ever been in before. There was no more denying it. That's when the real nightmare started, when my life got on a track I don't think I ever got off.

Course we didn't have no indoor plumbing. You had to follow a dirt path across the yard to get to the outhouse. It passed our kitchen garden and a pile of junk—old cans and jars and some pieces of equipment, plows and the like, we didn't use no more. It was the hottest time of the year by then, humid, and walking out there to the outhouse for the fiftieth time that day I wanted to lie down on the ground and have it swallow me up. The only thing that kept me going was the hope that, when I took down my drawers, I'd see the blood and everything would be over, everything would be back to normal, and I'd never, *ever,* sin like that again. So I went out there and sat down and bent over to have a look at my underwear, hoping with all my might that I'd started. There wasn't a whole lot of light, just what came through the cracks around the door and ceiling, so I had to lean over and look real close, and while I was like that with my head practically between my knees, all of sudden something in my nose burst and sprayed blood like a fire hose. It gushed all over my knees and underpants and floor, even on the door opposite, spattering everywhere like someone had been murdered.

Don't ask me why, but it was a sign to me. I read it loud and clear, as if God himself made an announcement right through the roof of that out-house. Sister Cora, you have got yourself into a right fix. You have made your bed, now it's time to lie in it.

That was the end of my smelling things like a bloodhound. From then on I was all stuffed up. I couldn't smell so much as a house on fire until after my little sweetheart was born. It was the end of my hope, too. Scared as I was, much as I wanted to die as I mopped up my own red blood with the pages of the Sears catalog we used for toilet paper, I told myself that I better get my ass in gear and figure something out. I cried the bit-terest tears on earth as I wiped down the walls and floor and threw those crumpled pages down that shit hole, but I finally got knocked out of the stupor I was in. I had to open my eyes and look around. It was a grim sight, to be sure. But there was no time to waste.

Back in those days, if a girl got pregnant, it was the end of the world. All your life you've heard fire and brimstone, the preacher pounding the pulpit and going purple in the face yelling about how you'll burn in hell, which is a hundred times worse than the very worst you can ever imagine. No matter if what's happening to you is common as dirt, if it's happening right that minute to thou-sands of other girls around the globe like it has since the beginning of time, you feel so alone, without a soul to help you. Living every minute of every day when that's happening to you is a lot different than *thinking* about it in the abstract. It leaves you speechless and plenty more besides. It leaves you shitless and breathless and just plain dumbstruck that it was so easy to get yourself in this fix and so impossible to get out.

My first thought was to get rid of it. On my own, of course, because back then it wasn't like now where girls do away with babies without a second thought, easy as blinking an eye. I was scared out of my wits just *thinking* about it because I knew what a horrible sin it was, but I was desperate to fix everything with nobody being the wiser. Only trouble is, I didn't have a clue how to do it. I had no money. I'd never been more than thirty miles from the place I was born. I'd heard a few stories, the barest scraps I'd caught from women or older girls whispering in corners, but the facts were sketchy, to say the least. Looking back now, I wonder why, desperate as I was, I never went to my mother, or at least one of my sisters. Ruby, who always took charge of everything. What I'm forgetting, I know I am, is how ashamed I was, and how scared. I couldn't look at myself, not my face in the mirror, or down the front of me, at my own body. I was so full of disgust, I wanted to throw up my own insides, to vomit and vomit 'til there was none of me left.

I never stopped. That's what made me the sickest. All that time I wanted to die from shame, when I hated myself so much I couldn't bear to look anyone in the eye or even raise my head from looking at the ground, I never let up with Edward. I couldn't. If anything, it got *worse,* more shameless, me at him so frantic, you would have thought my life depended on it.

I tried remedies: douched myself with vinegar, then poured the rest of the bottle down my gullet. Nothing happened, aside from a few burps. I walked out to what we called Indian Hill, a rise about a half mile from our house, climbed to the top, and threw myself down. I rolled over and over, bumping and bouncing. When I got to the bottom, I ran straight up and did it again. And again. Worst I got was a couple of bruises, some scrapes on my arms. I even drank iodine, but the nasty taste made me stop before I drank too much.

Truth is, I was fit as a fiddle. Life coursed through me and through that baby. I never felt better. I pictured things I could do: throw myself down a well, drink gasoline, jump in front of the train, hang myself from the big hickory tree over the creek, or just take off, sell myself into white slavery and never show hide nor hair around there again. But I didn't have the will, not at all. It occurred to me just to let things take their course, not to say a word and see what happened, and I tell you it was tempting, but I knew in the back of my head that I still had an ace in the hole, a last resort if everything else failed, and that was to tell Edward, and get married lickety-split.

I'd always wanted an old-fashioned wedding with folks from near and far come, and a dinner afterwards, and me the center of attention. I'd spent years choosing everything in my mind: what I'd wear, who'd be there, what we'd eat, and what everyone would say. Only thing missing was a face to put on the man who stood next to me, but once I met Edward, everything was in place. Before I got into my predicament, I pictured him getting down on his knees, giving me a ring, asking my daddy's permission, everything like a storybook. Well, all that went haywire. I had to make quite a few changes to my story—including facing the wrath of my ma and daddy and having everybody within shouting distance shake their heads whenever I walked by—but I wasn't the first girl around there who had to get married in a hurry. Long as you were married by the time the baby came, people tended to forgive and forget. I had to settle for less, but at least I had an out.

That was August. Ruby was getting ready to be married herself. Her and Calvin had set a date in September. Right before my eyes, she changed into a woman. She got a job in town as a clerk in the ladies' department of Tweeds. Calvin had a job with the government, working on the roads. That was during the Depression, so they were damn lucky to have jobs at all, not to mention good ones. They rented a three-room house on the edge of town, and Ruby learned to drive Calvin's Chrysler. She was in hog heaven making all the plans for her wedding. She bustled here and there like she was the most important woman in the world. All that time I watched, guarding my secret, living like a little girl with my folks. I couldn't help but imagine Ruby's face when I announced that *I* was getting married, too, and not only was I moving to town (which to us was the same as New York City), but *I* was going to live right in the middle of it, on Main Street, in the Dentons' house, which was practically a mansion.

All I had to do was work up the nerve to tell Edward. That took some doing, let me tell you. Long as I kept things a secret, I had a handle on what would happen—at least in my head. I could still believe that things might take a turn for the better, sort themselves out. But once I said those words out in the open, once I told him—well, that was a whole different thing. It would start a chain reaction that was out of my control.

I practiced it in my mind—pictured the words I'd use, the look on Edward's face, the way he'd take my hands in both of his and press them to his chest. Maybe his eyes would get a little teary, maybe it'd be hard for him to find his words. He'd surely take me in his arms, he'd tell me that—while maybe the timing wasn't perfect—this was still the happiest day of his life.

So why was I so afraid to tell him? He was an honorable boy, brought up right. He'd courted me out in the open, showed my ma and daddy plenty of respect. But every night I lay in bed with the sweat pouring off me, imagining all manner of things, scared out of my wits. Time was wasting. I *had* to tell him. I tossed and turned, half asleep, my worries falling into nightmare the minute I drifted off. I'd jolt awake terrified, cursing myself for not telling him that day, for letting another day pass while my grave was dug deeper. I'd swear to myself, *swear,* that the very next day I'd talk to Edward, I'd let him know. Then I'd fall asleep, and morning would come, and things wouldn't look so bad. Another day would pass and there I'd be the next night, terrified to death.

I finally reached the point where I couldn't face one more night like that. It was the last Sunday in August. I know because it was my ma's birthday. We'd all gone to church, then Jasper and my dad laid a big fire in the pit out in the yard. We had pork ribs, sweet potatoes, and corn. My pa bought salt and ice and we churned ice cream. My folks' brothers and sisters came with my cousins. So did some of the neighbors. Calvin was there with Ruby. Edward drove out in the afternoon. My pa split a big watermelon open and we all sat around in the shade, eating big bowls of ice cream and slices of melon, spitting seeds right and left.

I was in a lather. The night before had been worse than ever. I'd got to shaking so bad I was afraid my sisters in bed next to me would wake up. My muscles were sore from trying to keep still and, if that weren't bad enough, the last few days I'd had faint spells, where I had to sit down fast and put my head between my legs to keep from falling dead on the ground. With the heat and people talking, the smoke rising from the pit and the flies buzzing around, I felt like I was looking at everything through a haze. My ma was laughing at the flannel nightgown she'd got for her birthday. She was so pretty with her hair tied back to keep it off her neck. My daddy was across the yard with the other men, who stood under the tree where we chained the dogs. Edward was there, sitting on a milk stool with his knees wide apart so the watermelon wouldn't drip on his pants. I could tell from how easy my daddy and brother Jasper were with him, the way they talked and laughed, that they liked him. Calvin was there, along with my uncles and boy cousins.

We'd carried the dinner table outside and set it on the side of the house in the shade. That's where the women were, my aunts and girl cousins. Ruby and Crystal bantered back and forth the way they always did, and Ma was trying to cover things to keep the flies off. I was down on one end with my ice cream, stirring it into soup the way I liked it, not talking, just listening to everybody else. This is all going to end, I told myself. It broke my heart, because Ma was so happy that day. When I think back on it now, I realize she couldn't have been more than forty-two or forty-three years old, but back then I felt like I wanted to protect her, keep her safe because she was getting older. I had a high, tight feeling in my throat. I tried to concentrate on the ice cream, on all of us being together, for a little while more before all hell broke loose.

"Look at Toad," Crystal said. "She sure is enjoying that ice cream."

The minute she said that a big June bug flew out of nowhere and landed smack dab in the middle of my bowl. I'll never forget that, the way it looked, black and shiny, floating in the ice cream I'd just finished working to perfection.

Everybody laughed. Aunt Millie, my ma's older sister, said, "Here, Toad. Take mine. I'm full up to the eyeballs."

You might think it's funny, but I feel like those were the last few minutes of my girlhood, that when I finished that bowl of ice cream everything that had come before ended, and a new part began.

I looked across the yard and saw Edward was fixing to leave. He tossed the rind of his watermelon into the scrap heap a few yards away, brushed off his pants, then put his arm across Jasper's shoulders. My heart filled with love for him. He was practically part of the family already. Like my daddy and uncles, he was strong and trustworthy, someone you could rely on, someone who'd take care of you.

He came over and said good-bye to the women, even kissed my ma. I was so proud of him, happy to have all my cousins see what a good man I'd got, despite everything—including how fat I was.

I walked with him down to his car. Just before he got in, I said, "I need to talk to you. Let's drive down the road a ways."

He must have thought it was for the usual reason, but I was grim as we bumped down to the road. We didn't say a word and I didn't look to the right or the left, just stared through the wind-shield. My hands were clenched in the pockets of my dress, and my heart was pounding. Now or never, Cora Spring, I told myself. You have *got* to do this.

I had him pull off beside the road under the big willow that grew near the spring. The bugs were just starting to come out like they do before it gets dark. They were eating me up, but I didn't care. I waited for the engine to sputter and die, then I just sat there in the car, feeling the stillness of it, listening to the silence. I looked at the knobs on the dash, then out over the side of the car, at the ground, at the ruts that had hardened into place from all the other cars that had pulled out there.

I finally worked up the nerve to turn and look at him. I think he knew right then, just seeing my face. He always had the most blooming skin, blushed as a peach, all gold and pink, but when I met his eye the color drained from his face, from his hairline to his jaw, like someone had pulled the plug on him. He turned a putty color, like his face was made of clay.

"Edward, I'm in trouble. Deep, deep trouble."

The color rose back up his face just as fast as it had disappeared. It turned deep red, the flush men get when they're trading insults, the fever that burns their cheeks right before they fight.

"What kind of trouble, Cora?" he said. His voice was calm, but his eyes sparked. Veins showed in his forehead.

I couldn't talk to save my life.

"What kind of trouble?" he repeated, louder this time. "Cora, answer me!"

The ice cream I'd eaten crawled back up my gorge. I had to swallow hard to keep it down. It had soured, curdled in my stomach. My throat burned more than it had before. I couldn't get a word out. I just looked at him, begging with my eyes, praying that he'd understand without me having to say it.

He slammed his hands down on the steering wheel. I nearly jumped out of my skin. I'd never seen him mad before, not once. I remembered what I'd thought the first time I saw him, "This here's a man, a *man*." I thought the same thing now, but in a fearful way, like he was an animal whose ways I didn't understand, a wildcat or a bear. I'd seen plenty of men fight, saw them explode in fury with no rhyme or reason, saw them charge each other with no regard for nothing but to maim or kill. Edward was one of those, I saw. *Dangerous*. Different, way down deep, than any woman.

"Answer me, Cora! What kind of trouble you in?"

I couldn't find my tongue with him like that. All I could do was sit there and stare at him, terrified. All of a sudden, the four years between us felt like a lot—enough to make him seem like a grown-up who caught me doing something wrong. Enough for him to talk to me like I was a naughty child.

"You want to sit here and play guessing games with me?" he snapped.

He was just as scared as I was.

"The worst kind of trouble," I finally managed to whisper. "I think I'm in the family way, Edward. I think I'm up a tree."

He heaved a big sigh and shrunk down behind the wheel. His chest caved in, his head drooped forward like his neck had gone slack. He rested his forehead on the steering wheel.

"You sure?" he said, staring down at the floor of the car.

I waited for him to raise his head and look at me. When he did, I saw that he knew. Oh, he knew—just as sure as I did.

"Pretty sure," I mumbled. "I got all the signs."

"Goddamn it!" he yelled. He grabbed the steering wheel and shook it like it was the bars of a prison. "Damn it! Damn it! Damn it!" He shook so hard I thought the wheel would snap off. "No! No! No!" he shouted, pounding the steering wheel with his fists each time he said it. He turned and gaped at me wild-eyed. "What was we *doing,* Cora?" he hollered. "What was *I* doing? What was I *thinking?*"

His face was white now. No color at all. That's how mad he was. It made me calm, somehow. Or maybe it scared me so much I didn't make any quick motions or loud noises. "We're in love," I said in a tiny voice, barely moving my lips. "We weren't thinking."

That made him madder than ever. His eyes flashed. I thought sure he was going to hit me. I knew he wanted to. I closed my eyes, waiting for it to come. But instead he jumped over the side of the car, ran around to the front, and cranked like fury. The car started up and he came back around, hopped over the side again, slammed it into gear, and spun around in the road so fast and tight I thought the car was going to roll over. I grabbed the side.

He tore back up the road the way we'd come. His jaw was clenched and his eyes were on the road, grim. When we got to the lane that led up to my house he stomped on the brakes so hard I almost went through the windshield. He leaned across me and unlatched the door, pushed it open, then sat there with the car idling.

"Get out," he said.

"What are you doing?" I asked.

"I got to go, Cora. I got to get out of here."

He ran his hands through his hair and kept his eyes fixed straight ahead. The car jiggled underneath us. I smelled its exhaust. All those things I'd thought about—the poison, the well, the tree and the hanging—I thought of them now, but in a different way. The tree, I decided. Climb on up to the branch that hung over the creek. Tie the knot, slip it over my head, just slide off the branch. I even saw myself hanging there, bare feet dangling a few inches over the water.

"What are you saying?" I asked.

He turned and looked at me, looked me up and down. His lips worked like he was trying to make a decision, pursing, then pressing together in a tight line. Finally, his face softened. It melted, the muscles loosening around his eyes and mouth. He came back to himself. He was my Edward again, my boy.

"You go on back," he said, his voice tired, but tender. "I got to think. I got to figure things out."

I was so grateful I could cry. So relieved to have him taking care of me, knowing what to do.

"Go on back to your ma and pa," he said in the same gentle voice. "Go on," he repeated, since I didn't get out of the car. "Give me a day or two. Once I get a plan, I'll come out here and get you. Don't say nothing to nobody."

He leaned over and kissed me. That kiss was the best I'd ever had. It was a whole new feeling, kissing a man who was going to be my husband, who I'd be living with for the rest of my life. I stepped down from the car, turned back and looked at him, and remarked to myself what a fine man he was, what a prize I'd hauled in.

I shut the door and leaned over the side toward him. "You going to do right by me, Edward?"

"Course I am, Cora. You know I will," he promised before putting the car in gear and driving away.

A DAY WENT by. Two days. Five. The feeling of dread started to weigh on my chest, making it so I couldn't take more than little sips of air, barely enough to stay alive. It was so humid, breathing was like sucking warm water into your lungs. I was dizzy all the time, fading to black three or four times a day.

I looked for Edward in church the next Sunday, but he wasn't there. His family wasn't too regular, though—his ma being from the East and all—so I didn't place too much stock in it. The drugstore was closed on Sundays, so I couldn't go looking for him. He'd told me not to say nothing and I didn't. I went home with my family and waited some more. Each day the dread got worse. I started pulling at my hair, little clumps at the base of my neck where it wouldn't show. Jerking out those plugs of flesh gave me some comfort. I was almost out of my mind by then, but I kept talking to myself, telling myself to wait, to trust him, that he'd come through.

"Where's Edward?" my ma and daddy asked. "You two had a spat?" They was used to seeing him a couple times a week.

Most I could do was shake my head. "He's busy," I mumbled. "He'll be round." Ruby raised an eyebrow. She looked at Crystal and Jasper and snickered.

He wasn't at church the next week, either. His daddy was there, though. I figured Edward must be home with his ma. She must be having a bad spell, must need constant care. There had to be a good reason Edward was staying away. I just had to wait.

Toward the end of that second week I stopped Ruby before she went to work in the morning. Calvin came and picked her up, drove her into town on his way to his own job. I couldn't face another Sunday looking for Edward in church, wondering why he wasn't there.

"Listen here," I said. "I need to talk to Edward. Will you go round to Denton's and tell him to come out here?"

Do you know that Ruby didn't say a thing? Not one *word*. That was a miracle in itself, probably the first time in her life she held her tongue. I should have taken heed, should have known how far gone the situation was just from that.

When she got home that night, I followed her to our bedroom and shut the door. She got a discount working in the department store and had real nice clothes. I still remember the outfit she was wearing that day: a taupe suit with wide lapels, navy blue piping around the collar and sleeves. She always changed her clothes as soon as she got home. We didn't talk while she unbuttoned her jacket, while she took it off and hung it up, then unzipped her skirt and put it on another hanger.

She avoided my eyes while she unfastened her stockings and rolled them down her legs. I could see the garters under her slip while she stood there in her bare feet. It reminded me of the movie I'd gone to that first time with Edward, how that finger of his had worked its way up the inside of my thigh.

Finally, she turned and faced me. "I went to the drugstore and talked to Mr. Denton," she said in a flat voice. "Edward lit out. He's gone, moved up to St. Louis to go to pharmacy school."

RUMORS

The rain woke me up about 7:30 this morning, pelting my window like buckshot. The clouds were thick and dark and the wind was whipping. You could tell it had blown all night because there was a lot of junk on the ground—fronds from the palm across the street, sopping cardboard boxes that blew off the loading dock, newspapers turning to mush in the gutters. What a mess. Everything was drenched—the sides of the buildings, the streets, the jacarandas along the curb.

I watched the cars turn into the parking lot. Their headlights reflected in pond-size puddles. Their tires threw up a wake. The rain was letting up but the wind was still blasting, sending squalls across the puddles. Cooks and dishwashers, the girls who worked in housekeeping, the office staff and nurses' aides—they jumped out of their cars and sprinted like gazelles across the asphalt. I wondered how it felt to have a job, a place to go to every morning.

The blues came down hard. I missed Lulu, the way her eyes move behind her eyelids when she's dreaming. I started sniffling thinking how her paws flick and her muscles twitch like she's running. Sometimes she even barks. I wonder what she sees in those dreams, whether she goes back to wolf days and runs in a pack, bringing down a deer like on those nature shows. If it weren't for her, I'd have lost my mind. I bawled in earnest when I remembered the look on her face when Dean tucked her under his arm and carried her out to the car. I'm going crazy worrying what she's going through living with Dean's jackass grandkids.

One thing led to another and before long I made a list of everything that had ever been taken away from me. When I got to my crystal, I longed with all my heart to hold it against my cheek, or press the point into the pad of my thumb. You don't know how much comfort I got from that thing, and how much I miss it.

I was in such a state by breakfast time, I decided I needed to take special measures, so I tossed back a couple of pills. I been holding back lately, not taking hardly any, but my mood was feeling like the old, black times. I could barely drag myself to the dining room.

Ivy picked up on it right away, like the vulture she is. Soon as I sat down she said, "You're not looking so good, Cora. Is everything all right?" She never misses a chance to rattle my cage.

I looked over there to see what Vitus was up to.

Trouble is, there are so many women here, they swarm like piranha fish around a man. Even men who had to scrape the bottom of the barrel turn into Clark Gable the minute they walk through the door. Ten or twelve women swoon if those men so much as hiccup. And a man like Vitus— well, he can have his pick of anybody. Not just the old ladies, but the nurses and cooks and other women who work here. So I got to keep an eye on him.

Ivy doesn't miss a thing. She saw me looking over at Vitus, who happened to be talking to a woman at the next table. "I see your *friend* has a friend of his own," she cackled.

She likes to pretend that there's nothing going on between us, that it's all in my head. It drives me to the brink. Of course, she don't come right out and say it. She's got little ways of showing it, mostly with her eyebrows. Those damn drawn-on skinny lines can almost talk. They dance around on her big shiny forehead spelling out words that goad me to the quick. They've got a way of puckering up when I talk about Vitus that says she don't believe a word I say.

She's one of them who gets in that van that takes people shopping. "You should have seen that Vitus, riding along in the double seat next to Violet McKay. You'd think they'd been together all their lives the way he had his arm on the seat behind her and the way he helped her down the steps," she said, looking at me, of course. "They were shopping like honeymooners at the Save-On, giggling in the aisles, playing hide-and-seek, and filling a whole basket with treats that Violet paid for."

Well, my blood started boiling. I was ready to go wild, but I managed to control myself. "Now, Ivy, I have a hard time believing that," I said as calm as I could. "I am at a loss as to why you have to make up those stories." I started buttering my toast to show I wasn't bothered in the least, but damned if my hands weren't shaking.

Oh, her eyebrows shot up to the crown of her head. She leaned over the table toward me and hissed, nasty as a viper, "You know, they say he's been in other places before this. They say he was in two or three other facilities, and he was asked to leave."

I squeezed that butter knife until my knuckles turned white. How I wanted to bury it in her bony old chest! I leaned in closer and said, "You are full of shit, Ivy Archer! You don't know your ass from a hole in the ground!"

She gasped. "There is no need for that kind of language, Cora Sledge! I won't tolerate it."

Carolyn Robertson, whose head had been swiveling back and forth while she listened to us, rolled her eyes, shook her head, and gave a little laugh. At least *someone* was enjoying the show.

"Trouble with you is you're jealous!" I let loose. "Green with envy."

That got her. She slammed her silverware down on the table. Even old Krol perked up. He raised his head and stared at her with his milky blue eyes. Those jaws of his didn't miss a beat, though. He chewed with his mouth open, scrambled eggs sticking to his gums like moss.

"That got your attention, huh?" I said. "The truth hurts, don't it? You wouldn't know what to do with a man like Vitus! You wouldn't have the faintest idea!"

I laughed right up in her pinched face. Oh, it felt so good! Her mouth dropped open and those damn eyebrows flew right off her forehead and disappeared somewhere up by the ceiling. She gasped again, and clutched her throat like she couldn't get her breath.

I leaned even closer, moving in for the kill. "And one more thing," I said real low, pointing the butter knife to show I meant business. "If you don't quit tormenting me and spreading those filthy rumors, you're going to regret it, and I don't mean maybe."

She squealed like a stuck pig. That made me laugh some more.

She commenced to flail her arms and hop around in her seat. "Excuse me! Excuse me!" she yelped, trying to flag down one of the boys who clears the tables. "Help, please! I need help!"

What a ruckus. I just went on eating my toast like I didn't have a care in the world.

The big cheese, the woman who runs the place, was over by the entrance talking to the dietitian. She raised her head to see what all the commotion was about. Poison Ivy spotted her. "Yoo-hoo!" she yodeled, waving her arms like she was drowning. "Over here! Please! Help!"

"You turn my stomach," I said.

The boss lady started toward us, threading her way between the tables—which was no easy task, seeing as she has a butt the size of New Jersey. Chairs fell like dominoes. Good thing the dining room had started clearing out, or she might have knocked a few heads off on the way over.

She put her hand on the back of my chair and leaned toward Ivy. Her perfume made you want to retch. Up that close I could see that she'd gone outside the lines of her lips with orange lipstick.

"Yes, ma'am. What can I do for you?" she said, breathing heavy from dragging that ass all the way across the room.

Ivy puffed up like a hen. "Mrs. Sledge here insulted me." She pointed at me with one of her scrawny fingers. "She used rude, vulgar language, and she threatened me *with a knife.*"

"I did no such thing," I said, cool as a miner's ass. "Her mind is wandering."

Bigbutt turned to Carolyn. "What happened?"

197

Carolyn shrugged. "Don't look at me. They're both crazy, far as I can tell."

"That was uncalled for," I told Carolyn. "I didn't appreciate that."

"Ladies, breakfast is over," Bigbutt said. "What if we all skedaddle and go about our business?"

"You don't have to ask *me* twice," Carolyn said. She backed up her wheelchair, spun around, and rolled away. Old Krol stood up and followed her, his arms dangling like a zombie.

"If you don't make her leave the table, I'm going to leave myself," Ivy said.

"Go on, then! We're better off without you," I shot back.

"All right, ladies. That's enough!" Bigbutt clapped her hands like she was breaking up a dogfight. "Let's get moving, shall we? It's time to leave!"

WHEN I GOT back to my room, Vitus was waiting on the folding chair outside my sliding glass door. Since my money went missing I've tried to make sure all my doors are locked.

You can bet I was ready for a cigarette, so I went with him to our little bench near the fountain. "I heard a rumor about you at breakfast," I said after we lit up.

He blew out a puff of smoke and turned to me with that easy smile of his. "What was that, Woozy?"

"Well, there's two, really. One is that you was cozying up to Violet McKay at Save-On. The other is that you've been in places like this before and got kicked out."

He nodded and took another slow puff. "Who's Violet McKay?"

He wasn't the least bit ruffled, but I decided to test him. "You know damn well who she is. You had your arm around her on the shuttle bus."

"Sure it was me?"

He smiled, the rascal. "People say all sorts of things, Woozy. I'm surprised you listen to them."

"I haven't heard you deny it."

"Would that make you feel better?"

"You know what? It would."

"All right, then." He laid his hand on my knee. A jolt went up and down my leg, but I kept a straight face.

"You heard wrong, Woozy. It never happened."

He sounded as sincere as all hell, and I sure wanted to believe him. But something more important was happening. He let me ask those questions. He acted like I had a right to them. We'd never talked about the two of us, him and me, and the fact that he didn't get mad cheered me up.

"She didn't buy you nothing at Save-On?"

He scratched his chin and tipped his head to one side. "Not that I recall."

He crushed out his cigarette and gave me a sly

grin. I put mine out, too. I can't get enough of that man. When I'm around him, my whole body feels like it's covered with little mouths sucking in fresh air.

"Let's go inside," I said. "Talk a little."

I've never been one to leave well enough alone. Soon as we were sitting down, I started in. "You know, a lot of these old bats get the wrong idea about you, Vitus. To them you're fair game, spoils for the taking. I think it's time we tell folks about me and you. Let 'em know to stay away."

"Do you think so, Woozy?"

"Yes, I do!"

He gave me the smoothest smile. I reached over and gave him a little slap on the arm. "Listen here, quit teasing me. I'm serious. I don't like these women licking their chops over you."

"I hardly notice them," he said. "They're nothing to me."

"Tell them, then! Let them know, so they'll stay away!"

Vitus is real smart. I'm not used to it, after Abel. A whole new world opens up when you talk to somebody like Vitus, but it's got its drawbacks, too. You can't pull anything over on him.

"I wasn't brought up that way, Cora. My mother taught me that a gentleman treats all ladies with respect."

"Well, that's part of the problem. Just tell them to get lost. Tell them you aren't interested, that you're already spoken for. What's the big secret? I want to shout it from the rooftops. I want the whole world to know."

Me and my big mouth. Soon as I said it, I knew I'd gone too far. But instead of shutting my trap, I asked, "Are you ashamed of me? You too good? Is that it? Or is there something you're hiding? Something you don't want me to know? Or is it because I'm fat and you like that, but you don't want anybody else to know? What is it? Tell me."

Vitus kept his eyes focused on his lap and pinched the bridge of his nose between his thumb and finger. I dug myself in a little deeper and commenced to bawling, snotting and spraying in all directions. Lord, I brayed like a jackass. Aw, it was the last thing I wanted Vitus to see, the very last. I hated myself to the core, but that just made me cry harder. I covered my face with my hands and turned it loose.

Lord have mercy.

"Cora, please," he said after a little while. I felt his hand on my shoulder, coaxing, touching me soft. He rubbed real gentle, then he patted the top of my arm. I was afraid to look at him.

"They said you got asked to leave," I sniveled. I pulled a ratty little shred of Kleenex out of my pocket and blew my nose. "Lord knows why."

His hand stopped moving. "What are you talking about, Cora? What do you mean?"

I wiped my eyes and turned toward him. I know

I looked like hell. "That hateful one, Ivy, at my table. She said it. She said you was in places like this before, and you had to leave."

"People say all kinds of things, Cora. The woman at your table is lying. I don't know why she'd make up something like that, but it's not the truth."

"I know."

He talked in a soft voice, not mad at all. "Before I came here I *was* staying in a place like this, outside Phoenix. I left there because I didn't like it. It didn't suit my tastes. But as far as I know, that's not a crime."

I wiped my eyes. "No, it isn't."

He laid his hand over mine, even though it was gripping that nasty Kleenex. "I hate to see you upset like this."

A warm feeling washed over me. All the hard things inside—the rocks and claws, the hooks and hammers and broken glass—melted into warm, sweet jelly. It scared the life out of me to feel them dissolving, like being pulled out to sea by a powerful wave. I gave in, though. I took a deep breath and let them go.

PIE

Glenda showed up out of the blue today, didn't give a word of warning, just waltzed right through the door and sat herself down. I was writing here and had to slam this book shut and put it out of sight because if anybody gets wind of this while I'm still alive I'll have a lot to answer for.

She brought me some of the things I want. A nice outfit—pumpkin color with some gold in it—that buttons down the front. A floral print shift, kind of Hawaiian looking, and some maroon pants. "From Mervyns," she says. "Aren't they nice?" No sweatpants! And jewelry, too. A couple of papier-mâché bangles painted kooky colors, pink and orange and green. They slip over your hand and have earrings to match.

"And guess what," she went on. "I'm taking you out to lunch. To celebrate the new you. I just can't get over how much weight you've lost, Mommy. How good you look."

I'm not bragging, but she's right. All my life I've tried every diet known to man, ate nothing but birdseed or grapefruit or raw steak, and I couldn't shed more than a few pounds. Now they're just flying off me, and I ain't even trying. I got to say, I feel a whole lot better. So I decided to take her up on it.

"Where are we going?" I asked.

She grinned. "You feel like pie? A nice big sandwich on a roll, then a piece of Marie Callender's pie?"

She knows my weakness. They got ham there they slice real thin and pile up so thick on those rolls you can hardly get your jaws around it. Spicy mustard and Thousand Island dressing, with potato salad on the side. Boy oh boy. And those cream pies. I was already running the choices through my mind, trying to decide whether I was going to have the banana cream or the chocolate cheesecake, when I happened to glance at the sliding glass door.

Who should be standing there but Vitus?

I jumped like I'd been caught red-handed doing something I shouldn't. I tried to shoo him away, but he was already fooling with the latch. Glenda caught me looking and turned around. Damned if Vitus didn't slide open the door and walk right in. He went straight over to the TV, snapped it on, and settled himself in the armchair. Glenda's mouth hung open wide enough to catch flies.

"This here's Vitus," I said. "He's a friend of mine."

We been getting closer, me and Vitus. At night when he comes to watch TV, we might cuddle a little. And we been talking, kind of jokeylike, about busting out of here. Just for fun, we say what if I got my house back, we might live out our days there.

"Hello there," Glenda said. "I'm Mrs. Sledge's daughter."

Vitus can be charming when he wants to, but he's not a man to kowtow. Plus it was time for *The Price Is Right,* one of his favorite shows. He gave Glenda a halfhearted wave without taking his eyes off the screen, and that didn't sit well with her. She screwed her mouth up and squinted at him while he chuckled at his program like there was nobody else in the room.

"Let's get going," I said. "I'll just change my clothes and we can get a move on."

I hustled into the bathroom and stripped down fast as I could. Having the two of them sitting out there in the room together made me nervous as a cat. I put on the pumpkin-colored suit and ran a brush through my hair. No time for extras. I wanted out of there.

A commercial was playing when I came back to the room, and Glenda was giving Vitus the third degree, asking him how long he'd been at The Palisades and where he came from, if he had a wife, and who knows what else. Vitus didn't seem to mind a bit. He'd gone to my cabinet and gotten a bag of chips, which he munched like he was at a ball game.

"Well, well. What have we here?" he said when he saw my new outfit. He gave me his devilish look and twirled his finger like he wanted me to spin around. I obliged. When I came back to face them, Glenda's jaw was in her lap, poor thing. Vitus clapped. Then his program came on and he went back to watching.

"You ready?" I asked Glenda. "All I need is my purse."

She looked over at Vitus, who was chuckling again as he watched the TV and ate the chips. She looked at me. Then at Vitus. Me, Vitus.

"Better get going," I said. "Before it gets too crowded. I don't want to wait for a table."

"Don't we need to lock up here?" she asked, shifting her eyes toward Vitus. "With all the things that's turning up missing and everything?" She raised her eyebrows and nodded toward him, to make sure I knew what she meant.

"Where are you going?" Vitus said.

"Glenda's taking me out to lunch. Marie Callender's. One of my favorite places."

"Shall I come along?" he asked.

It *had* crossed my mind to invite him, but right then I wasn't in a mood to juggle the both of them. Glenda frowned her heart out.

"You better go get ready for lunch," I told him, winking so he'd know that I'd explain things later. "I'll see you when I get back."

He walked us out to the lobby. "Pleased to make your acquaintance," he said to Glenda as he held the door for us.

• • •

IT'S BEEN A long time since I was outside The
Palisades. Crossing the parking lot was like
heading out on a big vacation. It seemed like I
could see for miles in all directions—out, up, to
the left and right. The roads and stores and sky
spreading every which way, the wind flapping,
cars coming and going.

"Oh, my goodness! Lookee here!" I said when
Glenda got her keys out and unlocked the door to
a fancy new car. It's silver, with leather seats the
color of butterscotch. She was in a pout, but I
decided to ignore it. "When did you get this?" I
asked. "I feel like the queen of Sheba getting into
her carriage."

She shut my door without a word and stalked
around to her side of the car. I watched her
through the windshield. Her lips were pressed so
tight together they could have bent nails, and her
shoulders were way up around her ears. She has
always been so touchy. Tough titty, I said under
my breath. I decided to enjoy myself, no matter
how big a snit she was in.

Bells rang, air started blowing, and that damn
tinkly music she likes came on when she turned
the ignition. "Goodness gracious!" I said, hoping
to joke her into a better mood, but she sighed like
the weight of the world was on her shoulders. She
was grim as a hangman as she backed out of that
space and headed out of the parking lot.

"Bernie buy you this car?" I asked. It's a wonder I can even remember the names of all her husbands.

Her mouth twitched. I decided to take that for a yes. I ran my hand over the armrest, nestled down deeper in the leather seat, then flicked the button for the window to go up and down a few times. It opened and closed smooth as butter. The dashboard had as many dials and buttons as an airplane.

"Well, it's real nice." You can't say I wasn't trying. "Reminds me of that Lincoln your aunt Ruby had. You remember that?"

Not a word. Not so much as a twitch.

"You must feel pretty important riding around in this. What kind is it?"

"Acura," she said, barely moving her lips.

I finally took the hint and busied myself looking out the window. There was plenty to see: car washes, nail salons, restaurants from every country you can imagine, and so many cars I felt like I was inside a hive of metal bees. And with all I was seeing, what I remembered was the way this place was when we first moved to California. There where a man stood on the corner waving a sign that said HUGE MATTRESS SALE used to be a drive-in called Oscar's where the carhops came out and took your order on roller skates. Across from that, where a Mexican girl waited to cross the street with one kid in a stroller and another holding her hand, was where a dirt road used to cross the old trolley tracks. In the spring you could get off there and walk down the dirt road through meadows of purple owl's clover and those bright yellow flowers we called tidytips. Now there was a Shell station next to a Big and Tall Shop for men.

Glenda braked at a red light. She still hadn't given me the time of day. She's the kind of driver that leans way forward over the steering wheel, nose against the windshield. Since she was set on keeping quiet, I started jabbering about the rusted old Studebaker that we drove out from Michigan, how the last leg we drove all night because we didn't have money for a motel, and besides, we were excited because we were almost there. I told her how her and Dean sang "California, Here I Come" for two days. We'd crossed the border into California right around when night was falling, came down through the pass and across the Mojave. We smelled the orange groves in the Valley. By the time we got to San Diego it was the wee hours of the morning and we were dead tired, but we drove straight to the beach. We fell asleep in our seats, and when the sun came up the next morning, I felt like I'd reached the promised land.

"Are you listening to me at all?" I interrupted myself to ask Glenda.

"I've heard this before."

"Not like this you haven't. It don't hurt you to

listen. You got nothing better to do when you're driving, anyway."

"Well, go ahead then. Looks like I don't have a choice."

"The ocean spread out in front of us and the waves rolled in one after the other. I told myself I was never leaving this place. We took off our shoes and ran across the sand. I'll never forget how that water felt lapping at my legs. It pulled me like it wanted me to come farther, farther and farther until I was out to my waist right there in those stale clothes I'd been wearing for days. After all that driving and being awake and eating peanut butter sandwiches and drinking warm water out of a jug, I couldn't believe I was there, on the edge of the world."

"That's him, isn't it?" Glenda said.

I was dreamy, seeing everything like it was yesterday. "Who?" I asked.

She turned into the shopping mall where the Marie Callender's was. "The man you told me about. The one you say you love."

The parking lot had those humps that throw your innards up against your front teeth. "Mmm," I said, grunting as we took the first one.

"I don't like the looks of him, Mommy."

"Now why would you say that? Why would you pass judgment on a person you don't know the first thing about?"

She wasn't paying attention to driving. We

came within inches of a woman pushing a shopping basket, then a car nearly backed into us. "I just get the feeling that you might not be able to trust him," she said in her peppy way. "It's just a vibe I get."

That was Glenda, always using words like *vibe*.

"You just have a hard time imagining me with anyone but your father."

We hit another one of those damn bumps and my teeth smacked together. I nearly bit off my own tongue.

"Maybe, but I don't know. I wouldn't want to see you rush into anything."

She was getting me riled up by acting so patient and understanding. "Drop me off in front of the restaurant," I told her. "It's too far for me to walk. And can't we just go have lunch? If I knew I was going to get a lecture, I would've eaten the slop in the rest home."

"It's not a rest home."

"What is it, then?"

"Assisted living."

I snorted. "Well, I don't need that kind of assistance! I can help myself! And if I feel like helping myself to a man like Vitus, I don't see why it's anyone else's business!"

Glenda poked along like a turtle, creeping up one row and down the next. "Here we are fighting again. No matter how we start out, we always end the same way."

"Turn that damn music off. It's driving me crazy. I don't want to fight, either. I just want a nice lunch. Especially after you bought me this nice outfit and everything."

Finally, there was Marie Callender's with its ruffled curtains and hanging ferns and sweet smells floating out the door. I practically jumped out of the car while it was moving.

"Wait right there by the door," Glenda said. "I'll be there in a minute."

She must have given herself a talking-to while she was parking, because when she walked out of that ocean of cars she'd screwed a smile on her face. Her scarf was tied fancy on her shoulders and she'd put on fresh lipstick.

The hostess led us to a booth over on the side, with a window that looked out on the parking lot. They had those wooden venetian blinds and a bouquet of straw flowers on the table. I have a hard time getting into those booths and scooting around to the middle, but I managed.

No sooner had I opened my menu than Glenda started up again. "It's just that I'm concerned you're having some kind of reaction," she said. "I think that moving out of your house stirred up a lot of things. Emotions, you know. Unresolved issues."

I didn't want to hear words like *issues*. All I wanted was to read that damn menu. It has pictures that make your mouth water like a fire hose:

chicken pies, pot roast, sandwiches piled high as skyscrapers, and, of course, those pies.

"I think you're still mourning Daddy," she blathered on. She had on about twenty bracelets that clanged against the Formica table. "I don't think you've gotten over that yet. Now, with this different environment, and these other men around, you're acting out a lot of your grief."

I dug my fingers into the vinyl seat to keep from smacking her. I was just ready to let go and give her a good piece of my mind when the waitress showed up.

"Oh, goodness," Glenda said, snatching up her menu. She didn't have to look long since she always orders the same thing, Caesar salad, which is nothing but a bunch of watery lettuce with a few cubes of stale bread thrown on top. Even though she's skinny as a rail, she's always on a diet. She ordered dressing on the side. No pie.

All my life, all I ever did when I went into a restaurant was look down the column with the prices and order the cheapest thing on the menu. Just *being* in a restaurant was treat enough. It's a hard habit to break, even when you're not paying. But I told myself it was really that rich husband of Glenda's who was paying, and he had money to burn. He was more *my* age than *hers,* and anybody with a wife half his age should splurge once in a while. It wouldn't hurt him a bit, so I ordered the ham stack I'd been dreaming of and a slice of banana cream pie.

The waitress had no sooner turned tail and headed for the kitchen than Glenda started in about Vitus again.

"I think I made a mistake," I interrupted her.

Would you believe that she broke out in a big smile?

"With the *pie,*" I said real fast, before she got too far along in her celebrating. "I should have got the lemon meringue. That's what I *really* have a hankering for. Or the pecan. Lord, I loved having that at Thanksgiving. They got that chocolate satin pie and all them different cheesecakes. I should have taken my time. I should have been more careful."

Glenda tapped her fingers on the table. She wanted to strangle me just as much as I wanted to strangle her. "You like banana cream," she said after staring daggers at me a minute. "It's your favorite."

"That waitress came before I was ready and I just said the first thing that came to my mind!"

"Do you want me to call her over here so you can change your order?"

"I love lemon meringue. Remember that lemon tree we had when we first moved out here? Over by the gas meter, growing up the side of the house? It had the biggest, juiciest lemons in the world. Sweet as sugar."

Glenda waved her arm at the waitress and all of a sudden I saw the layers of that banana cream pie, so fluffy and rich, ready to melt in your mouth. "Never mind!" I spoke up. "It's too late now. I'll just live with it."

"I am *trying* to have a serious talk with you," Glenda said. "All those years you and Daddy spent together, then suddenly you're alone. It jarred something loose inside your head. Now you're trying to get that feeling back. But, like you just said, you're making a mistake."

"I was talking about the *pie!*" I cried so loud the old lady in the next booth spun around. "Listen here," I went on, lowering my voice. "I know you and your daddy were thick as thieves. You were his princess. The two of you worshipped each other and you got away with a million things he never tolerated in the boys. But you've got to understand—"

"He worshipped *you,*" she interrupted. "He loved you like life itself. You and him were like the same person."

"That's not the least bit true, Glenda. We were different as night and day. More like opposites."

"Opposites attract. They complement each other."

Lunch came. My sandwich was steaming. The smell would drive you wild.

"You don't know nothing about any of that," I said while the waitress refilled our water glasses.

"You don't know what went on behind closed doors."

"I was behind those doors, too. I was right there with you."

"Anything else I can get you?" the waitress said. She must be used to that kind of talk, because she smiled real big, not turning a hair.

"Fine, thank you," Glenda said.

Much as I wanted to tear into that sandwich, I blurted out, "I want my house back. Me and Vitus want to live together."

She gaped at me. I'd gone and done it again, jumped the gun and shot off my big mouth. To keep myself from digging the grave deeper, I sunk my teeth into my sandwich. Lord, it was good. I could shut out the whole world chewing on that sweet, salty ham.

The whole time Glenda watched me like I was a monkey in a zoo. "You're not eating," I said after a few bites. "Good thing you got a salad. Otherwise your lunch would get cold."

She answered in a raspy voice, "He *loved* you. He loved you *so much*. I wish I could find a husband who loved me *half* as much. How can you do this, after he loved you like that?"

Would I ever get to enjoy my sandwich? Glenda took up her fork and worried a few leaves of lettuce. She's always been a picky eater.

"I don't want to explain to you what it's like between me and Vitus, just like I don't want to

explain what went on between me and your dad,"
I told her. "Now, it's real nice of you to buy me
these clothes and take me here for lunch, but the
rest is really none of your business." I held out
my sandwich. "Do you want to try a bite of this?
It's real good."

"No, thank you." She finally took a bite of her
salad. "I'm just stunned. This is so out of the
blue, you wanting to move in with this man, a
person you hardly know." She shook her head and
stared down at her plate like some accident had
happened there—a car wreck or an earthquake.
"Into the house you and daddy lived in," she
added with a tremor in her voice.

"It's *my* house! I should have never left in the
first place, but I'll let that pass. I'm ready to go
back now."

Glenda was suddenly hungry. She got busy with
her salad, eating leaf after leaf without looking
up.

"I'm in better shape now. And it'll be easier
living there with Vitus than by myself. I want
Lulu back, too. I pine for that dog day and night."

Since she just went on eating like she hadn't
heard a word, I finished my sandwich. I was sorry
to eat the last bite, because God knew when I'd
get another one. I ate the potato salad, too, and
the slice of dill pickle.

Glenda ground her croutons between her
molars. When she was done, she wiped her mouth

and asked in a cold voice, "Are you planning on getting married?"

Even though I was scared to hear what would come out of my mouth next, I couldn't stop talking. "We're not sure."

The waitress brought my pie. It was beautiful, piled a foot high with a layer of yellow custard, a layer of bananas, and a big layer of whip cream. It smelled like heaven itself. Exactly what I've been dreaming about these last months while I laid in bed knowing that I'd have to get up and eat that same dog food the next morning.

I lifted up my fork, but didn't have the heart to dig into it. "All this talk has taken my appetite away," I said.

Glenda, the queen of sighs, heaved a big one. She rolled her eyes and slumped back in the booth like her spine had turned to Jell-O. I looked at my pie, and remembered what Marcos said about Renato. "I make love to him with my eyes." Well, I tried it with my pie and, lo and behold, it worked.

"How do you know you can trust him?" Glenda said, watching me take my first bite. "How do you know he's a good man? How do you know where he comes from or what he wants?"

"Maybe he just loves me for who I am. Is that so hard to believe?" I asked between mouthfuls. "Am I so terrible that a man can't want me for myself?"

"You know that's not what I'm saying."

"Sure sounds like it. That's the message I'm getting."

"Well, it's not what I meant." Her eyes followed the fork from my plate to my mouth. "How's the pie?"

"Nasty. I *knew* I should have got the lemon meringue. Why don't I listen to my instincts? This one tastes like something you pulled off the bottom of your shoe." I licked the fork. The whip cream wasn't bad. "You want a bite?"

She shook her head. "I'm sorry you don't like it. You don't have to finish it if you don't want."

"Flag that waitress down. I want some coffee."

When she'd filled my cup, I said, "I feel like my old self again, after all these years. Not my self that everybody knows, but from a long time ago. My whole self, before things happened."

Glenda didn't know what to make of that. To tell the truth, we weren't used to talking that way. No one was more surprised than me, but I wasn't done yet. "I know it's hard for you to hear this, after your daddy and all. Don't worry about him. Him and me had us a whole life together. This is apart from that. It's altogether different. This is just me, my whole self, at the end of my life."

She took a sip of my coffee. Her eyes welled up—I don't know if the drink was too hot, or she was hurt. "But *why?*" she asked. "What is it about this man that makes how you feel different?"

Well, I've been asking myself the same question, but I didn't think it was a good idea to let on. "I been hurting a long time," I started out, feeling my way. "I been . . . Well . . . you know. *Sick.* I wasn't well." I stopped to put the last few bites of pie in my mouth.

"I'm not sure I know what you mean," she said, narrowing her eyes like she didn't believe what I was telling her.

"Them pills and all. How I was sleeping. And my heart, it was breaking all the time. Slow breaking. I was so lonesome. Pining, deep inside. I couldn't tell no one."

"But how did it happen?"

"Something inside me perked up," I said with a shrug. "I don't know how else to explain it. Something woke up and took notice."

"But why *him?*"

"I never met no one like Vitus. He's from another country. He don't look at me like a regular man. He looks at me different. Like a *person.* A whole person."

"Daddy didn't?"

She was fired up, ready to defend Abel tooth and nail, so I had to be careful. "I'm not blaming your dad," I said, "but it was just different between me and him. Maybe I didn't let him. I don't know. He wasn't interested in the same things."

The waitress came with the bill. Glenda looked

at her watch and let go of another sigh. "I guess we should be going. I got to take you back so I can get on the road before all the traffic starts."

"Are you going to try and stop us?" I asked while she was taking money out of her wallet to pay the bill.

She made a big show of not answering me while she figured in her head, counted out the bills, and finally dug through the change compartment of her wallet to find a few pennies.

"The thing that bothers me," she said as she pushed the tray with the money and check to the edge of the table, "is that I don't know how this man feels about *you.* You've told me how *you* feel, but how does *he* feel in return?"

"That is none of your business," I snapped. "That is a private matter that has nothing to do with you."

She put her wallet in her purse and took out her keys. You can't believe how many doodads she has hanging off the key ring—charms, feather, beads, shells, even a little flashlight. Weighs a ton, and jingles like a mule team.

"You've been honest with me," she said. "Some people might think you've been *too* honest. So, I have to tell you right out in the open." She paused, then looked me square in the eye. "That man did not make a good impression on me."

"You're not a kid no more. You don't have to live with Vitus or do what he says. This is between him and me. I ain't asking you to call him *Dad*."

"Let's go," she said.

It took me awhile to scoot out of that booth, which may sound bad to you, but to me it's a big improvement because six months ago I wouldn't have been able to sit in it at all.

"Thank you for lunch," I said when I stood up. I brushed off my lap and straightened my top. "I appreciate it."

She was tight-lipped all the way home. I figured two could play the silent-treatment game, so I clammed up, too. While I looked out the side window, I got my revenge by picturing me throwing out those renters in my house, moving in, and getting all new furniture. I saw me and Vitus in the living room, him stretched out on the couch, me in the armchair, Lulu in her spot under the coffee table. "Woozy darling," he said in that gorgeous accent of his. He put his fingers to his lips and threw me a kiss.

THE FALL

After lunch day before yesterday I thought I'd take a shortcut across the courtyard instead of going back down the hall to my room. The gardener had washed down the pavement and before I knew what was happening my feet slipped (the soles of those damn gold slippers are slick as snot) and my legs windmilled and I got that sick feeling in the pit of my stomach that tells you you're about to fall. You know what I'm talking about? For one split second I thought I might save myself, but the next instant a voice inside said, Get ready girl, you are going down.

Well, I just couldn't believe it. When you're a kid, falling is no big deal. You do it every day. But let me tell you, at my age falling down is a major event. It's something you don't soon forget. Way too often it changes your life, and if you don't believe me, you should see this place, which is chock-full of old ladies who lost their homes and their freedom just because they slipped and broke a hip. They are stuck here for no other reason than their cat got underfoot or they missed the last step or they got up in the night and had a dizzy spell. One little flop and their lives might as well be over. If they're lucky they can still hobble around on one of them walkers, but like as not they're tied to the bed for the rest of their lives, which turns out not to be too long because who can hold up for any length of time like that?

Believe it or not, all of that was going through my mind while my arms were spinning like propellers and I was doing my damnedest to get my balance back. That falling took a long time. I finally gave up and thought, Here I am, I'm really falling and Lord knows it's going to be a bad one because the ground is coming up at me mighty fast and I'm not at all ready for it.

Last time I fell was a good ten years ago, when Abel was still alive. There'd been a frost overnight and I was going down the back steps when my feet flipped up over my head and I slammed down on my tailbone and bumped down the rest of the steps like a rubber ball. I'm talking hurt like you never felt before. Each stair I screamed louder, so that Abel came running with shaving cream still on his face. He found me splayed out at the bottom of the porch like a rag doll. Almost scared him to death.

I had time to remember that, too, as I was going down. Had time to wonder—while I flew with my arms straight out in front of me like Superman— just how many bones I was going to break and who was going to see me fall and whether I might need surgery once it was all over. Round about then I hit the sidewalk like a ton of bricks, hit harder than I even imagined I would, my hands first and then my knees. The jolt went up through every joint of my body, clanging the bones together like a pileup on the freeway, the cars smacking into each other *bang bang bang* in a chain reaction. My neck snapped back, my teeth crashed together, and the wind got knocked out of me. Just when I thought it couldn't get any worse, my teeth flew out of my mouth and skidded like a hockey puck across the pavement.

I crouched on my hands and knees like an animal and gasped for breath. My housedress was thrown up over my backside, but all I could do was moan and roll over onto my side. Wouldn't you know that a little knot of people just coming out of the dining room saw the whole damn thing? Bad as I was hurting, I saw those fogies push and shove to get a better look at me lying there like a beached whale. My teeth were two blocks away, over on the edge of the grass. I couldn't tell if anything was broken, if I'd had a heart attack, or paralyzed myself.

The gardener who'd caused the whole thing ran over and tried to help me up. He was no bigger than a gnat and I pulled him down on top of me. The show was getting better and better. I'd started to get my breath back by that time, and I could hear the crowd buzzing, excited as if they were at a circus.

"Somebody fell," a geezer said.

"That fat lady," another one had the nerve to add, as if I was already dead with no ears to hear.

One of the nurses' aides came running over, her and the boss lady with the big caboose. The more I got my wits about me, the more the misery sunk in. I covered my mouth with my hand and yelled, "Fetch my teeth! They're over there by the spigot."

Lord, what a production. My hands were smarting, my knees were throbbing, and my back was way out of whack. I'd smacked my chin on the cement and—before my teeth flew out—I'd somehow managed to bite my tongue. But all I wanted right then was to haul myself up and get out of the sight of those vultures who were ogling and whispering and drooling like they were at a peep show. The boss lady and the workers were cooing and clucking, asking me if I was all right, but for the life of me I couldn't say a word. I couldn't get up, either. The best I could do was drag myself up on my hands and knees and pant like a dog.

Then I heard Poison Ivy. She bustled her busy-body ass over to me and said in a voice loud as a bullhorn, "Don't move, Cora! Stay right where you are! Wait there 'til they come with a gurney."

Well, not much could have raised me, but when I heard that voice and crooked my head up to see her smirking down at me in her gold earrings and painted nails and perfect little pantsuit, I reared up on my knees like a stallion. "Get over here!" I hollered to two of those boys who clear the tables. I grabbed one under each arm and grunted and groaned and almost mashed them into the ground, leaning on them until I hauled myself up and stood.

"I don't need no gurney," I spat at the crowd. The gardener handed me my teeth and I jammed them in my face. "I can walk back to my room."

• • •

SO HERE I am, writing in bed. I got an ice pack on my knees, which look like they been through a meat grinder. The little finger on my right hand is swollen up to the size of a broom handle and I can barely bend my wrist. The palms of my hands are scraped up and pocked with gravel. My tongue feels like those cow tongues you see at the butcher shop, my one ankle is big as a tree stump, and my neck is so sore I can't turn my head. The icing on the cake is my chin, which is scraped raw. It keeps bleeding down the front of my nightgown like I tore up a live rabbit and ate it for dinner.

I'll tell you again, it's no joke to fall down at my age.

My first thought was to load up on pills and drift off to never-never land, but I wrestled with myself and fought off the urge. I did! All I took was a couple of aspirin; now I feel like there's a halo floating over my head while I sit here in bed. I can't believe I didn't snap my wrist or break a leg, and even though I feel like a truck ran over me, backed up, and did it again for good measure, I'm lucky. I could have ended up in B Wing, locked up in bedlam with those lunatics and half-deads. As it is, I'm still walking, still got my wits about me, and still making plans to get out of here.

A WAY OUT

Marcos brought me a big book of maps from the Day Room. I put it across my knees and use it as a writing table. I'm stuck here in bed all black and blue, so I'm making the best of it and catching up on my story. Better than laying here looking up at the ceiling.

A LITTLE MORE than a week after Edward lit out, Ruby got married. She'd been planning it forever, and it was a big event.

I can't rightly describe the state I was in except to say that I moved my feet and hands, I went through the motions of every day, but I hardly knew I was alive. I'd been like that since the minute I heard Edward had gone off to St. Louis without a word, leaving me holding the bag. I didn't know such suffering was possible, that every minute could be filled with such misery that my body felt poisoned, soaked with sorrow. How could he leave me like that? The sorriest thing was that I still loved him. I did. More than ever. I pined for him day and night. I couldn't get through one hour without wondering where he was, what he was doing, if he was thinking of me, of our baby. I touched my own mouth with my fingertips, pretending it was his lips. I handled myself, my eyes shut tight, imagining it was *his* touch I was feeling, *his* body next to me. Despite what he'd done, I yearned for him with every ounce of my being. I drove myself crazy, hoping any day now I'd hear a knock on the door and there he'd be, hat in hand. Saying he was sorry, that he'd thought better of things, had come to take me away.

Each day that got less and less likely, and I had to face the fact that I was in a stone fix. St. Louis could have been Timbuktu as far as I was concerned. I didn't have the first idea how to get in touch with Edward, and I don't think I would have tried even if I did. I missed my period for the second month, and I still didn't breathe a word to anyone. With Edward gone, I was more ashamed than ever, and I was clean out of options. I decided I couldn't live without him. I decided I didn't want to.

I made my preparations. I chose the rope from the coils we had hanging on pegs in the barn. I'd already picked my branch, the one that reached over the creek down by the springs. When the panic set in at night, or when I woke in the morning still in the same fix, I told myself that soon it would all be over, and that calmed me, made me able to get through another day. It wouldn't be right to spoil Ruby's wedding, so I'd wait until she was married. Then I'd put an end to my problems.

Her wedding was on a Saturday in the middle of

September. That morning was still and hot—every hour it just got hotter. The ceremony wasn't until late in the afternoon. By the time we all gathered in the church it was stifling. Women fanned themselves and babies fussed. All buttoned up in our fancy clothes, we could hardly draw breath, me most of all.

Ruby had her best friend, Karlene, stand up with her. Calvin had his brother J.D., who worked down in the mines along with half the men there in the church. Our family was up in the first pew on the bride's side, Ma and Daddy and me and Crystal and Jasper, with our aunts and uncles in the pews behind us, and our cousins behind them. Calvin's ma sat across the aisle from us looking like a big old grizzly who'd been forced into a dress made out of a ground tarp. She kept blowing her nose so loud you couldn't hear a word of what was being said.

I watched Ruby's back, thinking how she'd been with me every day since I'd been born, how we'd slept in the same bed every night, how we'd laughed and fought and ate together. Pretty soon I wouldn't be around anymore. I worked myself into a lather thinking how all those people there in the church would feel when they heard the news, how Ruby would go on with her married life and have kids who would never know me, their aunt Cora who died right after their mama got married. I started sniffling as I pictured all that life going on without me, but a lot of people were shedding tears, so no one paid me any mind.

I couldn't help but think that it should have been *my* wedding, that *I* should have been standing up there with Edward. It affected me so bad that when Calvin finally kissed the bride and the preacher turned them around to introduce Mr. and Mrs. Roberts to the congregation, I let out such a sob that Ruby looked down at me from the altar and raised her eyebrows. I cried the bitterest tears as they strutted to the back of the church together, man and wife, and I know everyone thought I was brokenhearted about losing my sister, but I was crying for myself, bawling my eyes out because there I was, only seventeen years old, and my life was over.

BUT WE DON'T really know squat about what's going to happen to us and where we're headed, do we? My daddy had rented Neosho's banquet hall, and after the wedding everyone headed over there. They'd set up big barbecues in the back and some of my uncles were already out there stoking them.

Even though Baptists aren't supposed to dance, my father hired a band—three boys playing fiddle, accordion, and guitar. There wasn't supposed to be liquor, either, but you could see it being passed round, mostly by the men who'd taken over the side of the room by the little stage.

The women were on the other side with the kids winding in and out of their legs. Folks danced in the middle, more and more by the minute, spinning and kicking up their heels. The younger kids played out front, chasing each other around in the dirt. There was quite a crowd, with so much noise and commotion you couldn't hear yourself think.

I stood in a corner with the girl cousins. I had plenty, not to mention second and third cousins and relatives once removed, so many that I couldn't keep track of them, not that there was any reason to try. They were watching the men across the room, making bedroom eyes at the ones they fancied while still keeping track of who was dancing with who, chattering about who was too big for her britches, how could so-and-so show up in such a getup, and generally being the biggest busybodies on the face of the earth. They were excited because Calvin's family was there and that was a lot of fresh blood for those girls to sort out, deciding which boys were worth paying attention to and which didn't deserve the time of day.

I stood there listening, nodding when I needed to, and following the dancers with my eyes, but I was so hungry I could hardly see straight. The woodsmoke from out back drifted in, making me slather like a calf. I didn't know how I was going to make it until they cooked that meat, weak as I was feeling. Ruby was dancing with our daddy and Calvin with Ma. Ma laughed up in his face like *she* was the one who'd just married him. My poor brother, Jasper, led Calvin's mother around the floor. That lumbering she-bear knocked dancers down like bowling pins. My sister Crystal was dancing with Martin Jenkins, a farm equipment salesman from Carthage who turned out to be the first in her long string of husbands. Calvin's oaf of a brother J.D. was making mincemeat out of the feet of Karlene, Ruby's maid of honor.

A breeze came up and the smoke blew in, but sweat still poured off everybody, who by then were revved up to high gear, swinging and shouting. The musicians played their hearts out, whooping up there on the stage, stomping their feet. Every minute more people streamed through the open doors. They joined the dancers or crowded along the walls, shaking hands with people they knew, waving across the room. By that time word must have gotten out to everyone within fifty miles that a party was in progress, because I starting seeing people I'd never laid eyes on in my life, boys and men mostly—some dressed in coveralls, horse shit still fresh on their shoes, others in what passed as Sunday best— faded-out poplin shirts buttoned up to their scurvy necks.

I couldn't hardly draw a breath, and the faint feeling came over me again, making the floor tip.

The thick smell of smoke and sweat made my stomach heave up and do a flip-flop. I leaned back against the wall and closed my eyes. When I opened them, there was Karlene, standing in front of me with a grin on her face.

"How you doing, Toad? Having a good time?"

Karlene had a pug nose and shiny brown eyes like a teddy bear. Her and Ruby had been thick as thieves since they were five years old. They were a tight little club of just two members, and much as I wanted to be a part of it, they'd never let me in, even for a minute. Karlene tipped her head and smiled at me like that was about to change. Her hair was plastered to her forehead with sweat.

"Listen here, Toad," she whispered in my ear. "There's someone here wants to talk to you."

"Who?" I said, quick as a shot. Edward was so much on my mind, my first thought was that he was there, or that he'd sent word. I got so excited I forgot about feeling faint, or sick, or even hungry.

"A boy. A boy who's interested in meeting you."

"Who?" I repeated.

"You sound like a hoot owl, Toad," Karlene said with a laugh. She'd been taking a nip. I smelled it on her breath. "He's a Sledge. One of the Sledge boys."

My heart sunk. Everybody knew the Sledges. They had a reputation in those parts for being rough and dumb, for wild behavior and breeding like rabbits. Sledge men were notorious for running up and down those country roads sticking their peckers in every knothole they could find. There was a slew of them. The oldest ones had kids older than their own brothers and sisters. They all had names from the Bible, which was funny since they showed up at every honky-tonk where they could drink and dance—and they all could *dance,* which was part of how they got in so much trouble. You could tell one a mile off. All of them had dark coppery hair, kinky as could be, black eyes, broad shoulders, and skinny hips. Wasn't no surprise that half the folks a hundred miles around looked just like them. Those Sledge men had been going at it for generations.

"What would I want with a Sledge?" I answered.

"Listen here, Toad. Don't you play high and mighty. He's a real nice boy. He works with Delbert down at the mine. He wants to know if he can talk to you, if you'll walk outside with him a minute."

Delbert was Karlene's sweetheart, so he must have put her up to it. My nosy cousins were listening in.

"Why?" I asked. "What's he want?"

"He *likes* you. Wants to get to know you better."

I guess word had gone round that Edward had lit out. It stung, but I reminded myself that I wouldn't be around to suffer much longer, so what difference did it make?

"What's his name?" I asked. "Where is he?"

Karlene smiled, like she'd won out. "His name's Abel. He's right over here."

She took my arm and led me away, pulling me through the crowd, stepping over and around kids. My cousins twittered and bobbed their heads, trying to see where we were headed. We had to dodge the dancers, who kicked out their feet and twirled each other around. Karlene was more tipsy than I thought. She stumbled, leaned on my arm, and laughed her boozy breath in my face.

"Your daddy know you been drinking?" I asked. He was one of the deacons of our church and would have given her what for if he knew.

"You hush your mouth, Toad, and listen to me. Abel is the sweetest thing. It is not going to hurt you one bit to talk to him. Look, there he is."

He was standing over on one side of the room with his arms at his sides and his legs together, like a line drawn on the wall. His pants were too short and his jacket too small. A good three inches of his ankles and wrists showed, making his hands and feet—which were already big— look bigger. That kinky hair of his was parted in the middle, standing out on either side like a hayrick. No wonder people said they was part colored. His face was covered with tiny flecks of rusty freckles that made his skin look like fresh-sawed cedar. He'd been waiting for us, you could tell. He was jittery, but he kept a poker face, not showing a trace of a smile as he turned and watched us come toward him. He was so beside himself that he took hold of both Karlene's hands when we got up next to him and held them like the preacher does when he's greeting people after service on Sunday.

"Toad, this here's Abel. Abel, this is Toad," Karlene said.

She pried his hands loose from hers, swung around, and snapped them onto mine like she was hitching up a carriage. Then she turned tail and tottered away, back into the crowd.

There I stood facing him, his hands locked on my hands, his black eyes fastened on my face. He kneaded and squeezed my hands. His thumb probed my palm. His head bobbed, his mouth opened and closed like a fish, and his Adam's apple worked up and down, but he couldn't for the life of him utter a syllable. His face was so earnest, and so scared, I took pity on him. I glanced over at the corner. My cousins' necks were craned three feet long so they could ogle us. They were chattering like monkeys.

"You want to go outside?" I asked. "Get a little fresh air?"

Boy, did he. He nodded 'til I thought his head would break off and bounce across the dance floor. He took my elbow and shouldered a swath through the crowd, butting like a billy goat. The fresh air out back was a blessing. There was a big open space behind the banquet hall, with the stables off to one side and the feed store on the other. A clump of sycamores stood in the middle, with two long tables beneath them. Some of the older kids were chasing a dog around them, jumping up on the benches and yelling their heads off. Close to the banquet hall, three of daddy's younger brothers were getting sides of beef ready to put on the barbecues, where the heat was rising in waves. A few cars had pulled up near the side of the building. A group of men I didn't recognize squatted down in the dirt alongside them, throwing dice. One of them looked up and jutted his chin at Abel when we walked by.

"You know him?" I asked.

"That my brother."

"What's his name?"

"That one?" He looked back like he hadn't taken note the first time. "Adam."

His voice was gruff, like talking was a trial for him. Like he'd been yelling all night, or was getting over a cold.

Another boy on the edge of the group looked up at us the same way. Abel gave a little grunt and nodded at him.

"That there's Esau," he said.

"He your brother, too?"

"Yep. Two more inside. Shem and Enoch. They dancing. We all come in the wagon."

Swooped down on the party like a swarm of locusts, I thought to myself. To him I said, "Goodness me. How many of you are there?"

"Fourteen born, but my ma raising ten."

He commenced to naming them on his fingers, those boys he already mentioned and a bunch of girls—Naomi, Sarah, Ruth, Dinah, and Rebecca. I looked at his hands while he counted them off. They looked like they were made of leather with big thick fingers and raggedy, scraped-up nails.

"Joe, he got killed down there at the mines. We lost two when the flu came round. And Baby Zillah, she caught the whooping cough. Never made it to her first birthday."

When we got to the strip of shade near the stables, Abel dragged a metal drum up against the side, pulled his hankie out of his pocket, and spread it on the drum for me to sit on. I looked him over. He wasn't bad-looking, but he wasn't no Edward. He looked strong, with a thick neck and ropy arms and legs, and that hair of his wasn't that ugly orange-red, but darker, a deep rust. There was nothing particularly wrong with him, but nothing really right, either. He wasn't the kind of boy I'd ever give a second thought to. And the way he talked! I marveled at that. He was a hick with a capital *H*. I know I ain't no Shakespeare, but next to him I spoke the queen's

English. When he got the hankie all smoothed out the way he wanted it, he made for me to sit, helping me like I was delicate as a flower.

It felt good to sit, and to be out there in the shade, breathing fresh air. When I was all arranged, he pulled those thin lips of his back in a smile. His teeth were small and yellow, with spaces between each one. Looked like corn kernels. Let's just say he was more handsome with his mouth closed.

I smelled the hay and horse shit in the stables behind us, heard the horses knocking around in there. "How come you sent Karlene over to get me?" I asked him. "I don't know you."

"Well, I know you. I remember you from school." He grinned at me with those sorry teeth.

"When? I don't remember you being in school. Not in the least."

He must have gotten all dolled up for this party, but he was sweating through that too-tight jacket. "I sure remember you," he said, shifting from foot to foot. "You was the prettiest girl in the whole school. And the smartest."

Everybody likes a compliment, but I am no fool. When I looked at his face and saw he wasn't just blowing smoke up my ass, that he really meant what he said, I had to wonder what was wrong with him. Even in my wildest dreams I never imagined I was the prettiest of anything. Smart, maybe, but not the smartest. Nowhere near, unless you were a moron, which seemed to be the case with Abel.

"I stopped school when I was thirteen, but I remember you," he said, dancing back and forth. A line of skin showed above his socks, which were creeping down into the backs of his shoes. "Went down and worked, you know. Worked there in the mines. Couldn't keep on there at school. But I always remembered you. Remembered you, then I seen you. In town a couple times. And at that Christmas pageant. At church."

He looked at me the hungry way you do when you're aching for someone. I didn't understand it since he didn't know the first thing about me. What was there he liked so much? I still couldn't place him. I thought again that there must be something wrong with him, but then I thought how I felt about Edward, and I took some pity on Abel, because sometimes you just can't explain these things. When my eyes shifted, he turned to see what I was looking at. His hands floated in front of him like big mitts, ready to pluck whatever I wanted out of the air. He'd talked himself dry. Now he just watched me, that idiot grin on his face.

"I better be going on back, then," I finally said, hoisting myself off that drum. His black eyes were making me squirm. They were about to bore a hole through me.

"Can I call on you?" he said. "Come out and see you?"

He was so hell-bent, I couldn't tell him no. I shrugged. "All right. If you want."

You'd think I gave him a million dollars. He took my hand and nearly squeezed it to death.

"I'll come on out there, then, Toad. I'll come see you."

ABEL CAME TO call the very next day. The day after and the day after that. The days were long that time of year. He came on up to our farm after his work, got out there God knows how, hitching rides, then walking three or four miles up to the house. One thing you can say about Abel is he was determined. Pigheaded as all get out.

Every time he came, he brought me something. A jumping jack he carved out of wood. All the joints—the shoulders and knees and elbows— were attached with little pins. You squeezed the sticks it hung on and it spun around, did tricks. It was real clever. He gave me a hankie with the edges embroidered in red, and hickory nuts he strung together in a necklace. He even brought me a kitten, an orange tom, mean as hell. Tiger, Abel called him. I grew to love that cat. He fetched anything you threw, like a dog. Must have been a Sledge, because within a year a slew of orange kittens was swarming around.

Not two weeks passed before Abel told me he

loved me. That just showed how much he knew. He didn't have the faintest idea how I was still pining for Edward, how I was worried sick about my predicament, and what I felt about him— which was pretty much nothing. I didn't have no room for that. It was the furthest thing from my mind. You wouldn't know it, though, the way he fawned and followed and mooned over me every chance he got.

"You got no reason to feel the way you do," I told him. "You don't know the first thing about me. You just dreamed up some crazy notion in your own head."

"I *do* know," he answered, kneading my hand like he always did. "It's all in them dark eyes of yours, Toad. I love everything about you. There's not one thing I'd change. You are *just* the kind of woman I want."

He must have mustered up every ounce of brainpower he had to string that speech together. To this day, more than sixty years after we were married, I *still* don't know what made him love me the way he did, come hell or high water. The best answer I got is once he latched on to something, he'd never let go, even if you beat him over the head with a skillet. He was just like a mule that way, dogged as the day is long.

MY MA AND daddy's house was on a little rise. You could see a distance out toward the west. Us girls' bedroom was right over the front door. You could sit on the edge of the bed and look out the window, down toward the bottom of the hill where the road was. The drive up to our house was rough, just a rutted double track, grown up with weeds. I sat there of an afternoon during that desperate time and watched the sun drop lower. It got so my heart sank when I spotted Abel at the bottom of the hill, small at first, making his way on up. I didn't want to see him, face his earnest eyes and big hands opening and closing, him wanting me despite everything, not knowing how miserable I was.

"Go on and leave me alone," I finally told him. "I've had enough of this now. There's no reason for you to come up here." There were plenty of girls who'd have been tickled to death to have him. I couldn't figure out why he was wasting his time with me.

"Just give me a chance, Toad," he begged. "*Please*. Get to know me a little before you make up your mind."

So here he came again right after supper, about seven in the evening. Toiling up that damn hill with his hair fresh parted and slicked down on both sides. I had the heartburn that evening. I kept burping, like I'd drank three or four gallons of sour milk. The last thing I wanted was to see Abel, but I'd given up on everything by then. I didn't even have the energy to go down to the creek like I'd planned, to tie the rope around that branch and slip the other end over my head. See, it was too much trouble even to kill myself. I threw my life to the wind.

That was the end of September. I was a good two months pregnant. It was harvest time, and dust from the threshers slung a haze in the air, making everything shimmer and glow. The sky turned orange as the sun sank lower, and Abel seemed to be moving slow, taking a long time to get up to the house. Maybe he was tired that night. I watched the dust rising behind him as he traveled along the lane, not really thinking of anything, just mad at how bullheaded he was, how he wouldn't take no for an answer.

I can't say how the idea came to me. I didn't piece it together in words, building it up bit by bit like you do with other ideas, with plans. No, this thought just arrived in my mind like something left on your porch that surprises you when you open the door and see it sitting there. The only way I can explain is, every step Abel took up that hill brought me closer to my answer. Just as sure as he was going to keep on walking toward the house, I knew I was going to go through with it. When he passed the pump, I made up my mind. When he got to the tree where we tethered the dogs, I knew it would work. Just as sure as he was going to keep on walking, was going to come on into the yard, step up on the porch, and knock on the door, I knew that things were set, that there was no turning back. By the time I opened the door, it was set in my mind, everything in place.

"Come on inside," I told him, and that was that.

RASSLING

We had baked fish and boiled potatoes for lunch, with green beans on the side. Boring. Poison Ivy was nattering away about the illegal aliens. You'd think she's Walter Cronkite the way she talks.

When we were done and everybody was leaving, I flagged Vitus down and said, "Just a minute. I got something else to tell you." My timing couldn't have been better because Poison Ivy happened to be walking by at that very minute and her eyes popped out of her head. I gave her a big smile and nestled a little closer to Vitus.

"I talked to my daughter about me and you," I said close to Vitus's ear. He isn't like lots of old men who got bushes sprouting from their ear-holes and nasty wax built up inside. His is just as fresh and clean as a baby's, smooth and good smelling. "She's way against it, Vitus. She objects to us being together."

"Is that right?" he said.

"I'm afraid so."

"Did she say why?"

Well, I couldn't tell him all the nasty things Glenda said about him—it would hurt his feelings, plus I didn't want things to get off on the wrong foot between him and Glenda. And, to tell the truth, I had to be careful what I said because I went overboard with what I told Glenda. Vitus and I hadn't really *said* we were going to leave this place together, at least not in a definite way. I didn't want to scare him off, but I have to admit I did want to know where he stood on the subject.

So I just said, "She wants me to stay like I always was. Her mother. She can't stand to see me change, do something different."

"That worries me," he said. "Do you think she'll make trouble for us?"

"I'm afraid she'll talk to her brothers. I'm scared that all three kids will put their heads together and plot against me like they did before." All the bile bubbled up fresh as ever and for a minute I hated my own children, I really did. "They are going to try and keep us apart!" I cried. "They are going to do everything in their power to make sure I'm shut up in this place the rest of my life, while strangers live in my own home!"

"Now, now, Woozy," Vitus said, patting my arm. "I'm not going to let that happen. When two people want to be together, nothing can keep them apart. Where there's a will, there's a way. Come on, you're upset. I'll walk you back to your room."

I invited him in when we got there, but I think what I'd told him tired him out because he kept yawning and rubbing his face.

"I apologize, Woozy," he told me. "I'm just so sleepy."

His room is no bigger than a closet, and that fiend Daniel who shares it is evil incarnate. Plus his single bed is nowhere near big enough for a man his size. So when he yawned for the fiftieth time and blinked at me like he could hardly see, I told him, "Climb up there on the bed. Take you a nap."

He slipped off his shoes and got up there, on top of the bedspread. I plumped up the pillow and covered him with the afghan Glenda gave me. He cozied up there on his side, his hands in prayer position under his head like an angel. I didn't want to watch TV or do anything to disturb him so I tiptoed over here to my dressing table and opened my book.

He don't sleep sprawled out like Abel did, his arms and legs thrown helter-skelter like a corpse. I have to pinch myself, seeing him there on the bed. *My* bed! I'd forgotten how nice it is to have someone in the room sleeping while you're up and about. It makes you feel warm and safe, like you're watching over somebody. I felt that way with my kids and even with Lulu. I loved it when she slept under the kitchen table while I had breakfast. I slipped my house shoes off and worked my toes into her ribs while I read the paper and drank my coffee.

Vitus's feet are sticking out of the afghan, so pink and sweet. I have half a mind to go over there and press my face against his soles, to take those toes of his right into my mouth! I got a confession to make. I want to suck, and lick, and bite Vitus all over. I want to eat him up! Things I never thought of before, things that in the old days might of turned my stomach. He just seems good enough to eat. I want to give his nipples a good, hard pinch! I want to suck titty on that man, nurse on him like a little baby! Take a wad of that fat that hangs over his pants on the side and sink my teeth into it! Shake it like a dog! I want some private time with his kneecaps! Push my tongue up his nose as far as it will go! Smell his belly button! Run my finger over his gums! Lick his armpits! Spread his cheeks and get a good look at his asshole! I want to suck his teeth and rub my tits in his hair! Oh, Lord. There's no end to the things I want to do.

It's been a long time since I felt this way about anybody. My first baby was like that. Like we were two bears in a cave, a cub and her mama. I wanted to breathe that baby's breath, I wanted to feel her next to me every minute. I never felt that same way about my other kids, and they didn't feel that way about me, either. I could tell. With Abel it was pretty much his mouth and his whang—the rest was a mystery to me. I didn't have no interest, and as far as I could tell, neither did he. As long as the one was sucking and the other was prodding, he was happy.

I can hardly contain myself. Vitus is like a new place I got to go. It's like my whole body is an ear, listening as hard as it can, straining toward a sound. The front of me itches to press up against him, to breathe him in with my skin.

WHAT A SCENE between laying down this pen yesterday and picking it up this morning. My God. There's so many ups and downs, I get dizzy just thinking about it. It's going to be tricky to do it justice, but I'll try my damndest.

I waited 'til Vitus was good and asleep, then I closed this book and tippy-toed across the room. I slipped off my shoes and crawled up next to him as quiet as I could. He didn't wake up. I stretched out on my side next to him. Our faces were but a few inches apart.

Can you imagine how thrilled I was to be there beside him on the bed, to feel his body so close to mine?

I don't think you can.

I was shaking. For a minute I just laid there, looking at his face and breathing in his smell. My skin pumped out heat like a furnace. It's a wonder it didn't char the front of Vitus's body.

I had an urge, oh such an urge!

He must have sensed me there, because his eyes opened. For a second we just looked at each other, eyeball to eyeball. He didn't move, didn't talk, didn't smile.

"Hi, sugar," I said.

For a minute I thought he was still asleep, because he stared at me like he'd never seen me before in his life. He sat up lickety-split.

I sat up and slipped my arm over his shoulder. "Did you have a nice nap?" I pulled him closer. He was still a little confused from sleeping. I put my other arm around him and gave him a bear hug. I was revved up. "Lie back down," I coaxed. "Let's have a little hanky-panky."

He finally smiled. "My, my, Cora. What did I do to deserve this?"

"Well, you looked so sweet sleeping here," I whispered in his ear, "I thought I'd come over and get me some of you."

He slicked his hair back and grinned. "Oh, you did, did you?"

"That's right." I laid back and pulled him down with me. "I've been waiting for this a long time."

He nestled on the pillow next to me.

"I hope you want me like I want you, Vitus. Because I want you in the worst way. The very worst."

He rolled onto his side and stroked my hair. It gave me the shivers. I reached around and got me a handful of ass.

His hand moved down to my neck, then to my shoulder. He petted so gentle, in big, slow circles. "You're such a beautiful woman, Cora. I can't take my eyes off you." He tapped the end of my nose with his finger.

Things were moving a little slow, so I rolled him onto his back and threw a leg over him.

He chuckled. "My goodness, Cora." He growled like a little dog. "You bring out the beast in me."

"Let it go. I can handle it."

He kissed me, soft and tender. That got me going full bore. His lips moved like powder puffs on my neck. It was real nice, but after awhile I wanted to move along. Maybe I was used to Abel, who'd chew your face off in ten seconds and eat your head for dessert.

I moved his hands down to my boobs. He started those circles again, not grabbing at all, just swooshing things around. I tried to enjoy that fancy stuff. I told myself to sit back, relax, and enjoy the ride. But I was in a lather. I clambered up on top of him.

He chuckled again, and made his little dog barks. After having just one man for all those years, it takes time to get used to a new one. But he was trying my patience. I squirmed around on top of him, tried to smarten the pace.

He didn't squirm back, or rear up against me, or grab my behind, or throw me over and climb on top. Nope. I was puffing like a freight train by then. His hands moved soft, up and down my sides. It shamed me to feel so crude, like a rutting billy goat. He knew how to take his time, how to make things nice. I loved smelling him, feeling his body against mine. But he was so still and quiet. Much as I hate to say it, I missed Abel's smutty talk.

"Loosen up, sugar," I whispered in Vitus's ear. "Let yourself go."

I decided to give him a little help. I snaked my hand down between us and hunted out his crotch. Lord have mercy! It was soft as pudding. Nothing but a pot of mush between his legs.

"Listen, honey," I said, "if you have a medical problem, just say so." I reared back so I could get a look at his face. His hair was jumbled up. His cheeks were red. "Are you just not able?"

Vitus shifted under me. "Cora, please. You've taken me by surprise, that's all. I wasn't expecting this."

"Well, get with the program, mister," I kidded him.

He smiled and gave me his devil look. "I'm a slow starter, that's all. Always have been. But once I get warmed up, watch out."

"I can help you with that."

I gave his balls the what for. He gasped. His poor eyes looked scared. "What's wrong?" I said, giving them little squeeze. I winked. "Ain't you a man?"

"Cora, please! I am a *gentle*man!"

I guess I embarrassed him. "Well, get over it! There's a time and a place for everything, and there's no room for a gentleman in this bed! You can have *anything,* Vitus! Anything you want!"

He was the exact opposite of Abel, who wanted sex every day of his life, right up until the end. He pestered me at all hours of the day and night. When we was first married, he'd even drive the ten miles home at lunchtime, do his business, then hop in the car and be back at work within the hour. I couldn't even *look* at his whang without it standing up to say hello.

Six months before Abel died, we got a new mattress to see if it'd ease the pain the cancer caused him at night. "I can't get no purchase on this damn thing!" he complained while he pumped away, sick as he was. Without the divots his knees had worn in the old mattress, he couldn't get up the speed he wanted, poor old devil. "There's no gription!" he cried. He punched the mattress with his fist and flung himself on his back, having a tantrum like a little boy.

I took pity on him. I got up and straddled him, finished him off in twenty seconds. That was the thing about Abel. He might want to do it five or ten times a day, but it never took him very long. "Thanks, Mommy," he said when I got off and laid down beside him. We both laid there on our backs and cried.

So I was confounded with Vitus. All those times a stiff dick was the *last* thing I wanted to see and now here I was *begging* for it.

He rolled me over, got on top, and commenced to kissing me again. Now we were getting somewhere. None of that rough kissing like Abel, but Vitus was putting his heart into it. Trying to make everything feel just right, I could tell. I tried to do it right, too. Showed him that I could follow his lead. We waltzed instead of doing a stomp dance. He commenced to stroking my hair again. He gave my boobs a little tickle. He giggled.

I reached down again and fished around in his pants to see if the situation had improved. Same old mush.

"What is it, Vitus? Is it my size? Are you shriveled up because I'm fat?"

He pushed himself off me, rolled to the side of the bed, and swung his legs over the side. "You know it's not that, Cora." He covered his face with his hands. "Sometimes I have trouble. There you have it."

I scooted over and rubbed his back. "Don't you worry, Vitus. I understand. There's nothing to be ashamed of. I've heard it happens to the best of men."

He turned around and looked at me. His face was so pitiful, my heart almost broke. "Will you forgive me? Just this once?"

"There's nothing to forgive, sweetie. I love you

to death. You don't have to worry. All that's not important to me." It was a lie, but a white one.

He took my hand and looked into my eyes. "You're one in a million, my girl."

He bent over to put his shoes on and mumbled something in a foreign language.

"What was that you said?" I hate for someone to say something I can't understand.

He straightened up, twisted around, looked me right in the eye, and repeated what he'd just said, slow and clear, all those foreign clicks and clucks and hisses buzzing around my head like a swarm of hornets.

My gorge starting rising. "What does that mean, Vitus? Say it in English."

"I said I don't want it to be like that for us, Cora. Not two animals lunging at each other. I want it to be special."

It was like the movies, where they swing a watch in front of your face to hypnotize you.

"You deserve better than that, Cora, much better. You'll see. Let me show you. I have it all figured out."

Trouble is, he's so handsome. It's hard to stay mad at a man like that. He was right. My life has always been so rough, barely scraping by. Same thing with love—it's always been the bottom of the barrel for me, whatever comes my way. I wouldn't know the finer things in life if they bit me on the ass.

He patted my hand between the two of his real soft, like he was making hamburger patties, then he leaned closer. He was wooing me, doing it right. I felt ashamed of myself all over again. Oh, what he must think! I wondered how he could ever love me when I'm so ignorant, so crude. *But he does.* I could see it in his eyes, the way they wandered over my face.

"Let's do something," he said. "Let's get away from here."

Words have always come fast and easy to me. No matter what happens, I always have something to say. Now I couldn't find my voice. I had to push with all my might just to get a few words out. They came out weak, barely a whisper. "What are you talking about?"

"Let's go where no one can say anything about us," he said. "Where we can do as we please."

I scooted over to the edge of the bed and sat next to him. "What are you saying, Vitus? Are you talking about a *hotel?*"

"No, Cora. No." He laid one hand on my knee, which made it hard to concentrate. "We both want our freedom. We don't belong in a place like this. We want to live our *own* lives."

Don't get your hopes up, I told myself. Part of me had already gone wild, though. It ran, jumped, and spun in circles. It erupted like a volcano. All those hopes I gave up a long time ago burst out in full force.

"We've talked about this before, but it's time to get serious. We both want out of here. If we put our heads together, I know we can find a way. We can get what we want. We can be happy, Cora."

"How? What are we going to do?"

"I know this is hard to believe, considering my present circumstances, but I actually have a fair amount of money. I've managed to save quite a bit over the years and I've made some good investments." He looked embarrassed and added, "But there are a few problems."

"Like what?"

"Remember I told you about my nephew who's sending me money?"

"Course I do."

"Well, it's a long, complicated story." He wrung his hands. After staring at the floor a minute, he lifted his face and gave me a sad smile. "I hesitated to tell you this, because people assume all kinds of things, but you and I need to be honest with each other. I want everything out in the open. So I'll tell you—and please don't think ill of me before I explain—but I was in jail."

My hands flew to my face. "You're kidding."

"No, I'm afraid not. Please, Cora. Let me explain. It was an immigration problem, really. I won't pretend I was completely innocent. I set up a business before all my paperwork was in order. I worked under the table, if you know what I mean."

"You went to jail for that?"

He nodded. "It was a misunderstanding, really, but a costly one. Not only did it delay my citizenship for quite a few years, it also led to losing all my assets." He held up his finger. "*Almost* losing my assets."

"Well, I'm taken aback, Vitus." I leaned away from him so I could look at him from a distance, to see if there was something I'd missed before. "I don't think I've ever known anyone who's been in jail. I never had any idea you'd been mixed-up in something like that."

"I know. Not too many do. I'm not proud of it." He hung his head, poor thing. "But that's not the worst of it."

"It gets worse?" I gasped.

"Yes. You see, I brought my sister and my nephew to this country about ten years ago. I set the two of them up. My sister's husband was no good, and he never came to this country. I helped my sister and nephew any way I could. And when I—" He gave me a pleading look. "When I was, you know, in jail, I entrusted my sister with my money and my business. That was my mistake. She took me for everything I had."

I thought he was going to break down. "I just don't know what to say. You never told me any of this. Why did you keep it to yourself?"

He could hardly meet my eye. He looked at the floor and mumbled, "It scares a lot of people away." Then he lifted his head, and I swear there were tears in his eyes. "I was afraid of losing your friendship, Cora."

I felt for him, I really did. But I had to get to the bottom of things. "How did you end up in this place? Was your sister behind that, too?"

He gave me an eager look, like he was glad I understood. "Yes. I had nothing when I was released from, uh, jail." He sure had a hard time saying that word. I had a hard time hearing it, too. "I was barely scraping by. My sister knew I'd try to get my money back, so she convinced every-body that I wasn't able to take care of myself. I had no credibility because of my conviction." The poor man was sweating. He paused to take out his hankie and wiped his forehead. "Plus she agreed to foot the bill if I went into the assisted care place in Phoenix. I thought that was the best course of action until I could get back on my feet."

"But how did you make your way here?" I didn't let up. It was a grave thing, him being in jail. I couldn't begin to get my mind around it. "How'd you come to this place? And how did you land—" I pointed to the ceiling—"up there?"

He managed to smile. "You're very tough, Cora. If I didn't know better, I'd think you were a detective."

I started to object, but he held his hand up. "No, no. I'm glad to have the opportunity to explain myself. I want to clear up any doubts in your mind. But I'm sure you realize it's painful for me."

"Yes, I can see that, and I feel bad for prying." It was no time to be polite. He'd earned himself a good grilling.

He nodded. "Before long, she took off with everything. She stopped paying the tab for where I was living. I had nothing, nowhere to go. I had a friend here in San Diego, so I got on the bus and came out. Things didn't work out as I planned, and I agreed to move in here. It's only temporary, though. Until things get straightened out."

I studied him. He looked right back at me. "Yeah, and how's that supposed to happen?" I asked. "You said you had a fair amount of money. You let on that if you got out of here you'd have enough to operate on."

"Ah, that's the second part of the story," he said, brightening up. "My sister passed on and my nephew Nick took the reins. He realizes that what his mother did was wrong. Unlike her, he has a conscience. Sure, he wants a share, but right now he's cooperating with my lawyer to restore at least part of what I had. We've made a lot of progress. I'm getting very close to having my independence again."

"You telling the truth?"

He smiled and raised his right hand, like a swearing-in.

"Funny, that's a lot like what happened to me," I said.

"That's why my heart went out to you when you told me your story. I thought we were two of a kind."

"But why didn't you say anything? If you knew that we'd both gotten stabbed in the backs by our own families, why not tell me?"

"I've had a hard time trusting anyone since then. You never know what people are capable of."

"Amen to that." I paused. This was the hardest conversation the two of us had ever had. I felt warm and cold by turns. "Do you trust *me?*" I ventured.

His face opened up. He edged a little closer. "I'm starting to, Cora. I'm starting to. And you don't know how wonderful it feels." He gave me a sly look. "And how about you? Do you trust me?"

"Well, that's a real good question, Vitus." I thought a little bit. "It's hard to know who to trust when those closest to you sold you down the river. Being in this place, too. Every time you turn around somebody steals you blind. But I don't want to be like that, Vitus. I want to trust at least one person in this world."

Vitus took my hand. A warm current flowed between us. We were both in the same boat. Our talk had brought us closer.

"Listen here, Vitus. I'm willing to take a chance

on you. I own my house outright and I got money in the bank. About twenty thousand dollars last time I looked. If I can figure out a way out of this damn place, we can go live there. You and I could set up housekeeping and have the time of our lives."

Was I really saying such a thing? I had to pinch myself. I felt like I was living in a fairy tale.

"Oh, no, Cora. I wouldn't think of it."

"Well, my God. Why the hell not?"

He pressed his lips together and shook his head. I pulled my hand away.

"Cora, that's where you lived with your husband. You have so many memories there. I wouldn't feel right moving in."

"Vitus, that is my home and will always be my home. *My* home. It's all I dream about. When I imagine getting out of this place, it's always so I can be back there."

"But Cora. We could get a new place. A place of our own, where we could start fresh. Soon as my money comes in, I can buy it. I can buy anything we want." He winked and squeezed my knee. "Within reason, of course."

"But why look for something else when I already got everything we need. Why spend the money? Why spend the time?"

Vitus stroked his chin. "You wouldn't feel funny living with me in the same house where you lived with your husband?"

"We'll clear everything out, repaint, get all new furniture and carpet—everything. It'll be different. It won't seem the same."

Vitus nodded. You could tell he was thinking real hard. "Okay. I see you have a point. Well, let's think about it. We'll see what happens. Everything will turn out all right."

"We can stay up late and watch TV," I said. "On Sundays I'll cook a big egg and bacon breakfast and we can read the paper. I want to get sheer drapes that go all the way to the floor and two new recliners. You can pick your own. And butter-colored walls in the living room. I've always wanted that."

"I like to garden," Vitus said. "Is there a place where I can work in the yard?"

"Is there ever! You can root around in the dirt to your heart's content."

I never felt so giddy in my life, even when I got married at seventeen years old. *Especially* when I got married.

"And I'll cook for *you,* Cora. Not to brag, but I'm a gourmet."

I wondered about getting married, but I didn't bring it up. I used to have fits about my grandkids living together with this one and that one and never getting married, but it's different for me. I'm old, and it's not like I'll be having more kids. Plus things are different nowadays. Everybody's talking about men marrying men and women marrying women and before you know it, people will be able to marry a damn goat if they want to, or a fire hydrant. So maybe it don't matter so much. After what I been through, it's the least of my worries.

"Now we just have to hammer out the details," Vitus said. "We need to figure out a way around your family so we can get you out of here." He looked off into the distance. "There are so many places I want to take you, Woozy. So many things I want you to see."

I was overcome, I don't mind saying it. Life welled up inside me just as strong as when I was twenty years old. "I love you, Vitus," I cried. "I love you like life itself."

"I love you, too, my darling." He raised my hand and kissed it. Not the back, but the *palm*. "We'll take them all by surprise, before they have a chance to get in our way." He moved closer and whispered in my ear. "It's now or never, Woozy. There's nothing to stop us." He pressed my hand between the two of his. "I've been looking for you all my life. I have to grab you fast, before somebody else does."

THE CULPRIT

I'm still trying to take in everything Vitus told me. Part of me thinks he got a bum rap and was swindled by his sister just the way I was swindled by my kids. The other part wonders if Glenda was right when she said there's something amiss with him. One thing's sure—I got feelings for that man, strong feelings. I'm in a real quandary. I didn't tell nobody, and I don't mean to. I'm inclined to feel that the past is the past. Everybody deserves a second chance.

But there's more big news. Speaking of jail, there's someone here who belongs there, certain as can be. Things are happening so fast, I feel like I'm in a speeded-up movie. I better get to telling before some new hell breaks loose.

Remember that crazy Mrs. Cipriano, who looks like a spider monkey? She weighs all of eighty pounds and has big bright eyes and bushy brown hair sprouting all the way around her mouth. She's fit as a fiddle, always scurrying and hopping like a sprite. I don't know if she dyes her hair, but it's still black, which makes her sunk-in face all the scarier. The fingers on her tiny paws are quick and sharp, made for getting into trouble. I don't know who buys her clothes, but she wears stretch pants about five sizes too big. They bag down around her knees like she just dumped a load in them.

The poor little coot is completely off her rocker.

Well, she's always been nosy about this book. If she ever sees me outside writing in it, she scampers over and watches with her glittery black eyes. She's so fast and nervous, I'm afraid she's going to reach out and snatch something, or jump on my shoulder like a squirrel. I always try to shoo her away, and like as not she's gone as fast as she appeared.

This afternoon I lay down for my nap around 3:00 or 3:30, like I usually do. I drifted off no more than fifteen minutes when my eyes flew open and there, not two feet from my bed, was that little spider monkey. She scared the living tar out of me! My heart jumped out of my chest and my legs gave a kick. She stood there at the dresser with her thin little back to me, her scrawny shoulder blades holding her shirt out like wings. The crotch of those stretchy pants hung to her knees. She was busy with something, her arms moving, but I couldn't see her hands or face.

I didn't realize I'd been holding my breath 'til I let out a big gasp. She whirled around, those huge crazy eyes of hers sparking fire. She clutched my fountain pen in one paw and the three quarters I'd left as bait in the other.

"Those are mine!" I yelled. "You put them right back!"

She's teeny, but I'm scared of her the same way I'm scared of a mouse running up my leg. She looks like she might bite, or scratch out your eyes. The bottlebrush around her mouth twitched. "Dis iss my pen," she growled, holding it up in her paw. "You stold it."

I scooted to the edge of the bed and put my feet on the floor. "That's mine!" I hollered. "You are all mixed up! Put them back right now and get out of my room! You got no right to be in here in the first place!"

She cocked back her hand like she was going to stab me with the pen. The bristle around her mouth split open and showed her little pointed teeth. "Mine!" she hissed, so fierce that I drew back. She'd scare the piss out of anybody.

I glanced over at the sliding glass door and saw it was open about a hand's width, enough to let that little weasel in. I must have forgotten to lock it before I laid down, and now I was in a fix. "This has gone far enough!" I screeched as I dragged myself to my feet. I stood up, and she changed her tune. Her nose came about to my belly button. The fire in her eyes turned to fear.

"Gimme that right now! Hand them over and get the hell out of here, or you'll be sorry!"

I managed to grab the pen out of her hand, but that varmint ducked and dodged and before you could spit she'd shot across the room and shimmied out the door with the quarters. I stumbled after her, yelling for her to stop, but by the time I got to the door there wasn't hide nor hair of her left.

"Help!" I yelled out into the courtyard. "I been robbed!"

I kept the racket up 'til one of the nurses came down from the station. I stood right there and told her word for word just what happened.

WEIGHING IN

Y ou seen those ads in the magazines? Before and after? They got some lard-ass whale standing there in shorts with her blubbery thighs rippling and her gut sticking out and tits flopping over her knees? Her hair looks like she's been through a cyclone and she's scowling like her cat just got ran over. Next to it is a picture of some little tiny thing in tight pants with a butt no bigger than a cupcake, boobs riding up under her chin, and stomach flat as a board. You couldn't pinch an inch anywhere. Her hair and makeup's all done up and she's grinning like the Cheshire Cat. Who wouldn't be, looking like that? You can't believe those two pictures are the same person.

That's me.

"Big day today," Marcos said when he came in to take my vitals and give me my hookah. "It's time for your six-month checkup."

"Six months from what? I been in this crap-shack nine months."

"Six months from your last checkup, Coralita. You were so bad back then you probably don't remember. Come on, you've got an appointment down the hall with Dr. Kildare."

I didn't want to go but Marcos insisted. It was his job to take me. "It's nothing, *señora*. Five minutes. You know that doctor—the less he sees of you, the happier he is. Come on. I will be your escort."

"You want to smoke first?" I asked.

He still had that hunted look, like something was bothering him. His hair was flat on one side, something he'd never have allowed before. He gave me the once-over. You could tell he wanted that cigarette. I was practically reaching for my pack when he sucked his teeth, then shook his head. "No. I can't do it, Cora."

"Well, why not?"

He put his hands on his hips. "Number one, it's against the rules. Number two, I don't have time."

I clucked my tongue. "Never stopped you before."

"Times have changed. Things are not as they used to be."

"What's that supposed to mean?"

For a minute I thought he was going to spill the beans right there. I saw him think about it, and my tongue was already out, ready to lap it up. Just as quick, he changed his mind. "I'm in a hurry," he said. "Let's go."

Usually, I'd walk, but since Marcos was in such a damn rush, I let him push me in the wheelchair.

"How's your loverboy?" I said once we were rolling.

"He moved out."

I turned around and looked up at him. From that angle, I saw right up his big nose holes, which opened and closed like fish gills from pushing me down the hall. The smell of his cologne rained down on me. He looked straight ahead, no expression on his face.

"How come?"

"Where are your manners, Cora?"

"I left them at home when they dragged me to this dungeon. Soon as I'm back there I'll be nice as pie."

He finally laughed. "Somehow I don't think so."

I laughed, too. "I just believe in speaking truth. So what happened? That boy doesn't deserve you, pretty as he is."

"Oh, Cora," he sighed. "I gave him everything he wanted. All he had to do was ask. Paid for everything. Took care of him. Still, it wasn't enough."

"Why don't you get you a nice girl? A *real* wife, not somebody who lives in France."

He'd just started in scolding me when who should come down the hall but that crazy little spider monkey. She capered and hopped. You half expected her to scale the wall, or jump up and hang from the lights by her tail. Lo and behold, when she got even with us she screeched and darted toward me like she was going to scratch my eyes out with her tiny paws.

I yelped. Thank God Marcos was there. He grabbed her arm, spun her around, and led her off toward the nurses' station. Damned if she didn't crank her neck around and make a face at me from the end of the hall.

"Close call," he said when he came back.

"She's the one, Marcos! She's the one that's been stealing!"

The wheelchair stopped. Marcos came around to the front and bent down in my face. He'd gone pale. "What are you talking about, Cora? What are you saying?"

"I'm saying I caught her red-handed! I'm saying she's the one that took my quarters and my crystal and my twenties! I woke up from a nap and there she was not two feet away with her paws shit deep in my things! What are you staring at?"

"Are you sure, Cora? Did you really see her?"

"Of course I saw her! Do you think I've gone round the bend? What in the world are you asking me for? I told you exactly what happened."

A few droolers parked in the hall to air out turned their heads and stared.

"What's gotten into you?" I asked. "You looked like you seen a ghost."

Marcos went around to the back and started pushing me way too fast.

"Slow the hell down," I called back. "I'm getting whiplash."

An old lady on a walker inched toward us. A glacier would have beat her down that hall.

"Why are you so surprised?" I asked to break the silence. "You act like you don't believe me."

"I'm glad you caught her in the act. What happened? What did you do?"

"I yelled enough to wake the dead, then I told the aide who came to see what happened. I expect they'll follow up on it. Call the police or bring her in for questioning. Search her room, maybe. Get her to confess."

Marcos sucked his teeth. I couldn't for the life of me figure him out.

"Park here a minute," I said when we came to the room where Ivy and those other old bags did their exercises. The door was open. "Let's take in the sights."

They were all standing on their tiptoes, reaching for the stars. So much sagging flesh and gnarled bones you never saw in all your born days.

"Looks like a rack of beef jerky hung out to dry," I whispered to Marcos. He had to wheel me away quick to keep from attracting attention.

The doctor was waiting for us. He is one cold fish. Gray hair and skin to match, little wire-rim glasses. Sour. Not an ounce of flesh on his bones. He didn't crack a smile when we came in.

Without any warning, he reached out with those bony fingers and started probing in my neck. The stethoscope was toasty compared to his fingers.

Marcos stood in the corner like a schoolboy being punished. I never seen him so quiet or so still. I kept my eyes locked on his while the doctor did all the usual things—took my blood pressure and my temperature, looked in my ears and down my throat, thumped me on the back and made me cough a thousand times. I could have been a mattress the way he handled me. Finally, he closed the damn folder and motioned me over to the scale.

Marcos weighs me on one of those newfangled things where your exact weight shows up in numbers. But that doctor had the old-fashioned kind with weights you slide along the bars. I slipped off my shoes and made a face at Marcos like I tasted something nasty. The doctor started fiddling with the weights, bumping them past the little notches, fussing and adjusting until I was ready to jump out of my skin. I was ashamed to have that bone of a man see I weighed more than *two* of him.

He thumbed through my chart—writing here and there, squinting at the pages, glancing up at me, adjusting his glasses—'til I thought I'd lose my mind. Finally, he pushed his glasses up on his nose one last time and fastened me with his icy stare. "Mrs. Sledge, according to these records, you've lost sixty-one pounds in six months. Your blood pressure has dropped twenty points. Your heart rate is down over 10 percent and you haven't refilled your prescriptions for tranquilizers, antidepressants, or sleeping aids."

I let out a bloodcurdling whoop and did a little stomp dance. Marcos's face flushed bright red. He put his hand over his eyes like he couldn't bear to see me make such a horse's ass out of myself.

"Do I have the right chart here?" the doctor said, flipping over some pages.

"Mrs. Sledge has worked very hard," Marcos said. "She's made a lot of progress."

"It's a lot of Marcos's doing," I added, winking at him to show I appreciated all those cigarettes and snacks he'd brought me.

"Well, whatever you're doing, keep it up," he said, not bothering to look up from the chart. I took advantage of it to stick my tongue out at him. He walked over and opened the door, and as he stood there waiting for us to leave he finally deigned to lay eyes on us. "I'll see you in six months."

"Like hell he will," I said to Marcos as soon as we were outside.

I WROTE AND wrote and here I am at the end of this book. The second! Lord God Almighty! The pages flew by. These last five or six I had to write so tiny to squeeze everything in, they're nothing but flyspecks on the page. I don't know how anybody's going to read it, but the way I'm feeling now I just got to keep going no matter what. If this place goes up in flames tomorrow all this working and remembering and writing I've been doing will be wasted. I been trying to think of a safe place to keep these books 'til I'm dead, but the only thing I can think of is to go out and bury them somewhere, which seems silly, so I guess I'll just take my chances.

Third Book

THE COMET

I called Emma and told her I needed a new book, and look what she got me.

"Why, Gamma, what did you do with the other two I gave you?" she asked in that silly little-girl voice of hers. "Are you using them for firewood, or what?"

Ha, ha, ha.

It seems like only yesterday she gave me the last one with the nautilus shell on the cover. "I'm making scrapbooks out of them," I told her, which is true in a way. She don't need to know nothing more because I don't want her snooping around or flapping her lips to anybody else in the family. "It helps me pass the time," I added, since I felt her hesitating on the other end of the line. Maybe she's getting tired of shelling out the money.

"Well, let me think. I—"

"I'm making a keepsake for the family once I'm gone," I interrupted. I guess she wanted me to beg. "You'll see."

The long and short of it is she dropped it off on her way to work. She's got a job at the blood bank, filling out forms for the people who come in to donate. I was at breakfast, so she left it at the office. One of them secretaries came to my room and handed it to me. I almost jumped for joy.

Oh, this one's a humdinger! The cover's pitch-black. On the front is a comet with a long tail. Smaller stars swirl thick as flies in the background and a crescent moon peeks out of one corner. It's all done in silver ink that gleams against the black leather like the real sky at night.

That last book has thick pages full of chunks and chips, like they were made of a dried-up salad. I practically had to *carve* the words into the page, jabbing with the sharp point of that cheap pen. This book is a whole other story. It's like a big, swanky Cadillac—you hardly feel the bumps in the road. The pages are bright white, smooth as glass. And the pen Emma got to go with it (yes, she remembered this time) is a felt tip with a thin silver barrel. *Elegant* is the word to describe it, like a movie star's cigarette holder. It glides over the glossy paper like a skater on ice. Writing is a pleasure, I tell you that. Sometimes I doodle just for fun.

I wish I could see everybody's faces when they lay eyes on all these pages, every one of them covered with words I wrote myself, with no help from anybody. I marvel at it myself. Sometimes I flip through just to see all that ink.

I can't help but think how miserable I was when I started that first book, the one with the lavender on the cover. I would just as soon have died as go on living.

What a whole different world it is now.

Still, with all that's happening here right now and so many things to think about, I got in the back of my mind that other story, the one that happened so long ago. It's with me night and day, in my dreams, in my every waking moment. I'm getting that story straight for the first time in my life. I'm *letting* myself see what happened, watching myself like I was in a movie. Sounds crazy, but for the first time I see a person who was struggling, groping in the dark.

THE HERO

I didn't lay a trap for Abel, didn't snare him like a rabbit. More like I saw how things could turn out and stepped aside so they could move in that direction. I'm not saying it was right. But I was operating on instinct then, doing what I had to do. It was sink or swim. You never know what you're going to do when your back's against the wall.

Abel turned out to be a gentleman. After all I'd heard about the Sledges, I thought he'd come on strong, but next to Edward, he was mild as a maiden. He didn't lay a finger on me, didn't even try. Oh, don't get me wrong. He was willing, *more* than willing. But he waited until I gave him the go-ahead. I didn't have much time to lose. All he needed was a little nudge. Once he got to a certain point, there was no turning back, and once he got a little taste, he had to have more. All hell broke loose then, believe me. That man thought he died and went to heaven.

It's no secret that sex is a whole lot different when you're in love with somebody. Hard as Abel tried, much as he flailed and flopped, it wasn't the same as with Edward. Only one thing got my attention, and it's not at all what you'd expect. Like I told you, talking wasn't easy for Abel. But I found out that the only time he had a lot to say was when he was making love. Then he couldn't shut up! That man was a regular motormouth, like taking his clothes off jogged something loose in his tongue. He talked a blue streak about what we was doing, how he felt about it, and what he wanted to do next. Good Lord, the things he said! It took me aback while he was saying it, shocked the shit out of me. But later, when I was alone, his words played over in my brain. It's like when they break a horse, the way they whisper to it constant under their breath. Don't matter what they say—it calms the horse down. Abel's voice lulled me. Those words spilling out of him made it easier for me, less like swallowing medicine.

But that's neither here nor there. The long and short of it is we'd been carrying on about a month when I told him I was expecting. I couldn't wait much longer, because I was starting to show, or at least *I* could tell. I was more than three months gone by then.

I'll never forget Abel's face. I was scared to death when I told him, remembering how mad Edward got, how he'd looked at me like he wanted to reach over and wring my neck. Well, Abel's eyes flew open like he'd stuck his finger in a light socket. I held my breath, and then damned if his eyes didn't light up and his mouth split open and all them spaced-out yellow teeth break out in the biggest grin I ever saw.

I was so surprised, I forgot myself. "Ain't you scared?" I asked. "Ain't you sorry?"

He took my hands and started mashing them up real good. If I wasn't so dumbstruck, it would have hurt. Damned if those eyes of his didn't get teary. "We just got to get hitched, that's all," he said, so choked up he could hardly get the words out.

I felt so many things, all at the same time. Relief, of course, because in one fell swoop my troubles were over. My baby would have a home and a father. My own hide was saved, too. I wouldn't have to face all them people with what I'd done and I wouldn't have to figure out what in the world would become of me. But part of me felt like I'd just got condemned to prison, a life sentence. Because there it was, my whole life, spread out in front of me. Even then I wondered how I was going to get through it, if I was going to spend every waking moment ruing what I'd just done. I didn't love Abel, but there he was, looking at me with all the love in the world. Oh, the shame! It nearly tore me apart. At the same time, I hated Abel for not being Edward. That's right, even then! Oh, it was a mess! I nearly cried out, I was so miserable.

Abel looked confused. "Ain't that what you want, us getting hitched? Ain't that what we been heading for all along?"

Gratitude and guilt don't mix, don't sit right on your stomach. They pull you apart, make you feel like heaving. But I made up my mind then and there, on the spot, that I'd do everything I could to try and love Abel. I had a whole lifetime to learn how.

My eyes were teary when I looked at him, but not for the reason he thought. I never planned to be with you, I thought to myself. All that thinking I'd done about Edward, all that imagining of our house and our children and our life together, that was all still fresh in my mind. I hadn't pictured one thing about being married to Abel, and I didn't want to start then.

"Yes, it is," I said. "This is where we been heading."

He put his arms around me and pulled me close. "You my baby girl," he rasped, "and I'm going to take care of you."

There, I've gone and done it, I thought as I pressed my face against his hard, bumpy chest. I'd pulled one over on everybody. I heard him breathing and felt his heart pounding and told myself, good or bad, everything was settled.

I TOLD HIM I was pregnant the first week in November. A couple days after that we told our folks we wanted to get married. We said we didn't want to wait, we wanted to do it right away. Maybe they got the idea, because nobody asked any questions. Only Ruby kept eyeing me. Part of me feels like she knew what was happening right from the beginning. We set the wedding date for a month later, a Saturday morning, the twelfth of December. It wasn't going to be nothing like Ruby's wedding. Just our families, with lunch to follow at my folks' house.

Everything was slapped together and rushed. We didn't have no place to live after we got married. The Depression was getting worse and even work there at the mine was slowing down, with more and more men trying to get the little work there was. Abel was hanging on by his fingernails and making next to nothing. So it got decided that we'd go live with his oldest sister, Dinah, once we were married. Her and her husband had a hog farm way out in the sticks, with a lean-to tacked on to the main house where we could stay. I dreaded it. They had five or six kids and I'd never met that woman in my life. Things looked bleak, but they were about to get worse.

Abel and I got to fussing. He couldn't see why

we shouldn't carry on with the sex like we had, but I told him we had to wait now, 'til after we were married. I was already thinking of excuses to keep him off me. That should have told me something. He tried to abide by it, but by that time he was too far gone. He'd gotten a taste and he couldn't do without. So, often as not, we'd end up bickering. I had my own gripes, the major one being piled up like kindling with his sister's family. I couldn't hold my tongue about how much I hated the idea, while he didn't see a thing wrong with it.

Round about Thanksgiving, he decided to go with his brothers to visit some kin in Tulsa, a last trip before he got married. Fine with me. I welcomed the break. Give me a chance to store up some patience so I could spend the rest of my life with him. So off he went with that pack of boys. They were planning to be gone three or four days.

It was mild that year. That far into November and we didn't have no freeze, or hardly any rain. With the banks failing and more and more people out of work, I got a sinking feeling that matched the one in my heart. People were getting desperate and there was no end in sight, just the days getting shorter and winter coming on. Meanwhile it was real pretty, the sky gentle and the trees going bare. My baby would be born in the spring. I couldn't begin to picture what my life would be like by then.

I was expecting Abel back the weekend after

Thanksgiving. You'd think he was going to the moon the way he acted before he left, almost crying, saying how much he'd miss me, and he'd be back before I knew it, Don't you worry, take care of yourself, I can't wait to see you again. I appreciated him caring so much, I really did. I just wished I felt the same.

So that Sunday after Thanksgiving, I was there in the kitchen with Ma and Crystal, helping fix our supper. We'd killed a chicken and I was plucking it. Jasper came round the back way and opened the kitchen door. He poked his head in and said, "Somebody here to see you, Toad."

Course I was expecting Abel. But Jasper had a funny look on his face. "He's over there by the stump. Said he'd wait for you out there."

He went back around toward the barn and I pulled the last few handfuls of feathers off the bird. It was a red hen, with black speckles across its wings. I handed it to Crystal and washed and dried my hands. When I opened the door, the wind was blowing, making the dry maple leaves cartwheel along the ground.

The stump was across the yard, over by a little copse of saplings. About as big around as a barrel, it had been there since I could remember. We split wood on it, and the top was crisscrossed with hack marks. He was sitting on it, hands in his pockets and shoulders slumped, looking down the slope away from the house.

I was halfway across the yard before I realized it wasn't Abel. The way he was sitting was different—his chest was sunk in, like his shoulders wanted to meet over his heart. As I got closer I saw he was taller and his hair was cropped close to his head, barely an inch long. It didn't have that copper sheen like Abel's, either. He turned and watched me coming toward him, but he didn't make no sign—didn't wave or nod his head, didn't even smile.

When I got up next to him, I could see why I'd thought it was Abel. The family resemblance was strong. He had the same square head, thick neck, ropy arms, and speckles covering his face. But this one's eyes were closer together, hard and shiny as a snake's. His mouth was pinched, puckered like it opened and closed with a drawstring. He was a few years older than Abel. Of course, I learned later it was his brother Enoch, the coldest man alive. He ended up working at the slaughterhouse, shooting steers in the head one after the other.

He didn't get up from the stump, didn't take his hands out of his pockets or look me in the eye. I had a thought that I'm ashamed of to this day. It came to my mind before I had a chance to stop it that Enoch had come to tell me Abel had been killed. I didn't have to marry him. I'd have the baby and live at my ma and daddy's instead of his sister's, and people would remember how me and

Abel were going to get married, how he died right before the wedding, how our baby never saw its daddy. Later down the line, I could marry someone else, maybe even Edward. Hope surged up in my heart before I had time to scold myself, before I could think, Now, ain't you ashamed?

There was chips and splinters around the stump, and a pile of cut wood nobody had stacked yet. Smelled nice, that fresh wood. Enoch stared down at it, and since he didn't say anything neither did I. He had big scuffed-up workboots on. The laces were knotted together in about a dozen places where they'd broken. I dug my toe in the chips, looked off toward the house where smoke rose from the chimney.

"Abel ain't coming back," he said so sudden I jumped. He didn't look up, just talked like he had a little speech he'd memorized, all in the same tone, without raising or lowering his voice. "He done cleared out. Quit the mine. He's up in Tulsa. Staying there, looking for work. Say to tell you he ain't coming back. Say to tell you, if you ask yourself, you know why. Say he ain't never been done like this before in his whole entire life."

"What do you mean?" was all I could say.

"Mean what I said!" he snarled so fierce I stepped back. "Mean he ain't coming back! Mean you ain't going to see him! Mean he's gone for good!" His snake eyes glinted. He pulled back his lips. He had a brown tooth right up front. His hands clenched on his thighs. He shoved himself up to standing. "You know the reason why!" he spit before he turned tail and hustled off down the slope.

I turned, too, and half ran, half stumbled toward the house. I leaned forward, faltering over the ruts and bumps. The ground passed under my feet, my cheeks jiggled and my jaw clacked. My mind was racing, too. I figured one of Abel's brothers—or maybe an uncle or older cousin— must have took him aside while he was in Tulsa. Must have said, Listen here, she's playing you for a fool. Man talk. Or maybe he just got to thinking on his own. Figured things out, put two and two together. Didn't matter how. I tripped on a rock up close to the house, almost fell flat on my face, but I kept on moving. I had to get inside. Had to hide.

The back door always stuck. I jerked it with all my might, pulled it open. Ma and Crystal looked up, surprised. I went to pieces, fell apart right there with the boiling water and chicken feathers and heat from the stove. Collapsed in a heap on the floor, fell to crying like the world was going to end.

THE REST OF that nightmare time is a blur. Ma took me upstairs and got me to bed, and that must have been when I told her, yes I did, I told her as best I could, that Abel had cleared out and I was pregnant, that my life was ruined and all I wanted was to be gone, dead, out of sight of everyone.

My poor ma. People say folks turn old overnight at times like that, but while my confession sank in, her face changed into a young girl's, a little lost girl who needed her *own* mother. "It's a grave sin you've committed, Toad," she rasped. She was right on the edge of crying, but she was mad as fury, too. She was disgusted with me, shocked at what I'd been up to. "A grave, grave sin. You better pray that Jesus can find it in his heart to forgive you."

She could hardly stand to look at me. That night I lay in bed so full of hate for myself, and with longing for her to love me, that I hit myself in the face and pulled my own hair. I cursed myself, sobbing into my pillow while I thought how my ma would never love me again, how she'd never, ever look at me and be glad I was her daughter.

I lay up there under the eaves all alone, wishing I'd never been born, moaning and crying in pure misery. There was a deep quiet in the house I'd never felt before, a sorrow like someone had died. I waited for Crystal to come up, waited and waited, until it got so late I realized that Ma must have made a pallet on the floor for her downstairs. I was too filthy for my own sister to sleep with, and that sent me into a new fit of wailing. In all my life I'd never slept in that bed alone, and there I was, left for lost, forsaken by my own family. I thought I could hear my folks talking down in the kitchen, their voices going back and forth. I wanted them so bad, but at the same time I dreaded having to look them in the face. The open window tempted me. I pictured them all hearing the thud, running out the front door, and seeing me spattered like a pumpkin on the ground.

The sound of the car starting woke me the next morning. It was a bright day, like nothing at all was wrong in the world. The car idled awhile, sputtered, then headed down the hill. I didn't stir from the bed. Before long I heard the pump working out in the yard, the kitchen door slam, the squawk of the chickens. I was dying of hunger by then, but I couldn't bring myself to go downstairs. Jasper's bicycle rattled down the hill. A metal pot clanked in the kitchen. Everybody was going about their business, and there I was rooted to the sheets.

I cringed when I heard footsteps creaking up the stairs. I slunk down and pulled the covers up to my chin. I could have died of shame when my ma opened the door and came in with a bowl of oatmeal. She looked so tired, it broke my heart. I didn't say a word, just peeked over the top of the blanket.

"Sit up here and eat something," she said in a cold voice.

I scooted up in the bed. The smell of those oats

made my mouth water. She handed them down to me, along with a spoon. She'd put milk and sugar on top, the way I liked. "Blow on it for me," I wanted to say like I had when I was little. I wanted to be her baby again, her little girl. But I just held the bowl in my lap, feeling the warmth through the blankets on my belly, where that baby was.

Ma sat on the edge of the bed. I wanted to throw myself on her, to bury my head in her lap. Instead I leaned against her ever so slightly, so she wouldn't notice.

"Your daddy left," she said in the same cold voice. "He's gone to pick up your cousin Gordon. They driving up to Tulsa. Going to find Abel and bring him back."

ONE OF MY jobs was taking care of the chickens. I had to feed and water them, muck out their coop, and collect the eggs. Every morning I dragged myself out of bed when it was just getting light and walked on down to the edge of the yard where the outhouse and chicken coop were about twenty feet apart.

The hens were locked up at night so no varmints could get them. By the time I got there they were raring to get out, crowding the door and fussing for the kitchen scraps I brought. I threw the food down, then went in to the boxes to get the eggs. A few hens were always still sitting.

It was dark in there, and it smelled like the chickens, which—you might be surprised to know—is a nice smell, like a warm pillow. Makes you want to curl up and take a nap.

Anyway, I was still sleepy, so I liked being in there where it still felt like night. It had been about two days since my daddy went to Tulsa to fetch Abel, and right then I was happy for any chance to be out of the house, because I couldn't bear for my ma to look at me, to see me in my shame. I put the eggs in a metal pail, then I stuck my hand under the hens that were still fluffed out on their nests. They were feisty, and might give you a peck or two.

I'd just begun to muck out the old hay and chicken shit when Jasper stuck his head in the door. He must have been about thirteen then. His voice was just starting to change and he'd grown about ten inches in the last year. "Better get your tail in the house, Toad," he said. "Dad's come home." He kicked at the chickens that clustered around his feet, pecking at his shoelaces. "He's got Abel."

It's funny what you remember. I pulled the rake one last time across the ground and, after all this time—over sixty years—I still can see those lines in the dirt. The little grooves perfectly spaced, the wavy pattern I'd made, the clean floor. I don't know why it gave me such pleasure, maybe because it was the last few seconds of peace before I'd have to set the rake back in the corner, leave the dark henhouse, step out in the morning sun, cross the yard, and walk back into the house to face the music.

Ma and Crystal was there in the kitchen, getting ready to make soap. The windows were steamed and the air was thick with the greasy smell of tallow. Crystal met my eye with a look that said she was damn glad she wasn't standing in my shoes. They both were sweating.

"They up in the sitting room," Ma said. "Go on in there."

The sitting room was really a screened-in porch at the front of the house. It was nice in the summer and evenings, when the breeze blew through. Now it felt like a gas chamber. I made my way toward it like I was a dead man walking, and really that's how I felt, like I'd given up everything, just surrendered to my fate. I raised my arm, took hold of the doorknob, pushed the door open, stepped inside. The hardest part was knowing they were looking at me, forcing myself to raise my eyes and see their faces.

They must have driven all night. My daddy, who was always so careful about his looks, hadn't shaved. I was surprised to see that his beard was gray near his temples and on his chin. He was a thin man anyway, but now his cheeks were sunk in and his clothes seemed to hang on him. He was tired, too, you could see that. All of it made him look like a hobo, like those bums we were seeing more and more often passing through town. But bad as he looked, he was nothing next to Abel.

It hadn't even been a week since he'd left, but he looked like a different person. He stood up against the wall with his legs together and his arms by his sides like he did the first time I'd ever seen him at Ruby's wedding. I remembered how he'd looked like a line somebody had marked on the wall, straight and narrow.

But his face! Oh Lord, his face. An outbreak of fever blisters covered his mouth and chin. From far away you might think he'd been eating a mess of berries, but up close you saw they were big open sores, swollen and oozing. His skin was deathly pale. Even his freckles were washed out, the color of some grub you'd find under a rock. And his eyes. They were sunk deep back in his head and they glittered like he was sick. You couldn't tell the expression. They were like a wounded animal's—a badger or a bear. Only other time I'd seen someone look like that was when my cousin Davis had run up from the river to get help when the man he worked with at the sawmill cut his hand off at the wrist. Abel had that same ravaged look, like he'd witnessed something he'd never get over.

We didn't say nothing, didn't make any move toward each other. Abel wouldn't take his eyes off my face. Much as I was suffering, my heart went out to him, honest to God it did. You could see in one second how bad he was hurting.

My daddy leaned against the windowsill, his arms crossed over his chest. He said in a weary voice, "Toad, Abel here says that baby ain't his."

There's times when it's no use talking. Words weren't made for those times. I was so crushed that I'd brought my father to look at me like this, to see me in this light. Him, a man who'd married my mother and had all of us right and proper, had brought us up and worked hard all his life, had never raised a hand to any of us, or showed us a bad example in any way. I turned my miserable face toward him and he knew without my saying that what Abel said was true, that I'd defiled our home and family in the worst possible way, not once but twice, with two different men.

I begged with my face for my daddy to do whatever he wanted with me because I was pure out of energy—to lie, to scheme, to cry, or to explain. Even to live. I was too weary and worn out. Whatever my daddy had in mind when he made me, I wished he could undo it now. Say, I made a mistake, and stamp me out. That's what I tried to tell him with my face, without saying the words.

It must have been a pitiful sight, because Abel gave a little whimper. I'd almost forgot him standing over there against the wall, but now he made a move toward me, like he was going to catch me from falling. My daddy held up his hand to stop him. I wish I'd never lived to see his face when he looked from Abel to me. I had no business being alive, no business being on this earth with other people.

"Get on out of here, Toad," he said. "Get out of my sight and leave us be."

I DON'T KNOW how long they talked in the sitting room. Not long. I walked out the front door and over to the side of the house. I was sick in the weeds there, my hands on my knees, the smell of the dry grass rising in the heat while I heaved. My eyes and nose ran. I went over to the car parked beside the house and sat down on the running board. Wiped my face with the hem of my skirt. Hung my head between my legs. Looked down at the dust.

They didn't see me when they came out, but I watched Abel walk down the hill, that straight body moving out of sight. This baby wasn't his, but it *could* have been, the way he'd been carrying on. I thought with shame how well I knew his body—his narrow ass with a dimple on the side of each cheek, the red hair on his legs, the knobby bones of his ankles, and his nipples, pink and tender as a little girl's on his broad white chest.

My father saw me when he turned back toward the house. All of a sudden there he was, his shadow falling over me.

"What you doing sitting there?"

I looked up at him, the underside of his jaw, his head against the sky. "Nothing. Just sitting."

He put his hands in his pockets and his foot on the running board next to me. He was wearing his Sunday boots, pointed with thin, oiled laces. They were scuffed now, dusty. I wondered how long he had been wearing those clothes, how he'd managed to find Abel and bring him back.

"That boy is one in a million," he said, looking off across the sky like he was scanning it for signs of a storm. "He saved your life. You're luckier than you deserve, and don't you ever forget it." He gave me one last look of sad, quiet disgust before he turned and walked away.

Me and Abel were married two weeks later, just like we planned. In my ma and daddy's eyes, he could do no wrong. They loved him 'til their dying day.

THE PROPOSAL

I expected Vitus an hour or so after dinner, like usual. Last night he was a little late. I started to worry, wondering what he might be up to. I went to the sliding glass door a couple of times to look out over the courtyard. Nothing but a few moths fluttering around the porch light.

No sooner did I sit back down than here he comes. He was carrying something, but when I went to let him in he put his hands behind his back so I couldn't see what it was. He bowed real low. "Good evening, madame," he said. "Tonight is very special."

He sat me down on the edge of the bed, pushed the armchairs to the side of the room, and spread a tablecloth on the floor in front of the TV. He set a big basket covered in colored paper and tied with ribbon right in the middle. He lit candles in glass holders, four of them, and set them on each corner of the cloth. Can you imagine? When he was done, he dimmed the lights. He got down on the floor there by the cloth and patted the ground next to him.

"Come down here, Woozy," he beckoned. "Come join me."

Don't think it was easy getting down on the floor, but after a lot of grunting and groaning, I managed. I felt so silly with my legs splayed out.

"It's a picnic. A surprise from me to you."

He got out his pocketknife and commenced to splitting the red cellophane on the basket. Inside was all manner of treats—three different kinds of sausage, two chunks of cheese, crackers, a packet of pistachios, dried apricots, chocolate-covered almonds, and more that I'm not remembering right now. It was all laid out in a bed of straw, and you could tell that none of it was cheap—even the basket, which was big enough to hold a good-size turkey.

I oohed and aahed and picked everything up and admired it. But that wasn't all, because Vitus winked at me and reached around the corner of the bed and brought out a bottle of wine! He pulled two plastic medicine cups out of his pocket, twisted the top off the bottle, and poured us each a cup.

I was nervous about drinking the wine with my meds and all, but Vitus clucked his tongue and shook his finger and raised his cup in the air. "To us!" he toasted, and there was just no way I couldn't drink to that, so I tipped back my plastic cup and took a slug. Not bad at all. He filled us up again, then he used his pocketknife to chunk up the sausage and cheese.

We had so much fun! The candles shimmered and shadows played on all the walls so you could almost forget where you were.

"Pretend we're on the banks of the Danube with the trees all in blossom!" Vitus said. He leaned over and kissed me on the cheek. "There are swans on the river," he whispered, gesturing toward the sliding glass door. "Sailing so white and graceful downstream."

My head was swimming. It was magic, like a dream. Every time I finished one snack, Vitus fixed me another. I liked the summer sausage and the darker cheese with the butterscotch flavor. I drank four or five medicine cups of wine. Wonderful as it all was, I couldn't get comfortable on the floor. My legs got pins and needles and my back started feeling like it would crack in half.

"This is a lot of fun, Vitus, but I need a chair," I finally told him.

He pushed my chair back to the middle of the room. I had a devil of a time getting up, but he helped me, and what a relief it was to have my butt on a seat and my feet on the floor. "Go on and get your chair," I told him. "That's enough now. Come on up here with me."

I was just getting situated with my crackers and wine when I saw Vitus down on all fours, crawling toward me! It scared the bejesus out of me!

"What's wrong?" I cried, sending all my snacks flying. Just my luck. During one of the happiest moments of my life, the man I loved decided to have a heart attack.

But Vitus only smiled. He raised up off his hands and walked the last few paces on his knees until he was right up next to me, close enough to lean against my legs. "I'm fine, Woozy," he said, beaming up at me. "I've got something to ask you."

Did my heart ever pound! I saw what was coming and it was like running flat out into a wall. I couldn't get a breath, couldn't do anything but gasp and put my hands over my ears. Don't ask me why, but I was scared to death of hearing what he was about to say.

"Cora darling, will you marry me?"

Well, it was right out of the movies. It just didn't seem *real*. I knew what I was supposed to say and what was supposed to happen next—I'd seen it a hundred times, read about it again and again. But, I have to tell you, at eighty-two you don't need those kinds of fairy tales, or at least *I* don't. I love Vitus with my heart and soul, but after everything what's happened in my life, I don't need to make a show of it.

I took his hand and pressed it between my own. "We don't have to get married, Vitus," I said while I stroked his arm. "It don't matter to me. It ain't like we're going to have kids or anything."

Damned if a little spot of red didn't bloom in each of his cheeks until his whole face was flaming. His hand went limp.

"Listen here, Vitus. I want us to be together. I want you and me to be in my house. To sit us down at that table in my kitchen and have our morning coffee. I want us to be able to walk out the back door and across the lawn and look over the fence there, down the hill toward the train tracks. It's a peaceful feeling, Vitus. And I want us to have our own bed, a brand-new mattress where nobody ever slept before that you and me can climb into at night and sleep side by side with the window open and the smell of jasmine coming in on the night air. Fresh sheets, all cotton. When I wake up at night, there you'll be.

We'll have the sweetest dreams, Vitus, and we'll live out our lives there, just you and me."

His eyes got moist. He blinked like words failed him. My heart filled to the brim. I leaned over to kiss him, but he brought his finger up to my lips. "I still want to get married," he said, quiet but stubborn. "I want to be husband and wife—legal, in the eyes of the world."

I'd hurt his feelings, the last thing I wanted. He's everything and more I've ever dreamed of in a man. I'd never have another chance like this. And if I don't marry him, somebody else will, and fast.

"I'm crazy about you, Vitus. If that's what you want, then let's get married."

He took me in his arms and my doubts disappeared like spit on an iron.

"What a moment this is, Vitus. I'll never forget it. But everything's moving so fast. This is a big change."

He finally got up off those poor knees of his and hobbled to the chair. When he'd sat down, he leaned closer to me and winked. "A big *adventure*. We'll have the time of our lives."

Well, this is just what I'd wanted, but now that it was happening, I was wary as a cat. Don't ask me why. Maybe I was afraid to be happy, afraid that once I let myself it'd be taken away and I'd be in a worse fix than ever. On the other hand, I didn't want to drive Vitus away. Let me tell you,

I was torn in two. "We haven't known each other very long," I said to gain time. "You sure you want to rush into this?"

"I've learned to listen to my heart, Cora. A long time ago I decided to say yes whenever life gives me a wonderful opportunity. Why waste time when we can be happy?" He leaned back in his chair and sized me up, top to bottom. "What is your heart telling you, my dear? To play it safe and stay here, in this room, for the rest of your life? Or to take a chance on love and make a life with me in our own home?"

Put that way, it was pretty clear. I wove my fingers through his and squeezed his hand in mine. "I know, Vitus. You're right." I was damn near crying from his little speech, and from the feeling welling up inside me. "All right, then. Let's do it. Let's get married. We'll show everyone. We'll have the last say."

NO MORE PUSSYFOOTING

I didn't waste no time announcing the news. This morning, the very next day after Vitus got down on his knees, I called Glenda. Maybe I wanted to lay it on the line before I could change my mind. Or maybe I was so happy I wanted to tell the world. You decide.

"Guess what!" I said the minute she answered. "I'm getting married to Vitus. You know, the man you don't like. I hope you change your mind about him because we're fixing to tie the knot."

The silence on the other end of the line like to deafened me. "You there?" I finally had to say. "Cat got your tongue?"

Glenda hemmed and hawed and choked and moaned and did everything short of chewing up her own tongue and spitting it back out before she made a human sound. "I just don't know what to say," she finally managed.

"Try congratulations. Or I'm so happy for you."

She *still* didn't say nothing. I imagined her sitting in her fancy house staring at the carpet.

"Well, I guess there's no point sitting here listening to empty space," I said. "I could do that on my own, right here in my room. If you can't think of anything to say, that's your business, but there's something I need to tell you. Those people need to move out of my house. We're planning on getting married pronto and we'll be ready to move in. If you don't tell them, I will. I need my things, too. All my belongings you packed up and stuck somewhere, I need those right away. Wherever you put them, I want them back. And Lulu. Get her back. I pine for that dog every day and I can't wait to see her again."

"That man is influencing you," Glenda said.

"That just burns me up! You act like I don't have no mind of my own! For months now, all I been telling you is I want to move back to my house. Nothing changed about that, Vitus or no Vitus."

She put on her patient, talking-to-an-old-coot voice. "It's not that easy, Mommy. We looked all over to find you the place where you're living now, and we were lucky to get you in. The people in your house are a young couple. They have a baby who's not even a year old—"

"What do I care about a damn baby?" I yelled. "That don't give them the right to stay there! I ain't senile and I ain't crippled! For all you know I could live twenty more years."

"Well, I don't know what to do," she said. "I need to talk to Dean and Kenny."

"Did the three of you do any paperwork behind my back? Get me committed or give yourself power over my business?"

"We *should* have. Dean wanted to."

"Did you do it?"

"No."

"Good! Then you don't have a leg to stand on." I laughed, long and loud. "You listen to me, Glenda. I don't want no trouble. We're family, and if we can do this without stepping on each other's feet, all the better. But if you spite me, I'm going to get me a lawyer and do what I need to do. It's a lot of trouble, and expensive to boot, but I'm not laying down for the way you're treating me. You understand?"

It hurt me to talk to my own daughter like that,

but my back was against the wall. Pretty soon I heard her blubbering. "I feel like I'm losing you," she sniffed.

"Why do you have to cry? Why can't you be glad for me?"

"Because we can't trust you to take care of yourself! You never have! All you ever did was pop those pills, stuff yourself with as much shitty food as you could get your hands on, lie in bed, and feel sorry for yourself! Daddy did everything for you and once he died you went straight down the toilet—or *farther* down than you already were, if that's possible! Why should you change now?"

That was more than I bargained for. I felt like I'd been cracked on the back of the head with a billy club. A million things crossed my mind, a million things I'd like to answer back, but my tongue lay on the floor of my mouth like a dead fish. The strength ran out of the arm that was holding the phone. I dropped the receiver back on the hook.

After a minute or two it rang again. I knew it was Glenda. I would have walked on broken glass before I'd give her the satisfaction of hearing my voice.

That settles it. I'm not pussyfooting around anymore. I'll do whatever I need to do to get my house back. I'm not going to worry about hurting anybody's feelings. They want to hear my story, they're going to hear it. I'm not sugarcoating nothing. They wonder why I done the things I did, why I behaved that way, I'm more than glad to tell them. I'm going to finish writing my story here in this book, then to hell with the lot of them.

BROWN INK

I was running a brush through my hair this morning when a knock came on the door that leads out to the hall. I'd only been up long enough to put on my robe, slip in my teeth, and wash my face. Nobody uses that hall door except Glenda, and I wasn't expecting a visit from her, so I wondered as I crossed the room who the hell would be coming round at that hour of the morning.

When I pulled open the door there was that woman, the boss lady I call Bigbutt, whose name is really Ms. Albert—at least that's what it says on her name tag. "Good morning," she said, real businesslike, and bustled right past me into the room.

I stood there in my robe while she helped herself to an armchair and pointed for me to sit down in the other one. I got flustered thinking maybe she was wise to me and Vitus and had come to break things up. Then it occurred to me that she might have got wind of my smoking and was going to tear me a new one over that. She had that makeup slathered on her face like always, and enough perfume to float a battleship. I could hardly draw a breath.

"I've come to talk to you about Mrs. Cipriano," she said.

That little spider monkey? I thought. But of course I didn't say it out loud. I just stared at Bigbutt, wondering what she had up her sleeve.

"She insists that the fountain pen is hers."

"I've had that pen for years and years," I said. I didn't let on that I didn't know when I got it or where it came from. "That woman was creeping around my room, hunkered down like an ax murderer while I was having a nap. She nabbed that pen right off my dresser and tried to stab me with it. If that wasn't enough, she made off with my quarters. What more do you need?"

Bigbutt smiled her fake smile. "Well, as a matter of fact, a few other residents have reported Mrs. Cipriano coming into their rooms uninvited. We searched her room and we *did* find a cache of quarters hidden in a vase."

"What about my twenties and my crystal? Did you find those?"

She shook her head. "Only the quarters. So we still don't know who's been taking things from residents' rooms." Her eyes wandered over my room like she might find some of it sitting on my dressing table, or hanging on my chair.

"My things have been disappearing since the day I got to this shithole," I said.

She hoisted her keister out of the chair and walked it over to the sliding glass door like she wanted me to get a good look at it. Her pants were like blue jeans, only dressier, with a high waist and little white flowers embroidered on the hip pockets—which is a lot of fancywork, believe me, because each pocket is big as a tablecloth. "We've contacted Mrs. Cipriano's family. Did you know she has seven children?"

Like I cared, though I was surprised that shriveled up little body could push out so many people. I pictured all her kids standing in a row with rings of bushy hair around their mouths, like their mother.

"In fact, one of her daughters is in my office right now." She spun her butt away from me and looked me in the eye. "In fact, I'd appreciate it if you came and had a word with us."

"I'm not dressed. I'm in no condition to see anybody," I sputtered.

"That's all right. We'll wait for you. Just come down when you're ready."

I DIDN'T SEE any use in objecting. Besides, I had nothing to hide. When I got to the office, there were three of them.

"This is Ms. Hoover," Bigbutt said. "She's the owner of The Palisades." She gestured to a woman who looked like the profile on a cameo, white as snow with done-up hair. Her nose was so high in the air it's a wonder she could find any oxygen to breathe.

"And this is Mrs. Carranza, Mrs. Cipriano's daughter."

That one didn't need an introduction. She was dark and quick like her mother, with the same nervous hands and sparkly eyes. She was in a right state, shaking in her chair and looking like she wanted to sink her fangs in my neck.

Bigbutt was putting on the dog for the owner. She pranced and puffed and patted her hair into place. "Mrs. Sledge, Mrs. Carranza here says that—"

Before she could say another word, that quivery daughter of the Spider Monkey gave a funny chirp and sprang out of her chair. She grabbed some papers off Bigbutt's desk and flew at me like a bat.

"What in God's name are you doing?" I asked, dodging out of her way. "What's that you're shoving in my face?"

"Letters!" she squealed. "Letters my mother's been writing me for years! They're written in *fountain* pen! You accused her of stealing! You made a lot of trouble, when all along that pen was hers! Here's the proof!"

She rattled the papers in my face.

"Your mother was creeping around my room

like a cat burglar. Those letters don't prove nothing. I expect there's more than one fountain pen in this world."

"Could you look more closely, Mrs. Sledge?" Bigbutt said. "Look carefully and see if you notice anything."

I didn't like the tone of her voice or the way she was looking at me. I took the pages. The sheets were thin, like what a Bible's printed on. There were no rules on the paper, but the writing went straight across, real regular, line after line. It was hard to picture the Spider Monkey copying all that out.

"Well, her handwriting's nice, I'll give her that," I said.

"What about the ink?" Bigbutt said. "The *ink,* Mrs. Sledge. It's *brown.* Brown ink."

A jolt went through me. A picture flashed in my head of that section I'd written in my book when I was practicing with the pen. Brown ink from here to kingdom come. I handed the pages back to the Spider Monkey's daughter like they stung my fingers.

"What color is the ink in the fountain pen you have?" Bigbutt asked.

"I don't recall," I stuttered. "Purple, I think." The three of them watched me like hawks. It occurred to me that I'd never even seen that pen in my top drawer until right after I got my second book. "Yes, that's it. Dark purple," I added. "Almost black."

313

Bigbutt's ears pricked up. The Spider Monkey's daughter clicked her fingernails. The ice queen owner glared. I can stare down a rattlesnake, and it's a good thing because all three sets of eyes were boring holes in me. I had no reason to feel like a criminal, but I started sweating bullets. Something was wrong, dead wrong, but I couldn't think with those vultures watching me. I hadn't meant to lie, but that's what had come out and now I had to stick with it. I wanted to get back to my room and hide that book and pen. If anybody asked about it, I'd say I lost it.

The owner, Mrs. Hoover, pushed off from where she'd been leaning against Bigbutt's desk and took a step toward me. "Are you all right, Mrs. Sledge?" she asked in her hoity-toity voice. "Is something wrong?"

I took a minute to look her over. She's making a lot of money off us old folks. I wondered what kind of person would get into that line of business, and what it was like to run a prison for people who'd got to the end of their lives and had everything they ever worked for taken away. Did she ever go up there to the second floor where those state men lived in that stink, using furniture that looked like it'd come through the Blitz? From the looks of the double-breasted jacket, fancy watch, and black pumps she was wearing, it was paying off. She must have seen on my face what was passing through my mind, because all of a sudden her face curled up like it'd been singed.

"Mrs. Sledge?" the ice queen repeated. "Is something wrong?"

"I'm not feeling so good. I need to lie down."

Truth is, I needed to hightail it out of there. Not only were those three witches getting under my skin, but the breakfast hour was nearly over, and I was hungry enough to gnaw the balls off a bull. I lit out of there like lightning. If anybody would have told me that I'd be covering ground the way I am now, I would have laughed in their face. But I sprinted down to that dining room without hardly noticing, when before I felt like I was trudging halfway around the world dragging a boulder behind me. By the time I got there, most everybody had cleared out. Some of the droolers were waiting to be wheeled back to their rooms. The busboys were going around with plastic buckets cleaning up the dirty dishes, and a few lost souls were still sitting at their tables, finishing up the last scraps.

My heart sunk. Vitus's table was empty. *My* table was a different story, though. Poison Ivy and Carolyn were sitting down, and four or five other biddies were clustered round, clucking away.

"Here she is," Ivy said the minute she saw me.

I don't know why I never noticed it before, but for the first time I realized her hair is a *wig!* That damn little helmet of hers had slipped forward so it almost covered her eyes, while in the back a patch of her poor old skull showed, sporting a few straggly gray hairs like a mangy dog. She was trembling.

"What's wrong?" I asked. "What's going on?"

Carolyn Robertson's wheelchair was right next to me. "She got robbed," she whispered. "Somebody took all her jewelry."

Some of the uppity women from Ivy's exercise class turned on me like a pack of dogs, but knowing that Ivy wore a wig gave me some confidence. At least I got my own hair.

"They walked right into my room and took everything!" Ivy wailed. "It's worth *thousands* of dollars! *Tens* of thousands!"

"That's too bad," I said. "But don't look at me." A plate of buttered toast was sitting there, untouched. "Anybody mind if I eat this?" I helped myself to a slice.

Ivy's gang tried to calm her down. I couldn't keep my eyes off her poor scrawny neck where the wig rode up. It looked like a plucked chicken. The toast was cold and soggy, but I was fit to be tied, so I started in on the second slice.

"My friend had some of his clothes stolen last week," Carolyn said.

Ivy shut up her bellyaching long enough to stare daggers at Carolyn. "That's hardly the same thing. This was *heirloom* jewelry. It's priceless."

Carolyn shrugged. She turned her chair around and wheeled off.

I thought it would be a good time to make my get-away, too, so I grabbed those last two pieces of toast and came back here. I sat right down and wrote this, start to finish, while it was all fresh in my mind. Three whole hours! Now I got to hurry up and get out of here, or I'm going to miss lunch, too.

ALICE

Some kind of trouble out in the hall woke me up. Nurses were yelling, then somebody was running, then there was a lot of banging around—doors slamming and equipment rattling. They must have called the paramedics, because pretty soon the sirens came blaring, and a bunch of feet rushing in, and something rolling, like a gurney. And moans and pleading, and—oh my God, it was like someone being led away to the gallows.

After that I laid here listening into the dark for hours with my eyes open, imagining all kinds of things and feeling my blood run chilly through my veins. I couldn't sleep for the life of me. My heart kept pounding and I couldn't keep my legs still. So finally I got up and turned on the light, and now here I sit, at three o'clock in the morning, in my armchair with the throw over my knees and my book in my lap.

So I'll get on with my story.

● ● ●

TURNED OUT WE never did have to live with that sister of Abel's. We got married on December 12, 1931. One of his brothers had gone up to Pontiac, Michigan, and got a job in the GM factory. Come up here, there's work, he told Abel. We had us our last Christmas at home, then we headed up on the train with nothing but one big suitcase apiece. Abel got a job the day after we got there, wet-sanding car doors on the factory floor. We rented a one-bedroom apartment in a fourplex close to downtown. A brick building. We was up top, with a rickety little porch off the kitchen that looked down on the roofs of the warehouses and shops.

White, white, white. There was nothing but snow and ice when we got there in the dead of winter. I'd never been in cold like that, or seen cities like those up North—big, hard cities hunkered down by lakes and rivers. I was only seventeen years old, and there I was married to a man I hardly knew, pregnant with another man's baby, living in a city I'd never seen the likes of in my life. I looked out on those white fields and roofs, that open gray sky and the bare branches of those leafless trees and said, This is your blank slate, Cora. This is your new life, where nobody knows you from Adam.

Homesick as I was, much as I woke up every morning craving the smells of my own house, the sounds of my family moving around with their morning routines, the back door slamming and the smoke from the stove, my ma standing in the open door, looking off across the yard as she drank her coffee, part of me felt like I was just waking up and looking around, seeing the world for the first time. I longed for everything about Neosho—the cottonwoods that grew down by the water, the smell of alfalfa in the evenings, the creek where I could sink up to my ears and feel the current whiffling past my legs—but I was also relieved to be away from everyone who knew me, from those eyes that would judge and condemn me. I thanked God for those hundreds of miles between me and where I started out, and felt free in a way I'd never imagined. Alone there in Pontiac with Abel, I started to feel the wholeness of myself, who I was and who I might be. I finally could do what I damn well pleased. At least it seemed that way, right at the first.

The spring thaw came and things started poking up through the snow. A curb, a mailbox, a hedge. Like the place was showing itself to me, little by little. Every day was something new, a stretch of sidewalk or a big rock down at the corner, buds coming on the trees and the rain washing away the dirty snow. The city grew curves and lines. It got color. And my baby was growing, too, getting a mind of its own, making its presence known. Everything was opening up, getting fuller.

And Abel. Well, I started getting attached to

that donkey's ass. *My husband,* I said to women in the store, to the landlady who came around to collect our rent. I was proud to have a man who was working, I'll tell you that, what with so many people starving, down and out with no place to go. I tried so hard to love him. I made a list in my head of everything he'd done for me, all the ways he took care of me. I practiced getting excited when he came home from work, smiled up at him, kissed him real sincere when he walked in the door. I cooked for him, kept that crooked little apartment real nice, made curtains, put new paper on the cupboard shelves, cleaned around the baseboards. I got myself up special if we had a night out.

Other women looked at him, then looked at me like I was lucky. Wishing *they* had it so good. Maybe they wondered how a fat woman like me could snag such a thin, handsome man. So I busted ass, tended to every little thing, made him happy in bed at night. And oh, was he happy. Hard as he worked, tired as he was when he came home at night, that man was glowing. I almost envied him. He was in love. And me, I did my best.

I couldn't make myself fall in love, but I got to liking him, maybe even loving him. I appreciated how strong he was, how he carried on no matter what, how he'd die before he'd give up. He was good-natured as could be, woke up with a smile on his face every day. He never complained, and he'd do anything for me. Yes, despite everything that had happened, I was number one on his list. He didn't breathe a word about Edward, or the baby not being his, or how I'd double-crossed him.

We had us some fun, me and him. All day he squatted down in the noise and dust, wet-sanding that metal. His hands were scuffed and raw. He was hollow eyed by the time he got home, all done in. He threw himself down flat-out beat on the divan and had a beer, then we'd have dinner, and by the time it was over he was better, ready to go downstairs and play cards with the young couple who lived below us, or to go out walking, looking in the shop windows. A couple times we went dancing, or out to the pictures.

Abel took to that place just like I did. He wouldn't say, but I think he was glad to be away from his family, too. All them brothers and cousins and uncles living back in those hollers, all of them ignorant as mules grubbing their living out of the dirt, mucking around in the mud one way or the other, either the mines or some farm, just like their daddies and their daddies before them. That's what he had to look forward to, and he'd gotten away.

Everybody was in the same boat. They'd swarmed there from all over the country to work in the factories. There was Polacks, Italians, and

Irish, all those Catholics who wore hankies on their heads when they went to church. There was colored people by the droves living over on the other side of town, and all manner of people we'd never seen the likes of in our lives.

I guess they hadn't seen nobody like us, either, because every time I opened my mouth, somebody's head would snap around, and they'd ask, "Where you from?" I got so tired of that question. If I acted like I didn't know what they were talking about, they said your *accent,* the way you *talk.* They looked at me like they were surprised I had shoes on my feet, that I could read a street sign or eat with a knife and fork. Abel got it, too. People in the shops and banks and barbershop treated us like backwoods hillbillies who couldn't write our own names. That was a tie we had, me and Abel, something that kept us close. We were each other's little piece of home.

Things were so new and so much was happening, I started to forget about Edward. Only when I dreamed about him could I remember the feeling he gave me, how strong and joyful it was. Then I'd wake up raw, longing again to see his face, to feel him standing next to me. But those dreams got fewer and farther between. Things might not have been the way I'd dreamed of, but all in all it was a happy time.

And there was my baby I was waiting on, that precious little face I longed to see. *Alice.* I haven't let myself say that name for so long, much less write it. Shaping it, writing the mountain of that first letter, lifts the corner on a whole world of sorrow.

ALICE WAS BORN May 20, 1932. An easy birth and a perfect baby. Women stopped me on the streets to exclaim at her. Even men said, Isn't she a pretty one? Men, you know, don't usually notice girls 'til they're older. She was a quiet baby, content and calm. She grinned every time you looked at her, and laughed out loud if you clapped your hands.

She was six months old on November 15, 1932, exactly one week after Roosevelt was elected president. Tuesday, the most run-of-the-mill day of the week. Not laundry day, or prayer-meeting day, or market day, or the Sabbath. Tuesday is the day you're most likely to forget about, the day you don't expect anything to happen. I'll never forget how ordinary that day felt. You'd think you'd know, that you'd wake up with a bad feeling, but I was heedless as the day is long, going about my business without a care in the world.

It was the first fall we'd spent in Pontiac, and I didn't know what to expect. People from around those parts remarked on how funny the weather was, frost and freeze one day, warm as summer the next. The morning before there'd been an icy crust on the porch when I went down to hang the clothes on the line behind the building. I nearly slipped on my ass. But that day, Tuesday, the sun came out bright and warm, melting everything. Water dripped from the corner of the roof, beating a hollow in the mud below. By eleven o'clock, the sidewalks were steaming.

That's when I put her down for a nap.

We lived in a square brick building that had four little apartments, two on top and two on the bottom. We were on top, just a living room, a kitchen with barely enough room for a table, a bathroom with beige tile, and a bedroom that looked out over the backyard, which was muddy right then, the grass worn off except around the edges. A boiler in the basement heated the water and ran the radiators. They clanked and banged like crazy, and kept it too warm in there, so we had to leave a window open, even in winter.

The bedroom was only big enough for our bed, a dresser, and the crib squeezed in the corner by the closet where we hung our clothes. I had just given Alice a bath in the kitchen sink. She kicked her fat legs and splashed with her hands, giggled when the water hit her in the face. What a doll. I loved her like life itself, couldn't wait to see her each and every morning, marveled that God had seen fit to give her to me, to fill me with such joy. I loved the way she clung to me when I lifted her out of the sink, her skin so soft and her hair smelling so good. I carried her to the crib, diapered and dressed her. That day, that Tuesday, I looked forward to her going to sleep because I was tired myself. She still wasn't sleeping through the night. I wanted to go in the living room and lie down on the divan with a magazine.

I opened the bedroom window a crack to let in some fresh air, then I leaned over the side of the crib and rubbed Alice's belly. She liked that while she was falling asleep; it comforted her. She had the sweetest way of holding onto your hand while you did it, her little fingers caressing and squeezing yours while she looked up in your eyes.

She always fought sleep, jerked herself awake just before she went under. She didn't want to miss anything. I'd have to stroke her belly again, so tight and firm in her gown, 'til finally her eyes drooped closed and stayed shut. I tiptoed out, let down the blind in the living room, and stretched out in the breeze from the window. I don't think I read two words of that magazine before I fell asleep.

It feels so strange to write this down. To pick out the words and set them down next to each other so they make the sentences that tell the story of what happened, when all these years I've only seen it in pictures, only seen myself wake up from that nap, open my eyes, blink at the sun coming through the blind, smack my lips a few times, and sit up, looking at the white face of the metal clock that Abel wound every night before he went to bed and set on the little table beside the door where he put his keys and the change from his pocket when he came home from work. It was just before noon. I've seen myself, so many times, straighten my hair and pull down my dress, get up off that divan and walk into the kitchen for a drink of water. Not knowing. Not having the faintest idea.

Do you know how I despise myself when I picture me standing there looking out the window over the sink, when I lift that glass of water to my filthy lips? A bloated, ignorant sow slopping herself without a care in the world. What if I wouldn't have drank that water before I walked into the other room? What if I would have checked, just once, instead of sleeping like a lump of lard on the divan? But no, I drank that water, then I walked to the icebox. For shame, I lifted the tinfoil off the roast left over from the night before and pinched me off a hunk of meat, the fat congealed white and waxy over it. I loaded it in my mouth and chewed. I helped myself to a few more bites. Even that wasn't enough for me, so I pried loose a red potato stuck in the fat on the bottom of the pan. I stuffed that in my fat mouth, too, crammed it into that disgusting hole in my face while I stood there in front of the icebox, chomping like a cow. I've watched myself hundreds of times in my mind, and every time it nauseates me, fills me with such disgust that I wish I could come up those rickety back stairs to the kitchen, burst through the back door, and stab myself over and over with a butcher knife.

I went over to the sink, washed the grease off my hands, and dried them on the dish towel. I wandered back into the living room and folded the clothes I'd brought in off the line earlier that morning. I rolled Abel's socks into balls, smoothed out his undershirts on the coffee table, and folded them neat as the packages you buy at the store.

Well, my goodness, I thought to myself. Alice is having a good long nap today.

I wasn't the least bit uneasy. Much as I loved her, the peace and quiet was nice. So many times I've wondered, What if I hadn't gone down to check the mail? What if—instead of taking my time wandering down to the mailbox at the curb, instead of looking up and down the street, sniffing the air, and watching the women standing at the bread truck parked down on the corner—I would have gone into the bedroom and checked on her. Leaned over the crib, picked her up. One minute could have made all the difference.

So when I see myself dawdle on the stairs going back up, taking a minute to squint into the kitchen of the apartment downstairs, wiping my feet a few extra times on the mat on the top landing, I want to yell, Hurry up, you stupid bitch! Go in there and look! What on earth is wrong with you? It's torture to watch the movie of myself thumbing through the mail, slitting open an envelope, and sitting my fat ass down on the couch to read. The kind of movie where the train gets closer while someone's on the tracks, but there's not a damn thing you can do but cover your eyes. I almost go crazy thinking back, seeing myself those last few minutes before my life changed forever. It's agony watching as I wet my finger on my tongue to turn a page, as I lift my head to look out the window at the maple tree that had dropped all but a few of its leaves.

Well, let's go see if she's waking up, I thought, still ignorant as a stump.

I can't let go of the moment when I walked into the deathly stillness of that room. The feeling of panic is still in my body, lodged in my joints and tissue like a disease. Yes, I finally figured out that something was wrong. Oh, I knew the minute I set foot in there. I felt the angel of death, as if its wings had left a smell, a flutter in the air. A hum that was still thick and fresh. I ran to that crib and picked Alice up, plucked her from under her blanket and held her up, saw her head flop over to the side, saw the color of her face, like the livid sky before a thunderstorm.

I couldn't even scream. My breath stopped at the hollow of my throat. I made an animal sound, the croak a pig makes when you slit its throat, the strangled gurgle of blocked pipes. I shook her, shook her to wake her up, shook her so hard her head snapped back and forth, shook her 'til my own teeth rattled, shook her until I knocked something loose inside me, my own crying and screaming, and I bawled, *No! No! No!* because in my head I was thinking, This is not my baby. This cannot be my baby. This could *not* have happened to my baby, not *my* baby, not Alice.

I put her up over my shoulder and pounded her back, praying that she'd stir, cough, sputter, raise her head. She was so close to being there alive in that room, so close. If I wanted it bad enough, it would happen, she would come back, so I pounded, pounded and prayed, found my voice and screamed for her to come back, to wake up, screamed her name and called on Jesus, yelled for him to help me, to help me oh please.

When she didn't move, I squeezed her to me like I wanted to press her into my own flesh, like I wanted to meld the two of us into a living statue, a block that would harden together and never move again. I felt her little muscles, her perfect bones and flesh, and I just could not believe, *could not believe* that such a thing was possible, much less that it was happening, had happened, that it was happening to me right then, right that minute, and that I was still alive, standing there holding my baby, my little Alice, who was dead.

Do you know how many questions I've asked myself? Why she had to die, why I couldn't keep her safe, why she had to be born in the first place. Was there a reason? Did someone plan it? Why did it have to be Alice, rather than any other baby in the world—the Rasmussens' down the street, who was born blind, or the Sheas', who already had eight and let them run wild in the streets all hours of the day and night, dirty as beggars.

But the biggest question, the one I've asked myself every day since she died, is whether it was my fault. Whether I caused it, the way I tried to get rid of her, tried everything I could think of— drank that vinegar and douched with it, too. Threw myself down Indian Hill, bounced all the way to the bottom. All the schemes I had, the thoughts that crossed my mind, shameful things I can't even mention. I wanted her dead. I torture myself with that, think of the times I prayed for her to go away.

Not a day has passed that I haven't seen myself standing in that room with Alice clasped to my chest like that. Part of me stayed there, never left. Never went howling out of the room with her still pressed against me, never ran screaming to pound on the door of the next-door neighbor, who pried Alice out of my arms and laid her on her kitchen table and, when she saw there was nothing she could do, ran and got the neighbor downstairs to go fetch a doctor. The part of me who stayed in that room never saw the doctor take one look at Alice and turn to me, seeing that *I* was the only one who needed looking after. He guided me back to my apartment, where he put me to bed and stayed with me until someone went and fetched Abel from the factory.

I can't get past that picture. I see it like somebody else is frozen in that pose: a big woman with the limp body of a baby pressed against her, standing in the hot bedroom of a rented apartment in a cold city far from her home. All those things that came later—the bleak, nightmare weeks that followed, and that winter I spent in bed, sleeping as much as I could, waking only to eat and use the bathroom, to moan and roll over and sleep again—seem to have happened to half a person, the woman I came to be. Having more kids, moving out here to California, all the Christmases and heartbreaks and, yes, even the joys I've had since then, don't keep me from craning my neck around and looking back at that same old scene, like maybe I'll see it different this time. Maybe this time she'd cough, and stir, and draw another breath. Those maybes, along with the what-ifs, won't leave me alone. To this day, I open my eyes every morning and hope that none of it really happened.

THE GHOST

I had another restless night, and the strangest morning.

I don't know what time it was, long after midnight, when the raccoons started raising hell in the Dumpster outside my window. They banged on the metal, squabbled and fought and caterwauled like banshees. It must have been three o'clock when I finally drifted off, and that's when the worst started. Writing about Alice plunks me right down in the middle of those tormented times. Those memories prey on me, lay in wait for me to fall asleep so they can get busy spinning out a nightmare.

I dreamed I was reading the newspaper, turning over the pages and looking at the photographs. "Oh, look! Here's Alice!" I said to Abel, who was stretched out on the couch like always. Sure enough, there she was, all grown. Turns out she'd never really died. I just *thought* she had, so we buried her and she grew up without me knowing it, and made a life of her own separate from me. Having her grow up without me felt worse than her being dead, and I started bawling, crying so the tears sprayed like a fountain on the carpet around my armchair.

"Now look what you've done," Abel said. "That rug's going to mildew and stink to high heaven."

Then came the same dream that's tormented me for decades. "Oh, lookee here, what's that?" I say to Abel. I see a bundle, something covered with a blanket, or a newspaper, or dried leaves—beside the road, in the tool shed, or at the back of a closet. I lift up the cover even though I know I shouldn't, even though the part of me that knows this dream so well is hollering, Don't you lift that cover up now, you'll be sorry! But I go over and lift up the edge of the blanket and there is Alice, half dead or taken apart by some animal or starving or struggling for breath, but always deformed and frightful, looking up at me with eyes that are feverish and in pain, eyes that aren't human. I started up from that dream feeling like I couldn't contain the terror, like if I had to live with it for more than a minute or two I'd have to do myself in.

Well, I got up and peed. Drank me a glass of water. I walked over to the window by the bed and watched the sky, which was lit a murky orange from the fog. I was afraid to go back to sleep, so I sat in the armchair by the TV. I tried to take my mind off the dream by thinking of Vitus, and how he was going to straighten everything out so we could be together. But my mind was too much in the past with all those old hurts that go so deep—my ma and daddy and sisters, and Abel and Alice, and all those places I lived and things I suffered. When I got too cold to sit there anymore, I got back in bed and said a little prayer for God to ease my mind. For the millionth time I told Him I was sorry, and I begged Him to lift the burden from my back.

When I could hear the traffic start up, I knew it wouldn't be long before morning. I was completely done in, so tired that I drifted off to sleep again and didn't wake up 'til way after nine o'clock when the light was streaming through the window over my bed making the blankets hot, and the delivery trucks were spitting diesel fumes at the loading dock, and the gardener with a leaf blower was making a ruckus out in the courtyard.

I was weak from all those dreams, shaky and light-headed. My pillow was wet—whether from crying or drooling or sweating, I can't say—but it was irksome, so I flipped it over and hoped for some relief. By that time the whole world was awake and moving around: the cleaners coming down the halls with their carts, the boy with the trays for those that eat in their rooms, the lunatics singing and shouting in the hall, and the TVs blasting upstairs. I felt empty of everything, a husk rattling in the bed. I wished one of them girls would come in here and vacuum me up along with the flakes of dry skin and pussy hair on the floor so I'd be lost with the lint balls and the cobwebs.

I had no choice but to open my eyes. The haggard sky was framed by those flouncy flowered curtains that Glenda bought to match the bed-spread. My eyes fixed where the curtains pucker just under the curtain rod, and there was Abel's head. That's right. Just his face with no body attached, looking down at me like the Wizard of Oz. You might think this part was a dream, too, but you'd be wrong. It was the real thing, I swear. I could see the flower pattern of the curtains through his skin, so I knew he was a ghost.

I wasn't scared, not in the least. After those terrible dreams, I was glad to see a familiar face. Abel looked to be in a good mood. He nodded and gave me a friendly smile, showing his little yellow teeth. I could tell, without him saying a word, that he'd come to take care of me.

"I have had the most hellacious night, Abel. I have been afflicted and tormented past my wits' end."

He just nodded. Maybe he can't talk with the state he's in, maybe he can only listen. Or maybe he don't want to. It was hard to make out the expression on his face with the pattern in those curtains. But I felt such comfort having him there, seeing his face after all that time.

"What have you been up to?" I asked with a chuckle. "Where you been?"

His face got fainter and fainter until I couldn't make it out no more, but it left me feeling better, almost like I had a good night's sleep.

PAPERWORK

After the grilling I got from Bigbutt and her henchmen, I couldn't quit worrying about that fountain pen and the brown ink I'd used in my book. I got scared that someone would find them in my room when I was gone, then they'd think I stole that pen and everything else, too. I was so spooked at dinner last night that I hotfooted it back here in a panic, determined to hide them.

I love the look of these books, every damn page covered with *my* writing that *I* labored over sitting alone here in this room, casting my mind back to all them places, recalling things I didn't know I remembered. The books are thicker when I fill them than they are when they're brand-new. The pages suck up my life and get fat with my thoughts. Trouble is, this place is small. There's nowhere to hide anything. It would kill me to get rid of these things, but I was in such a state about getting caught red-handed that I was ready to run out there to the loading dock and pitch the pen and the second book, where I'd used the fountain pen, over the side of the Dumpster.

That's when Abel piped up. "Don't you dare, Toad," he said. "Just take that book and slip it under the rug there by the bed. Nobody'll find it. Get you some Scotch tape and stick the pen on the underside of your nightstand."

That's just what I did. You can't see the book at all under the rug, and no one would think to look under the nightstand for the pen.

"Thanks, you old son of a bitch," I said. "You always come through in a pinch."

NO SOONER HAD I finished than here comes Vitus. I hadn't seen him for a few days, which had been bothering me, sure as shit. He was in such a hurry his lips barely scuffed my cheek when he came through the door.

"I'm sorry I haven't been to see you, Cora," he said. "But I've been busy, very busy." He was excited the way men get when they have an idea in their head. "Wait until you see this. Look, Cora. It's the application for our marriage license." He grinned from ear to ear. "Can you believe it? I have it all right here."

He pulled my little lamp table over between the two armchairs and spread the papers out. "We just fill these papers out and take them in to the city clerk. That's it! Then we can get married."

"Well, I'll be. Where'd you get these? How'd you know what to do?"

He leaned back in the chair and looked real proud of himself. "The computer, it's all right there. My buddy ran them out for me. You just go to the computer and get everything you need."

"What buddy? I never heard you talk about no buddy."

"Cora!" he said, shaking his head. He touched my knee. "My friend Bruno. He's from my own country. He is a wizard with the computer. He got us everything we need. Here, take a look."

He handed me the papers. It wasn't complicated. They just wanted to know the usual stuff— my name and birthday and Social Security number, the place where my ma and daddy were born, and when Abel died.

"Don't we have to get blood tests?" I asked.

Vitus grinned. "No, my darling. Not in California. You just need your ID and the death certificate from . . . from your, uh—"

"From Abel?" I helped him out.

"Yes, your first husband. You need to prove you're no longer married to him."

"Hard to be married to a dead man. What about you?"

"All my paperwork is in order. I have everything I need."

I looked at him, trying to see him like a regular man, like a man I was seeing on the street for the first time. What would I think if love hadn't changed my heart, if the way he turned his head or pursed his lips didn't touch something deep inside me? I couldn't tell. All I saw was the love of my life, a man like no other.

"What's wrong?" Vitus said. "What's going on in that mind of yours?"

He notices everything.

I wavered. I wanted to tell him about Bigbutt and the pen, but it seemed puny next to what we were talking about now. And something else was bothering me, but I didn't know if I could say it. I gave myself a little talking-to, saying this man is going to be your husband, you better open up your heart to him.

"What, Woozy? Tell me."

"Let me ask you something." I cleared my throat and wiped my hands on my thighs, trying to get up my courage. "Don't get mad now, I just gotta ask."

"Go on."

"Well, are you a citizen here? Is everything aboveboard?"

He studied me just as close as I'd studied him. I get the flutters when his eyes are on me. I got to pat my hair and tug down my blouse to make sure everything's in place.

"What are you asking me, Cora?"

"Well, I read about people who get married just to stay in the country. That's not what you're doing, is it?"

"Is that what you think, Cora? Do you think I could do something like that?" He didn't yell, or even raise his voice, but his tone made me grab tight to the arms of my chair. "It doesn't say much about how you feel about me, Cora, and—forgive me—but it doesn't say much about your idea of yourself, either. This is below you, Cora. It really is."

I couldn't help myself. Hard as it was, much as it hurt, I kept on. "I need to hear it, Vitus. I need you to say it."

"I am a citizen of the United States."

"I'm sorry, sugar. I just had to ask. I feel better now. I'm so used to things going wrong, I think something's amiss if they're going right. I don't know why I have so many doubts when all my dreams are about to come true."

He waved his hand. "It's all right. I want to put your mind at rest. Is there anything else you want to ask me?"

I looked him over. Everything seemed right. Still, coldhearted as it seemed, I had to ask. "And when's your money coming in? When is your nephew going to give it to you?"

You know, he didn't turn a hair. He just nodded and said, "I don't blame you for wondering, Woozy. I'd do the same if I were in your place. My lawyer is in the process of drawing up the paperwork right now. Soon as that's finished, my nephew will sign. I have his word on it. So I'd say in three or four weeks everything will be set. Anything else?"

I shook my head. "We got a problem, though. I told my daughter she needs to get those people out of my house, but I might as well have been talking to a wall."

"Hmm." Vitus rubbed his chin. "Do you have any ideas what we should do?"

"I don't know the first thing about those people living in my house. Not their names or how to get in touch with them. I wouldn't know how to go about getting them out."

"Right," Vitus said. He leaned toward me and put his elbows on his knees. "Well, as I see it, the easiest thing would be if your children cooperated. They must have the rent agreement, or whatever it is. It would save us a lot of trouble if they dealt with the renters."

"Well, I could talk to them again and let them know I mean business. My daughter told me they haven't done anything legal to take things away from me. Seems like I still got a right to my house."

"You sure do. If your kids make trouble, we'll have to play hardball. Step in and take some measures. Let's give them a chance to do the right thing."

"All right. I'll talk to them. Too bad they're not kids anymore." I laughed. "Back then I could have whupped their little asses into shape."

Vitus chuckled, then he looked deep into my eyes. "I so want to be with you. I can't wait to be married to you. I don't want to waste one day that I could spend at your side."

No one has ever said anything like that to me before. I choked up, but I didn't want to let on. My heart felt like it was hooked in to his.

"All right, darling," he went on. "Here's how it

works. After we fill out these papers we have to take them to the city clerk. You're supposed to file them in person, but because it's hard for you to get around, they'll let us mail them in. Once they're filed, we have ninety days to have the ceremony."

"You sure know your stuff. But what about getting married? How're we supposed to do that? Do we go to a church? Or a justice of the peace? Are we going to invite people and wear fancy clothes and dance and eat cake? And how're we supposed to get wherever we're going?"

Being locked up here, I'd started thinking it's impossible to get out. I never imagined strolling out on my own and doing whatever I wanted. But looking at Vitus smiling at me, his head tipped to the side and his eyes twinkling, made me feel like someone had opened a gate, and on the other side was the whole world. All I had to do was walk through.

"We can do whatever we want, Cora. My friend Bruno will take us where we decide to go. He has a car."

"Well, what's in it for him?"

"He's a very good friend of mine, Cora. He lives here in town and he wants to help us. But guess what else." He took my hand and stroked it ever so gently. "There's an easier way. We don't need a clergyman, or a justice of the peace, or anybody like that. All we need is someone who's certified to marry us, and we can do it anywhere. Right here in your room if we want."

"Here? With this ugly hook rug and the flowered comforter I hate? Right here at the foot of my bed, with the television and the toilet not ten feet away?"

"Or out in the courtyard, if you want, where we first met. With the birds singing."

"I've never heard of such a thing. And who are we supposed to get to come in here and marry us?"

"Bruno! He's certified to perform the ceremony. Anyone can be a witness. We can even ask someone who works here—one of the boys who clean up the dining room, perhaps?"

"Bruno! Bruno! Bruno!" I snatched my hand away from him. "This isn't right!"

"Cora, my dear," Vitus said in a soothing voice. He started stroking my hand again. "Settle down, my love. Listen, it doesn't matter. Whatever you want, that's what we'll do. This is all just paperwork, just a technicality. All that matters is that we'll be together. We'll be protected, so that nobody can come between us."

I couldn't go no further. My nerves were in tatters. Much as I tried not to, I started crying. "Why do we have to do all this when all I want is to go back to my house? All I want is to have breakfast with you and sleep in the same bed! I don't need all this! It's too much trouble!"

Vitus went to the bathroom to get me some toilet paper. He took my hand and pulled me out of the chair. Gently, so gently. "Come here, darling," he said, leading me over to the bed. "Come here and lie down." He helped me up on the bed, took off my shoes, fixed the pillows under me, and—when I was settled on my side—slipped off his own shoes and got up there beside me.

I lay there sniffling. It troubled me that all the time I was married to Abel, he took care of everything. When he died, my kids took over. Now here I was, handing the reins over to Vitus.

He snuggled up against my back and put his arm around my waist. Lord, it felt so good. He wormed his stocking feet under mine and whispered in my ear, "Let's feel your feet, Woozy. I think they're getting cold." He pulled me a little closer. "Are you getting cold feet, darling? Have you changed your mind about me?"

It was the most delicious feeling having him cuddled up behind me like that, whispering in my ear. I've thought long and hard about the way I acted in bed with him before, and I've decided not to bother him about the sex anymore. There's plenty of time for that later. I won't say we're like brother and sister, but we're not exactly rutting. He stroked my hair and touched the back of my neck with his lips. I'm telling you, there's nothing in the world like it. All the time he sweet-talked me, little whisperings and sighs and baby talk.

Until you've been treated like that, you don't know the meaning of love.

"Don't worry, my dear, I'll take care of everything," he whispered. "It's just busywork, papers and such. It's nothing, you'll see." His lips moved against my ear. "If you want, there's a little chapel where they'll marry us. It's downtown, near the bus station. We don't even have to make an appointment. We just drop in and it only takes a few minutes. Soon as our paperwork is done, we can stop by there and make it official."

He makes me feel so good. I snuggled up against him. He's got a lot more meat on his bones than Abel did. I didn't say a word, just laid there listening to the sound of his voice. He even sang a little, a beautiful song in his own language. It was heaven to be comforted like that, so loving and soft.

I imagined touching the porcelain light switches in my house again. Hearing Lulu coming down the hall toward me, her toenails clicking. It's been less than a year since I lived there, but it seems like forever. So much has happened, I feel like a different person than when I left. I'm going to feel like I'm seeing a long-lost friend when I walk through that door.

The last thing I remember before I drifted off to sleep was telling myself, You just go whole hog, Cora Sledge. Throw caution to the wind. Go for broke.

I woke up a few hours later still laying on top of the blankets wearing all my clothes. Vitus was gone. The bedside lamp was on. There was a note on the pillow next to me. *Will you marry me on October 25?* it said. *It's a Friday, Cora. Our lucky day.*

WHEN I WENT to bed, I called out to those flouncy curtains, "Come on out here, Abel. I need to talk to you."

I didn't see his head up there where it was before, but I started talking anyway, asking him what he thought I should do, reminding him how the kids had put me here against my will and how I'd wanted to die, but now things had taken a turn for the better, on account of Vitus and how I got myself together, giving up all those pills and losing weight and walking around on my own two feet. Pretty soon there he was, up in the flounces at the top of the curtain.

"I hope you don't mind, Abel," I told him. "Me going with another man and all. I hope you don't hold it against me, taking him into the house you and me lived in all those years. You're dead, after all. And I was faithful as a hound the whole time we were together. You know it's true."

Well, he gave me to understand that those things don't matter to him anymore, which is what I thought in the first place. Jealousy and who's married to who—he's got bigger fish to fry in heaven, and he loves me in a whole other way than when we were husband and wife.

It's not like he *talked*. I just saw his face and knew exactly what he wanted to tell me. Don't ask me how, but his meaning couldn't be clearer if I heard every word with my own ears. After a little bit his face started fading until he was gone, and I was left laying there in bed, looking up at the window but feeling real peaceful, like—one way or another—everything was going to work out. I drifted off to sleep knowing that Abel didn't take no offense at me and Vitus, that he was guiding me from above.

THE INTERROGATION

Sunday morning my kids showed up like the Gestapo.

I don't like the church services here, which are what they call *nondenominational*. That means it's a mishmash of a lot of religions, with a preacher who wears a collar like a Catholic and works down at the drunk shelter during the week. It's a free-for-all, with the lunatics from B Wing herded into a row of folding chairs, the droolers parked in the back, and old ladies coming out of the woodwork to warble and pray. There's so much rigmarole and shifting around and moaning and singing, you think you've already died and gone to hell. It doesn't have much to do with

Jesus, I'll tell you. So on Sundays I just take my folding chair and sit outside my door by the courtyard. I look at the plants and birds and pray a little. That's my church.

That's what I was doing yesterday when I see three people coming down the walkway. I didn't pay them much mind because a lot of people have visitors on Sunday. I didn't recognize them until they were right up next to me.

"My goodness, don't you know your own kids?" Dean said, before he bent over and kissed me.

"Well, I wasn't expecting you."

"What're you doing sitting out here all by yourself?" he asked.

"I'm just biding my time, taking in the sun." I looked him up and down. "My God, Dean. How much weight have you put on?"

I'd say he'd gained about thirty pounds since the last time I saw him. His face was puffy and he had on them khaki pants that aren't real flattering anyway. The side pockets stood out like elephant ears and his gut hung over the waistband. Kenny, he was just as cute and slim as he's ever been, though he looked like he'd lost a little more hair. Glenda—well, it hasn't been long since I've seen her. She was wearing one of her circus outfits, something more fit for a clown than a woman.

They all made a big fuss about how good I looked—how much weight I'd lost and how I looked younger, better'n I've looked in years. It didn't take a genius to figure out they had something up their sleeve. We went inside and the boys milled around while Glenda and I sat in the armchairs. Turns out they'd already been to the office and spoken to what they called the *administration,* which I took to mean Bigbutt. Glenda told the boys about Vitus first chance she got, and here they all came to put out the fire.

"We want to meet this man," Dean said.

I don't know where he gets his manner because nobody in my family, or Abel's either, ever put on airs. But Dean swaggered around like John Wayne with his hands in his pockets and a scowl on his face.

"It's a free country," I said. "Be my guest."

Not that they needed *my* permission, because as it turns out they'd already gotten Vitus's room number from the office, and off the two boys went, leaving Glenda to guard me.

"You happy with yourself?" I asked her.

"Seems like they got the right to meet the man you want to marry," she said. She switched the TV on to a cooking show. That big fat guy from New Orleans was stuffing a fish with shrimp and oysters.

"Glad I don't have to do all those dishes he's dirtying," I said, but Glenda was giving me the silent treatment. She chewed a hangnail and kept her eyes on the screen until the boys got back.

They walked in sober as judges. Dean went so far as to take a little notepad out of his back pocket and ask Kenny, "How do you spell the last name?"

"K-O-V-I-C," I butted in.

Dean sat down on the foot of my bed and Kenny leaned against my dressing table. After a lot of throat clearing and pants adjusting and head scratching, Dean said, "Mom, we really hope you'll reconsider this whole thing."

"Are you the spokesman for the group?" I asked him.

He was a bully when he was younger, always tormenting the other two. Now he was acting the big man. He needed to trim his eyebrows and the hair in his nose.

"We're just trying to protect you, Mom," he said. "You could lose everything. Your house. All your savings."

"Far as I'm concerned, I already have. Somebody's living in my house, and it sure ain't me. I expect I have some money, but I'll be damned if I know where it is. And my things—my dishes and furniture and knickknacks—they're not getting much use, are they? Looks like I only stand to gain by marrying Vitus. Looks like, if anything, I'll be getting back control of what's rightly mine."

Hoo-ee, he didn't like that. The color rose in his face, and he leaned back on the bed like someone slapped him. The truth hurts. Glenda and Kenny looked down at the floor so as not to embarrass him any more than he'd already embarrassed himself. Their fearless leader had just put his foot in his mouth.

"You don't know anything about him," Dean went on. "You don't know where he's from or what he's done in his life. Why he's here, who his family is. Nothing."

"I know enough," I said. "Me and him has spent plenty of time together. I know all I need to know."

"I'm tempted just to go ahead and let you do it," Dean said. "Let you marry that man and live with the consequences."

"Why don't you do that, honey? Why don't you just let me go my own way, since you don't have much of a choice about it in the first place?"

Nobody had anything more to say, so we just sat there and eyeballed each other. The boys milled around like cattle. Glenda couldn't keep her teeth off that hangnail. I found myself wishing Abel was there. He had a way of making us feel more like a family, like people who liked being with each other.

"Don't let me keep you if you have things you need to do," I finally said.

The boys had flown in from out of town just for the day. All three kids lined up at my chair like I was a department store Santa Claus. They took turns bending over and kissing me on the cheek.

"Good-bye, my darlings," I said. "I love you, no matter what."

I CLOSED THE door and flopped down in my armchair. I was beat. The silence was heaven. I hadn't been sitting there more than a minute when Vitus showed up at the sliding glass door.

"How did it go?" he asked as he sat down across from me.

"Well, what do *you* think?" I asked, maybe not as nice as I could have. "They declared war. Everybody dug their heels in and nobody gave an inch. We're on our own, Vitus. I'm surprised you have to ask."

He looked taken aback that I'd talk so rough to him, and I was sorry for it, but I'd plain run out of sugar. "I don't know what you said or did," I went on, "but they came back here with their minds made up. They're more against this thing than ever. We can't count on them for nothing."

"Well then, we'll just proceed," Vitus said. "I'll have to call my lawyer." He came over and laid his hand on my shoulder. "I'll do it first thing tomorrow. We'll get him to evict those tenants of yours right away."

I hate to pit Vitus against my kids, but that's the way it's shaping up. I haven't talked to him yet today to see what the lawyer said or what we have to do. Things are moving. It feels like I'm getting swept along in a fast current and there's not much I can do but keep my head above water and hope for the best.

TWO DAYS AFTER the kids were here, Glenda phoned me up first thing in the morning. "Your fiancé is wreaking havoc!" she yelled. Those are the words she used, *wreaking havoc.* I got a kick out of hearing her call Vitus my *fiancé.* It made me feel so young and adventurous, like I was about to take off on a honeymoon.

"His name is Vitus. You better get used to it."

His lawyer got through to the renters living in my house and told them they have to move. Now! So they went into a tizzy and called Glenda, who called me and went apeshit about how she couldn't calm them down and what is Vitus, the Russian mafia, and what kind of threats did he make to those people? "That man is ruthless!" she said.

But guess what? They're packing up! Moving out! Glenda tried to smooth their feathers, but they don't want no part of whatever's going on, so they'll be out of the house in thirty days.

There was a ringing in my ears when I hung up the phone. The wheels are in motion, I told myself. Here we go.

THE WORD

Dead.

I practiced saying that word every day after Alice was taken from me. I repeated it like a drumbeat in time to my footsteps, my breathing, the smack of the broom against the rug I hung from the clothesline as I beat, dust flying as I swung and hit, again and again. Dead, dead, dead. It was the sound of the spoon clanging the edge of the jar as I knocked out the last bit of jelly, Abel's rhythm when he pushed into me at night. I wrote it on the scraps of paper that passed through my hands, the pen sliding over the slippery surface of magazine pages, catching on the bumps and pits on dry edges of newspaper. In the fog on the bathroom mirror, in the dirt that spilled out of my shoe onto the kitchen floor. In the dust that piled up on the coffee table and sideboard, dust that comforted me from where I lay in bed, making the shiny surfaces softer, hiding the reflection of my own face.

Right in the middle of *dead* are the first two letters of *eat,* and I didn't stop, didn't lose my appetite. Nope, I kept on eating, but for a long time, months and months, all I wanted was white bread, Webers, slice after slice washed down with milk, big cold glasses of it. Soft and bland and white, all white. I ate the slices one by one, plain, or maybe I laid them in a saucer and poured the milk over them, ate them with a spoon like pudding. I might take two or three slices and wad them up into a ball, press them together and roll them into a globe, eat it like an apple, just for a change. Or spread a slice with butter and sprinkle on a little sugar—white, of course—for dessert.

I could eat half a loaf a day, easy. You'd be surprised. Some days I ate more. It plugged me up, that's for sure, in more ways than one. I had this hunger deep down, but the minute I thought of eating anything, I got queasy as hell. Anything save for that bread and milk. I still cooked for Abel, pork chops and fried chicken and meat loaf. Lots of potatoes: fried, mashed, or boiled. In the morning, eggs and bacon, or he ate some cold cereal if I couldn't get out of bed. He was never big on vegetables, maybe just a can of creamed corn now and then. Green beans.

"Try some," he prodded, pointing with his fork. "Just a little." He was grieving, too, real deep. I could see it. When we got married, I prepared myself for him to pay Alice no mind, but from the day she was born he was tickled to death, like she was his very own.

"Don't want none," I said, pressing my lips together to keep from heaving.

Dead. I repeated the word so much, it lost its meaning. I stared at the letters 'til they looked scrambled. How did you spell it? Daed? Ded?

Dead, I told myself, trying to get it through my thick skull. *She's dead.* I couldn't get used to it. Instead, I was losing my mind.

My aunt Alpha, the same one who used them crystals for scrying, told me a story about how my sister Emerald died. God gives every baby a choice whether to live out their life here on earth or to go up to heaven as an angel, she said. Some babies choose to be an angel even before they're born, when they're just a tadpole in their ma's belly. Those are the miscarriages. Others make it out into the world, but once they get a look at how things are, they decide they don't want no part of it. Those are the babies that die. They only get one year to decide. After their first birthday the deal's off, and they're stuck with this world and the family they were born to.

So that's what happened to your sister, my aunt explained. She saw there was something better for her in heaven, so she decided to go straight there and live with Jesus. She'll be waiting for you when you die, Alpha said, but for now you two got to be apart. She won't have no mumps or measles like you. She won't have to step on no rusty nails or get stung by bees or spanked by your ma for being bad. She'll never be cold or dirty or hungry. *She's* the lucky one, Alpha said. *You're* the one with a row to hoe.

That almost got me to hating my sister Emerald, feeling jealous that she was sitting up in heaven eating candy and floating on clouds while I had to get up early and tote water or sleep squished between Ruby and Crystal because I was low man on the totem pole. How come Emerald decided she was too good for us, that she had better things to do than stay down on earth and pull her share of the weight?

So I figured maybe that's what happened with Alice, my little angel. She saw what I'd done, how she was born in sin and how I'd tried to get rid of her, how her daddy took off, and how Abel loved her, even though she didn't belong to him. She saw the shame in my heart, how I'd made a mess of everything, and she said "No thanks, this is not for me."

That was one story, a simple one, the kind a young girl might believe. But I had a better one, even though it was simple, too. That story went like this: This was my punishment, exactly what I deserved considering the things I'd done. That little girl was taken away because I wasn't worthy of her, not with my lying and cheating and adulterating. God took her to a better place instead of leaving her with a no-account mother who'd tried to murder her before she saw the light of day.

THAT WAS NOVEMBER. A few months later, not long after Christmas, Abel got a job at the plant in Flint. I was glad to move, to get away from those neighbors in Pontiac who saw what happened, from the women who gave me sorrowful looks wherever I showed my face.

We rented a little house with a screened-in porch and two bedrooms, with a yard all our own. We didn't know a soul in the whole place, and each new person I met was one more who didn't know my story. I aimed to keep it that way. Abel and I didn't talk about it between the two of us, either. It got so just the *thought* of having to say her name sent me into a panic, even though she was in my thoughts every minute of every day. It was lonely inside that cocoon of silence, but it was the only way I could carry on.

It's so strange to say her name now. To write it down knowing that someone else will read this, will finally know her story. It's a peculiar comfort to me after keeping that secret so long. Alice would have been one year old on May 20, 1933. Not long after that I found out I was pregnant again. Dean was born the following March. When I was in labor, the doctor asked, "Is this your first, Mother?" I bit my lip and nodded, crossed my fingers that my female parts wouldn't give me away.

Glenda was born in Flint, too, and then Kenneth came after we moved out to California in 1941, when Abel got a job in defense, working on the B-1 bomber. Every one of those kids is the spitting image of him, like all I had to do with it was sit on them nine months until they hatched out. I don't mind, to tell you the truth. It's the least I could do, all things considered. I love them, of course. And I did everything a mother should do: made sure they were clean and clothed and fed. But I always thought of those three as *Abel's* kids, the ones I gave him.

Mine was gone.

Yes, she was all mine. She grew up inside me, in my thoughts. I marked all her birthdays, and every time one of my kids did something special—got a tooth, or took their first step, or started school—I imagined Alice doing it, pictured in my mind what she'd look like, what she'd say. Those kids right in front of me, with their squabbling and snotty noses, they couldn't measure up. Especially Glenda, the only girl, the *other* girl. I feel terrible about it, but the love I felt for Alice was too powerful.

It got the best of me.

THE NECKLACE

We were just tucking into lunch (beef stew, green beans, and a cube of orange Jell-O) when they sent those boys around with baskets of rolls. They do that sometimes to make us feel like we're in a restaurant.

Who should come around to our table but Marcos's pretty boy, Renato, with his butt-hugging pants and pouty little smile. He leaned over and I took a roll, then old Krol, then Carolyn. Poison Ivy sat there with her tight-lipped smile and helmet hair, waiting her turn. When Renato held out the basket, she stretched her claw toward it, but just when she was ready to snag a bun she let out a bloodcurdling scream that would raise the dead. My God! Chairs around us scraped, dishes rattled, heads spun in our direction.

"What in the world?" I hollered.

Old Krol lowed like a calf. His paw closed on the bun he was holding, squashing it to nothing.

"Goodness gracious!" Carolyn squawked, rocking back in her wheelchair.

Ivy put her hands around her neck like she was choking the life out of herself. She juiced the volume on her screaming 'til I thought the windows would shatter. Those who were able stood up at their tables to get a better view. Renato drew back like he'd been scorched. Even the droolers took note. A few of them stopped sucking their lunch up those straws long enough to flop their heads in our direction.

"She's choking! Somebody help her!" Carolyn yelled, which surprised me, seeing as how she felt about Ivy.

Bigbutt, who's always hovering around some-where, came bustling across the dining room, using that hind end of hers to cut a swath through the tables like Moses parting the Red

Sea. "What is it, Mrs. Archer?" she yelled. "Do you need help?"

Ivy still had her hands around her own neck. Her eyes bugged out. Her screams quieted down to a bunch of short grunts like something out of a dirty movie. It embarrassed me to hear it.

Bigbutt leaned down in her face. "Are you all right? Should I call someone?"

"Oh!" Ivy moaned. "Oh!" She turned her terrified eyes toward Renato and pointed one of her talons straight at him.

He took a step back, looking like he'd seen a ghost.

"What is it, Mrs. Archer?" Bigbutt asked. She gave Renato the once-over, looking at him from stem to stern.

Ivy grasped her throat again, then she pointed to Renato's. She looked around at each of us like we was playing charades but none of us got it, so she did it again. Patted her own throat, pointed to Renato's.

"I don't understand," Bigbutt said. "What are you trying to say?"

She deserved an Oscar. Ivy gasped like she'd just crossed the Sahara. She croaked, gulped, contorted her face, and finally rasped, "My necklace. He's wearing my necklace."

"Oh, for God's sake," I said, falling back in my chair. "You ought to go onstage."

I must have been the only one who made out

what she said because both Carolyn and Bigbutt turned to me.

"What is it?" Carolyn asked.

"What did she say?" Bigbutt said. "I didn't catch it."

Krol went back to eating his roll. The mash in his mouth sloshed around like laundry in a washing machine.

"She says that boy is wearing her necklace," I said, pointing to Renato. "Looks like her mind is wandering again." I flapped my hand at Ivy. "She's lost another marble."

Wouldn't you know it, Ivy found her tongue. She leaned over the table and practically spit toward me, "You keep quiet, Cora Sledge. No one asked your opinion. Everybody knows you aren't in your right mind." Then, just like Dr. Jekyll, she turned back to Bigbutt and said in a whisper loud enough to be heard across the ocean, "He's wearing my necklace. The one that was *stolen*."

Everybody looked at Renato. He'd been standing there the whole time with that straw basket in his hand. His big fawn eyes were startled. He raised his hand and laid it over the necklace, like he was trying to hide it.

"That Mexican stole my jewelry!" Ivy screeched. "He came in my room and robbed me blind! There's the proof, right around his neck!"

"I'm not Mexican," Renato said in a voice so

soft and breathy we had to lean forward to hear him.

"Chinese then! Whatever you are, I don't care. You're a thief, that's all that matters! Taking advantage of the people here! Stealing from underneath our noses!"

"Mrs. Archer, there's no need for that," Bigbutt said, laying a hand on Ivy's shoulder.

"That's right, Ivy. Hold your tongue," I couldn't resist scolding. "No need to show your true colors."

"You are just like a dog, Cora," Ivy sneered, "attacking with the rest of the pack."

"Ladies, please," Bigbutt said before she turned to Renato and asked, real stern, "What is your name?"

The way he tucked his long black hair behind his ears before he answered made me remember the first time I'd seen him, that night I'd journeyed upstairs to Vitus's room. It seemed like ages ago. Thinking about how I was then—struggling to walk a few feet, scared to death of my own shadow—it dawned on me how comfortable I've got here, how I've learned the ropes and got to know people. By God, I'm a different person! This is the first time in my life I've done anything on my own, with no one around telling me what to do.

"My name is Renato," he said softly. "Renato de la Cruz."

"My goodness!" I exclaimed. "Sounds like a movie star."

"I'd know that necklace anywhere," Ivy said. "It's one of a kind."

For the first time I gave it a good look. It was silver, but not shiny—more like pewter. The links were rectangles, about the size of a grain of rice. It laid real pretty, each link adjusting itself separate from the others, hugging the curves of Renato's throat like a road snaking over bumpy terrain. Poor Marcos. I could see how he might get hooked on that boy. Everything about him made you want to peel his clothes off to get a look at what was underneath.

"I didn't steal this necklace," Renato said. "It's mine."

His voice stayed low and soft, but his eyes looked scared. Knowing how he'd treated Marcos, I thought he might be capable of anything.

Ivy smelled blood. "Check the clasp," she snapped at Bigbutt. "There's a cloisonné bead on either side of it, taken from a strand that's been in my family forever. They're crimson, about the size of a peppercorn."

Bigbutt's upper lip was sweating. Old Krol had lost interest long ago and was shoveling stew down his gullet, but me and Carolyn were on the edge of our seats. You could have heard a pin drop as Bigbutt raised her eyebrows at Renato, asking him if she could check the clasp.

364

He nodded.

She stepped around behind him. He bowed his head. She hesitated a minute, then moved the hair off his neck. It was better than the movie theater. Carolyn and I held our breath while Bigbutt looked down at the clasp.

"I'll stake my life on it," Ivy said.

Bigbutt was wearing a blue-and-white-striped dress that looked like a sailor suit. The top fit tight across her big boobs. It was V-neck, with a bow that tied at the bottom of the V. Soon as she saw the clasp a spurt of color squeezed out of her cleavage. It spouted across her chest, shot up her neck, and flooded her face, turning it bright red.

"Notify the police!" Ivy growled. "Right this minute!"

Bigbutt took a deep breath.

Renato shook his hair back in place and turned around to look at her. "This necklace was given to me," he said. "It was a gift."

Oh no. Unless that boy was a good liar, I had a fair idea who'd given him the necklace. The bottom dropped out of my stomach. I saw then how much I cared about Marcos, and how I'd looked the other way whenever something suspicious turned up. I hadn't wanted to believe he'd be capable of something like that. But as I cast my mind back on how he'd acted—how mad he got when I called him on that money he kept, how he knew every corner of my room, how he'd buttered me up with cigarettes and snacks—I felt like a fool. It broke my heart. I'd trusted him and look what happened. All for that boy. He loved him the way I loved Vitus. He'd do anything—lie, cheat, and steal—to win him back.

Ivy made all manner of fuss. I got to hand it to Bigbutt. She kept things under control. "Mrs. Archer, we'll take care of this, I assure you," she said. Then she turned to Renato. "Would you please come with me to the office?" Before we knew it, the two of them headed off across the dining room, that boy following Bigbutt like a little lamb.

QUESTIONS

The day after Ivy's fit here they come again from the office. They marched me back to Bigbutt's.

Her henchmen were gone. She was all alone, sitting at her desk. "Please, Mrs. Sledge, have a seat."

"What is it this time?" I asked as I plopped down in the chair across from her. "Somebody get murdered in their sleep?"

She gave me her tight-ass smile. "I just want to ask you a few questions, Mrs. Sledge. We're trying to get to the bottom of things here."

"Wasn't me," I said by way of a joke.

She pressed her lips together like she wanted to

cuss me out. That mood passed, though, and after a minute her smile fell back in place. "I'm sure you know we have a situation here."

I sucked my teeth. "I'll say. More'n one, if you ask me."

Her desk was full of fussy things—a vase of silk flowers, a froufrou bowl of paper clips, Kleenex, hand lotion in a pink pump bottle, and a figurine of a girl swinging on a swing. She had a lot of framed pictures, but they were turned toward her so I couldn't see what they were. The room was filled with stink from one of those things you plug in the wall.

"Mrs. Sledge, I'd appreciate it if you cooperated with me. We have a few leads based on what some of the other residents have told us."

"Well, maybe I can help you. Let's see. I've had money stolen from me here, plenty of it. I lost a keepsake that cannot be replaced, a gift from my father, a one-of-a-kind object. I pay good money for this room and I shouldn't have to guard my possessions like I'm living in a ghetto!"

Her smile got tighter and tighter. You could tell I was working her nerves. "All right, then. Do you have any ideas who took your things, Mrs. Sledge?" she asked in a voice you'd use on a half-wit. "Does your woman's intuition tell you anything? Have you noticed anything suspicious?"

"Nope."

"Nobody at all who raises an alarm?"

My hackles went up. She meant Marcos, but he's like my kids. I can bellyache about them all I want, but don't let anybody else bad-mouth them, or I'll come out swinging. I wanted to throw her off the scent 'til I could talk to him myself, but at the same time I wanted to know what she had on him. I figured the roundabout route was best.

I leaned across her desk and pointed right at her. "You listen here. I caught somebody red-handed, taking something off my dressing table right under my nose, but I guess that ain't good enough. People come and go all the time. Those girls are in here changing my sheets and cleaning my sink—not to mention the half-assed job they do—and I can't tell them one from another. At night people I don't know from Adam are up and down the halls. Most of them look like they're straight out of Sing Sing, or living on the streets, or just stepped off a boat or sneaked across the border, but if you need—"

"What about Mr. Dominguez?" she interrupted.

"Mr. who?"

"Dominguez."

"I don't know anyone named that."

"Mr. *Dominguez,* the gentleman who administers your treatments during the week."

"You mean *Marcos?*"

"Yes, Marcos," she said through gritted teeth.

Once her sweetie-pie routine wore thin, you

could see how tough a cookie she really was. I was glad *I* wasn't working for her, mopping floors or cooking meals. I bet those that did hated her guts.

"You think he's the one doing the stealing?" I asked, like the thought had never entered my mind.

"I didn't say that," she answered in a way that told me it sure as hell *was* what she meant.

"Well, has somebody said something? Did you catch him red-handed?"

"We haven't caught anybody," she said, real snotty. "We're just trying to put two and two together."

I hate a person who acts so important. Her perfume was putting me in a bad mood, too, reaming out my nose holes like the Roto-Rooter. "Until you tell me what's going on, I can't do a thing for you," I said.

All this was bad for my blood pressure.

"We have reason to believe that Marcos Dominguez might be involved in what's been going on. Have you ever given him any money, Mrs. Sledge? Have the two of you exchanged any personal items?"

"I'm not saying. It's nobody's business but my own."

"Did Marcos give you that fountain pen?"

"No, he did *not!*"

"Are you aware of the, um—" She paused and

crooked up her nose like she smelled something nasty. "Of the *relationship* between Marcos and Renato de la Cruz?"

I crossed my arms over my chest. "Maybe I am and maybe I'm not." I glared at her. "And since there seem to be so many questions flying around, I got one for you. What happened to that boy after Ivy Archer had a conniption fit about her necklace the other day?"

"I'm not free to discuss that," Bigbutt snapped.

"Well, here's another one, then," I said. "What about my rock? Did you find that?"

She gaped at me like I was speaking in tongues. "What are you talking about, Mrs. Sledge?"

"My rock. My crystal that was stolen out of my room. Did Renato have that, too?"

She huffed. "Well, I can see you can't be of any assistance, Mrs. Sledge." She got up and came around her desk. I followed her big caboose to the door. "Thank you for your time. Let me know if you have any more concerns."

I wasn't about to let her cow me. "You just remember who's working for who here," I said as I walked out the door. "Next time you get your paycheck, you think about where it's coming from."

I TALKED TOUGH, but inside I was quaking. I wanted to give Marcos the benefit of the doubt. After all we'd been through, he deserved one last chance to explain himself. I started down the hall toward my room, but when I looked down at that cloudy white linoleum the most horrible fear took hold of me. I don't know why. I can't explain it. The sheen from the lights overhead made the floor look like dirty ice, and all of a sudden I felt like I was walking on a frozen pond. I was sure that something lay at the bottom of it, a monster in the murky water, whose shape and size I couldn't rightly see. I was terrified it was going to rise up, come crashing through that ice, grab me, and pull me down to the bottom. Lord knows what came over me. Sweat poured down my sides, my knees trembled, and my teeth started chattering together.

I had to make an emergency stop in the lobby, which was right on the other side of Bigbutt's office. I sat there bug-eyed and tried to get my senses back. After a while I was able to look around, to get my breath and my sweat under control. An old woman in a robe was sleeping in her wheelchair over by the door. She had a stuffed white kitten on her lap, poor thing. The only other person there besides the receptionist was Old Man Speck, the one who has to wear a bracelet around his ankle so he can't escape. He was pretending to read the newspaper but his eyes were on the entrance. When he saw me watching, he grinned and gave me the thumbs-up.

You won't believe what happened next. One of

those girls who works in the office doing paper-work and whatnot shot into Bigbutt's office. Guess who was right behind her.

Marcos.

Well, I just couldn't believe it, but I guess it made sense. The office girl came out and shut the door, leaving Marcos inside. I leaned closer to the wall and strained my ears. Sure enough, I heard a murmur. I couldn't make out what they were saying, but I could hear Marcos's voice—his Mexican accent and the showy way he talked, like he'd watched too many of them soap operas. His voice rose and fell, then I heard somebody who had to be Bigbutt gurgling like a rainspout.

I decided to wait there so I could talk to Marcos when he came out. I had to hear his explanation—no matter what it was—with my own ears. The receptionist, a bottle blonde chomping on a wad of gum, glanced my way. One of the cooks was outside on the walk, smoking. Drops of rain sparkled on the glass door. Beyond that was the parking lot, then the street, then the wide world beyond. Hard to believe I'd soon be out there, coming and going at will, a free person like everybody else.

The front door opened and in walked the UPS man pushing a handcart loaded with cardboard boxes. On top sat a gift basket just like the one Vitus brought to my room the night he proposed. My asshole pinched down to the size of a toothpick. The deliveryman went to the reception desk, leaned way over, and commenced to bill and coo with the receptionist. Maybe Vitus was planning another surprise picnic in my room, or maybe he was on one of those plans where you get some treat—apples or candy or dried fruit—in the mail once a month. Maybe his nephew sent the gift basket or maybe—a cold chill went through me— he had a lady friend on the outside. Now what made me think that? You put those thoughts right out of your mind, I told myself. My hackles went up, though. I couldn't help it.

Soon as that UPS man went on his way, I hoisted myself up and went over to the receptionist.

She popped her gum. "Yes, ma'am?"

"I'm in room 136. Cora Sledge. That basket wouldn't happen to be for me, would it?"

That jaw of hers never slowed down. She worked the gum over while she looked at the tag. "Nope," she said. "Sorry."

"Is it for Vitus Kovic, then?" I asked, real innocent. "I know he's expecting one."

She squinted at me. "You the one who was expecting one last month?"

"What?"

The phone rang. "Never mind. It's not for me to say who it's for," she said before she picked it up. "We have rules here, you know."

I was getting ready to tie into that girl when

Bigbutt's door flew open and Marcos charged out like a bull. He stomped past the reception desk and bolted out the front door. I liked to kill myself running after him.

Old Speck dove for the open door. The alarm went off and the receptionist came running. I didn't heed nothing. While she tried to drag that old fool back in, I trotted after Marcos, yelling his name at the top of my lungs.

He had nice clothes on. Black slacks and a white shirt, pressed to perfection. He was all the way to the curb before he turned around.

"What are you doing out here? What do you want?" he snarled.

"I need to talk to you, Marcos." I grabbed hold of his hand. "Right now! You got some answering to do."

He shook my hand off like it was something nasty. "I'm leaving this place, Cora. I just quit," he said, and made to walk away. "Go back inside. You shouldn't be out here."

He stepped off the curb and started into the parking lot, but I grabbed hold of him again. "Don't you walk away, Marcos! I'm asking you, now. I'm telling you!" Lord knows why I felt so desperate. "What happened, Marcos? What's going on?"

"I'm sick and tired of this place. It's crazy! I've had enough!" he shouted. He looked at me a minute, and his face softened. "I don't need this kind of treatment. Now let go of me, Cora. Don't make a scene."

"Marcos, wait!" I panted as I stumbled after him. "Stop, please! Listen, stay a little! Talk to me! Just a minute!"

We must have walked down half a row of cars before he finally stopped and turned around. Droplets stood on all the cars. The colors looked brighter, the reds and blues.

I still had feelings for him. I just couldn't believe he was the culprit.

"What happened, Marcos?" I reached out toward him. "I don't understand. How can you leave without saying good-bye? How can you go, just like that, after all we been through? Can't we at least have a cigarette together?" I saw them in his breast pocket. "For old time's sake?"

He shook his head and sighed. "All right. One last time, because we are soul sisters." He looked out over the cars. "But let's get away from this place. Come on, over here."

He dragged me across the parking lot, all the way past the strip with the trees, over to the main road. I was huffing and puffing by then, fighting to get my breath.

"I can't take another step," I said once we got to the sidewalk. "I'm fit to die."

"There's a bus stop. Let's sit down."

Soon as we sat down on the wooden bench, a bus pulled up and the people who were waiting got on. The bus pulled away, leaving us in a cloud of stink. The back of the bench had an advertisement for kids who needed adopting. There were three of them—a brown one, a black one, and a white one—with the words TAKE US HOME! painted across the top.

I was so winded I couldn't smoke. I couldn't even talk. I sat there getting my breath and watching all the cars speed past. The sun had come out but the streets were still wet, and the cars sprayed a mist on our faces. The wet bench seeped into my backside, but I was so glad to be sitting I didn't care.

"You're going to get that white shirt dirty leaning against that nasty wet bench," I said when I could finally talk again.

He stared with wild eyes at the traffic like he might throw himself into the middle of it. He felt around his chest 'til he found his pocket, pulled out his cigarettes, lit two, and handed one to me. We smoked without talking for a few puffs. Another bus pulled up and opened its doors. We shook our heads. The doors slammed shut and it pulled away.

"You should have seen this place fifty years ago," I said. "Nothing but marsh and a few little farms."

He wrapped them big lips around that cigarette. The backs of his hands were furry as a badger. After what seemed like forever, he said, "They found some of the stolen things in Renato's locker."

"Why, that little—"

Marcos held up his hand. "He says they were gifts." He flicked his cigarette butt out into the street.

I was hoarding mine, sipping it down to the nub.

"He is in nursing school. Only one semester left. He will be an RN and can get a good job anywhere he wants. He takes care of his mother and sister, who's still in college."

"I had no idea!"

"Why do you think he's at The Palisades all hours of the day and night? Working hard, trying to hold it all together until he finishes school?"

A big truck blasted its horn. I jumped a mile. Marcos mumbled a curse in Spanish. "Throw that away," he said, nodding at my cigarette. It had burned down to nothing in my hand. "They found out about me and Renato." He gave me a look.

"I didn't tell them. I swear I didn't."

"It doesn't matter. Maybe they knew all along. Maybe *everyone* knew. I don't care."

"But I didn't tell. You have to believe me. It wasn't me."

"They think I stole those things and gave them to Renato."

"Well, did you?"

Marcos lit two more cigarettes. He handed me one without looking at me. "No," he said so low I could barely hear him.

"You sure?"

He gave me a look, halfway between steamed and hurt. "What do you think, Cora? Would I do something like that? I thought we knew each other."

"Then why are you taking the blame?"

He waved me off. "Once they make up their minds, there is no use arguing. It makes no difference whether I stole those things or not."

"The hell it doesn't. Did you or didn't you?"

"I already gave you my answer, Cora."

"If you didn't do it, just tell them."

"They found stolen jewelry in my locker, too."

What a bombshell. For a minute I was speechless. "Well, how'd it get there?" I said when I found my tongue.

Marcos shrugged. "I don't know. Someone put it there."

"You know, Marcos. I hate to say it, but this is sounding more and more far-fetched. Did that boy accuse you of giving him those things? Is he trying to save his own pretty ass?"

Marcos shrugged. "He only said they were gifts. He won't say who gave them to him."

"Is he lying? Who could have given them to him?"

"You know Renato. Everyone is in love with

him. It could be anybody." He took a puff. "Or not."

"Well, just say it ain't you! They can't fire you for nothing!"

"I already quit, Cora. Let them think it's me. I don't care." He rubbed that sad face of his with both hands. "It's best for me to leave, anyway. Get out of here. It's painful to see him, to watch from a distance. It's not good for me."

I don't care about the facts. Just looking at Marcos, knowing how he treated me, made me almost sure it wasn't him. "But it ain't right! Why should you take the blame if you haven't done nothing?"

He stopped looking at the sidewalk long enough to meet my eyes. "If they think he accepted them from me without knowing they were stolen, he can stay at The Palisades long enough to finish school. It will be my gift to him. My last one."

I couldn't believe my own ears. "Why in the world would you give him that when he did you so wrong? And he could have stole them himself for all you know."

"This is love, Cora," he said softly. His beautiful smile spread across his homely face. "Love makes its own rules."

The half-smoked cigarette fell out of his hand and lay there by the toe of his shoe. I was dumbstruck. All I could do was stare at that smoking butt until a drop fell on the pavement beside it, then another, and another. Lord Almighty, he was crying. He pinched the bridge of his nose as the tears fell thick and fast, splashing on the gum-scarred sidewalk.

I couldn't think of one word to say, so I laid my hand on his back between his shoulder blades. He didn't make any sound, but I could feel him jerk. I thought how many times *his* hands had worked *my* back, thumping and pounding, jarring loose all that mess in my lungs so I could breathe a little easier. It was his job, true. He got paid for it, but he didn't have to touch me the way he did, so giving. I felt it every time.

"Listen here, Marcos," I said, raising my voice so he could hear me over the traffic. "I need to tell you something. You been a true friend. You showed me a kindness you didn't have to. You might not know it, but it made all the difference in me getting well. If it weren't for you, I wouldn't be sitting here right now with the cars blowing past me and this wet bench soaking my ass."

His poor eyes were blood-red when he turned toward me. "Thank you, Cora. Thank you." He pulled my hand off his back and kissed it, three times. "You are my queen."

"You are a giver, Marcos," I said, tearing up myself. "You just can't help yourself."

Saying that gave me a full feeling, like I just ate a five-course meal. When we stood up, I grabbed

Marcos and pulled him tight against me, never mind all those cars driving by seeing my wet behind and thinking, Look at that poor old fat woman peed her pants and that man is hugging her anyway.

"Where are you going?" I panted between steps as we walked back across the blacktop. "What are you going to do?"

"An agency will hire me to make home calls. They're always looking for someone. I won't have anybody breathing down my neck while I do my work."

"Well, that's real nice," I said, though—truth be known—it made me jealous as hell to think of Marcos taking care of other people, laughing and talking with them, maybe even calling them *my queen* and watching soap operas on their TVs, while he never laid eyes on the likes of me again. "I guess you got your life all laid out," I said when we were almost to his car. "Guess your time here with me was nothing but a fart in the wind."

"I will remember you in my prayers, Coralita," he said, pulling his keys out of his pocket. "I will never forget our time together."

"Don't come no farther." I gave him a little shove toward his car. "I can go the last few steps myself. Go on home, now. I love you, sugar. Thank you for all you done."

I blew him kisses as I walked away.

Those hound-dog eyes rested on me one last

time before he threw me a kiss and went to his car. I'd gone about ten paces when I turned and called out, "Say there, Marcos! My crystal didn't show up, did it?"

He shook his head. "No sign of it, Cora."

Did he do it? Was it him, my Marcos? I racked my brain all the way back to The Palisades. I was beat by the time the front door swung open and the smell I know so well now, Lysol and piss, hit my nose. The air was hot and close. The nutcase with the leg bracelet was still in the lobby, his sneaky eyes ogling the door.

"Why'd you come back?" he called out when he saw me. "You crazy?"

"Must be," I said as I marched past him.

MY HANDS SHOOK so bad when I got to my room, I could hardly fit the key in the lock. I know exactly what I would've done in the olden days, and don't think I wasn't tempted. The only way I could resist those pills calling out from my drawer was to crawl straight into bed and pull the covers over my head.

I slept in fits and starts all the way 'til dark. Didn't bother getting up and going for supper, just laid there wondering about Marcos, trying to put two and two together and figure out if he was guilty or not. If so, what drove him to it? Maybe he loved that boy so much he didn't care what happened. How'd he pay for all that gold that was always hanging off him? Where'd he come from and what was he doing here? Lots of questions and no answers.

Something else was bothering me. That gift basket. Sometimes when you're halfway between sleep and waking little things blow up and bother you more than they should. The long and short of it is I tossed and turned late into the night. My mind was troubled, swirling like a maelstrom. Must have been about midnight I fell asleep.

I woke up right before it started to get light, about six or so. Reason I know is I heard a bus and they don't start running 'til then. I must have dozed off one more time, a light sleep, and the dream I had was so real I remember every detail.

Me and Vitus were at the altar. We said our vows and when it was time to kiss, I turned to him and he was wearing a veil! *You crazy thing!* I told him. *The groom doesn't wear a veil.* I raised it up to kiss him, and who should be underneath but my dog Lulu! The whole congregation burst out laughing, and when I turned around I saw everybody was from Vitus's country—men in ragged black suits with funny scarves around their necks and women wearing babushkas on their heads. Lots of them were missing teeth. They were jabbering in their own language, laughing and clapping and generally raising hell. I looked around for a friend or someone from my family, but I didn't see a soul I knew and that filled me with the biggest sorrow, a kind of homesickness in the pit of my stomach. It was too late, though. I'd said my vows. And, as luck would have it, when I turned back to Vitus, Lulu's face was gone and his was back. He was still wearing that veil, though, and missing teeth like the rest of them.

THANKSGIVING

I feel like something's coming to a head here at The Palisades, the wind picking up like it does before a storm. With it blowing all around me, it's a comfort to cast my mind back to the past. It calms me, puts me in another place. For so many years I did everything in my power not to think of it. The more I write this story the better it feels, almost like it happened to somebody else.

RUBY WAS THE one who said her name right out in the open, after so long a time. Her and Calvin came out from Neosho to spend Thanksgiving with us. We'd been living in San Diego a good ten years by then. They liked being out there by the ocean—to them it was a vacation. Turned out Ruby couldn't have no kids, which is why she built that real estate empire of hers, out of frustration, and why she loved *my* kids so dear. She spoiled them rotten, brought them piles of toys for Christmas, things Abel and I could never afford. She took them to ball games, out to lunch for hot roast-beef sandwiches, loaded them in her Lincoln and took them to the drive-in movie, where she bought them anything they wanted at the snack bar. They loved her to pieces, and who could blame them? It was a twenty-four-hour party when she was there.

That was after the war, when we were living in temporary housing they'd built for all the people who'd come to work in defense. Calvin and Ruby slept on a foldout couch in the living room. She was hooked on those pills by then—like me, only worse, because every day her and Calvin downed a quart of gin between them, no sweat. She wore tinted glasses so you couldn't see her eyes. If she ever took them off, her pupils were big as silver dollars. She walked around with her hands stretched out in front of her like a sleepwalker, feeling along the walls. But I'm no one to talk, and besides, I'm getting off track.

We were all there on Thanksgiving Day, getting ready to sit down to dinner. Two of Abel's brothers who had moved out there to San Diego were there with their wives and kids, so we had a full house. I'd put all the leaves in the table and set a door on a couple of sawhorses for the kids. People were stirring around, finding their places, and pulling out chairs. I was fussing with the turkey, trying to siphon the grease out of the roasting pan so I could make gravy.

It was hot in there with the oven blazing. I was

sweating. Everyone was talking at once. The littler kids were racing around the table. All of a sudden it got quiet. I didn't pay any attention at first because I was still wrestling that bird, but I heard, or thought I heard, Ruby say, "She died right around this time. She would have been twenty years old this year."

The hair raised up on my arms and the back of my neck. Every part of me came to attention, but I told myself I must be hearing things. Ruby would never say that, not in a thousand years. Still, it was awful quiet in there. The turkey was nice and brown on top. I sucked up another baster of juice and squeezed it into the skillet.

"Who?" Glenda said. She was a teenager, but she was still sitting at the kids' table. She's always been the kind who wants to know what the adults are up to.

"Alice," Ruby called over from the main table.

That word ricocheted from the walls of the kitchen like a bullet. It bounced off the Wedgewood stove where I was standing with the turkey, flew over to the sink where the dishes were piled high, rattled the silverware and glasses on the table, and smashed up against the window in the back door. I spun around. People at the table looked stricken, like someone had done something shameful, come to the table naked or blasted a big fart. Some stared down at their empty plates, others had their eyes fastened on me, waiting to see what I'd do. I looked at Ruby. She was already crocked, her glasses cockeyed, her head lolling around. But the look on my face sobered her up real fast.

I was hot already, but I got hotter, like someone turned the thermostat up in my body. Sweat rolled down both my sides into the elastic of my underpants. It felt like bees were swarming in my chest, hundreds of them beating their wings inside me, buzzing, ready to take off. When they were about to tear open the middle of my chest and spill out in a black cloud, Glenda piped up again.

"Who's Alice?" she said, innocent-like.

Something barely balanced inside me, a million glasses stacked in a shaky tower, came crashing down, shattering one after another. I screeched and slammed the roasting pan down on the counter. That bird—and it was a big one, eighteen or twenty pounds—jumped in the air, and floated there a minute like it might flap those roasted wings and fly out the window before it came down with a splat in the pan, spraying grease all over the front of me.

The floodgates opened. I couldn't hold nothing back. Tears came streaming and next thing I knew I was crying at the top of my lungs. A few people gasped. Chairs scooted on the floor. I headed for the kitchen door, threw myself against it, and stumbled out onto the porch. I had to get away.

Last I heard as I ran down the steps was Abel yelling, "Let her go! Let her go!"

I staggered out over that bumpy crabgrass, past the rusty old swing set and the patch of ivy that kept coming up no matter what I did to it. I lurched all the way out to the back of the lot where the tumbleweeds and wild oats grew, and wrapped my fingers in the diamonds of the Cyclone fence. I lowered my head against it and cried my heart out. It took me aback that I was so affected. I just couldn't believe I was sobbing like that, but I was, and there was no stopping it. It shamed me that I was acting like that in front of all those people, but just when I got control of myself, a new wave of bawling washed over me.

I was finally starting to settle down when here comes Ruby picking her way out over the grass, her hands out in front of her like she might slip on ice, liable to fall and crack her skinny ass. She was panting by the time she came up beside me and put her arm around my shoulder and laid her head against my face.

I could smell the booze on her breath.

"Listen here, Toad. Get on back in there. Everybody's waiting on you."

"I ain't going in there," I sniffled. "I can't."

"Now, don't you give me that. Yes, you can."

She'd put on fresh lipstick to come out there. It was deep red, running just outside those thin lips of hers. Ruby still looked good, way prettier than me, and—except for a potbelly—she was still slim.

"Tell them go on and eat," I said. "Don't wait for me."

"You know I can't do that, Toad." She was trying to be nice, on account of the wrong thing she'd done inside.

"Tell them to go on home, then!" I said, stamping my foot. "The party's over."

Ruby chuckled. We'd gone to Newberry's the day before and bought little pouches for our cigarettes. Mine was a deep red satin and Ruby's was plaid corduroy, with a little pocket for the lighter. They snapped open on top like a change purse. She took hers out and tried to pinch up a Tareyton with her long nails, painted to match her lipstick. Her hands shook so bad she couldn't home in on it. Just when I was so impatient I about snatched them out of her hand, she managed to pull out two cigarettes and light them with her big silver lighter.

We didn't say a word. We just smoked.

We leaned against the fence and looked down toward the house while we dragged on our cigarettes like we had all the time in the world. I imagined the circus going on in there, Abel telling everyone to settle down, Glenda going to her room to sulk, the relatives trying to decide whether to leave or stay. Clouds sailed over the house. A few seagulls circled way high up like they do when it's going to rain.

"You know, I see that son of a bitch all the time," Ruby said.

"Who?"

She turned and looked at me, her tweezed eyebrows riding up over her glasses. "Who the hell you *think* I'm talking about? Edward!"

"I'll be a monkey's uncle."

"He moved back to Neosho five or six years ago. Parades himself all over town. Married some mousy thing from up in St. Louis. He has two boys, teenagers."

"You never told me that." I gave her a little slap on the shoulder. Somewhere along the line I'd stopped caring about Edward without even noticing it. I laughed at the sheer wonder of it.

"I didn't think you'd want to know." Ruby sure could smoke. I turned and watched her wrap those bloodred lips around the filter and suck like her life depended on it. Her cheeks went hollow while she inhaled so long and deep you'd think she'd turn herself inside out. She added in a lower voice, almost like she was talking to herself, "I never run into him but I don't think of that time back then. All that trouble."

"Feels good to get out of that goddamn kitchen," I said. The Tareyton was hitting the spot. For no reason at all, I suddenly felt cheerful. It was like old times, me and Ruby sneaking a smoke together. I glanced at her out of the corner of my eye. She had an extra flap of flesh under her chin now, and jowls starting on either side of her mouth, but she was still the finest thing west of the Mississippi.

"What's he look like?" I asked her.

She laughed her deep rattling smoker's laugh. "Ugly as ever. Wears his pants up under his armpits. Butt's as broad as a barn."

We finished our cigarettes and stomped the butts out in the dirt. Ruby shoved her plaid case back in her pocket, then she grabbed my hand and crushed it in those claws of hers. "I love you to death, Toad," she whispered in my ear.

We headed back across the yard to the house.

The two women, Abel's sisters, were bustling around when we came inside. One got the turkey on a platter and the other made gravy. The bird smelled good. Abel set to carving. I was hungry. We loaded up our plates and tied into that food and nobody said one word about what had happened.

THAT NIGHT I was in the bathroom in my slip getting ready for bed when a little knock came on the door. We only had one bathroom for all five of us, so everybody was always fighting to get in.

"I'm almost done," I called out, grouchy that someone was disturbing my few minutes of peace.

The door opened a crack and there was Glenda, peeping in with those eyes of hers—just like Abel's, always wanting something. She was his little princess. He was hard on the boys, but Glenda could do no wrong, far as he was concerned. Sometimes I was almost jealous.

"Can I come in?" she said in a meek little voice.

I didn't bother answering because I knew she'd come in no matter what. She closed the door behind her, put the toilet lid down, took a seat, and there we were, the two of us, shut in the bathroom together.

That poor thing. She was at that age where her face was breaking out. She had pimples across her forehead and chin. Those she hadn't picked into scabs were whiteheads. She was tall and lanky like her dad. About the only thing she didn't get from him was that damn kinky hair. Hers was straight as a stick, oily and limp. Her bangs needed cutting. She peered up through them at me like a puppy looking through a fence.

"You put your medicine on?" I asked, meaning the cream she used for her pimples.

She nodded, watching while I used a cotton ball to take my makeup off. I knew what was coming, but I let her do the asking. My feet ached. I was dead tired from cooking all day.

"Dad told me who Alice was."

Every time I heard that name the swarm of bees started revving their motors in my chest.

Thousands of tiny wings fluttered, the buzz building to a roar. I tried not to go off the deep end this time. I took out the moisturizer and started rubbing it on.

"What did he tell you?"

"She was a friend you had. Somebody you loved."

I kept my eyes on the mirror and took my time smoothing the lotion on my face. "That's right," I croaked after a minute. Something had me by the throat. "It's not something I like to talk about."

"I'm sorry she died, Mommy."

You could tell by her face that she really was. I wiped my hands and stroked that poor greasy hair of hers. Her part zigzagged back and forth across her skull. I wondered what Abel and the boys were doing out in the living room. Probably watching Roller Derby.

I bit my lips to keep from crying. "You're a good girl, Glenda," I said. "You're my sweet baby. I'm lucky I have you."

She beamed up at me. "Alice. I like that name."

The word, especially in her mouth, pierced my heart. It took a minute before I could answer. "Don't say that name, honey. It makes me too sad."

NOBODY DID, IN all these years. I never told Glenda the truth, never ever. I wonder what she'll think. Soon as I'm gone, the whole world will know what I did and what I lived with, how I kept that secret all to myself, nursing it every day. And if I caused that baby's death, then so be it. I've asked her pardon so many times. I've prayed and prayed to be forgiven. I'll have to answer for it, one way or another. More than I already have in this life.

Edward died in a rest home back there in Neosho, the very same place they put Ruby. She went crazy the last few months she was alive, had to be tied down and sedated because she was living her whole life over at the top of her lungs, unspooling everything that happened in speeches that went on day and night for more days than I care to remember. She hollered about things that were long gone and forgotten. I pray that don't happen to me. Maybe if I write it all down I won't have to shout it from the rooftops.

One thing I learned from this whole mess is never to forget that life can slap you in the face any time it feels like it. For no reason at all, it can say guess what and the next thing you know everything has changed, everything that you thought was true and right and forever don't mean squat. You'll be doing the most ordinary thing in the world, clipping a hangnail or opening a can, when *bam!* you're flat on your back. The world looks different from there, a place you never expected to be, and you never see it coming. People don't think of that while they're making their kids' lunch or bending over to pick up the newspaper.

I still see myself that morning when everything changed. The radiators clanking, the curtain lifting with the breeze. The rungs of the crib and the creases in the blanket covering Alice. That stirring of air from the life just taken, and me there in the room, alone now, the phantom gone, the door closed in my face.

THE RING

I'm fighting this feeling. Trying to think of a way out. An explanation. If I write it here, maybe I'll understand, notice something I didn't see before. But all I want to do is scribble all over the page, turn it black, tear it up into tiny pieces. No, I keep telling myself. It can't be. But I got to do what I been doing all along. Put down one word and see what comes after it. Lay them down like bricks and hope they tell a story.

VITUS HAD BEEN making himself scarce for almost a week. He looked at me across the dining room like he never saw me before in his life. He didn't talk, didn't walk me back from meals, didn't come to my room, didn't throw me a kiss or pick a flower on his way across the courtyard.

The jitters grew in me 'til my knees were shaking and I had to slide my feet along the floor like I did when I first got here. I didn't realize how much Vitus has come to mean to me until he pulled away. Oh, I knew I loved him. I knew he'd changed my life. Knew I'd never had feelings like this before. I knew all kinds of things, all the ways he'd turned everything I knew upside down. But I never knew, not really, how he'd worked himself into my flesh. How him pulling away was like jerking something out of me, something I need—a heart or a spleen. The color drained from everything like someone had pulled the plug.

Then at breakfast yesterday he passed me on the way out of the dining room and—just like that first time—dropped a wadded-up pellet in my lap.

Be careful, it said. *Don't talk to me. Not now. Wait until I say.*

That note made me do exactly opposite of what he wanted. The minute I read it I was desperate to talk to him, so desperate I didn't care what happened. Soon as breakfast was over, I laid for him like a panther. I cornered him by the elevators when he was going up to his room. "What in the world is going on?" I cried.

"*Shhhh,* Cora," he hissed, looking up and down the hall. "I *told* you. This is dangerous. You need to wait. Let *me* come to *you.*" He caught me by the arm and tried to spin me around and push me away from him.

"You need to talk to me," I said, loud as I

pleased. I shook his hand off my elbow. "I'm not about to carry on like this. Whatever's happening, I need to know. I don't care what it is, I can't live like this. This is no way to behave, considering we're about to get married."

The laundry room was just around the corner. He took hold of my elbow and steered me toward it. They got ten or twelve machines in there, going all the time. He dragged me inside the hot, noisy room. One of those Mexican girls was taking sheets out of the dryer. She gave us a puzzled look, but didn't say a word, just went on with her work. Vitus hustled me into a corner.

"What're you handling me like this for?" I jerked away from him. Tears started in my eyes. "I never seen you like this. What is wrong with you?"

Clothes thumped around in the dryers. A detergent smell hung in a cloud of steam. Vitus clenched the muscles in his jaw and looked into my face like he was trying to see right through my skull to my brain.

"Someone's after me," he whispered. He scanned the room like that somebody might be hiding behind the hampers of dirty laundry or the shelves lined with Clorox and Tide. "They're checking up on me. Sticking their nose in my business."

"Who is?"

"I don't know." He breathed hard like he was

spooked, downright scared. His eyes narrowed. "Do you?"

"Of course I don't! I don't have the faintest idea what you're talking about."

"Are you sure, Cora?" he said in a low voice as he worked his fingers into the flesh of my upper arm.

"You let go of me, Vitus! No man has ever laid a hand on me. How dare you do that?" I was beside myself. "What's gotten into you?"

He let go of my arm and leaned in close, searching my face. "Don't you trust me, Cora? Do you still have your doubts? Haven't I answered all your questions? Have you stopped loving me?"

"If you only knew how much I love you," I said, rubbing the place he'd gripped. "I turned myself over to you. I gave you my heart. And now it sounds like *you're* the one who doesn't trust *me*."

He stared at me a few more seconds, then turned and watched the girl, who was folding the sheets. When he looked at me again, he must have decided I was telling the truth, because his face had softened.

"Why would anybody do that, Vitus? You sure you aren't imagining it?"

"Oh, no. It's happening all right. Something's going on that I don't understand. It's hard to know who you can trust." He rubbed my arm where he'd squeezed it. "I'm so sorry, Woozy. I never want to hurt you. Will you forgive me?"

The girl started loading her cart with the folded sheets. She kept glancing at us, probably trying to make up her mind whether or not she should call security.

"I just want us to go back to being the way we were when we were courting," I said.

"We will. Don't worry. It will be even *better* once we're living together in our own home. You'll see. But right now we have to be very careful. Someone is working against us. Until we're married, we have to watch our backs. Not make any mistakes. Do you understand, Cora?"

The girl finished loading the cart. She gave us one last look and pushed it out the door.

"I wish I didn't love you so much," I said. "I wish you didn't make me feel like my insides are melting together. If you ever go, or if anything ever happens to you, I'll never get over it."

Vitus pulled me toward him. "Listen, Cora," he whispered in my ear. "I was saving this surprise for later, but I want you to have it now. It's something that seals the pact between us. Something that means we're bound forever."

He stepped back and reached into his pants pocket. "Close your eyes and open your hand. Keep them closed, now."

I felt its weight, its coldness, when he dropped it in my hand. A shiver went through me. It felt like a dead thing, a lizard or a fish. I almost let it fall to the floor. Oh, I knew what it was. I could tell. But the coldness crept up through my arm to my shoulder. It spread across my chest. When it reached my heart a dread set in, something I couldn't explain.

"Open your eyes!"

I looked at him first. He was beaming. I let my eyes fall to the ring lying in my hand. The band was gold, set with a square green stone the size of a Chiclet.

"What's this for, Vitus?"

"It's a ring, Cora. To show the world you're mine."

"What kind of stone is that?"

"It's an emerald, Woozy."

"I had a sister named that," I said, so low he didn't hear me.

"What are you talking about, Woozy? What's wrong?"

"Emerald," I said louder. "I had a sister named Emerald."

He must have thought I'd quit my senses. "I don't know what to say," he stuttered. "I thought you'd like it. I thought you'd be tickled pink."

He had reason to be flummoxed, and to tell the truth I myself didn't know why I felt the way I did. It struck me as odd that he just pulled the ring out of his pocket, instead of handing it to me in a nice box, tied up with a pretty ribbon. More than that, I thought of my crystal, the way it felt in my hand. Alive. This stone was so cold, so still, like it was pulled up from the bottom of any icy ocean instead of dug out of the warm earth.

Inside me a faint bell started ringing, like a burglar alarm you hear far away. "Where'd you get this, Vitus?" I asked.

"Why, Cora! I'm just stunned. This ring was my mother's. My father gave it to her. It belonged to *his* mother."

He looked insulted, and hurt, too. Unless he was the best actor in the world, I was way out of line. But I had a feeling, a feeling that wouldn't turn me loose. The picture of that gift basket riding in on the delivery man's cart wouldn't leave me alone.

"Did your other wife wear it? The first one? Because I don't want no part of a dead woman's ring."

He gave me a hard stare, but I looked him right in the eye, didn't move a muscle.

"You're taking all the joy out of this, Cora. I had such a different idea of how this moment would be. But if you must know, my mother died after I was married. I'd already given my wife a wedding ring. She never wore this one. Does that satisfy you?"

I couldn't think with all those machines running, sucking in the fresh air and blowing it out thick and hot. The old feeling seeped in—that I was making a mess of things, that just when my life was starting to turn around I was stabbing myself in the back. It's a sickness, I told myself. A disease.

I took Vitus's hand. "I love you. I'm a sorry old woman who's falling apart. I don't know whether I'm coming or going. All this getting-married stuff is putting my head in a spin. I hate to put you through this. It's not your fault. It's me. I'm all mixed up."

"I know, darling. I know. That's just what happened to me when I brought you in here. We're both under a lot of strain. It's almost over, though. Things will get better."

I still had the ring in my hand. He peeled open my fingers and took it out. "Don't you want to put it on? Don't you want to wear it so everyone can see?"

Hard as I tried to talk myself out of it, that ring gave me the willies. "Maybe later," I said. "I'm too overcome right now."

I CARRIED IT to my room and slammed the door behind me. I commenced to pacing around the room, waving my arms and muttering to myself. Yes, I was out of my mind. The thought that kept creeping into my head made me want to rip my scalp off. But I couldn't keep it at bay. That ring was fishy, and it might not be the only thing.

"Abel," I called. "Get your ass down here. I need your help."

I'm finding I appreciate him better now that he's dead. I come to rely on him for big decisions. Makes sense he's smarter now that he's in heaven. All his pigheadedness is gone, too.

Well, here he comes. This time his face was reflected in the sliding glass door, instead of floating up there in the curtains.

"You take that ring and you put it way down in the toe of your shoe, Toad," he said. "Those nice pointy-toe high heels you never wear. Push it way down in there and stuff a hankie on top of it. Don't say a thing. You watch yourself, girl. Listen to your gut. You're skating on thin ice."

Poof! He was gone.

Like always, I felt calmer after seeing him. My mind was peaceful, so I could ask myself questions straight out.

What if Vitus *did* steal that ring? What if he took it from Poison Ivy? Maybe he did it for me. Maybe he wanted to get married so bad, he'd risked himself for me. So what? That's right. Sure, it's a crime and he shouldn't have done it, but everybody needs a little forgiveness. I haven't lived a perfect life myself. If Abel wouldn't have taken me to his heart, covered up what I did, forgave me for it, and made the best he could out of our lives, where would I be now?

Maybe it's time for me to spread a little of that around.

THE TRUTH

I'm just going to say what happened. It's all I can do.

After breakfast, I took my cigarettes and went and sat on the bench out there in the courtyard, the same one where Vitus and I had our first chat. I was feeling blue, to tell you the truth. I've been doubting and arguing with myself and making every excuse for Vitus in the book. He's been avoiding me again. Since our talk in the laundry room last week he's been sneaking around, slipping me a note now and then to say our wedding's on course, but otherwise not a word. Maybe I'm just feeling sorry for myself, but I keep expecting the ground to open up and swallow me. I jump at the slightest noise, see shapes out of the corner of my eye. My fingers tingle. It's like when I first came here. I lie awake listening to the night sounds, the moans and screams and banging around. All these people locked up here together, away from the outside world. Forgotten. Left to suffer in their minds.

I'd almost finished my cigarette when here comes that girl with bad skin that works weekends at the front desk. "Oh, there you are, Mrs. Sledge," she said. "Your family is here. They've been looking for you. I showed them to the Day Room."

Here we go, I thought as I followed her down the hall. She pushed the door open and stepped aside, and there in the room full of jigsaw puzzles, board games, and a slew of dog-eared magazines was the whole posse—Dean, Glenda, and Kenneth.

The boys looked up. Glenda fluttered over to me. The hair on my arms prickled. Not one of them could meet my eye.

"I get the feeling you got something to say," I said. "Don't bother beating around the bush. Just tell me."

That damn Dean had the nerve to pick up a *People* magazine and act like he was thumbing through it. Glenda and Kenny glanced at each other. I walked over to an armchair and sat down. Might as well be comfortable.

"Go on," I said. "Get it over with."

They shifted around, but nobody spoke up.

"Go on!" I yelled from my seat. "Something's up, or you wouldn't be here."

Glenda knelt down in front of me, right on the floor. "Mommy, we've come to talk about that man." She put one hand over each knee. "The man you said you wanted to marry."

I sealed my lips. I just looked at her.

"You know who I'm talking about?" she asked.

"Course I do. You think I'm senile?"

Both the boys came over and stood behind Glenda. They stuck their hands in their pockets and shuffled their feet. The tension could of parted your hair.

"He's not exactly a nice guy," Kenny started off. "He's nobody we want you to associate with."

"I've heard all this before," I said, smacking my hands down on the arms of my chair. "I been through this with Glenda more than once, and I been through it with both of you." I looked each of them in the eye. "I'm a grown woman and I'll—"

"You're not going to marry him," Dean broke in. "You're not going to have anything to do with him."

He said it so bossy and final I could have slapped him. I was about to give him a piece of my mind when the look on his face stopped me cold. I'd seen it before.

"Listen here, if you got something to say, why don't you just say it. I'm not in the mood for guessing games. And get your hands off me," I told Glenda. "I don't feel like being touched."

Glenda walked over by the door. Dean maneuvered himself into the middle of the room, spread his legs like he was in a shoot-out, and put his hands on his waist. The room felt like it was closing in on me.

"We looked into this man's background," Dean began, giving me a stern look. "And since you don't want us to beat around the bush, I'll just say straight out he's a con man and a criminal. He's duped a lot of people just like he's duping you."

"What do you mean, you checked into his background?" I yelled.

Dean yelled right back, "I mean we hired someone!"

"Who? Who'd you hire?"

"A private detective. A professional. Somebody who found out all the things this man, this *Vitus,* has done in his life. It's not a pretty picture, Mom, believe you me."

Pressure built in my ears like I was going up a mountain. I looked at Dean's red cheeks, at Glenda's white face and open mouth, at Kenny's nervous eyes skittering toward the window. Bright light flooded from it, bleaching everything out. Within seconds I could hardly see. All there was were dim shapes moving around in the glare.

Dean's voice came out of the haze. "Do you need to know more, Mom? Do you want me to tell you what he's done?"

I sneered right at him. "You don't need to tell me squat, because I already know. I know he's been in jail. I know some of his business dealings were a little shady. How do I know? He told me, that's how. He laid all his cards on the table. So there."

Dean's hands opened and closed. He was about to cut loose when he waved his arms in the air and stormed toward the other side of the room.

"You tell her!" he shouted at Glenda. "Maybe you can talk some sense into her."

"I'm sick to death of all this," I said. Any second now I was going to blow a gasket. "I'm not the fool you think I am. You're afraid you won't get my money, that's all. You're scared you'll lose the house."

Glenda licked her lips and took a few steps toward me. "Vitus is a criminal," she began like she was reciting a lesson.

"You already said that! I told you it ain't news to me. Tell me something I don't know or don't tell me nothing." I clamped my hands over my ears. "I don't want to hear it!"

"You have to listen, Mommy. You have to hear this. I know it isn't easy. But you need to know. You have to know what kind of man Vitus is."

"I know what kind of man he is. He's a *wonderful* man. A *smart* man, a *cultured* man. He's a beautiful man like none I've ever met before. And he loves me! Oh yes, he does. He loves me heart and soul. He loves me like no one's ever loved me before. And I love him!"

I fought my way up out of the chair and stumbled toward the door. Kenneth stepped in front of it. Dean took hold of one of my arms and Glenda the other. I'm not proud of it but I swung in all directions. I landed one upside Dean's head and another square in the middle of

Glenda's chest. I fought like a tiger and the rest of them grappled with me 'til Kenneth finally managed to clamp me in a strong hold with my arms pinned to my sides. Glenda bawled, "Mommy! Mommy!" Dean grunted and swore, trying to push me up against the door. It's a wonder the whole place didn't come running to see what was happening.

"That's enough!" Kenneth shouted while I fought to free my arms. "You stop this right now!"

He dragged me over to the chair and pushed me down into it. Glenda fell into the other one. The boys stood there panting, sweat running down the sides of their faces. "This is ridiculous!" Kenny said. "Everybody calm down!"

We did, believe it or not. We all sat there and got our breath. When things had settled down, Kenneth was the one that talked. "Listen, Mom. We're not doing this for fun. We don't like it any more than you do. But you have to understand that this man is dangerous. We have *proof* that he's conned plenty of women. You're lucky we found this out before he took everything you have. I know it's hard, but you have to believe us."

"Say whatever you want. I don't care. You've lied before. You've done everything in your power to strip me of what's rightfully mine. You're just trying to get me in my weak spot.

You'll say anything to keep me here. Well, I won't have it. I happen to know that Vitus didn't take anything. I got proof. People are talking against him, but I know it's not true. I'm going to marry him no matter what you say."

"No, you're not," Dean said. "We've already spoken to the administration here and told them what we found out. They're making him leave, pronto. Some nephew of his is taking him back to Arizona. He's lucky he's not going to jail. Far as I'm concerned, he got off easy."

I stared straight ahead and concentrated on not listening. There was a bronze globe on the table in front of me, a battered box of checkers, and a couple of encyclopedias squashed between stone bookends carved to look like horses. "You can talk 'til you're blue in the face," I said. "It doesn't change the way I feel."

Dean was working up a good head of steam. He'd puffed up to twice his normal size and his face had turned from red to purple. "If you insist on associating with him, we're going to make sure he ends up in jail!" he bellowed, pointing his finger right in my face. "We'll have the law on him in two seconds, believe me. Only reason we haven't is to spare you the humiliation. But you don't seem to care. So if—"

"Can it, Dean, will you?" Kenneth broke in.

I stood up and screamed right back in Dean's face. "I'm getting married! Do you hear me?" I poked my finger at him same as he'd poked his at me. "Ain't nothing nobody can do about it. You can't keep me in this place. I'm getting out of here. Going back to my home!"

Dean and I stared bug-eyed at each other, too mad to say another word.

"You can't marry Vitus, Mommy, because he's already married," Glenda said in a tired voice. "Not once, and not twice, but three times over."

The room dipped and spun. I dropped into the chair. "I don't believe you," I said for the hundredth time. I stared up at them before I covered my face with my hands.

I pressed my face against my palms, trying to turn the whole world dark, but there was no stopping it. Every doubt that had been nagging at me busted out in full force. One thing after another, all with sharp teeth and a stinging tail. I sobbed, emptying everything out—every scrap of pride, hope, and strength. Any glimmer I ever had that my life might change, that things might turn out all right, that the cloud hanging over me might disappear. In that ugly Day Room where everything had been fingered to soft edges by the hands of cast-off old people, I cried until all the fight drained out of me.

"Go on. Go out and leave us," Glenda whispered to the boys.

I don't know how much time passed before I raised my head and blinked through the tears.

Glenda was there, kneeling on the floor beside me. She leaned over the arm of the chair and rubbed my back.

"I'm sorry, Mommy. I'm so, so sorry."

I took the Kleenex she handed me. "Are you lying to me?" I asked her while I wiped my nose.

"No we're not, Mommy. It's all true, I'm sorry to say."

"It's not true, Glenda. I know for a fact." I held my breath and took the plunge. My back was against the wall. "I know who took those things. It wasn't Vitus."

She looked up at me and I could tell she was hurting, too. Her eyes filled with tears. "Listen, Mommy. There's something else I need to tell you."

Oh, the feeling in my stomach. I'd give anything not to have lived through that moment. "Don't tell me," I managed to say. I could tell by the look on her face that whatever it was would tear me apart. "I don't want to know."

She took my hand. "You need to know. It's hard for me to tell you, but in the long run I think it'll help you."

I put my hands over my ears. "No, it won't. I don't want to hear it. Please, I'm begging you. Don't tell me."

"Listen, Mommy. Please." She pulled my hands down and held them tight. "You have to hear this. You have to know."

I didn't have any pride left. I looked at her with the tears and snot running down my face.

"He said *you* took them, Mommy. That *you* stole those things."

"He did not! I'm tired of your lies. I'm tired of all of you talking that way about him. It's just not true!" I heard my own voice shouting, but it didn't seem like me that was doing it.

I tried to cover my face again, but Glenda wrested them back down to my lap. "This is the truth, Mommy. You have to believe me."

She waited for me to quiet down before she took a big breath and said, "He said he's seen you wearing jewelry you stole from that woman at your table."

"He did not!"

"Yes, he did. He told that woman there in the office. He swore you did."

"No, no." I held my head in my hands.

"He said you roamed around at all hours of the night, looking for something to steal. He claimed that men upstairs had seen you. That they'd vouch for what he was saying."

I just stared at her.

"He said he saw you writing with the fountain pen that woman said you took."

Snot ran down the back of my throat. It hurt to swallow. "What else?" I rasped. "What else did he say?"

Glenda looked down at her hands and shook her

head. "Isn't that enough? Do you need to know more?"

"Yes." I sniffed. "I need to know everything."

"He said you gave him things you stole from other people's rooms."

"He said he loved me," I said. I was truly bewildered. "We were happy. We had so much fun together."

Glenda looked at me with real pity. "I'm sorry, Mommy."

I was pleading with her now. "We had so many plans. We were looking forward to spending the rest of our lives together."

Glenda shook her head.

I cut loose and started sobbing my heart out. She rubbed my back in circles, then massaged the back of my neck. "He could have taken the house and every last penny you have," she whispered in my ear. "If you married him, he'd have a right to it. He would have stolen you blind. God knows what else he might do. I know it's hard to believe, Mommy. He's a criminal. You just didn't see it at all."

I gave that Kleenex the biggest workout of its life. That sad little tissue wasn't equal to the job, believe me. My heart was ripping in two. I was stunned. Vitus, my Vitus! How could he do it? *How could he?* But much as I tried to close my mind, the doubts I'd been having got sharper and clearer every second. All those things I'd pushed

414

away, made excuses for. How could I not know? Poison Ivy was right. I was the worst kind of dupe.

"Am I that stupid?" I bawled. "Am I that much of an ignorant old fool?"

"No, Mommy. No, you're not." Glenda wrapped her arms around me, pushed my hair back from my face, wore a track on my back with her rubbing. "You were following your heart, was all. You thought you were in love."

"I went whole hog," I wailed. "I didn't hold back, and look what happened. I'm pitiful, just pitiful."

"Mommy, listen." She was trying to keep her voice calm, but I heard the worry in it. "No one thinks you took those things. But did he give you anything? Do you have anything he stole that could get you in trouble?"

I stopped crying all at once, the way you do sometimes. My heart slowed down, kicked into its normal rhythm.

I lifted my head and blinked at her. "Nothing," I said. "He didn't give me nothing."

THE PATH

Yes, I took the pills. I swallowed them, closed the blinds over the sliding glass door, then I went to the bed and shucked off my pants. I got under the covers with my blouse on. I closed my eyes, and asked Jesus to still my heart and turn off my mind.

I mourned Vitus something terrible.

For five days I didn't go outside my room. They brought my meals here; I set the dirty dishes out in the hall. I didn't want to see Vitus or anyone else. I didn't bathe, comb my hair, or change my clothes. My mind was working all that time, trying to make sense of how I've been so taken in, trying to understand how I come to be like this, all the air let out of me, the lowest of the low. I played back things Vitus had said and done. All those tender moments, the way we laughed. I tried to understand what kind of person could do what he done, and—worse yet—how someone like me could mistake it for love. What was you thinking, Cora Sledge? I asked myself. When are you going to grow up and look life in the face?

I woke up in the early morning and heard rain falling outside, all the rest of the world asleep, and I thought, *Not yet.* I am not ready to go away yet. So I lay there and waited for the light to come, and when the room got brighter, I dragged myself up and ran a bath and sank down to my chin. I lay there in the water, feeling that weight-lessness, and looking down at my poor old boobs and belly. I wondered whether Vitus was still here, or whether they made him go away like my kids said. The longer I stewed in that bathwater, the more I needed to find out.

When I was clean and dry, with fresh clothes and combed hair, I felt light, like those astronauts floating around in space. Nothing much mattered, but I didn't care. I went to the phone and dialed The Palisades. That's right. Asked to speak to Vitus Kovic. Clever, wasn't it? You know what they said? Yes, he is still here.

I KNOW VITUS'S habits like the back of my hand. I knew where to lay for him.

The dining room's at one corner of the court-yard. Kitty-corner from that is the stairway to the wards upstairs, so after meals he always walks diagonal through the middle, right past our bench and the Cupid fountain. That's where I was sitting when lunch ended.

People started trickling out—a few biddies from Ivy's exercise class who think they have to move faster than everybody else, the Spider Monkey hopping and skipping, and that woman who drags the Chinese man around, calling him her husband. A couple of aides pushing some droolers. Part of me hoped nobody'd see me there waiting, but part didn't care. I been an outcast all my life, so why change now?

Pretty soon here he comes. He was wearing his sweat suit, the green one with white stripes. The newspaper he always swipes from the lobby under his arm, that little bounce to his step. Heading back for his afternoon nap. My heart ached looking at him, it really did. His silver hair on his collar, them long legs. He looked up, sniffed the sky, and smiled like the wind and sun were made just for him.

You are some kind of fool, Cora Sledge, I told myself. Sorry as the day is long.

About halfway to the bench he saw me. He paused with one of his big sandaled feet hovering in the air like he might turn tail and go back the other way. I didn't move, didn't lift my hand or change my face, just kept my eyes trained on him. Wasn't but a second before that foot came down and he started moving forward again, heading straight for me. Boldness itself. When he was about ten paces away, I saw he didn't mean to stop. He aimed to sail right past me like I was no more than a skunk flattened on the road.

"It's our wedding day, Vitus," I called out. "You set to get hitched?"

He made to speed up and cut a wide berth around me. I hauled myself up to my feet. "Don't you pass me by, Vitus, or I'll raise all manner of hell!" I stepped out in the middle of the path and dared him to take another step.

"I'm leaving here, Cora," he said, raising his hands like I was holding a gun on him. "They're coming to pick me up this afternoon."

"It's a good thing, because I never want to see your sorry ass again. How could you treat me like you did? How could you play me for a half-wit all this time? You think I'm some fat hillbilly don't know any better?"

He gave me a nervous smile and made to start moving again. I do believe he was afraid of me. I don't know what it was about the expression on his face, the shifty way he looked around me to the place he wanted to be that gave him away, but all of a sudden I knew as sure as I was born that everything I suspected was true.

"Not so fast, Vitus. You should thank me for covering your ass with my family, otherwise you'd be in jail. So you listen to me. It was you that took Ivy's jewelry and my money, and everything else that went missing around here, wasn't it? You even stole that goddamn gift basket. It was you that put that fountain pen in my drawer. And you who put those things in Marcos's locker. You wanted me to wear that ring so I'd get caught and accused, just like Marcos. You sold me down the river without a second thought, Vitus."

He didn't bother denying it. He looked me right in the eye and said, "Are you finished with your little rant, Cora, so I can be on my way?"

"No, I'm not! You have a hell of a nerve." I stamped my foot. "You were fixing to do more, playing Romeo and cozying up. You were going to take me for everything I have. You are a snake, Vitus, slithering around on the ground. Shame on you!"

He shrugged, like he didn't care one iota what I thought. I was shocked at how cold-blooded he was. I was so disgusted I spit on the ground in front of him.

"You've always been crass, Cora," he said in his smooth voice. "But now you've outdone yourself."

I was ready to light into him when the thought hit me. I sank down on the bench. "It was you that gave that boy that necklace, wasn't it? Were you trying to play him, too?"

He just smiled. His eyes teased me, like he had a secret he dared me to guess.

My mind inched toward the truth. I could feel it stretching, trying to reach it. Finally, it grabbed hold and everything stopped, stood still.

"You're that way, aren't you, Vitus? You're like Marcos and that boy."

He didn't have to answer. I knew it was true.

"Well, that explains a lot, don't it?" I said. "I should have known, the way you acted."

The smile didn't leave his face. "That boy loves me, Cora," he said quietly. "I'm going to take care of him."

"You're an old fool!" I spat. "Worse than me."

He chuckled and shook his head. "Well, that's debatable. But maybe we *are* in the same boat."

Would you believe it, after everything that had happened, I was jealous of that boy? I felt it coursing through me, envy and shame, wanting and hating. I still loved that devil! My heart ached that he didn't love me back. I wanted to throw myself down on that same path where we first met and grovel on the ground. But I couldn't move. I sat on that bench like a stone that fell from the sky. And Vitus, he must have seen how I was rooted there, just as sure as the tree growing beside me, because he took a step, and then another, and before I knew it he'd moved around me, keeping on that same path, walking out of my life forever.

I had just the tiniest bit of breath left in my lungs. "At least I loved you true," I said as he walked past.

"Everybody makes mistakes." Without turning around, he raised his hand and twiddled his fingers good-bye.

THE KEY

You'd think with the state I was in last night, I wouldn't sleep a wink, but I'll be damned if I didn't slumber like a baby. Abel's voice woke me up. "It ain't over, Toad," he said. "You got things to do." I opened my eyes in time to see his face up there in the curtain for just a few seconds before it faded away.

"Easy for you to say when you're dead as a doornail and not a care in the world!" I called out. I must be losing my mind because I laughed before I swung my feet over the side of the bed and stood up.

I knew Abel was right.

I didn't bother getting dressed or putting in my teeth. I walked right over to the phone and called Glenda. I didn't waste time with any hello how are you's, or would you look at this weather. "Listen here," I said, soon as she answered. "Whatever happened with Vitus is done and over. I admit it's a right mess, so there's no use rubbing it in. But I still want out of here. I'm ready to go back home. If you love me, you'll help."

After a big, fat silence, she asked, "How come you always call *me* about things like this? How come you never call Dean or Kenneth?"

I'd sure like to slap her. "Glenda, you know that's neither here nor there! You're my daughter. I expect you to understand. If you think it'll do any good, I'll call Dean and Kenny, too. I'll call the goddamn president of the United States. What I'm asking is simple. Those people have already moved out. All I want is to go back to my home where I belong. I just want to live in peace in my own home."

"Look what happened last time," she mewled. "Look how you were living before we put you in The Palisades."

"That's all past. I won't give you any problems now. I'm on the straight and narrow, I promise."

Oh, I ate crow by the shovelful. She tried my

patience, but I managed to hold my tongue and stay civil. "Look at me," I said. "I lost all that weight. I'm walking like I haven't for years. I'm off them pills. My mind is clear."

"What's wrong with where you are? It's a nice place. We don't have to worry about you. What if something else happens? We might not be able to find something so good again."

"They got nurses that'll come out to your house," I told her. "If it makes you feel better, I got a special man who knows me, who'll come give me my treatment and take my signs, just like he did here."

"Well, I don't know."

My nerves were wearing thin by that time. "How'd you like to live here where it's half hospital, half prison? Can you imagine what it feels like to sit and stare at these four walls, all the time knowing that my own house is empty, just waiting for me to come back?"

Glenda sighed. Of course she sighed. "I'll think about it," she said.

"Think fast," I said. "I'm hanging on by a thread."

I hung up the phone and paced like a tiger. Lord, I was restless. That's when I realized that getting married to Vitus and moving out of this place were mixed up together in my mind so I couldn't tell one from the other.

"I need to get back there to the house!" I called

up to the ceiling. "That's *our* house, Abel! Those kids got no right to keep me from it!"

"I didn't work my ass to the bone all those years for you to be taken away from your home," Abel answered. It was full light now, and I couldn't see him proper, but his voice was still coming from over by the window. "I never meant for you to be shut up in a prison. It ain't right. Don't let them kids jerk you around, Toad. Take matters into your own hands. Do what you need to."

Soon as he said that I had the feeling deep inside that he'd work for me, pull strings from the other side. Just like that, the idea popped into my head. It was so simple, I laughed. Vitus, I thought. He gave me the key. He might not have known what he was doing, but he set things in motion, bought me my ticket out of here.

THE HOLE

It's late. The building's quiet and the rain has started again. It's pattering on the loading dock outside the window, dinging the metal Dumpsters, and plopping in the bushes and trees out in the courtyard. I lugged myself over here to my dressing table, and took out this book. My heart thumps along like a broken-down mare for a few paces, then speeds up like a jackrabbit for a few more. But I need to finish my story. Need to get the last words out. Hard as it is, I got to get to the end.

We buried Alice in November. It had been freezing and thawing off and on for days and the ground was a mess: churned up and muddy in places, crunchy with ice in others. I watched the points of my oxblood pumps make their way across it out there in the cemetery, walking careful so I wouldn't slip. I stared at the earth that was going to swallow up my baby, thinking of it different than I ever had before because that's where she'd be forever, sleeping under that gooey tan soil that sucked at my feet and stuck to my shoes. The ground was uneven and the dirt churned up from the people walking ahead of us. I stumbled a few times, holding onto Abel's arm, and thinking how different this here dirt was, thin and ashen, weak compared to the sweet black earth back home that smelled of leaves and animals, that was thick and alive, warm as a stove. I moved my feet so slow all the others had to hang back to wait for me, but it was the best I could do seeing as my baby was going to be buried here in this unfamiliar soil, this bleak lifeless ground where none of her people had lived before.

We came to a stop and I realized that everyone was gathering around, that they were making a ring around the thing my mind had been fighting all along. But I stopped, and I looked, and there it was, the hole in the ground, the small rectangular void in the hard cold earth. Abel knew what I was thinking because he braced his feet, dug his fingers into my arm, and jerked me back. Nothing in my life could have prepared me for the sinister sight of that gaping pit.

Seeing a wood box lowered into the ground with your own child inside is something you can't fathom unless it happens to you. Just as awful as the grave was the heap of sodden earth piled beside it, the mountain of dismal clods and rocks. Rain spattered, coming in gusts like someone was tossing it by the handful. The sky was purplish gray. Beside me Abel's breath rasped in and out. He must have felt sick because he breathed out a sour, decaying smell, like his gullet was rotting. All the time I told myself, No, they are not going to put my baby down there they are not going to lower her down they are not going to cover her up and leave her there, in the cold and dark, all by herself.

I don't remember much about walking back to the car. I hadn't worn my pumps but a few times. They gouged blisters on the backs of my heels and I felt them biting deeper with each step, the blood soaking into my hose, running into my shoes. Abel had bought them for me, along with a matching purse. I'd been so proud, but now they were caked with muck. I panted across the oozing ground, clutching my purse, feeling like I might drop any minute. When we got to the car, I looked at the drips pelting the mire along the curb and remembered how I'd stood on the second-story porch the day Alice died and looked down at the hollow the rain made in the mud as it fell from the eaves. Two days later, here I was. A different person in a different world.

Later on I imagined her in a cutaway picture, like a slice had been made in the earth and I could see all the layers—pebbles and clay and stone, with a thin shell of grass on top. In the middle, like a strawberry in a Jell-O mold, was Alice, her hands folded on her chest, her eyes open, staring up at nothing, quiet by herself underground while the rest of us went about our business there on the surface, under the sky.

SHAME'S LIKE A plant that needs repotting. When it fills up your whole body, sends its roots and creepers into every ounce of flesh so there's no room for anything else—then it sends runners out in all directions, looking for new soil to grow in. You get to hating not only yourself, but everybody you know. You get to thinking they're the ones that's shaming you, like the crime was theirs in the first place. Pretty soon everything is tainted. You don't know if the shame is coming from inside or outside, but nothing is right and nobody is worth loving, or even liking. You don't want nothing for yourself, but what other people has burns you up, makes you mad that they can still enjoy listening to a song or visiting friends or taking a Sunday drive. This is what I'm starting to realize as I write all this about Alice, like my eyes have been slowly opening.

Talking about Alice has been like burying her all over again, but this time I feel like I'm putting her to rest, like she can finally sleep. She can stop this feverish living inside me and go be with her own kind, go to that other place and leave me be.

Now that I have told my story, it's like I was looking down on myself from up above, like there's no ceiling to my room and from the sky I saw me in the middle of this cinder-block square, sitting here in this chair with my book in front of me. It has been my lifeline, the rope pulling me back to myself.

Cora Sledge, I forgive you. I pity the girl you were and the shame you've suffered. I'm not feeling sorry for you like I've done year after year. I'm opening my heart to the sorrow I feel. Though the tears are sluicing down my face and I'm rocking back and forth here in my chair, I feel a calm because I forgive you. A space is opening in my heart. I didn't know how much pain there was until now, when it melted away and peace came in to take its place.

THE EMERALD

I never rightly saw how beautiful that emerald was, but when I got in the back of my closet and pulled the ring out of the toe of my shoe, I gasped at the pure green—deep and sparkling as the clearest lake. That jewel is like a cat's eye, like the gems on the casket of King Tut, heavy as a golf ball. I felt it gazing back at me, like I was swimming in its emerald light.

That Poison Ivy. She must have some big bucks.

I dressed special for dinner. The pumpkin-colored pantsuit and the gold slippers, the big papier-mâché earrings. I brushed my teeth, took extra time with my hair, and painted my face. When I was all ready, I slid that ring on my wedding finger. Then I set sail, strolled to the dining room with my head held high.

I haven't taken any meals there for over a week. When I sashayed in like a queen, the talking stopped and heads spun round. All eyes were on me. Word sure does get around. You could tell everyone knew about Vitus. Their eyes gleamed like wolves. Out of habit I looked over at Vitus's table. They'd already plugged in a man I'd never seen before—a fat round man with bright red cheeks and oxygen tubes in his nose. My heart gave way. Still, I sucked in a big breath and headed for my table.

Carolyn glanced up and nodded, then fastened her eyes on her plate. Old Krol never missed a beat. His jaw moved in a circle like the wheels on a locomotive. He stared at me, placid as a cow in a field. Oh, but Ivy! My Lord! She was outraged. She's the type of person who never tolerates no mistakes. Far as she's concerned, certain people are not fit to show their faces in polite society. Her eyes burned, her nose curled up, and her lips puckered so tight you'd be hard-pressed to fit a needle between them. She could not believe that I had the nerve to go on living, much less sit down at her table to eat.

"Evening, everybody," I said as I settled into my chair.

They brought my plate: Salisbury steak, mashed potatoes they never get tired of spooning out, and that nasty succotash I can hardly stomach. I smiled all round and shook out my napkin. Cut my meat in little pieces, flashing that ring and ignoring Ivy who sat ramrod stiff in her chair, staring at me like I was a polecat climbed up in the chair and said please pass the salt.

"Your food is getting cold," I told her, nice as could be.

I swear she was quivering.

"Something wrong with your meat?" I asked. I ate my own like it was a thick, juicy T-bone instead of something you pulled out of a plugged drain. Ivy still didn't see fit to answer. She just stared. They came round with the bread and I helped myself to a piece. Took my time buttering it. Meanwhile I was giggling to myself, trying to picture what she was going to do at the moment of truth.

Right before I was sure something was about to give, she managed to unscrew her lips and spit, "Your friend left here, I see."

I looked at her mild and sweet and gave her my best smile. "Well, you must be talking about Vitus. Yes, he's moved on."

That ring gave me special powers.

"I heard they made him leave, heard he was mixed up in all kinds of things," she hissed. "*Illegal* things. Things you'd never dream of."

I laid my knife and fork down and wiped my lips. "Hmm," I said. "Is that so?"

She rose up like a cobra. "Yes it is, and you know it! He was up to no good from the minute he got here! Horrible things!"

"Really? Well, people say all kinds of things," I said with a shrug. "It don't make them true."

"He stole, he lied, and he debauched! He was the worst kind of man, a charlatan through and through! There's even rumors that he had dealings with some of the boys here!" Her shrill voice rose over the clatter of plates.

I tipped my head to the side like a puppy. The calmer I stayed, the madder she got, until she worked herself into a class-A tizzy. I put my hand under the table so I could draw it out at the perfect moment. Carolyn was watching us now, her eyes as big as saucers. Krol scratched his bony head.

Ivy leaned over the table and hissed like the viper she was. "Only you, Cora. Only *you* would fall for someone like that. You're the laughingstock of this place. Everyone knows. Everyone's talking."

I took my time. Sucked my teeth, shifted in my chair. Then I pulled my hand out, put my elbow on the table next to my plate, and rested my chin in the palm of my hand. The ring was on full display. I raised my eyes up to the ceiling and waited for things to take their course.

Ivy was in high gear, but I stopped listening to her, or at least I stopped listening to the words, though her voice droned on like a buzz saw. Pretty soon she slowed down. She sputtered, then she coughed, then she choked like a car running out of gas. That's when I let myself look at her. You know, you don't often get that kind of satisfaction. The expression on her face was worth waiting for. It was one of the brightest moments of my life. The way I remember it, her eyes were crossed. Her tongue hung out of her mouth. Best of all, she was *speechless.*

I wagged my hand from side to side to make the ring sparkle.

She bolted up, staggered back, turned tail, and

ran off across the dining room. That's right, *ran* through the tables, dodging and weaving like a football star. Last thing I saw was her skinny ass flying out the door.

"What was that about?" Carolyn asked.

I chuckled. "Maybe nature was calling."

Carolyn laughed, too. "Looked like her pants were on fire."

You can guess what happened next. Wasn't five minutes when here comes Bigbutt. Made a bee-line for me. No sign of Ivy. Least I had time to finish my dinner.

"Mrs. Sledge?"

"Yes, ma'am?"

"Where did you get that ring?"

I held it at arm's length and admired it, turning it to catch the light. "Pretty, isn't it?"

"Yes, it is," Bigbutt said through tight lips.

"Family heirloom," I told her. Course I didn't say *whose* family.

"Could you please get up and come with me?"

I trotted behind her all the way to her office. She shut the door and commenced to questioning me, but I was like Jesus in front of Pilate. The less said the better. I didn't deny nothing. Didn't admit to nothing, either. I let her use her imagination, and it worked like a charm. Wasn't long before she let me go. "We'll take this up tomorrow," she said, looking at her watch. Tuckered out, poor thing.

I hadn't been back in my room fifteen minutes when the phone rang. There's Glenda, I told myself, and sure enough there she was, fit to be tied.

"Mother, *what* is going on?"

"Since when did you call me mother?"

"They said you stole something."

"Better come get me, then. No telling what I might do next."

"That darned woman just gave me an earful. Says you are not cooperating at all. I can't keep coming down there to straighten things out. What happened? What did you do this time?"

"Like I said, I ain't fit to be around these people. I need to be removed from the premises."

I kept up my Jesus act 'til I wore her down to nothing.

"Just say you didn't take the ring. Tell them that man gave it to you and you didn't know it was stolen."

"Why would I do that?"

"I give up!" she finally yelled. "Do anything you want! I wash my hands of you!"

"Hallelujah!" I shouted.

The little click when she hung up sounded like a key unlocking a door. I did a jig in the middle of the rug, then I looked over toward the window. "My days here are numbered, Abel," I called out. "I'm on my way!"

THE EMPTY BED

Life's got a force all its own. After all the fighting I did—scratching, hollering, and begging—to get out of here, all to no avail, all of a sudden everything's happening on its own, as if by magic. Nothing can stop it. I don't have to lift a finger. All I do is sit back and watch it happen.

Guess who's the biggest help? Ivy! Just goes to show you. Turns out her family *is* important. Turns out they give plenty of money to this dump, God knows why, but once Ivy went crying to them they called Bigbutt and all kinds of hell broke loose. If that wasn't enough, Ivy got all her fancy buddies in the exercise class to complain, too. The Palisades can't unload me fast enough. Bigbutt and Glenda been burning up the phone lines trying to come to some agreement, but yesterday Glenda called and said I'm leaving here, going back home, at the end of next week. Home! I'm beside myself. I can't believe I'll be walking through the door of my very own house. Every five minutes I need to pinch myself.

In the meantime, I been missing Vitus something terrible. Oh, I know what he did. I know how he played me, lied to my face. How he used me. Don't matter. He was a revelation to my heart. Something was stopped up inside me. Meeting him was like pushing a nail through the crust in the nozzle on a glue bottle and finding there's some sticky stuff, still good, left inside. The world came alive. I wanted to live again.

I'm hankering for his smell, for the size and weight of him. For his voice and every little thing about him, right down to his toenails. I loved seeing him across the room, waiting for him to show up at my door at night, running into him by accident in the hall. Like I told him, I loved him pure, and no matter what he did or didn't do, that feeling made me well. It brought me back to life.

But enough of that. Guess what?

I got it in my head that I needed something to remember Vitus by. It was a crazy idea, I know, all things considered. I couldn't sleep on account of I'm so excited about getting out of here, so after tossing and turning 'til one in the morning I finally got out of bed and put on my slippers and dressing gown. I got the little penlight Glenda gave me out of my bedside table and dropped it in my pocket. Go on, girl, I told myself. You're getting kicked out of here anyway, so what's the harm? I got my key and locked my room behind me and headed down the hall.

I knew not to go by the nurses' station at that hour, so I went the other way, past the Day Room. I know it's hard to believe, but I'm already starting to miss this place, thinking about all that's happened here, the ways I've changed, and what I've been through. I'm proud of myself for coming out the other side. Anyway, I put my head in the Day Room and thought of those jigsaws with their missing pieces, the ugly plaid uphol-stery on the banged-up chairs, and all those dusty magazines—and damned if a soft spot didn't open up inside me, like I was saying good-bye to an old friend. I couldn't help but think of that first late-night trip I took up to Vitus's room, when I could hardly put one foot in front of the other. Now I prance like a pony. Look at you, I said to myself. Just look.

I made it all the way to the elevator without seeing a soul. It was quiet as the grave up and down the hall, just the buzz of the lights and now and then a diesel bus outside. The elevator door slid open as soon as I pushed the UP arrow. It wasn't until I got inside and the door slid closed again that I wondered what in the world I was doing.

There I went again—down, down, down, to the bowels of the earth, even though it was one floor up. When the door slid open, I'd traveled back to the time when lunatics were chained to the walls of deep, dark dungeons. The empty corridor stretched out in front of me. A dark echo clanged in my ears. The smell of piss and sweat was thick. Down toward the end of the hall someone yelled, the icy sound of a nightmare.

I stepped out in the hall and started walking.

They slept with their doors open. Maybe it was

a rule. So much snoring and groaning and grinding of teeth you never heard. I passed a room with the TV on, another where, back in the dark, a man naked except for boxer shorts sat on a metal chair, elbows on knees, staring out into the hall. His eyes glowed. I scooted past. A couple of empty wheelchairs were parked at crazy angles against the wall. A gurney and a mop bucket on wheels. Watch your step, I told myself. All you need now is to fall and break a hip right when it's time to go home.

Vitus's door was open like all the others. His roommate, Daniel, hadn't shown his face in the courtyard since I don't know when. He could be dead for all I knew. Somebody else might already be in Vitus's bed. I snuck my head around the corner and blinked into the dark. Streetlamps from the parking lot gave a little light, enough for me to see the white sheets of the bed nearest me and the curtain pulled down the middle of the room. A machine was running. It sounded like a steam train just starting up, one long hiss then a short burst, over and over.

I took a step inside the room. Somebody was in the first bed all right, lying on his back, wearing what looked like a gas mask over his face. A tube like from a vacuum cleaner came out the bottom. It shuddered in time to the machine. It was enough to make your blood run cold, believe me. When I leaned in for a better look, a jitter ran through the body. It was Daniel, though there was even less of him than there had been before. His shark teeth were covered by the mask and his eyes were closed.

I could barely draw breath. I tiptoed past the foot of Daniel's bed and paused right before I got to the curtain. Vitus's TV was gone, but the dresser it had sat on was still there. I listened hard as I could, but all I heard was the breathing machine. I took one step, then another, and finally, holding my breath, I peeked around the edge of the curtain.

The bed was empty. The mattress and pillows had been stripped and the dirty linens tossed in the middle of the bed. In the dingy light from the streetlamp you could make out the thin stripes running lengthwise down the mattress, the scoop in the middle where the padding was beaten down, a saucer-size stain up near the top. The headboard had iron rungs like the bars of a jail. There wasn't another thing in that little space between the curtain and the window, not a chair or a calendar, not a slipper or a rubber band or a used Band-Aid. Only that banged-up, four-drawer dresser.

I stood in the narrow space between the window and the bed. The breathing machine went on regular, and I wondered how Vitus slept with it going all night, whether he got used to it, maybe even got comfort from it. Just one more thing I didn't know about him. I looked at that sad narrow bed and wondered if he laid there dreaming about Renato the way I dreamed about him. I laid across the mattress, pulled that pile of sheets toward me, and breathed in the smell. *Him.* Good-bye, my darling, I whispered as I buried my face in the linens.

"Hey, what're you doing over there?" a voice growled on the other side of the curtain.

It was so close, I shot through the ceiling. I peeked around the curtain and there was Daniel sitting up in bed. He'd slid the mask off his face. His skin was the color of skim milk. He flashed his fangs at me.

"I'm looking for something," I said, trying to pull myself together.

"What?"

"None of your business." I couldn't help but stare. "Why you wearing that?" I asked, pointing to the gas mask. "What's wrong with you?"

"Sleep apnea, girlie. Emphysema. This helps me breathe." He shoved the mask toward me.

"Well, put it back on before something bad happens!"

"What about you?" He leered. "What's wrong with you?"

"What do you mean?"

His lips drew back so far his whole skull seemed to show. "What's wrong with you that you didn't know about Vitus?"

"I gotta go," I said.

I started for the door, but for some reason I turned around and walked back. I went to that dresser and yanked open the top drawer. Empty. The second one stuck. I jerked again, harder this time, so hard that when it gave, the thing inside rocketed across the bottom and slammed against the front of the drawer. I froze, my feet stuck to the floor. I held my breath and fished around 'til my fingers crept over the smooth facets, the sharp edges, the pointed end. There was no mistaking its hard weight, the perfect way it fit in my hand. Even in that light I could make out the crystal faces, the frosty scenes etched inside. I pressed it against my cheek, let it work its icy fingers into my molars and jawbone, passed it along my forehead, the bridge of my nose. I held it against the pulse in my neck, then I clasped it between my palms and squeezed tight, warming it with my grateful prayer.

MY PRAYER

Abel was waiting for me to wake up this morning. "You dodged a bullet there, Toad," he said as soon as I opened my eyes.

You think he'll visit me once I'm back at the house?

Today is my last day here at The Palisades. That's right, Glenda is coming to get me this evening, going to drive me home.

Guess who's going to be there to greet me. Lulu!

"She's about to drive that family crazy," Glenda said. "Chewed up a whole couch and won't stop digging holes in the yard." I can't wait to throw my arms around that dog and bury my face in her fur.

Can you picture me sitting at my own kitchen table, drinking coffee out of my own cup? Feeding Lulu at her spot by the washing machine? Climbing into my own bed at night and in the morning stepping out on the porch and looking out across the yard?

There's some blank pages left in this book, clean and white without a thing written on them.

I got no more use for it. I am going home.

I'm going to take all three books, seal them in an envelope, and write OPEN UPON MY DEATH on them. I'll put them in my linen closet where I keep all my best pillowcases and towels, things that's too nice to use. When I die and you come to clean out my house, you'll find them. You can do whatever you want. I've pictured you reading them and finding out the truth. If you see any mistakes—spelling or wrong words—you can fix them. You have my okay.

I PRAY NOW like I did when I was a little girl— not needing to understand. I ask for simple things. Let me not hurt. Let me not be hungry, or cold. Please keep my loneliness at bay.

I used to pray to keep my ma and daddy safe, but that wasn't no use. I prayed for gifts at Christmas and to win the school prize. I prayed to be slim, so no one would make fun of me. That didn't happen, either. I asked Jesus to protect my kids. Look what happened.

Now I have a new prayer. Heal my heart. Please, I ask. Calm its pain, soothe its scars. Keep it open, Lord, despite everything—reaching for life, ready to love.

Acknowledgments

Karen Stough generously lent her prodigious editing skills to an early draft of the manuscript. Nina Friedman's intelligence and gift for spotting errors have improved my work, including this one, for decades. Michelle Echenique encouraged me to quit my day job. Her unwavering camaraderie and enthusiastic response to an early draft kept me on course. Angie Chau and Diana Ip scrutinized this book with writers' eyes. Vicente Lozano sacrificed time from his own writing to proofread mine. Sandra Cisneros and the Macondistas remind me of the reasons we write. My family provides the people and the places, the secrets and silences that are the bedrock of my stories. Their love cheers me on.

Stuart Bernstein has been lavish with his encouragement and advice. My work and I have both been enriched by his talent, friendship, and nose for fun. Shaye Areheart opened the door once again and made a place for me at her table. Sarah Knight adopted this book and nurtured it as if it were her own. She challenged me to reveal the bones beneath the fat. Her vision, energy, eye for detail, and persistence improved the manuscript more than I could imagine.

I began this book during a writing residency at Hedgebrook, where the generosity of the foundation and the kindness of the staff allowed me to dream big as I started my journey. The munificent award from the Astraea Foundation both kindled my self-assurance and gave me the means to devote myself single-mindedly to this book.

Carla Trujillo wouldn't stop pestering me to write this story. She welcomed the characters into our house and indulged their demands for months on end. Her laughter showed me I was on the right track. Her abundant praise, obstinate confidence in my abilities, and eagerness to conspire in the creation of this book made everything possible.

About the Author

LESLIE LARSON's critically acclaimed first novel, *Slipstream,* was a Book Sense Notable Book, winner of the Astraea Award for Fiction, and a finalist for the Lambda Literary Award. Her work has appeared in *Faultline,* the *East Bay Express, Writer* magazine, and the *Women's Review of Books,* among other publications. She has been a writer-in-residence at Hedgebrook and an instructor at the Macondo Writers Workshop. She lives in Berkeley, California.

Center Point Publishing

600 Brooks Road ● PO Box 1
Thorndike ME 04986-0001 USA

(207) 568-3717

US & Canada:
1 800 929-9108
www.centerpointlargeprint.com